Doom Fox

Also by Iceberg Slim

Airtight Willie & Me

Death Wish

Long White Con

Mama Black Widow

The Naked Soul of Iceberg Slim

Pimp: The Story of My Life

Trick Baby

Doom Fox

Iceberg Slim

WITHDRAWN

With an introduction by

Ice-T

Grove Press
New York

Printed in the United States of America

Library of Congress Cataloging-in-Publication Data

Iceberg, Slim, 1918-1992
   Doom Fox / Iceberg Slim ; with an introduction by Ice-T.
     p. cm.
   ISBN-10: 0-8021-3588-9
   ISBN-13: 978-0-8021-3588-9
   1. Title.
 PS3552.E25D66   1998
 813'.54—dc21   98-22265
                                                        CIP

Design by Laura Hammond Hough

Grove Press
an imprint of Grove/Atlantic, Inc.
841 Broadway
New York, NY 10003

Distributed by Publishers Group West

www.groveatlantic.com

08 09 10 11 12   15 14 13 12 11 10 9 8

Introduction

In order to enjoy any Iceberg Slim novel you must first open your mind and be ready to appreciate three things:

1. The life that he describes is real. Attempting to believe otherwise is a denial of street reality.
2. Iceberg Slim was an actual pimp who turned into one of the greatest black writers in American history.
3. The dialogue will sound like another language from another planet—in the same way the words of the Bible or Shakespeare may be hard to decode.

Even before I knew who Iceberg Slim was, I knew the man's words. Ghetto hustlers in my neighborhood would talk this nasty dialect rich with imagery of sex and humor. My buddies and I wanted to know where they picked it up, and they told us, "You better get into some of that Iceberg stuff!"

So we did. We found the books, and we started passing them around to each other. They were unlike anything I had ever read. Once you open an Iceberg Slim book you're instantly taken into a world of hustlers, pimps, con artists, and bad, fast women. The stuff I loved! My friends and I felt like we were part of this cultlike underground, 'cause they let us in on something real—Iceberg's words. Those words had a profound effect on my career and life.

As a young boy growing up in L.A. there were many directions my life could have taken. I moved to Los Angeles from New

Jersey to live with my father's sister after he died. My mother had died when I was in the third grade and this move was an attempt to give me a stable environment to grow up in. I was bused to an integrated junior high school in Culver City. When it was time for me to start high school I decided not to ride the bus, but to walk to Crenshaw High. This was one of the most dangerous schools on the entire West Coast. At the time, the school was controlled by gangs and violence. The only way to survive in this environment was to either bow and become prey to the gang bangers or join. Attempting to just stay clear of the drama was simply not an option. I became connected to the L.A. gang known as the Crips. Although I was never a hard-core member (doing drive-bys, killing, etc.), I wore the colors of the gang and only associated with Crips.

I'd been reading Slim's books for a while in high school before it really dawned on me just how much they meant to me. Here was a man that I could relate to because he spoke *my* language. The language of the ghetto. He wasn't writing from the perspective of some brother who got outta the hood, but from the perspective of an insider. He talks about situations that they might be going through or have been through or are watching their parents go through.

Typically, black authors—by the time they've made it— already speak a different dialect and kids can't relate to them as easily. But Iceberg Slim was true to where he came from. He ruled the streets of Chicago for twenty-five years and he chose not to write about what he didn't know. He knew pimping. He knew hustling. He knew the streets.

And he gives it to you straight-up. That's one of the most valuable aspects to his work. He shows you the positive *and* negative sides of the game, which is very rare. For instance, a lot of rappers today don't take that route. They try to make the gangsta lifestyle look like something to get into. Iceberg Slim, on the other hand, would give it to you straight, like, "Yeah, I had a lot going on and I was having a lot of fun, but at the same time, I was strung out on heroin, damn near dying, my mama died, and my friends are dying all around me." So it wasn't just some flamboyant trip through life. He's basically saying, "If you wanna go for a ride, you better be ready to accept the consequences." In that sense, he kept it real. Ironically, that's one of the main slogans in rap and hip-hop today: Keep it real. Iceberg Slim always kept it real.

So if the role of the artist is to tell you what he sees, then Iceberg Slim is a true artist. In all his works, Iceberg—as a junkie and a pimp—takes you out into America's ghetto streets and shows you the real deal. He doesn't glamorize the lifestyle to make himself look good. He shows you the dark side to the hustling life, the side that leaves you strung out, messed up, and dying inside. He shows it to you because he's a true hustler.

A real street hustler—whether he's out there selling drugs, pimping, or robbing banks—would never tell a child to do like him. They know they're victims of circumstance. It's the fakes that try to coax kids into getting into trouble. In my book *The Ice Opinion: Who Gives a Fuck?* I talk about how criminals have a code of honor, just like any other sector of society. The more honorable criminal understands the reality of his situation. He's out there trying desperately to survive, and he doesn't have that many options. He's repulsed by the game but he figures, while he's playing it, he may as well be the best player and take pride in being the best. Only a true player like Iceberg could have expressed this paradox as openly and completely as he does.

If Iceberg Slim had written books about how he was this invincible player and never got caught, I couldn't have identified with him. You can't identify with that when you're sleeping in the back of your car 'cause you got no place else to sleep. But when he says that he was down, out, broke, on drugs, you say, "Wow, shit, then what happens. . . ." It's this honest portrayal of his situation that makes his books so dynamic, especially to young black kids. They hear the truth in his words.

That's the attraction. The inspiration is the fact that he wrote these stories at all after what he lived through—that he had the ability to turn himself around and become a writer gives kids the courage to say, "Yo, I can get out of this and I can make something of myself." He did. That simple fact changed my entire life.

I was embracing the pimp lifestyle. I wanted to be one more than anything in the world. Then I turned back to Slim's works and realized that after all the real-life experiences that pimping gave him, he defied the odds and became an important writer. He took his experiences on the street and used them to elevate himself to immortality. It was a revelation, because nobody tells you when you're young that being a criminal or a pimp or a gangster can lead to anything positive.

I realized, if I'm idolizing this guy, I should follow in his steps and change my game. Like him, I wanted to be somebody who didn't just die there out on the streets. I decided that though I was out on the street doing wrong, I could take my experience and turn it into something else, possibly something constructive.

I knew I couldn't be a writer like Slim, but when rap music came along it hit me: The same way he could take his experiences and put them on the page, I could take mine and bring them to the mic. So by the same method he became a writer, I became a rapper. I even took on the name Ice in tribute to him. My job was to show the hustlers from my generation what he showed me: that they too can take it to the next level.

I spoke from the inside about the hustler lifestyle. I rapped about guns, drugs, gangs, and fast women. And like Slim, I spoke about the fact that I see life as being hard for a black person. Although I also try to tell people to overstep these hardships, I truly believe that everything I'm doing and every struggle I deal with would not be so hard if I weren't black. That's just part of the game. I see white artists come out and do something almost identical to a black artist, but make far more money and be accepted more broadly. Maybe one day that will change. But if the key to a good artist is telling it like they see it, you can't criticize them for showing you the ugliness under the surface. Certain black artists don't want to go there, they see things differently because they come from a different place or economic situation. But Iceberg and I came from the bottom.

When I started rapping I was condemned for my words and approach. So what. I was able to show an entire subculture of young criminals like myself another lane—music. There were other rappers out there, but none that came directly from the game. I was the real thing: a robber, pimp, burglar, etc., well known in L.A. and respected in the street by the shot callers, drug dealers, and gang members. Why? Because they all knew me, or knew of me. When I was able to make the transition into the rap scene another lane was open. A legit lane. A new style of rap was even born— Gangsta Rap. Since then thousands of young brothers have stopped hustling on the streets and stepped up to the mic to tell their stories.

That's the most important thing Iceberg Slim did. Not only did he show the world the game, but he showed young men like myself that no matter where you come from, you can always go on to that next level. Rappers like myself, Jay-Z, Nas, Notorious B.I.G., Tupac, Mobb Deep, etc. carry on the legacy of Iceberg Slim. To me he is the father of what they call Gangsta Rap. We call it Reality Rap. The thing is, it just may not be your reality.

But it's ours. What's really key to Iceberg Slim's longevity as an artist is that his stories are still relevant today, and still reflect the ghetto experience. It's over thirty years since he wrote his first book, *Pimp*, and nothing's changed. The song remains the same.

Doom Fox, Iceberg's last book, written twenty years ago and unpublished until now, offers up the dark side of human instinct: an ugly underworld of addiction and greed in its various forms. Critics might say the same thing about *Doom Fox* that they sometimes say about Slim's other books: that it's negative. I say that street life is negative. Change the conditions of the ghetto and the stories will change.

Two decades after he wrote it, *Doom Fox* remains fresh to the game. The language may be a little different, the players might dress a little differently, and some of the commodities that are traded have changed, but what he calls "The Life" is still the same roller-coaster ride it's always been. My advice is read all of Slim's books. His skills as a writer are unmatched by anyone, in my opinion. Nobody reaches his level.

So, to all you squares: Welcome to the Game. To all you players: Kick back, pour some Crystal, and enjoy *Doom Fox*. Iceberg—rest in peace.

Ice-T
Los Angeles, February 1998

One

*J*oe "Kong" Allen's lifelong stepfather massaged his shoulders and said, "Son, this is your first big one. Watch your temper!"

The opening bell of the main event heavyweight bout clangs feebly in the smoke-choked din. Joe's shaved bullethead shimmers beneath the inferno of ring lights like a black mini-pond. He shuffles his six-six juggernaut of steely muscle toward his older, crouching, weaving opponent. Joe's left jab blurs as it drums violently against the choirboy face of the bobbing target.

Joe's father ruefully shakes his graying head as he watches a handsome lemon-hued dandy prance down an aisle with a ravishing sloe-eyed beauty awiggle in a tight pink dress.

A corner of Joe's eye snares the comely couple as they seat themselves at ringside. Recklessly, he swivels his head to stare, for an instant, at them. His mouthpiece flashes starkly in his brutish face as his heavy blue lips pop agape in flabbergast. He scowls to see the rosebud lips of the Creole late teener shape, "Good luck, Big Bro."

Her companion, a relative of Joe's opponents, shouts, "Take care of business, Cous!"

"Reba took Melvin back again. She lied again!" Joe screams mutely to himself.

Freddie, his mulatto opponent, scalpels a red rill across Joe's nose with a left hook. Then he pops a right cross against Joe's jaw that blinks his eyes. The crowd explodes bedlam to see the underdog pretty boy let the monster's blood. Freddie grunts fero-

1

ciously as he rams in close and hammers lefts and rights into Joe's solar plexus.

A drunken hag screeches, "Knock out the ugly sonuvabitch, Doll Face!"

Joe clinches, gasps savagely, "I'm gonna run you back up your mammy's pussy, Bitch Face."

Freddie whispers, "No way, Kong Ugly Ass! Say, ain't your mama a fucking gorilla? And by the way, eat your heart out, Big Bro. I know you ain't hip to the latest. Cous and Reba is planning to tie the knot."

The burly referee hollers, "Break! C'mon, break!" He steps in to separate them.

Freddie flees with a smirk. Joe lunges to attack, his face hideous. Freddie backpedals and slips Joe's storm of hooks and jabs with deft moves of his head. Freddie cutely hitches his candy-striped trunks as he dances and jabs Joe's wounded nose. Joe traps him in a corner, pounds his midsection and face with both fists. Freddie's mouthpiece sails to the canvas. Freddie gouges a thumb into Joe's eye and clinches. The referee retrieves the mouthpiece and parts them at the bell.

Joe drops his arms and is turning away when Freddie loops a hard right to Joe's temple. The blow splatters blood on Joe's white satin trunks from his leaky nose. As the referee moves between them, Joe whirls and bombs a right hand to Freddie's jaw. The impact is like the pop of a Saturday Night Special. Freddie crashes to the canvas, motionless on his back, his jaw crookedly askew.

Joe slips through the ropes to the arena floor. He spits out his mouthpiece and bares his teeth as he strides down the aisle toward the dressing rooms through a strident gauntlet of boo birds, beer cans, and profane heckling. He goes through a door into a corridor leading to a row of dressing rooms. He pauses near his dressing room to rip a poster off the wall depicting him in hideous caricature looming above a crowded arena in the manner of the movie Kong threatening a city.

He enters his musky dressing room, leaps to sit atop a table. He makes monster faces in a cracked wall mirror. Self-hatred ambushes him. "Hey, Big Bro, you gotta be the ugliest nigger in L.A." he flogs himself aloud.

His torch for Reba sears him. He remembers his pain and rage, his wild hopeless palpitation for Reba through the years at Manual Arts High School. He relives visions of Melvin, Pretty Melvin, the fickle humper, the dapper campus god, cruising with Reba plastered against him in his low-riding purple chippie catcher. He remembers how the lovers' frequent breakups sent Reba to him for solace, how each time his secret dream, to move from Reba's play big bro to her main squeeze, had to be deferred when Melvin swooped to reclaim her.

Joe sheepishly averts his eyes when his father and his ancient trainer, Panther Cox, come into the room to silently remove his gloves and scissor away the bandages from his hands. He leaps from the table after his father attends to his damaged nose. He strips and steps into the shower. They smoke cigarettes and ignore him as he dresses himself in forest green gabardine, his favorite color. The handsome, mocha tan face of his stepfather is bleak with disappointment as he furiously puffs his cigarette.

Joe packs his working gear into a bag, moves with it in hand to the door, turns, gnaws his bottom lip. "Papa, I'm gonna take a cab . . . Hey, did that jive nigger get himself together?" he says with a flippant inflection laced with concern.

Elder Joe sighs. "Yeah, Freddie's all right. That was a sweet right hand . . . too bad you threw it between rounds. You get yourself together?"

Young Joe nods as his eyes inspect the scabrous wall above his handlers' heads.

The black granite face of Panther Cox softens as he moves to jab Junior's shoulder. "Damper your temper for the rematch and you're a cinch to K.O. that pussy in two . . . Sure you don't want me to drop you off at home?"

"Naw, Panther, thanks but I got some private thinkin' and a run to make," young Joe says as he opens the door.

Joe Senior says, "Son, don't let that run take you past your mama's curfew. I ain't in the mood to hear Zenobia hassling tonight."

"Me neither, Papa. I'm gonna cross fingers that she don't spot this beak."

The trio laugh as they step into the deserted corridor resonated by the roaring of the crowd to action in the fill-in bout. Young Joe falters, trembles uncontrollably as a pastel vision materializes through an arena door.

Reba steps in front of Joe to halt him as his companions nod and move on to the exit doors. She clutches his sleeve. "I'm sorry you didn't win, Big Bro," she whispers in a smoky contralto.

His heart booms as he gazes down into the enormous hypnotic green eyes set deeply in the high-yellow fawn face, framed by coruscating hair leaping in great voluptuous waves from the temples.

He finds his voice to croak fiercely, "I'm sorry too, sorry I didn't break the nigger's neck. Oh yeah, congratulations if the rumor is true 'bout you gonna get married."

She averts her eyes for an instant before she stammers, "Big Bro, I uh . . . didn't go back this time to Melvin because I really wanted to. Why, it's been almost three months since I quit him the last time, since I even saw him, talked to him . . . I'd been hanging up the phone on him dozens of times. Yesterday Daddy made me talk to him and take him back. I'm hip Melvin is rotten, no good . . . except in bed."

Joe sneers, "Who you hunching? Shoot! That chippie crazy humper is sho 'nuff got you in a cross. He must have a wart on his tongue and a zigzag dick. Girl, I pity you."

"Please, Big Bro, don't be mad 'cause I broke my word for the zillionth time. But I got to marry Melvin." She flutters a hand sporting a three-carat stone under his eyes.

Joe yanks his sleeve from her grasp. "Look, girl, I ain't got no right to be mad if you married the Devil. I don't care if you screw that turd on Fifth and Hill at noon. I'm cutting you loose, Li'l Sis. You ain't none of my business no more. Get hip to that, girl!"

She sobs, "Fathead! Can't you understand? I got caught . . . I got a baby!"

He stares at her slack jawed as she turns away to bump into Pretty Melvin coming through the arena door.

"Hey, Sugar Mama, what's going on?" Melvin asks as his hand snakes in to caress a switchblade imprinted against the pocket of his yellow slacks.

Joe hurls his gym bag to the floor. His crouched frame twangs killer brute force. Joe's voice is ragged with emotion as he warns, "Nigger, I dare you to pull your shank. Go on! So I can ice you! Take your duke outta your raise. Bitch Face!"

Melvin's delicate mouth twitches as he recoils and eases his empty hand from his pocket. Reba seizes his arm and tugs him through the swinging door.

Joe shouts to their backs, "Pussy, you better treat her right! Don't you give her no grief, nigger, 'cause I'll make your ass mine!" He presses his face against the door glass.

Tears well as he watches them walk away through the smoky haze to ringside. He goes to the street, whistles a passing cab to a stop for the trip to L.A. South. He waves at Panther Cox and his father leaving the parking lot across the street in Cox's new red Buick convertible.

Twenty minutes later he arrives to a light show of neon. He walks through a hubbub of honking cars and moiling people peacocking Central Avenue in summer finery. They are celebrating a salubrious July black ghetto Christmas. Saturday Night.

Jouncing bosoms that poke and peep from gauzy cleavages ache Joe's starved scrotum. He ducks into the Blue Pit Bar, a mecca for whores. A gamy meld of steamy crotches and clabbered perfume stings his nostrils. He seats himself at the crescent bar jammed with raucous whores, tricks, and hustlers. Pimps perch and swivel necks, hooded eyes aglitter in leather booths along the wall like gaudily feathered vultures.

The voice of Dinah Washington, street cult princess of pathos, wails "Unforgettable" from a Seeburg jukebox spewing neon flame into the gloomy murk. After three double whiskeys Joe sits, alternately staring bitterly at his uncomely reflection in the back bar mirror and darting doggish eyes at the connoisseur rear ends and curvy gams of two mulatto barmaids inflating black satin leotards.

Joe leans to eavesdrop the contractual rap of a dwarfish mudkicker reclining her fat bottom on the stool beside him with a corncob pipe–sucking Popeye the Sailor–type white man at the bar beside her.

She says, "Sweetie, I ain't gonna go three way with you for no sawbuck. You gotta gimme fifteen."

He says, "I'll spring for that if you can guarantee a tight back door and quim."

Her big eyes flash indignation as she gives warranty. "I got sanitary, tight, hot, and sweet as bee pussy merchandise, Lover Blue Eyes."

He shrugs. "I'll try a ride . . . I hope you took a recent crap."

She grins, stands as she says, "An hour ago, Lover Dong. C'mon, trail me."

Joe watches in the mirror as the pygmy hooker leads her trick to the street. His eyes glue to the mirror as an apricot-colored creature with a steepled mass of matching hair walks in and seats herself on the dwarf's vacated stool beside him.

"Hi, Miss Fine. Can I buy you a drink?" he says with a heated quaver.

Her sly eyes trap his in the mirror as she lights a cigarette and purrs, "Sure, heartbreaker, you can buy a lonesome girl a taste."

In the sorceress blue glow of the room, her face is Della Robbia angel fresh and innocent. Joe thinks, she's gotta be the finest chick I've ever seen—'cepting Reba, he amends. He decides to check out her frame and pins. He pays a barmaid for a planter's punch.

"I'm Delphine," she says as she turns to straw-sip the drink and gaze into his face.

"I'm Joe . . . Allen," he says as he shoves several quarters toward her across the bartop. "Wanta hear some sounds?" he asks as he dips his head toward the mute Seeburg.

She shapes a little girl lost smile as she spins off the stool to her feet with sinuous ease. Joe and the booth gallery of mack men ogle her crotch-revving curves as she prances regally to pop Joe's quarters into the Seeburg. Hamp's "Flying Home" blares from the box.

Sausaged in copper satin, she fires the blue haze back to her stool. "Like that number, Joe?" she says as she sips.

"Yeah, and you too," he says tipsily as he launches a hand against her escapist thigh.

"Don't be naughty Joe, so soon . . . I don't know you at all."

He says hoarsely, "Look, girl, I ain't trying to freebie you out of nothing. I'll lay some ends on you in front for some poony."

She smiles contemptuously.

"Don't play me cheap, girl!" he exclaims as he rips his wallet out and flashes his ninety-odd-dollar bankroll.

She curls her lips. He unfolds a bank statement with a thirty-six-hundred-dollar balance. She hawk-eyes it before he shoves it and the wallet back into his pocket, and decides to play him to a tap-out.

Her eyes slit and rake him in ersatz pique. "I don't sell my body! I'm no whore, Joe," she spits out as she swings her head to stare stonily into the back bar mirror. "I liked you Joe, right away . . . I thought you were different . . . but you're like all the other lousy dogs, thinking I'm just a hunk of meat with a hole, thinking they can screw me for money. Well, nobody has and nobody ever will. I'm a down on her luck girl. But a lady, Joe," she pitches in a hurt monotone.

After a long moment Joe says, "Delphine, I'm sorry I . . . uh got down wrong . . . Why you come in here? I was forced to think you sold pussy 'cause this joint is 'ho stomping grounds."

She faces him, eyes wide with grifter shock. "It is!? I'm a stranger in L.A. I couldn't know . . . had a hassle with my landlord. I just wandered in here for a drink and the company of noise and people to get my lonely self together."

She darts an apprehensive look about the room. She leans close to Joe, shivers, and stage whispers, "Oh Joe, I'd like another drink but I'm afraid to stay."

A soot black stringbean, with a Mephistophelian visage, struts through the door adazzle in puce gabardine. Tongues of frozen fire lap the blue mist as his gem-infested hand pats his glittery helmet of processed hair. He brakes his puce alligators, bares his shark teeth in recognition, stares at Delphine's puzzled face in the back bar mirror. He seats himself in a booth behind her. She is certain she's seen him before but can't remember where.

Joe flings the fourth double whiskey down his gullet, hooks an arm around her waist as he orders a fresh round of drinks. "Be cool, pretty lady," he slurs, "'cause bad Joe Allen is body-guarding you."

Doe eyed, she says, "I like you again, Joe . . . very much." She leans to brush his lacerated nose with feathery lips. Excitement quivers him as he opens his mouth in a smile revealing gigantic, snowy, perfect teeth. His solitary claim to beauty.

She cuts an eye back at the stringbean. "Let's try another spot, Joe."

"Okay, baby, soon's I get back," he says as he rises from his stool, pats her now receptive thigh. He hurries down the aisle to a pair of john doors gothically stenciled KINGS/QUEENS in luminous paint aglow at the rear of the room. He enters, dances in the crowd around the urinals as he awaits his turn.

She fidgets, stares into the mirror as she sips her drink. She stiffens to see the stringbean's image swoop in the mirror. She struggles when he armlocks her beneath her breasts as he bites and sucks the nape of her neck.

She makes wild cat-spitting protest, butts him hard between the eyes. The pimp gallery hee-haws as he flings her away and cocks a diamond-knuckled fist to bomb her out. She whirls her bottom, feral faced to brace him. Her bodice bursts silver flame as her hand streaks out with a clicking naked switchblade.

He defuses his fist to finger-stroke his forehead. He grins hideously as he documents his moniker with a raspy whisper, "Peaches! You blind? I'm Whispering Slim from the Big Windy."

She shuts the blade, returns it to its spectacular nest as she rummages her memory with a quizzical face.

To jog her recall he spills, "Girl, your mama, Big Louise, worked my girls in her joint when you were just a teenybopper. I pushed a pink La Salle to pick up my money. Why shit, seven years ago I was in the Mellow Fellow Bar when Jelly Drop copped you and turned you out on the fast track. Later that night, you and Drop snorted up my cocaine. Remember, girl?"

She smiles bitterly, remembering that Louise had really turned her out at twelve with an elderly white trick who paid Louise a C-note to go down on her.

She nods, says softly, "Yeah, I remember . . . How is L.A. treating you, Whispering?"

He hunches his bony shoulders as he waggles his riotous diamonds under her nose. "L. A. the sweet bitch is sucking my dick and teasing me with the motherfucking moon. How you doing, Peaches?"

She shrugs. "I been traveling, fighting back since I got my monkey's ass kicked at Lex last year."

Poisonous charm softens his face as he leans in. "Girl, you the prettiest trick ball blaster there is . . . I'm taking qualified applications for my stable. You got a shot to be queen bitch."

She says, "I'll think about it, Whispering . . . My customer is on the turn," as she spots Joe exiting the Kings room.

Whispering says, "Girl, don't think so long that you blow your shot to star as my woman. Oh yeah, I got a wire your papa beat his life rap, got croaked last spring in Joliet penitentiary about a faggot." He turns back to the booth.

Guilt and sorrow pang her. Guilt because for months she had neglected to write him and send him money for cigarettes and necessities. Sorrow because he was the only human being she had ever loved and worshipped.

She stands as Joe reaches her, totters a bit, shutters her eyes for an instant to fake intoxication. He embraces her waist to steady her.

She mumbles against his chest, "I just can't deal with liquor, Joe. I'm sorry if I'm embarrassing you."

Siren zephyrs of Paris perfume waft from her bottle curves to swoon him giddy, rut his basso profundo squeaky. "Hush, baby lady, you cool," he says as he kisses the crown of her apricot glory.

He pays his tab and shepherds her to the cacophonous street under the gimlet gaze of Whispering Slim.

"Outlaw Bitch! I got your boss. Hoss!" he exclaims aloud as he fingers a packet of pure "H" taped behind his knee.

She leads Joe to a new '47 Lincoln Continental cabriolet convertible sheening like alabaster in the razzle of neon. She makes a mental note to explain the car in her con tale.

Joe glowers behind her as he remembers her crack about being down on her luck. She's rich, Joe tells himself, she's a liar like Reba. Maybe she ain't no lady. Maybe she's a nasty stinking rich 'ho. All of 'em is liars.

She unlocks the door curbside, says "You drive, Joe" as she gives him the keys and eases into the machine.

Whispering watches through the bar plate glass, rises to follow them. Joe steps into the street, leaps back an instant in time. A mortal enemy, Leski, a killer cop, hurtles past in his personal Chevy. He has a smirk on his boyishly handsome face, marred by a slightly askew nose. Joe remembers that he broke it six months before after disarming Leski when he tried to arrest him at gunpoint on G.P. Joe recalls that it had taken six cops to beat him into submission for arrest.

He gets into the Continental, studies the controls for a moment before he violently guns the machine into traffic. She pushbuttons the top down, stares at his grim profile.

"Delphine, how do you score for your grits and greens and the dough for wheels like this?" he asks in a sullen voice dripping sarcasm.

She smiles delight at the cue to pitch her con tale—spun from desperate fantasy to escape the trauma and shame of her sleazed childhood in the carnal phantasmagoria of her hated mother's brothel, the shock and misery of her loving and beloved father's imprisonment for a bank stickup-murder when she was twelve. "I've been a waitress in Hollywood until several days ago. My father gave me this car for my birthday in April . . . a week before a stroke killed him . . . ," she muses sadly.

She pauses to light a cigarette.

"Where we going?" Joe asks at a red stoplight.

"Just let's ride," she says.

As Joe pulls away on the green, she continues the con tale. "Marva, my mother, one of Chicago's leading black socialites, died when I was born. Father was one of the most respected doctors in the city . . . Set me up, a month before his death, in the plushest beauty shop and boutique the South Side had ever seen . . . left me a mansion and two hundred thousand dollars that were confiscated by the government for back taxes they claim he owed. My lawyer is sure we can get most of it back." She shrugs. "That could take years. I'm flat broke, Joe. But I'm a fighter like Daddy. I'll—"

Joe interrupts. "What happened to the shop and boutique?"

"A numbers banker, my landlord, put a torch to the building when I wouldn't go to bed with him . . . his building was insured. I wasn't. I dream of setting up a shop and boutique in L.A. when I get financing. Wish I could sell the car, but I borrowed thousands on it in Chicago to pay for my grandmother's cancer treatments. She passed last month . . . left me alone. Oh Joe! I'm so lonely and confused." She sobs as she scoots against him.

He loops an arm around her shoulders, pulls the car to a halt at the curb. Grifter tears flood her eyes as she clings to him. They kiss deeply and long before they disengage.

"I'm so afraid here alone in L.A." She sighs.

"Ain't nothing to fear with Joe Allen here in your corner," he says stoutly as he pulls the Lincoln into the snailing traffic.

"Take me home, Joe, and hold me," she whispers.

His heart maniacs as he croaks, "Where!?"

"Two blocks ahead, turn left," she says as she adjusts a frilly garter on a maddeningly sculpted thigh.

As they inch down the avenue, they stare at a colorful pot-pourri of people spilling to the sidewalk from the front door of the Club Alabam, premier black and tan cabaret. White tourist nigger watchers, sepia hustlers with their gaudy women mill on the sidewalk. Familiar figures from the silver screen, resplendent in evening clothes, saunter to chauffeured limousines parked on both sides of the avenue.

A one-armed Uncle Remus panhandler costumed in a tattered soldier suit hustles the sidewalk. He doffs a battered officer's cap, bows his nappy white head, flashes a Halloween pumpkin grin to acknowledge stings from several of the movie luminaries.

Joe stomps the Lincoln forward as traffic unclogs. Sudden Santa Ana winds blast Delphine's steepled mane loose into a streaming banner of flame. Joe drives blindly for a long moment, gazing at the celestial radiance of her profile haloed in the neoned ambience. A corrupt angel gracing the night. He heaves a sigh as he thinks, Maybe Delphine is a finer fox than Reba. He cruises the Lincoln left into her block.

She says, "Pull in here," when they reach the middle of the block.

He parks, keys off the ignition. His heart arrests for an instant when she says in a stricken voice, "Oh Joe! We can't go to my place."

"Why, baby?" he murmurs.

She shakes her head as she stares at a three-story redbrick building with a manager sign gleaming starkly in a lighted first-floor window. A corpulent image, reading a book, is silhouetted against a window shade.

"Because she's up waiting for me!" she exclaims.

"Who?" he asks even as he remembers her remark in the bar about a squabble with her landlord.

"My landlord . . . She swore she'd throw me out and plug my door if I didn't come in tonight with every penny of back rent . . . Darling, guess we have to rain-check the rest of tonight's pleasure . . . Drive yourself home, Joe . . . Just lend me a pillow so I can bed down in the car."

Panicked by the thought that his bankroll will not cover her problem, his voice splinters, "How . . . uh, much uh . . . you owe her?"

"Four weeks . . . Eighty dollars," she whispers hopelessly.

He digs out his wallet, extracts the amount, lays it in her lap. Tears glisten her green blinking orbs as she scoops up the score, idly juggles the bills in her palm, turns to gaze into his face with tremulous lips.

"You're beautiful and wonderful, Joe . . . but I can't take money from you . . . money you might need, when we've just started our friendship," she says as she leans to slip the money into his shirt pocket.

"Delphine, I ain't gonna worry about you sleeping in the streets. You gonna put the hurt to me, girl, if you don't take it." Joe snatches the bills from his shirt pocket and shoves them into her bosom.

"All right, sweetheart. I don't ever want to hurt you . . . but remember, this is a loan. I'll pay you back. Okay?"

He nods, starts to open the car door.

She says, "Joe, you better not show until I've squared up the old witch. Lock up the car and come in when I signal 'all clear' from the vestibule."

She kisses him torridly and leaves the car. Shortly, Joe sees the obese shadow rise and disappear.

At the manager's door Delphine smiles apologetically when the frowning manager opens the door and grunts, "What the hell is done gone wrong now in your apartment, Miss Starks?"

Delphine says, "I'm sorry if I disturbed you, Mrs. Lee. I would appreciate it if the exterminators came in and went over my place. I saw a roach this morning."

The old woman snorts, "You kill him?"

"Yes, I did, but there may be others."

The crone jiggles her braided hog head in exasperation. "Oh shit, Miss Starks, he wasn't nothing but a scout. Don't bother me no more 'less you see some sho 'nuff roaches." She slams the door.

Delphine goes to the vestibule, dips her head at Joe through the door glass. Joe gets out with his gym bag, locks the car, goes up the sidewalk to join Delphine in the vestibule. His scrotum spasms as he follows her lush swaying derriere. They go up clean but frayed red carpeted stairs, through the odor of reefer, to her moon-splashed door near an open back door at the rear of the shadow-haunted second floor. The squealing of rats feasting on garbage in the alley below pierces the night air. She fumbles in her bag for the key.

The ominous bellow of a swain who thinks he's cuckolded issues through a nearby door. "Gloria, I ain't gonna ask you but one more time. Where you been and whose jism is this in your drawers. I'm gonna cut your chippie head off if you don't confess."

A fist impact sound is followed by the hysterical screeching of a woman. "I ain't been nowhere but Mama's. That ain't come! I swear, Franklin! Mama said that's pus from my ovaries from you punching your long dick in my guts night and day. Please, Daddy! Don't beat me no more."

"I pity her," Delphine says, as she unlocks her door.

Joe turns and starts to go down the hall. "I got to stop that nigger from abusing her, or maybe wasting her."

She seizes his sleeve. "He won't kill her. It happens all the time with them. She'd probably scratch out your eyes if you tried to rescue her."

She pulls Joe into her rose-lit trick lair and shuts the door. He blinks in the dimness, redolent of jasmine incense, as they move to sit on a blue satin couch. Her foot nudges his gym bag on the carpet.

"I think I know, but what do you do to score for your grits and greens?" she growls in comedic mimicry of his basso profundo question in the car.

They laugh.

He says, "I'm a pro fighter and I go on my old man's plumbing gigs when his arthritis lays him up . . . which lately is too often for me."

She flicks on a table radio beside the couch, stands, arms open as Jimmie Lunceford's sizzling music plays. He rises, takes her in his arms. They dance frenetically to the end of the number, then deep-tongue, locked together.

"Whee, babee, your kissing drives me mad," she moans.

She sucks his bottom lip as she unfastens his fly and feather-strokes the crown of his blood-bloated organ with her fingertips. His monster lunges into the rose glow when she nibbles through his shirt at his nipple.

She disengages, says, "Excuse me, heartbreaker," as she goes into the bedroom.

He stands palpitating for a long moment before he crams his organ into his pants and plops down on the couch with gluey palms. He glances at the luminous face of his wristwatch glowing eleven p.m. He remembers Zenobia's strict curfew. He fidgets nervously.

The bathroom phone rings as Delphine is stripping for a shower. She picks up and croons, "Delphine's house of ecstasy. What is your desire and name, darling?"

A guttural, accented voice says, "Otto vants to come over tomorrow."

She frowns, "Who?"

The trick says, "Otto! I love your vunderful pee-pee and spanking my ass red. Remember?"

She says sternly, "Motherfucker, where in the fuck you been hiding? You bring that fat little ass over here to be punished at noon. You hear?"

He makes lappy sounds and gurgles, "Gorgeous mean lady, I heard you!" before he hangs up.

She showers, applies thick makeup to her inner thighs to camouflage a scabrous network of needle tracks. She colognes herself, brush-flogs her six-inch forest of pubic silk into butterfly wings that hover above her liver-lipped snare. She puts a stack of Duke Ellington records on a record player turntable. "Satin Doll" oozes dulcetly as she pulls back a black silk spread on the red-sheeted, satin-canopied bed. She clicks off all light except for a hidden purple glow behind the bed. She goes nude to the doorway.

Joe peeps at his watch for the dozenth time, stares at it, decides to defer the blastoff of his aching nine-week cherry, decides not to further fracture Zenobia's curfew. He stands. Delphine's splendor magnetizes his eyes. His twenty-year-old hooligan heart pummels his rib cage.

Her feline green eyes are phosphorescent, compelling as the crotch butterfly wings that shadow her notorious, pulse-stomping thighs.

Trancelike, he zombies across the carpet void to take her outstretched hand, follows her into the purple maw of her trick trap.

A ghetto mile away, ebonic Zenobia Allen, seething matriarch, sits in her living room on a black horsehair sofa glaring through a front window at the deserted street. Joe Senior's employer's white panel truck with HOFFMEISTER PLUMBING stenciled on its sides, is parked in front of the Allen's neat, pink stucco house. A sign, REAR FURNISHED HOUSE FOR RENT, is in a front window.

The ravages of stoop slavery in broiling cotton fields and L.A. day work ache and twinge her joints and muscles. She flinches as she soaks and moves her sore feet, deformed by bunions, corns, and calluses, in a steamy bucket of Epsom salts water. She wears a wilted white uniform worn since seven a.m. A lance of street lamp glows her bunned white hair in the unlit half darkness.

The religious hymn "It's True 'Cause Jesus Told Me So" choruses joyously from an antique console radio. An antique grandfather clock disgorges a grimy plaster bird that stridently cuckoos midnight before it ducks back into its hidden nest.

She reaches to the carpet to place a heavy leather belt in her much too ample lap. She plans to chastise Young Joe with a lick or two for breach of her curfew rule.

She frowns as she thinks of Joe Senior. She is certain he is cheating on her. She wonders what her rival is like. "Some lowlife chippie half that old fool's age," she says aloud. I am feeding him with a long-handled spoon, she tells herself. But in time she, with the Lord's help, will trap and punish him. She smiles grimly.

Her ruined doll face hardens as she remembers the imperious white woman who mercilessly berated her, called her "imbecile girl" when she slopped sauce from a serving dish onto the damask tablecloth. She turns on a floor lamp and picks up her Bible to read for cleansing of herself. She needs a defense against a return spew of the bitter bile of humiliation, rage, hatred, and mayhem that had, in early evening, leapt in her throat. Her hands had palsied uncontrollably with the compulsion to pulp the patrician face of her tormentor with a massive pewter candelabra.

"Thank you Sweet Jesus for chasing Lucifer and saving your sinful chile," she exclaims aloud.

She reads several verses before she puts the Bible aside. She sighs to remember how wonderful it was to be her own boss as she stares at a blown-up photograph on the fireplace mantel. It is an exterior shot of the bannered and bunted gala opening of the Down Home Cafe ten years before on upper Central Avenue, now three years defunct, a casualty of softhearted credit policy and Senior Joe's raids on the cash register to bet long-shot nags that always ran out of the money.

The Allen house front windows reflect the posh house of Reba's father, Baptiste Rambeau, across the street. A battery of hidden spotlights shower pastel light on its redbrick two stories, set back on a landscaped expanse of manicured jade lawn ringed lushly by a profusion of tulips, lilac trees, and scarlet roses.

At a brightly illuminated den card table, slight, porcelain-hued, French Negro Baptiste, attired in gold silk pajamas, sits painstakingly marking a deck of cards. A widow's peak of indigo mop gives his near pretty face a softly Satanic cast. His widely spaced green eyes are ferret bright as he pen-etches the cards with invisible ink that only he will see with special glasses. Susie, his toy Manchester terrier, watches him from the carpet with bubble eyes radiant with love.

Erica, the white, petite blonde manager of the corner drugstore, sits in panties across the table smoking a cigarette and gazing infatuated eyes at Baptiste, her short-term lover. Her eyes shift to lock on a puckered scar gleaming lividly on the side of his neck.

She remembers with a shiver the carnaged scene she'd witnessed in San Francisco six months before. A razor-wielding poker loser inflicted the wound when he heard the telltale whistle of a tap-out "second" flawfully dealt by Baptiste because his dealing thumb had spasmed. The thumb spasm was due to a tendongrazing bullet wound inflicted a year before in the master bedroom of the Rambeau house.

Erica watches him complete his handiwork on the last of a dozen decks. He carefully reseals it in its original cellophane wrapping.

As he packs the decks in their cardboard container he says, "Well, Erica love, there they are, hopefully gaffed above detection. I should sting those rocky-assed poker-hustling chumps for the eight grand I need so I can save this house . . . By the way, darling, it wouldn't surprise me if our marks arrived before ten. Your store must be open when I send one of them to buy decks for the play, across your counter."

She says, "Da Dee, I'll open the store at nine." She rises and goes to sit in his lap.

Susie whimpers jealously. Erica measles his face with vermilion lipstick. He gnaws gently on her raspberry nipples as the heel of his hand grinds against her crotch.

Her blue eyes wall as she gasps, "Oh Da Dee! Let's go to bed."

He shakes his head resolutely. "After I've rehearsed dealing." He pecks her cheek and eases her off his lap to her feet.

Susie leaps to his lap. Erica pouts her mouth as she goes back to her seat. She props a large mirror on the tabletop before him. He shuffles a used deck, false-cuts it, palms cards with magician finesse for several minutes. Then he deals "seconds" soundlessly, pulls cards from the bottom and middle of the deck with such skill that even he cannot detect himself in the mirror. His gimpy dealing thumb does not so much as twinge.

High hopes of self-confidence seize him for an instant before doubt and depression snare him. He stares at the circles of discoloration on his fingers, denuded of his hocked diamond rings to raise a bankroll for the crucial play in the morning with his fat but sharply wary prey. He remembers again the threat of bank foreclosure on his house for months of delinquent mortgage payments.

He rises and leads Erica and Susie through the posh house to the second-floor master bedroom. Fear drums his temples as they undress and lie embraced on the emperor bed. What if the pressure under play with heavyweights causes another failure in my dealing thumb, he asks himself as he strokes the razor scar on his throat. He stares, with a bitter grimace, into an open walk-in closet across the room. Susie stares glumly at the couple from the carpet.

He relives the climatic shock of Reba's party for her high school graduating class: He had needed Philippa, his beloved wife, to assist him with the mob of teenage revelers. She was not on the first floor. Perhaps she was upstairs, he had thought. He was at the top of the spiral staircase when he heard a muffled catty yowling from the direction of the master bedroom.

He entered it, heard Philippa's voice ecstatically crying out from behind the closet door. "Fuck me! Fuck me! Goddamn! Oooeeee! I'm coming!"

He had crept to the lighted closet door, put an eye to the keyhole. Philippa, hostess gown hiked over her naked buttocks, was on her knees in a corner of the closet. A brawny terminal teen jock, his trousers and shorts looping his ankles, was pumping into Philippa dog fashion.

Initially paralyzed by painful shock for a long moment, rage galvanized him to arm himself with a pistol from a nightstand. He had flung open the door and fired on them, missing them in his wild excitement. The jock had sprung on him to disarm him. In the struggle, the pistol discharged, grazing a tendon in his dealing thumb. Disarmed, he fled the bedroom from a volley of shots, to a hospital. When he got back with the police, Philippa and the jock had vanished.

It had been easy to divorce her on desertion grounds. He remembers the recent rumors that the curvaceous and predacious Philippa had bewitched an elderly owner of a string of mortuaries in his native New Orleans and moved into his mansion with her young jock passed off as her orphaned nephew. Baptiste heaves a sigh of loss as he rolls between the eager thighs of Erica. Sensitive Susie retreats from familiar porn to the closet.

*J*oe Junior, while driving Delphine home past the Club Alabam, had unknowingly passed his stepfather, ensconced with a black L.A. socialite-divorcée. They occupy a second-floor room of the Dunbar Hotel. The hotel is mere yards from the Alabam; it is the West Coast mecca for black sportsmen and celebrities from across the nation.

Joe Senior lies in bed with his buxom secret sweetheart as he smokes the first cigarette after a passionate love bout. He feels marvelous, so young and virile as he always does when in the company of the refined, regal, and sensitive Marguerite Spingarn. Could be my arthritis is in my head, he thinks. I gotta cut Zenobia loose, soon. Guess it's the old girl's frozen pussy and her Holy Ghost and the fire that are jinxing me.

Marguerite coos, "How do you feel, honey dear?"

He glances through a window at the full bright moon, says, "Like I could leap up there and slice off a hunk of moon cheese to make you a double stacked on toast sandwich with french fried onions like you used to order in the Down Home Cafe."

They laugh. She nibbles his earlobe and whispers, "I love you, Joe Allen . . . and your marvelous lovemaking."

He says, "I love you too, angel. You made my life like a beautiful Technicolored movie the second I saw you walk in the Down Home Cafe."

She sighs. "Ironic isn't it that if Jay hadn't brought me to the cafe—'Let's go slumming for country goodies,' he said—I'd probably never have met you, perhaps would still be married to him." She finger-combs her shoulder-length mane of luxuriant auburn hair. Gem stones on her tapered fingers wink light like pastel fireflies. Her finely boned velvet chocolate face is serious as she asks, "How's Joe doing?"

"Fine, just fine, except for a setback in the ring tonight," he answers.

"How is Zenobia wearing her new retirement?" she says.

His throat constricts with remorse that he had told her the lie. "Just great. Her doctor said her blood pressure problem is getting better all the time."

She caresses his face with fingertips. "You deserve a billion kisses, Joe . . . That makes me so happy . . . I don't feel quite so guilty now about us. It's all so wonderful that you are now a partner in the Hoffmeister Plumbing business and Zenobia is regaining her health. Oh Joe, I'll be so thrilled, so happy when she's well enough so you can tell her about us and get a divorce." She peppers his face with kisses.

A leaden ball of tension inflates his chest as he struggles to make himself blurt out, "It's all lies! Lies so you won't quit me. I still ain't nothing but an old loser nigger flunkying for Hoffmeister and digging in filth for seventy-five a week."

But instead he mumbles, "Yeah, it is wonderful that things have finally turned around for me, for us." He avoids her eyes and slides from the bed to flee to the bathroom with the roil of sudden diarrhea.

He sits on the stool pressing his palms against his pounding temples. Finally he rises, flushes the toilet. He steps into the shower. As usual he cleanses himself only from the shoulders down to preserve and savor Marguerite's scent about his head. He is toweling off when Panther Cox, his bosom crony, sticks his head through the door of the adjoining room, his battered black pug face radiant with erotic conquest.

"Say, buddy, you leaving?" he asks.

Joe nods.

"Gimme another half hour with my fox and I'll take you home."

"Okay, Panther, take your time."

Joe steps into the bedroom. Marguerite is pillow propped in bed, languidly smoking a cigarette, watching the street below. She gives his strained face a concerned look as he gets into bed. He props himself within her encircling arm, cheek to cheek beside her.

"Hon, are you ill?" she asks.

"Just an upset stomach and a lightweight headache . . . had rough paperwork in the office today," he lies again as they look through the open window down at the street, ahum with cars and jaywalking Nigger Christmas celebrants.

Her fingertips stroke his temple as she says, "Hon, I've had a lovely time with you. Let's go home. Panther and his lady can take a cab when they are ready to leave."

Now he thinks he doesn't want to leave, wishes he hadn't complained but decides to terminate the evening to avoid further painful discussion and backup lies about Zenobia and the dismal state of his affairs.

"All right, sugar, after we finish your cigarette," he says softly.

She puts her cigarette to his mouth for a draw. Then she stiffens against him as she points excitedly at the street.

"Oh, there's Judge Evans with Rob and Helena!" she exclaims.

He sees, for the first time, her spitting-image lawyer son emerging, across the street, from a sparkling new black '47 Fleetwood Cadillac accompanied by his reddish tan Kewpie doll wife, Helena. Her father, a platinum-haired giant with a mahogany-hued fierce buffalo nickel Indian face and noble bearing, comes out from behind the steering wheel to lock the car. The men's flawlessly tailored ice cream silk suits sheen richly as they escort Helena, shimmery in orange taffeta, across the avenue.

Waves of class inferiority and paranoid jealousy rock Joe Senior as he wonders if Marguerite has a secret interest in the Judge since she exclaimed his name first before he emerged from his car.

She pecks his cheek. "Darling, I'm going to surprise them and join them for the Alabam's last show," she says excitedly as she scrambles across him to the carpet.

He puppy-eyes her as she dances a transient rigadoon of joy before she prances her Jane Russellish curves into the bathroom. He hears her click the lock on Panther Cox's adjoining door. Then he hears the pianissimo thunder of the shower. His idolatry of her, the terror of losing her aches his gullet. The thought of the suckling artistry of her mouth quivers his organ as he inhales the pungent spice of her plum-tinted sex nest clinging to his thick mustache.

Jealousy racks him when she returns to carefully apply fresh makeup at the dressing mirror. She's prettying up for the Judge, he tells himself. I'm just her ghetto jock she'll dump when she finds a muckety-muck like the Judge to punch the right buttons in bed. Their eyes meet in the mirror. She smiles lovingly. He smiles grotesquely.

She speed-dresses herself in her crimson chiffon dress and matching sling pumps. She appraises herself in the mirror, says, "This dress nearly perfectly matches your lovely new convertible. Don't you think, hon?"

He mumbles, "Close, baby, close."

She hides her long auburn glory beneath a floppy-brimmed black leghorn hat. She slips dark glasses over her sable eyes to complete the disguise leaving that she'd employed when they'd checked in down in the crowded lobby.

She comes to the bed, leans to kiss his forehead, says, "Promise me you'll go straight home after you drop off your friend and his lady . . . I don't want some prowling floozy stealing a smidget of my sugar. Promise?"

He says, with an inanely serious face that overrides flippancy, "I promise. But c'mon, baby, you know I wouldn't give up your sugar to Lena Horne with a tommy gun."

She laughs. "I know that, precious. And believe me, Clark Gable himself couldn't get into my pants with a blank cashier's check and Spanish fly, forever lover mine."

Unwittingly, her remark inflicts a fresh wound of paranoid jealousy and inferiority, for he is convinced she's fantasized opening her black thighs to the castrating white king of Hollywood. They kiss, lightly, to preserve her makeup before she leaves the room. He lies catatonically on the bed staring down at the roistering people on the street.

He is flayed by his central problem: how to divorce Zenobia and marry his socialite goddess, Marguerite. He thinks solution will be nearly impossible. Impossible not for his lies of new affluence—Marguerite, he believes, will forgive him those. But impossible because Zenobia knows his twenty-year secret and can condemn him, return him to a Georgia chain gang for life by dropping a nickel in the phone to the police.

Finally he hears Panther Cox and his girl giggling in the shower. Arthritic pain wobbles his knees as he leaves the bed and goes across the room to the clothes closet. A glance in the dresser mirror at his tortured face stoops him with despair and the full weight of his sixty years.

Several blocks away, Delphine's nightstand phone jangles Joe Junior from his drunken slumber. He stares at it groggily, glances at naked Delphine stirring feebly in deep intoxication. On the fourth ring, he knocks a dead soldier fifth of gin from the nightstand as he picks up.

He mumbles, "Hello."

He hears the rasp of the caller's breathing before he hangs up. Joe looks at two a.m. on the face of his watch.

He reaches to call Zenobia, decides he'd better try to slip in and cool her out at breakfast. He showers, feels the rash of Delphine's suck and bite bruises deliciously atingle. He remembers the sweet ferocity of her teeth gnashing, torso whiplashing, fake multiple orgasms under the womb stroking of his weapon. He feels himself, sees himself for the first time, the consummate lover, a sepia Apollo as he towels himself before an enchanted door mirror: duped by Delphine's lather of flattery and spurious ecstasy, choreographed down to her every rapturous howl.

As he dresses, he gazes at her face, childlike in repose, impulsively tells himself he's in love. He studies the phone dial to memorize her number. He leans across the bed to kiss her lips, is swooned, for an instant, by the raw perfume of their love stew. He gazes at her as he backs from the bedroom. He leaves the apartment, makes sure the door is locked behind him.

He whistles as he goes down the hallway, sees a young guy in shabby sports clothes shred a note, then bang a fist against a door at the end of the hallway before he goes down the stairway. Joe glances at a metal plug sticking from the lock of the punched door. Joe passes the young guy sitting forlornly on the stoop as he leaves the building.

Whispering Slim ducks down in his puce and gold Cadillac parked across the street as Joe goes down the sidewalk toward Central Avenue for a dab. Slim leaves his car, strides across the street, passes Delphine's Continental, to the sidewalk in front of Delphine's building. He stares at the manager sign in a lighted front window. He goes past the young guy on the stoop into the vestibule, retraces back to the stoop.

"Hey, Li'l Bro, how you doing?" Slim inquires warmly as he leans into the troubled face of the youngster.

"Ain't doing no good . . . My landprop plugged my slammer . . . ain't even got the geeters for a crib in a flophouse," he murmurs disconsolately.

Slim scoops a handful of silver coins from his trouser pocket, clinks them together in his palm as he asks, "You know the apartment number of the fox that owns that white Continental?"

"Yeah, two-fifteen at the end of the hall," the loser spills as Slim dumps the coins into his shirt pocket.

Slim goes to Delphine's door, shims open the spring lock with the blade of his pocketknife. He locks the door and cat-foots across the living room and stares at Delphine's supine form. His blind left eye rolls unfocused in his head. The eye was damaged when he was dumped in a trash bin when he was a week old by his junkie mother.

He fans out his five-grand bankroll in C-notes and fifties on the nightstand beside a half ounce of high-grade heroin, cellophane packaged. He picks up her switchblade from the nightstand and tosses it away beneath the bed. He searches the drawers of the nightstand, her purse, the bed, and beneath the mattresses for her hideout weapons. He slides his skeletal frame into bed, jiggles fingers in her rectum and semen-frothed vulva to awaken her to his presence.

Stone harlot to the pelvic bone, she reflexively humps his fingers in her sleep for a long moment before her eyelids flutter. He removes his fingers, wipes them on her lips. He inserts a C-note, tightly rolled lengthwise, deeply into her vaginal tunnel. Her eyes open, stare balefully into his face, then pop wide in shocked furious alarm. She emits a venomous wildcat-attack hissing sound. His spindly legs scissor-lock her thighs as he seizes her wrists before her clawing talons can shred his face.

"Let me go! You'll have to waste me to freebie-fuck me like a chippie. I'll kill you! Let me go, sonuvabitch!" she shrieks as she struggles mightily.

His lupine lips curl contemptuously as he whispers, "Bad Outlaw Bitch, Slim ain't yenning to highjack none of your stinkin' 'ho cave. I'm buying a ticket to your ears, 'ho. Now gander my ticket and listen." He dips his head toward the C-note peeping from between her thrashing thighs.

She stares at it, ceases struggle. She darts a greedy glance at his bankroll fanned out on the nightstand. He flings her arms free and unscissors her thighs.

"Motherfucker! Don't ever play this angle on me again," she pants as she retrieves the C-note, unrolls the bill to examine it. She impounds it inside her fist. "How did you find me, get in here?" she asks.

"A little bird snitched and your door was open . . . ," he replies.

She says, "Let's get this transaction straight, Slim. You're turning a pure conversation trick. Right?"

"Yeah, cold-blooded 'ho mama, that's right," he says as he turns to pluck the dope packet from the nightstand. He unfolds it. A loaded syringe gleams atop the powder. He dips a thumbnail into the contents and snorts a mini-pile of dust up his nostrils.

"Pure smack of brown for this pimping stud of clay scored from down old Mexico way," he chants with slumberous eyes rolling ecstatically toward the top of his long head.

She taps her wristwatch. "You're blowing your half hour, Slim," she says with a quaver as she stares hooded electric eyes at the packet of dope on his chest.

He props himself up, gazes into her eyes as he spiels his game in a sugary whisper: "Star, you ain't been outta my skull since the Mellow Fellow Bar. Remember that night in Chi when Jelly Drop copped you and I made you high? I told Jelly I got to buy! For that pimp's dream, the limit is the sky. He said, 'Nigger, I ain't selling. That gold mine young freak is worth no telling.' I vowed that night I'd kick the Windy's baddest asses, swim through an ocean of mildewed shit gasses to make you mine. Miss Fine! I got a stable of ten. Four African thieving queens, pocket magicians. Three blonde silks, boosting and grifting technicians. Three sissies, pretty and prissy, stone mudkickers from Dixie Missi.

"Now, Sugar Baby, 'cause I love ya, your spot ain't in between but at the top, the motherfucking queen! And that ain't all. I got enough bankroll, if you fall, to raise you for murder one with a telephone call. Get hip and flip for that!"

She coyly averts her eyes, to stroke his hoodlum ego, murmurs, "It's you I think I'll choose. But, like I told you in the bar, Whispering, I'll think about it, let you know."

He grunts as he picks up the loaded syringe. He flicks on the nightstand lamp, eases the syringe needle into a wrist vein. She stares at the red flood of his blood into the syringe. He pumps it empty into his vein, withdraws it and lays it on the pile of powder.

"Goddamn! This is some sweet shit," he moans with closed eyes.

She kisses his nipple nearest the packet. Her nose quivers as she hovers it above the powder. He seizes her hair and jerks her head away as she swoops her nose into the dope.

"Ask me for my dope, cold-blooded 'ho mama," he whispers savagely as he wraps up the package and starts to slide from the bed.

"May I have a pinch of your smack?" she asks sweetly with radiant eyes.

He starts to cook up a shot in a bottle cap with water from a glass on the nightstand.

"I don't want to start banging again, Whispering . . . Just lay a pinch on me for my nose."

He shakes his head as he draws the syringeful from the bottle cap. "Turn over, girl, if you want it."

She flops on her belly. He hits a vein in her buttock, drains in the contents of the syringe.

She moans into her pillow. "You rotten bastard! . . . It's soooo gooood."

He snatches his C-note from her unwary hand.

She screams, "Give me back that trick money!"

He grins, "Bitch, we ain't turned no trick. We done had a smack party."

He slides from the bed, dresses, stuffs his bankroll and dope into his pockets.

She rolls to the edge of the bed with dope-glazed eyes, mumbles thickly, "Leave me a light taste of that shit."

Stony faced he says, "Uh-uh, 'ho mama . . . Connect with me in the Blue Pit if you wanta score or be my woman. You dig?"

She nods stuporously as he turns and splits the bedroom.

Three

*D*ivorcée Marguerite Spingarn and her Club Alabam companions leave after the last show to have seafood at a Pico Boulevard restaurant. Afterward, Judge Evans, recent widower, drives them through thickets of extinguishing neon into the quietly lighted environs of Marguerite's impressive white stone house on tree-embossed Normandie Avenue in a still predominantly white-upper-middle-class neighborhood. Her real estate brokerage sign glows its pale blue neon in a front window. The fragrance of honeysuckle, ringing the house, pervades the night air.

Marguerite's all-day visitors, Rob Spingarn and his cutie-pie wife Helena, sleepily kiss Marguerite and the Judge good night. They go, arm in arm, to their new blue Chrysler sedan, parked in Marguerite's driveway behind her new fuchsia Caddie convertible. Marguerite and the Judge watch the ruby orbs of the Chrysler taillights disappear. Santa Ana winds lute a mournful dirge through a trio of weeping willow trees sighing counterpoint on Marguerite's spacious lawn.

"Happy kids, aren't they, Maggie?" the Judge says softly.

"Yes . . . Jay and I were happy like that . . . in the beginning . . . hope their happiness train never derails," she says as she flicks flame to a cigarette, exhales a gray poltergeist of smoke through an open window.

His amorous soft brown eyes gaze adoringly at her dusky, sloe-eyed loveliness as he takes her hand, kisses her fingertips. "Maggie, you, we could be happy again. I've been hellishly lonely since Ora passed last year . . . I . . . uh, have had, for many years, bountiful affection and admiration for you, as you must know. I've been in an airy fugue all evening in your company. My dear, I adore you! I must see you again and again. May I? Maggie, we are like canaries in the snow."

Her elfish face is serious as she studies his face with tender eyes for a moment, kisses his cheek. He reaches to embrace her.

She moves away, whispers huskily, "Cazzie, I've enjoyed you very much this evening . . . perhaps too much . . . Call me."

She flees the car and dashes up her walk, a scarlet sprite luminous in the starlight. He watches her tipsily fumble her key in the lock, blow a kiss before she enters the front door of the house. He drives happily away for his Malibu home.

Joe Allen Senior quietly keys into the Allen living room, glances at snoring Zenobia seated on the horsehair sofa, feet still immersed in the bucket of Epsom salts water. He removes his shoes, tucks them beneath an arm, goes up the stairway to Joe Junior's vacant bedroom.

He steps across the hall into his bedroom. The walls and dressertop are covered with rare posters and photographs of his idol, Jack Johnson. He gazes reverently for a moment at a mirror polished brass bound Bible that sits enshrined on a gold satin pillow on the dressertop. Beside it sits a bust portrait of his beloved, spit-image, lynched, preacher father. He undresses, liniments his aching knees before he puts on his favorite lounge ensemble of lavender pajamas, robe, and bedroom slippers. He returns to a living room chair near a front window to look out for Joe Junior.

He shifts his eyes to Zenobia, cruelly spotlighted in a klieg of streetlamp. He compares her jowly face with Marguerite's taut facial planes, Marguerite's pearly dazzle of teeth with Zenobia's snuff-browned teeth rotted and jagged in her agape mouth oozing snuff spittle at its corners.

He scans, compares the cables of varicose veins on Zenobia's tree trunk limbs with the smooth sleek legs and thighs of Marguerite, Zenobia's pendulous breast globs with the girlish jut of Marguerite's confection peaks. He stares, compares Zenobia's ballooned belly deformed by soul food suet with the sexy concavity of Marguerite's fashion model waist.

He sighs, shakes his head. How could it happen? Where did Zenobia's cute face and pulse-lashing figure go, the years, his own youth? He shudders and is panged by pity for himself, for her. He goes across the carpet, pauses to stare at her shambled face. He feels only sterile affection for his faithful, cantankerous, broken old doll as he goes past her to the kitchen to brew a cup of coffee.

In the feeble glow of the kitchen night-light he gazes at his lean six-three frame magnified into a gigantic ceiling-high shadow on the wall above the gas stove. He thinks that only in Marguerite's presence does he feel himself so heroically magnified. His ancient Zulu maiden—Dutch slaver roots are revealed dramatically in the blue flare of flame beneath the coffeepot that flickers his square cast, sensual-lipped Afro visage. Red highlights glint his near silky hair.

He stares at the gas flame, remembers long-ago festive flame: Succulent odors from a sharecropper's barbecue in celebration of the end of World War One waft into a boxcar. He sees himself leap off a freight train into heavy brush outside Macon, Georgia. He sees himself, a half-starved bedraggled murder fugitive from the chain gang, sneak into a sharecropper cabin on a knoll overlooking a frenetic scene.

Sweat-shiny celebrants, in Sunday best overalls and calico, dance and sing to the music of tambourines and banjos around browning carcasses of pigs spitted above crackling flames that grenade sparks into the clamorous night air. A sea of the plantation's cotton in blossom sparkles like ermine beneath a ceiling of crystal stars.

He thinks of how he exchanged his striped convict pants for field-grimy overalls found beneath the bed in the cabin. He remembers his wild anxiety crouching in the shadows waiting for the cabin occupants, rehearsing what he'd say to win support and compassion. At midnight, he presses himself deeper into the cabin murk. He remembers his high-grade erection watching the approach of an outrageously voluptuous and beautiful barefoot girl of thirteen agleam like sealskin in the moonlight, moving up a forested path to the cabin.

She lights a kerosene lamp and discovers his presence. He stifles her startled scream with his palm, blurts out his fugitive tale. She weeps to hear it, shares remnants from the barbecue feast with him. She tells him her name is Zenobia. Her child's face is unforgettably sad as she tearfully confides that she is an orphan married to a cheating, brutal husband three times her age. He has gone off to the cabin of his octoroon girlfriend on a nearby plantation, she tells him as she shows a snapshot of the grossly ugly fornicator.

She gives him an army blanket, buttermilk, a bag of cracklins and corn bread. She leads him to a hiding place in a stand of magnolia trees. He remembers Zenobia, hesitant to leave, gazing into his eyes. Then sudden erotic chemistry melds them, humps them furiously together on a bed of wild daisies. He remembers he didn't see her again until ten years later in 1928 after several stints on plantations and dozens of clandestine redneck-sponsored prizefights for miserly fees in Georgia and Mississippi.

Rediscovered, she is despondent, pregnant, and freshly abandoned by Cecil Brown, her second cousin common-law husband. He sees her drinking herself into a stupor in a blind pig moonshine joint in the hills outside Vicksburg. Sees himself rescuing her from mass rape by a hovering, hooched-up gang of cotton slaves. He remembers his heart cavorted at the sight of her again, the lovely vision she was in Salvation Army peach lace when they married six months later in a country church. He remembers that a year after Joe Allen Junior was born the family made it by Greyhound to the promised land, Los Angeles.

And now the sound of Zenobia muttering in her sleep dissolves Joe's reverie. He pours a huge mug of coffee, heavily laced with scotch, goes back to his chair at the window. Shortly, he rises to soundlessly open the door for Joe Junior. They go up the stairway to Junior's room.

"Damn, Li'l Joe, you had me worried . . . better put on your pajamas before Zen wakes up," Senior Joe says as he sits on the side of the bed, sips from the coffee mug.

Young Joe quickly shucks out of his street clothes and is putting on pajamas when his father says, with a knowing gleam in his eye, "You sonuvagun! Those bite marks and scratches on your back tell me you've had a ball with a hot-butt chippie."

Young Joe frowns as he sits beside his stepfather. "Pops, you got it wrong . . . I had a ball with a pretty, high-class business lady from Chicago. She's got Reba skunked on the figure side," he says as he air-sculpts Delphine's curves with his palms.

"That's great, son! I'm glad you finally realize that Reba isn't the only pretty girl in the world. I always hated to see you busting your heartstrings over Reba since you were twelve with never a Chinaman's chance to be anything to her except a play brother."

Young Joe exclaims, "Oh, me and Delphine got a groovy thing going from the git-go. She told me I'm the most striking-looking stud she's ever met and the best in bed. She's lonely, cried and told me she needs me. Pops, she sho 'nuff makes me feel gooooood!"

Senior Joe's eyes narrow suspiciously. "You just saw . . . uh, met Delphine tonight for the first time?"

"Yeah, so what, Pops? You and Mama had to meet the first time."

"You sound like you falling in love too soon, Li'l Joe. She might blow cold and dump you like they sometimes do. She could mess up your fighter's head, son, if you start dreaming a dream that can't come true like with Reba."

"She's for real. She wants to be my fox. She ain't in love with another stud like Reba."

"What kinda businesslady is she?"

"Had a beauty shop in Chi, gonna open one in L.A. She's got boo-koos of dough her father left her tied up in court."

"She older than you?"

"Near my age, maybe a year or two older."

"Ah! That's bad. She could be a fooling thirty, hardened and laid a zillion times. They come pretty but rotten like that, son, high-jiving and looking like angels fresh from heaven."

"She ain't jiving! Why you signifying 'bout her so tough, Pops?"

Elder Joe upends the mug of scotch-laced coffee, says, "I'm worried that the lady is too fast for you, which is bad news for a young fighter who is prepping his body and head to be heavy-weight champion of the world."

He drapes his arm around Junior Joe's shoulders, slurs with visceral passion, "Don't get trapped now in your young life like I was and blow the chance to live like a king with a worldful of luxuries and fabulous broads panting to lay poontang on you after you become champ. Don't wind up like me in the funky ghetto reaming shit for the white boss for chicken feed and trapped in hell with a Jesus crazy old—"

The hurt, shocked expression on his stepson's face as he jerks from his embracing arm abruptly sobers him, checks his scotch-loosened tongue. Sweat bubbles his forehead as he creaks to his feet, says shakily, "I'm sorry, Li'l Joe . . . That wasn't my heart speaking about Zen . . . just my scotch."

Young Joe stares up at him shaking his head incredulously as tears flood his eyes. He whispers in a ragged monotone, "Pops, I can't dig you, cracking you in hell and bad-mouthing Mama after all the years she's been in your corner, slaving to make it with you. Pops, you don't love Mama, don't wanta be with us?"

"Son, you know I love and cherish you and Zen," elder Joe whispers with anguished downcast eyes.

"Pops, me and you been tight like you my real pa. But we gonna fall out if you ever call Mama bad names again."

Elder Joe says, "Son, it won't happen again. I promise. Can you forgive me?" He extends his hand.

Young Joe stares at it, says, "I don't know right now, Pops."

Elder Joe turns and leaves the room with leaden feet.

Junior follows him into his bedroom, embraces him, says, "Pops, I forgive you. You still my main man."

As they disengage, elder Joe says, "And you mine, son."

Young Joe says, "I'm not going to bed and leave Mama down there sleeping in her clothes."

Elder Joe says, "I'll go down and wake her up," as he picks up his pearl gray suit coat to put on a hanger.

Young Joe snatches the coat and stares at the crimson smudge of Marguerite's lipstick on a lapel. "Oh Pops!" he exclaims with a contorted face.

He flings the coat to the carpet, stomps on it, says harshly, "Nigger, you done gone crazy?! You know Mama's got high blood pressure. Heavy stuff like that lipstick could give Mama a stroke. Nigger, don't waste my mama!"

They freeze at the sound of Zenobia's ponderous feet on the stairway.

Elder Joe stage-whispers, "Panther Cox's girlfriend branded my coat dancing with me. I ain't never played around on Zen. I swear, son!"

Young Joe dashes across the hall into his bedroom and eases the door shut. He gets into bed and cuts off the nightstand light. His need to believe in his stepfather forces him through a wall of doubt to accept the lipstick fable as truth.

He listens to his parents' conversation: "Midnight Creeper, is my chile home in one piece from the prize ring?"

"Yeah, Zen, except for a light scratch on his nose that don't matter a hill of beans."

"I didn't nap until after midnight. I done told you and told you I don't want my chile in them streets prowling late at night."

"We were off the streets, inside playing whist at Panther's with a few fighters and handlers . . . Junior's been asleep a long time."

Junior Joe hears his mother grunt dubiously, go to her bedroom for a moment, then go into the bathroom. He drifts into sleep listening to her draw a tub of bathwater.

Later, refreshed by her long nap and bath, Zenobia makes up her face. She leaves the bathroom with her bulk swathed in a tentlike white satin bathrobe. She opens Elder Joe's bedroom door as Joe is coming out. He pecks her forehead.

She follows him to the kitchen, stands beside him as he brews coffee, croons, "Big Joe, I brought you some of that catered choclit moosie from the white folks' party you crazy 'bout."

"Thank you, Zen. I'll eat it tomorrow," he murmurs as he stares at the coffeepot.

Her demolished doll face, thickly made up, is gargoylish in the murk of night light. She gazes cow-eyes at his dimpled cheeked profile, almost boyish in the sorceress soft light. Rare passion pings and fires her cold loins for the first time in almost three months.

"Big Joe, I been on a two-week diet and dropped almost six pounds. I ain't gonna stop losing 'til I get myself down to that tantalizing size you like when we opened the cafe. Remember how the customers flirted with me and made you salty?" she says as she massages her epic blubber against his buttocks.

"Yeah, Zen, I remember. You were something else, old girl . . . You can lose it, dear heart," he says as he pecks her forehead. He flees with the mug of coffee to the nearly empty fifth of scotch in a cupboard.

Rejected, she balefully watches him scotch-spike the coffee, says peevishly, "Guess I'll go to bed so I'll be feeling pert for church . . . hope you gonna go with me so I can prove I still got a husband."

With fake reluctance creasing his face he says, "Wish I could, Zen, but I got a lagging factory boiler to connect for Monday operation . . . maybe next Sunday, baby."

She waddles across the kitchen, evil eyed, to face him, ropy veined hands on her hips. "You been saying next Sunday for six months. Do that boiler after church. I ain't taking it no more. Joe Allen, you going to take me to church this morning. I'm not going alone!" she commands as she stomps toward the kitchen doorway.

"I don't want to go. I'm not going, Zen. Whatsa matter? Your main man, Sweet Dick Jesus, too busy to take you?" His calm, steely voice and taunt halt her, bring her back.

She tiptoes, eyeball to eyeball. "You blaspheming snake! You 'shamed of me, ain't you?! Bet you ain't 'shamed of that conning gutter skunk you hooked up with that's got you primping and thinking you young and cute."

She wiggles her nose, almost touches his face as she sniffs his mouth and his mustache. He recoils.

She exclaims, "Aha! I smell her pussy stink on your mustache!"

He shapes a controlled little smile, laughs hollowly. "Zen, what you must smell is the catfish I had at Panther's place. And I'm not gonna apologize for being fairly well preserved and keeping myself up. Don't blame me 'cause your hair turned white and you let yourself get fat and old . . . 'Sides, I'm gonna love you anyhow 'til the last breath I draw," he placates as he sees her eyes cloud with rage and her fists knot and quiver at her sides.

"You lyin'! I been knowing you foolin' 'round. And I ain't old yet. I ain't but forty-two. Shoot! You sixty. You old 'nough to be my papa. You old gray-butt, pussy-eatin' devil." She savagely waggles an index finger beneath his nose. "Don't you never let your mouth call me old again. I look old 'cause I gotta slave for the white folks, 'cause you wrecked the Down Home Cafe bettin' race horses and good-timin'.'"

"Zen, I swear on Mama's sainted soul, you smelled catfish. Zen, you hurt me when you get carried away by your imagination . . . I want to make it with you but you make it so hard," he says as he moves with a sadly solemn face and his laced mug of coffee toward the doorway.

She scrambles to block his way. She seizes the lapels of his robe, stares up into his shifting eyes. "Awright, fess up and promise me you ain't gonna midnight-creep no more and you ain't gonna see her no more and I'll forgive you . . . ain't no reason we can't make it swell together like we usta. C'mon now, Sweet Patootie, fess up and promise!"

He musters the guile to focus his wayward eyes on hers with unblinking, wounded innocence. "Zen, there's nothing to confess. You can't forgive an innocent man. You can't get yourself together, Zen . . . How can we make it?"

She stoops with a grunt, jerks up his right pajama leg. A circular chain gang shackle scar blackens his ankle.

She looks up into his face, says in a deadly monotone, "We better make it 'cause you mine, slick Mister Sweet Man. I tried to give you your last chance. Now ain't no more. When I catch you with her I'm gonna send you to get your leg jewelry back."

She straightens up, glares at him. Her blood pressure sky-rockets. She clutches her chest, gasps for air before she staggers away to leave him alone, paralyzed by the doomsday import of her threat.

Four

A warrior Sunday morning sun pierces a pall of smog with a volley of golden spears, illuminates the high-walled Beverly Hills estate of the interracial Sternbergs, Pretty Melvin's parents. Reba Rambeau, asleep in a sky blue stucco guest cottage behind the opulent French castle–styled main house, is awakened by the spastic gymnastics of her captive fetus.

She grimaces as she massages the top of her abdomen with the heels of her hands to assuage discomfort from the Flamenco stomp of the fetus' feet inside her rib cage. She glances about the lavish gold and lavender motifed bedroom. She stares at sleeping Melvin's face framed by a tousled mop of silky sable hair on the pillow beside her.

She remembers the myriad times since she was twelve that she had orgasmed in secret shadows with Melvin in the black ghetto home of the Sternbergs when his doctor father and receptionist-RN Eurasian-black mother were working long hours in their Central Avenue office.

Hatred twinges her for the exquisitely fashioned face of the promiscuous humper that hooked her, broke her heart a score of times. She rummages her mind for the generic term that fits his affliction. She grabs and mashes his testicles to awaken him when she recalls it. Satyriasis. He knuckles his great startled hazel eyes open like a little kid, reflexively swoops his head to suck her nipple like a ravenous baby.

He groans ecstatically, "Oh! I love you, Ice Cream Cone."

She finger-combs his hair, thinks, Damn! I love this rotten sweet sonuvabitch. He licks a trail to her pubic enclave.

She whispers, "Darling please, I'm not fresh," as she gently pushes his head away.

He scoops her up into his arms, carries her to the bathroom. They brush their teeth, make love in the mammoth black marble bathtub before they return to bed.

Her yellow fawn face is serious as she asks, "Mel sugar, we can be so happy if we're true and faithful to each other. I vow and promise now because I know I will . . . Will you promise?"

He shapes his chippie-rutting lopsided little boy smile. "I've had my run and I'm ready for pasture in the tall sweet clover with you and whatsit's name. I promise to be true always, sweetmeat."

He uses an intercom phone to order a breakfast of crêpes suzette and Bavarian sausage. A white thatched twig of a Scotsman serves them on a silver service.

In lounging robes they go to don bathing suits in the cabana at the edge of the kidney-shaped pool. Their laughter, as they frolic, shrills the morning air, attracts the critical eyes of the elder Sternbergs, breakfasting in the second-story master bedroom above the pool.

Their faces are permanently etched haggard by the twenty-three years of their daily ten to sixteen hours of treating multitudes of black patients and delivering their offspring at ungodly hours in ghetto hospitals. Often without pay.

Once voluptuously Junoesque, Mai Ling Sternberg, Hong Kong exotic dancer in her teens, is an emaciated semi-invalid. Ironically, diabetes struck her near the peak of the Sternbergs' stress-ridden climb to riches and a white socialite practice second to none.

She muses in a soft soprano voice, crisped by a faint British accent, "Saul, Reba has certainly grown into an attractive young woman . . . prettier I think than she was when we delivered her . . . I'm sure I'd like her as a daughter-in-law . . . Are you certain their marriage is unviable for Melvin's future and our own best career and social interests?"

His corrugated LBJ look-alike face is pained as he stares at the cavorting couple through an open louvered window for a long moment before he says, "Mai, you know my affection for Reba and my empathy for her rocky childhood, torn between two neurotic parents. Now Mai, as you know I've got no claim to pristine roots. My mother was a ragpicker when top price was two cents a pound. My old man was the only Jewish wino bum it has ever been my great displeasure to know."

"Neither have I that claim," Mai says sadly. "My father a hanged opium smuggler, my mother a permanent asylum inmate before my seventh birthday."

He says, "Mai, aside from the basic disadvantage of marriage at this time to Melvin's launching into premed school this fall, candidly, I must say, I'm reluctant to inflict Melvin as a husband on her. I'm convinced the boy is just not emotionally ready to handle the responsibilities and strictures of husband and father."

He pauses to lift their breakfast trays off the bed to the carpet. He reaches into a humidor atop a blond Chippendale nightstand near the window. He takes a lighter from the pocket of his gold brocade smoking jacket, lights the panatela. He sighs pleasure as he exhales a gust of aromatic smoke.

She smiles, kisses his blue-stubbled jaw. Phantom vestiges of her almond-eyed café-au-lait splendor mystiques through the drawn mask of her illness in the soft maize blush of infant sun.

She says, "Have you had a chance to finish the investigator's reports?"

He says, "Yes, late last night, and they depressed me."

"Why?" she asks. Then, in the same breath, "Does Mel know about the reports?"

He shakes his head to the second question. He says, "Well, Baptiste, poor guy, got only an ace-deuce shot at life from the beginning . . . His father appeared as a prosecution witness in the murder conviction of the leader of a New Orleans voodoo sect. Three-year-old Baptiste saw the execution of his mother and father and six older brothers and sisters. He was kidnapped by the killers and forced into a life of transvestism, perhaps perversion, certainly crime by the new homosexual 'fagin' leader of the sect.

"At fifteen, he was an accomplished cardsharp, pickpocket, and ravishing female impersonator baiting tourist tricks for muggers in the French Quarter. There he met Philippa, an orphaned teenage whiz at the badger game played with a Baton Rouge–based pimp and con man on johns during Mardi Gras. Her mentor got swept up in a police net. Philippa and Baptiste fled, in tandem, to hustle the golden west, San Francisco.

"At twenty-two, in L.A., he married Philippa, pregnant with Reba, to dramatically prove that against all odds he was heterosexual with a heart still miraculously vulnerable to the grand passion. After we delivered Reba, he retired Philippa as strictly mother and housewife. Since then he has earned their living as a journeyman card swindler with only an occasional dip into an unsuspecting pocket. He lost Philippa last year, as you know, to that Williams kid after gunplay . . . All these years we thought the guy sold roofing and siding contracts."

Mai Ling heaves a heavy sigh. "Baptiste is certainly no paragon father-in-law for Melvin . . . but I'm thinking it's unfair that Reba should suffer the consequences of her father's flaws. I cast my vote loud and clear for Reba as our daughter-in-law. She and the baby can be cared for here while Melvin is in premed. Perhaps Baptiste has reformed."

Maximal irritation flickers Saul's face. "Sweetheart, it can't work. Baptiste had his throat cut up in San Francisco last year while plying his craft. The guy is a predator in concrete. Why, if we brought him into our lives, he'd leech on to our friends and associates to infiltrate their card games. He'd fleece them and sooner or later be unmasked as a cheat. We would be excommunicated and disgraced with him."

She says, "But they love each other!"

He smiles wryly. "She loves Melvin, you mean. He loves to go to bed with her, as he does with any exceptionally endowed female that catches his Don Juan eye. Face it, Mai, we love the boy and I suspect we cushioned him too much, gave him too much. I think we ruined him in the ghetto with tailored clothes and fancy cars. He was like a despot king of teenagers, with his pick of the choicest girls and the ego-bloating worship of his subjects. I repeat, Reba does not deserve having our adored mixed-up son inflicted on her as a husband."

Mai says, "Perhaps she would accept care and support here unmarried . . . Since Melvin decided to join our church last month he seems less flighty. He could be on a moral turnabout. I've always believed he wasn't hopeless . . . Perhaps the influence of the church will result in his maturity to become Reba's husband in the near future."

Saul shakes his grizzled head. "Love, I don't think Melvin's church motivation was spiritual redemption but rather because I convinced him that his future medical practice needed the bedrock of a church congregation . . . And I think it may be too late to indefinitely defer the wedding, after the ring and her expectations . . . her Creole pride, you know, and the predictable shock of disappointment with fallout resentment for us as guiding culprits." He gnaws his bottom lip in thoughtful speculation. "There are two possible equitable solutions."

"Yes, like what?" Mai asks with a skeptical face.

Saul says, "I'm going to test Melvin's gut feelings about Reba and the marriage. I'm not planning to sacrifice my dream that he become a physician. Purely to test him, I'm going to tell him we've decided that premed school and marriage is not a good mix, that if he chooses marriage, then our only support will be the gift of a modest house that he must maintain on his own and a job changing tires for Greyhound that I will arrange with Murray, the foreman, down there . . . Well, dear, would you bet that diamond pendant on your lovely throat that he'll choose Reba or choose employment as a nine-to-five tire technician? Of course, we won't really force him to that."

She sighs. "That's a helluva test and choice to make for a man who gets a manicure every Friday . . . I hope he comes through with colors flying, love."

"And you know I feel the same. I'm pulling for him to take Reba but I wouldn't bet on him to go that way." Saul glances at his diamond-dial Patek Philippe wristwatch. He kisses Mai and gets out of bed. He does ten push-ups on the carpet before he will shave and shower for his usual Sunday visit to the black ghetto Universal Holiness Church of Reverend Felix and his child prodigy preaching son, Reverend Felix Junior. It is Saul's practice to mingle with and communicate with old friends there and slip generous checks to those in need.

Mai says, "I feel great, doctor darling! May I go with you?"

Saul rises from the carpet and goes to the bed, kisses her upturned face. "Next Sunday, pet, for sure." Then, as he turns to go to the bathroom, he adds, "If you're still feeling chipper later I'll take you to evening services at Saint Mark's."

She puckers her lips and makes a kissy sound to his back.

*A*t 8:50 A.M. Baptiste Rambeau walks Erica Swenson to a backyard gate. He dips his head toward the carton of marked new decks of playing cards she carries. He says, "Now honey pie, be sure to double-staple the decks of cards into a sack that one of my poker guests will come to buy. That way I'll know up front if he's switched in bust-out cards of his own. Give me a call right after he gets back. That way I can cancel the game off your call as an emergency without tipping that I'm hustler wise, that I'm not a mark."

They kiss.

"Will do, Da Dee," she says as he opens the gate.

As she steps into the alley he adds, "Oh say, as a double block against hanky-panky with the package, step out to the sidewalk and watch him all the way until he gets back here. He could have decks and a staple gun on him or stashed in a car."

She nods, glances at his throat scar, livid in the light, says "Do be careful with your . . . uh, guests" as she goes down the alley.

Baptiste watches the morning sun explode platinum fireworks from her tailbone-length mane until her girlish figure disappears.

He goes to his living room, yanks open heavy red velvet front window drapes to a shower of bright sunlight. His hands are jammed into the pockets of his red silk dressing robe as he paces the snow white carpet of the dazzling red and white furnished room.

All of it, the entire house furnishings, forfeit collateral if delinquent payments on a loan from a finance company are not made soon, he reminds himself with a painful scowl. He brakes his pacing, smiles satisfaction as he watches Pretty Melvin Sternberg's black Jag sedan pull to a stop in front of the house, behind the Rambeau dove gray Packard. He almost trots through the front door down the walk to the car. He warmly embraces black mohair–suited Melvin. Then he kisses Reba as she emerges through the car door held open by Melvin.

"How you doing, Mel?" he exclaims as Melvin pumps his extended hand.

"Fine, just fine, Mister Rambeau, and you?" He kisses Reba's upturned lips before she goes up the walk.

"I'm doing wonderfully well, son, thank you . . . How about coffee or something?" Baptiste croons as he beams the beatific smile reserved for fat marks.

"Thanks, Mister Rambeau, but not this time. I'll be late for a Bible class I teach at Saint Mark's Church across town," Melvin says as he goes to get behind the Jag's wheel.

Baptiste watches him sprint the Jag to the corner drugstore before he returns to the house. He finds Reba at her machine in her sewing room at the rear of the house.

"Have the muckety-muck rich folks set the date for the wedding?" he asks with gleaming eyes.

"Not yet," she says. "Melvin and his folks are finalizing the reception plans."

He watches as she completes the final stitching on her new choir robe. A craft her mother, Philippa, taught her. A half dozen neatly bagged and tagged garments hang on a rack beside her to be picked up by well-paying customers of her newly launched enterprise.

Baptiste glowers behind her as she starts to rehem one of the taller Philippa's daringly cleavaged dresses. "Baby dear, what are you doing with that vulgar dress?" he says in an echo chamber voice.

The reek of suppressed outrage in his voice swivels her on her chair to face him with enormous green eyes wide and quizzical. "I'm shortening this elegant dress of Mother's to wear . . . It's from Saks and awfully expensive."

He grunts. "You're telling me. I paid the bill. Look, baby, please, for me and your own dignity, don't wear that thing to church. Your mother's dresses wear lousy on you."

"I'm wearing it later. Melvin is taking me to a late afternoon cocktail party in Hollywood. This dress will be great. Okay, Daddy bunny?"

His brows hedgerow. "Girl, I don't want you to wear it—none of Philippa's things anytime, anywhere. Is that clear!?"

Her eyes slit and chill. "Baptiste, you can't dictate to a woman with child and a husband on the turn what she can wear. Is that clear!?"

She turns back to whir the machine. He lights a cigarette and stares at the yellow daisy–appliquéd black chiffon dress draped on the machine. He tries to recall why he despises this particular dress so much.

He mumbles to her back, "Reba, I meant what I said. You can't wear that dress!"

She chants in sync with the beehive hum of the machine like an impudent child, "I can, I can, I can, I will, I will, I will," as she completes the alteration. She stands, pulls the dress on over her slip. She smiles wickedly as she looks at herself in a wall mirror.

He glances at her reflection, suddenly remembers that Philippa wore it the night of a midnight cruise: Suspicious of her long absence, he left a dancing partner to search for her. He caught a young chef humping her in a gallery pantry. He remembers he lunged to attack them with a cleaver. He was restrained and manhandled by crewmen, then locked up until the ship docked at dawn. She got home the next midnight. He flinches to remember how they fought and screamed at each other.

His stare is poisonous as he sees Philippa's mint image in the mirror. Out of control, he snarls, "Reba, you're not wearing that goddamn nymphomaniac bitch dog's dress!"

She whirls. "Baptiste, are you drunk or just gone nuts!? I'm wearing my mother's dress," she says with bared teeth.

He screams, "The hell you will!" as he seizes the plunging bodice and rips the dress off her, tears it into ribbons.

She flails her fists against his face and chest as she shrieks, "I hate you, Baptiste! I hate you!"

He flings the shredded dress aside at the sound of the doorbell. He ducks the barrage of her tiny fists into the hallway. She skims his hair with a flowerpot before she slams the door behind him.

He pauses to compose himself for a long moment before he goes to the front door. He takes his special card-mark reading glasses from his robe pocket, slips them on. He opens the door to admit his dapper poker guests with a shark smile.

He pumps the hands of the portly trio as they enter. An alien, lean, fox-faced figure looms in the doorway as he is closing the door. Baptiste's head roars as he tries to place the vaguely familiar stranger's face. Could he be a fellow shark he met on one of his cross-country swindle junkets? Or even a member of the gaping crowd the night his throat was slashed by the San Francisco sucker? Baptiste's gluey hand shakes the stranger's hand, then closes the door.

Cabaret owner Dudley says, "Bap, meet my nephew, Clarence Jones, owns a poolroom up North."

The group seat themselves on chairs and couch. Baptiste stands, avoids the inscrutable stare of Clarence's deep-set maroon eyes as he asks, "Gentlemen, how about refreshments before we put our bankrolls in competition?"

Lefty Hicks, Draw Back Davis, and Dudley request coffee. Dudley's nephew, ice water. To match his fucking eyes, Baptiste thinks as he leaves for the kitchen.

When Baptiste returns to place the refreshment tray on the cocktail table before them, Draw Back says, "You got fresh decks, Bap?"

Baptiste says, "No, we need some. Maybe the drugstore on the corner is open." He leans to dial the phone on the tabletop. He hears Erica answer, says, "Madame, you got Bee decks in stock?"

She says, "I miss you, Da Dee. Good luck."

Baptiste says, "You have? Thank you, ma'am." He replaces the receiver, says, "Gentlemen, I'll slip on some slacks and make that run to get the cards."

Clarence rises, says, "Bap, don't go to that trouble. I'll make the run."

Baptiste enjoys an interior guffaw as he reaches into his robe pocket to take out his two grand blood money boodle of fins and sawbucks thinly wrapped in C-notes and a fifty.

He gives Clarence the fifty, says, "A half dozen decks will get us started."

Clarence goes through the front door. Baptiste sits on the couch, reaches a pawnshop-denuded hand to get coffee.

Lefty Hicks snickers, "Bap, you get lifted for your rocks?"

Baptiste laughs. "Yeah, Lefty, I lifted them myself last night to start some painting upstairs."

Baptiste initiates preaction chitchat. "Gentlemen, it's a pleasure beyond your imagination, to have your company this morning."

Across the street, Zenobia is seated on the horsehair sofa with her bare feet in Junior Joe's lap. He is in pajamas. She is made up and in her Sunday lace-trimmed pink slip intently watching him razor-blade off Epsom salts water–softened corns to give her an unhobbled gait for church.

Upstairs, Senior Joe writhes in nightmared sleep. Chain gang horror images and sounds stomp his psyche. He sees again the power-maddened white convict trusties on horses riding shotgun on the crew of convicts leveling and chopping away brush from the narrow dirt road for widening and paving.

He hears the profane admonitions of the trusties to laggard convicts—"Awright Mammy-fuckahs, shake yuh lazy nigguh asses"—as they lash puffs of dust from the striped-shirted backs of the offenders.

He sees the trio of guards crouched in tree-shaded points of vantage with leashed bloodhounds and cradled carbines. He sees himself, the water boy, stop along the line when he sees the truck bringing the noon lunch of fatback and black-eyed peas pull to a stop beside him.

He hears himself shout "Got to let 'em down, Captain" to the wrinkled, leather-skinned redneck on a knoll above him, who shouts back permission to defecate. "Awright, boy, let 'em down."

He hears again the stentorian voice of the Captain yell, "Awright, yuh bastids, line up single file for eats."

He sees himself go across the road just far enough into bushes so that his chest is visible. He squats, strips off his shirt, hangs it stretched out on brambles. The instant the Captain's eyes stray to the convicts lining up, he dashes fifty yards to a river, plunges in. He swims a hundred yards downstream to the rear of the crew.

He hears the distant muffled voice of the Captain shout, "Awright, Joe Henry, wipe yuh black ass," when he emerges from the river.

He goes to watch a truck from a stand of trees at the edge of a slight bend in the cleared and leveled road. He sees the cleanup squad of convicts, the guard and black trusty driver of the brush-loaded truck march around the bend toward the main crew. He leaves cover, worms himself beneath the mountain of brush on the truck bed. Minutes later, he lies in the stifling darkness listening to the hounds' banshee howls of frustration in the forest beyond the river.

After what seems like eons, he hears the driver start the truck, back it up, turn around, and go toward a ravine to dump the load several miles away. He sees himself leap from the truck and roll into brush near railroad tracks. He sees himself hiding there with a thunderous heart until nightfall, when he hops a freight train bound for Macon, Georgia, and young Zenobia's sharecropper shack on the outskirts of the city.

And now a nightstand alarm clock bombs him awake. He jerks rigid from a fetal ball of trauma. The clock nearly slips from his sweat-greased hands as he picks it up to silence its din. As always when he awakens, he thinks of Marguerite Spingarn, remembers they have a late afternoon movie date.

I've got to stop seeing her for a while, maybe even break off completely with her. She's too risky with Zen suspicious, he tells himself. He rises, goes to the bathroom across the hall. Diarrhea keeps him on the stool for long moments before he brushes his teeth and showers.

He returns to the bedroom and compulsively goes to the closet, removes from a boot toe a nightclub shot of himself with Marguerite. His hand is tremulous as he gazes at it. He groans, I have to see her today. I can't do without her.

He takes from the closet a freshly cleaned plaid suit of moss green, tan silk shirt, green silk tie, and a pair of tan Stetson shoes. He dresses himself. Then he slips on plumbing boots and coveralls, buttoned to his Adam's apple, over his natty outfit. He goes to the living room.

On his way to the kitchen, he pauses at the sofa to peck Zenobia's forehead and say, "Good morning."

Junior says, "Morning, Pops."

Zenobia grunts. She says, "If you wait a while, you can drop me off at church."

He says, "Now, Zen, if I do that I'll be late on the job at the factory I told you about."

She stiff-arms his belly. "G'wan, Mister Midnight Creeper, I'd rather go in a classy Packard then in a funky plumbing truck anyways."

He goes to the kitchen, gulps down a glass of orange juice. He pecks Zenobia's forehead on his way to the front door.

As they watch Senior Joe drive away, Junior says, "Mama, you look tired. You oughta take my nest egg in the bank like I been begging you, use it to let you loose from killing yourself for the white folks."

She says, "Hush up, Li'l Joe. You gonna need that money and more'n that to marry and start a family, soon I hope." He is about to tell her about Delphine when she says, "Don't court no pretty grief givers. Best to court a ugly chile 'cause she's maybe gonna sho 'nuff love you. Pretty peoples oughta hitch up with pretty peoples . . . You sure ain't ugly, you 'tractive in your way. But chile, you sure ain't Mister Valentino. And another thing, you got to quit that ring fightin' and get a solid job . . . Why don't you go to church with me? The Lord might show you a wife."

Terminal pain screws up his face. "Mama, please don't ask me. Them niggers shouting and talking in them spooky tongues gives me the heebie-jeebies, and the hives. Remember?"

He narrowly escapes his kneecap from the kick of her foot heel. "Hush up and call your play sister. Tell her her play mama wants to ride to church with her."

"Aw, Mama! We on the outs. I don't wanta talk to her. I'll dial and you talk to her," he says as he takes the phone off the end table behind him to place in her lap. She leans, hugs, kisses him.

He dials, then hands her the receiver. He goes to the vacant two-bedroom rental house in the rear. He punches a light bag on the service porch converted to a mini-gym. Then he goes to plop down across a bed in one of the bedrooms to fantasize, for the dozenth time, his sexual romp with Delphine. He is catnapping when he awakens to soft lips on his cheek. He stares up at Reba aglow in her choir robe.

She says, "Hi, Bro, I hope you're not still mad with me."

Swooned by her perfumed presence and moonlit voice, he stammers, "Naw . . . uh, I ain't mad . . . uh, wasn't in the first place with you, but with Melvin and his cousin that teed me off way back in the ring."

She leans and kisses his hops, says, "Bye-bye."

Through a haze of excitement he sees her leave the room. He leaps from the bed, goes to the front house living room. He stands at a front window and watches Reba drive Zenobia, gussied up in black taffeta, away to church. His head is chaotic as it struggles to unravel the riddle of his flaming love for two women at the same time.

Within fifteen minutes, Reba drives into the car-clogged church parking lot. Immediately that she parks, the child prodigy preacher, Reverend Felix Junior, leaves a knot of members on the church steps. A breeze whips his flowing black satin robe on his greyhound frame as he hurries to the Packard with a radiant smile on his breathtakingly attractive peach-hued face. His Persian cat eyes are afire with precocious passion.

He warmly embraces Reba and Zenobia emerging from the car. "Good morning, ladies, good morning," he says in a voice surprisingly rich in timbre for a ten year old.

They chorus, "Good morning, Reverend Felix."

"Father, thank the Lord, is well enough today to preach his first sermon since his stroke three months ago. Praise the Lord!" the Reverend exclaims as he escorts the women toward the church.

Zenobia breaks off to go toward the front door of the church as the Reverend and Reba enter a rear door leading to the pulpit and choir section behind it.

As they go down a hallway, the Reverend embraces Reba's waist and squeezes her close. "I missed you so much since last Sunday, Sister Reba . . . Too bad services can't be held every day so I could see you," he says petulantly.

"Reverend Felix, that's very flattering for a pregnant, soon to be married woman to hear, especially from a handsome gentleman half her age."

His rosebud lips pout irritation. "Please, Sister Reba, call me just Felix when we're alone, if you don't mind."

She says, "I don't mind a bit, Felix," as he opens the door into the packed church.

He goes to sit, dwarfed in an ornately carved high-backed chair behind the pulpit beside his septuagenarian father. Reba takes her first-row seat with the choir behind the pulpit.

A scarecrow deacon, in shiny black suit and high, starched, yellowed white collar, comes behind the pulpit to welcome the congregation and to announce the singing of the hymn "Rock of Ages" by the risen choir. An elephantine woman organist accompanies the choir's spirited rendition of the hymn to the rapt thousand souls.

The Elder Felix is presented by the deacon to cacophonous applause by the brightly feathered congregation. He feebly rises and takes his position behind the pulpit. A wizened, destroyed yellow leprechaun of a man.

His sermon on the awesome risks of not requiting God's love and the shirking of one's obligation to contribute hurtfully to the Lord's work, the church, is sufficiently impassioned to produce the usual quota of shouters and talkers in tongues. And a collection bonanza.

After services, Saul Sternberg chats briefly in the parking lot with Reba and Zenobia, among many others.

As Reba is driving down Avalon Boulevard past a used car lot two blocks from the Rambeau and Allen homes, Zenobia says, "Chile, it sure is a beautiful day. Let me out. Think I'll hike home to pump some blood."

Reba pulls over to stop at the curb.

Zenobia kisses her cheek. She says, "Thank you, baby daughter, for the ride," as she exits the car.

"See you, Play Mama," Reba says as she pulls the Packard into traffic.

Zenobia stands and watches the Packard turn off Avalon Boulevard before she limps down the sidewalk to the used car lot. She threads her way through a maze of cars to a gleaming black '37 La Salle. She sweeps excited eyes over the tall prepossessing machine.

The florid fatso owner comes to her side. "Good afternoon, Mrs. Allen," he purrs. "Have you come to get your La Salle today?"

She says, "Today is the day my car is mine," as she digs in her bosom. She extracts a thin roll of bills. "Mister Slater, my figuring tells me I owe you thirty-six more dollars on this deal. That's right, ain't it?"

"That's right, Mrs. Allen. The battery's charged and you can drive off," he says as he hands her the key and scribbles a receipt for the bills she hands him. He then hands her the pink slip.

She takes it and says, "Mister Slater, what you charge me to park my car on your lot?"

With a puzzled expression he says, "I really don't know . . . anything you think is fair."

"How about five dollars for 'bout three weeks. Ain't thinking I'll need to park longer'n that," she says as she tenders the five.

He shrugs. "Fair enough."

She touches his coat sleeve before he turns away. "Mister Slater, I got a special reason that I don't want none of the peoples in the neighborhood knowing I done bought a car. Don't tell nobody and I'll 'preciate it."

"Don't worry, Mrs. Allen. It's our secret." He turns away.

She keys into the car, sits and turns on the ignition. She listens to the fairly smooth engine for a long moment and is reminded that the La Salle will be her first car since the Down Home Cafe days, three years before.

She smiles grimly as she whispers, "Look out, Mister Midnight Creeper!" She gets out and locks the La Salle.

As she hobbles home on relapsed feet, Baptiste sits tensely in his den stud poker arena. The fact that his table stakes two grand bankroll has been under constant siege convinces him that his opponents are bust-out gladiators of considerable skill themselves. He suspects that their betting attacks and play against each other are simply ploys to camouflage their plan to bust him out, then divvy his bankroll among themselves. He is also intimidated by the butt of the holstered pistol that peeks from beneath Clarence's suit coat.

Baptiste peeps at a hole card king of clubs followed by a second face-up king of diamonds dealt by Lefty Hicks to his left. He sees through his "reader" eyeglasses Hicks' hand: spade ace in hole with heart ten showing. Draw Back Davis': spade jack in hole with diamond deuce showing. Dudley's hand: spade deuce in hole with diamond eight showing. Directly across the table he sees that Dudley's nephew, Clarence Jones, has a pair of red treys.

Baptiste has placed Clarence as one of the sidewalk gawkers in San Francisco when he was taken to the ambulance with his throat cut.

Baptiste folds on dealer Lefty Hicks' fifty-dollar bet after the third card when Lefty Hicks deals himself the ace of hearts to pair with his ace in the hole. Draw Back Davis, dealt the diamond jack to pair with his spade jack in the hole, calls. Clarence's uncle Dudley folds. Baptiste's eyes slit in suspicion behind the tinted windows of his glasses to see Clarence call Lefty Hicks' fifty-buck bet and raise it to a C-note with only the pair of treys and a third card, king of hearts. Draw Back and Lefty Hicks call Clarence's C-note raise.

At the conclusion of the hand, Draw Back and Lefty Hicks throw superior hands into the discard when they let Clarence raise them out with his ace of diamonds high, pair of treys hand. Baptiste tells himself his guests have not only been in cahoots to bust him out and drain him broke against the bandit percentages of their four hands against one, his, but now are throwing their bankrolls to Clarence for the buck power to muscle him broke. To counteract their conspiracy, Baptiste vows to himself not to bet past a C-note unless he has the deck in hand.

At nine p.m. Baptiste finds himself head to head with cigar-chomping Clarence Jones. Baptiste, with close to twenty two hundred dollars before him, glances at the eight-grand bankroll stacked in front of Clarence. Draw Back, Dudley, and Lefty Hicks smoke cigarettes and drink coffee as they sit around the table and hawk-eye the seesaw action.

At eleven p.m. Baptiste has, on his deals-stacked hands, jumped Clarence's cuts of the deck back to original mortal cinch arrangement. On Clarence's deals, he has only called cinch bets. He has dealt seconds with wizard expertise to amass a four-grand pile of bills before him. Half of what he requires to save his house, furniture, and Packard.

They ante a sawbuck apiece. He watches Clarence riffle and stack the cards. He cuts. Clarence picks up the deck to deal. Baptiste enjoys an interior chuckle to hear an almost impercep-tible whisper of the cards as Clarence jumps his cut. Baptiste peeps at his diamond jack hole card followed by a second face-up club jack. He knows Clarence has a pair of nines, suspects, is almost certain, the third nine is stacked to fall before or on the fifth card.

Baptiste bets a double sawbuck. Clarence calls, deals the third card, a diamond ten to Baptiste, a spade queen to himself, bets a C-note. Baptiste calls, is dealt a heart ten for two pair. Clarence deals himself a spade king. Baptiste bets a token C-note, is called and raised five bills. Baptiste folds with his two pair to escape the third nine he is convinced Clarence has stacked to fall to himself on the fifth card.

Clarence spills the deck to the tabletop face up as he reaches to pull in the pot. He lights a fresh cigar as they ante. His eyes are bright with cunning as he watches Baptiste pick up the exposed deck and shuffle it.

Baptiste feels his pulse sledge as he shuffles the deck and stacks a bandit hand. Clarence cuts the deck, gets red kings wired. Baptiste peeps at his diamond queen hole card pairing his face-up space queen.

Clarence bets a C-note, is called and raised two bills. He calls, gets a heart queen, Baptiste a spade king. Baptiste bets two bills, is called and raised five bills that he calls. He deals Clarence a spade ten spot, himself a diamond eight spot.

The deck wobbles in Baptiste's hand. His stacked hand has gone awry. His fifth card, the third queen of hearts, is on top! Oh well, what the hell. I'll just have to deal the thieving bastard a second, Baptiste tells himself with a dealing palm popping sweat.

Clarence bets five bills. Baptiste calls and shoves his nineteen hundred dollar tap-out raise into the pot. Clarence rises to his feet, leans his long frame across the table, takes a deep draw from his cigar as he stares into Baptiste's eyes.

Clarence says, "Bap, there ain't no help for you here," as he taps the top of the deck—Baptiste's winning third queen—with the fiery tip of the cigar.

Baptiste ashens as he stares at the pinpoint scorch on his money card. Clarence's trio of confederates exchange ecstatic glances.

Clarence says, "Bap, I hope that accident with my cigar didn't jinx me," as he lets himself down into his chair.

He counts out nineteen hundred, shoves the bills into the pot with a fiendish grin on his foxy face. The gallery of victors smirk and stare at Baptiste as he sits trancelike looking at the deck in his trembling hand.

"Bap, I'll give you a grand on your jewelry upstairs or two grand on your house if you think you've got the better hand and want to raise me," Clarence taunts. Then, "C'mon, Bap, deal out the hand and pee your pants," as Baptiste slowly shakes his head.

Baptiste's hand shakes as he flips the queen of hearts to Clarence. He turns the heart ten spot intended for Clarence, hurls the deck to the tabletop and rises on trembly legs.

He manages a tortured smile, says hoarsely, "Well, gentlemen, looks like that tramp Lady Luck has crossed me."

His guests rise. Clarence says, "Here's a double saw, Bap, for your lonesome pocket."

Baptiste scowls. "Thanks, but I don't need it. I've got walk-around dough upstairs . . . I'll get in touch with Draw Back to set up another session in a couple of days."

He heads the quartet to the front door, opens it. He shakes their hands as they file out. He shuts the door, goes to a front window. Despair slumps his shoulders as he watches them drive away. Don't panic! Don't panic! he shouts to himself as he collapses onto the sofa.

He stares blankly into space, immobile, slumped like a graven image of defeat until Susie the terrier scratches and whines at the front door. He heaves a sigh, gets to his feet with laborious effort. He opens the front door, follows as Susie goes to her potty spot in bushes at the edge of the sidewalk.

He glances at his watch and sees it is half past midnight, sees the lights of the corner drugstore extinguish. He idly watches elderly Havelik, the store owner, and his burly son exit and lock the front door in a wash of streetlamp. He watches them go to their car with the usual brown paper sack containing store receipts clutched in the son's hand.

Excitement reels Baptiste as he remembers that Erica, in her shop prattle, mentioned that on the last day of the month, when customers pay up their credit accounts, the Haveliks carry nine, ten thousand dollars with them when they close. Baptiste tells himself the heist of that paper bag is his only out. He has to save the house.

His head vibrates as he mulls heist angles, disguises, and choreography. He and Susie go down the walk into the house.

Five

Two weeks later at noon, Delphine, Young Joe's goddess, is awakened by the belly claw of her embryo monkey. Her great gray eyes anxiously sweep the drawn-drape purple murk for the presence of the gibbering sex fiend demons who have tortured her in her sleep. Her apricot mane is a tousled frame of flame about her wickedly pretty face as she slides her naked arsenal of golden curves to her preprepared speedball mix of "C" and "H" in a syringe on the nightstand.

She pillow-props herself, bends her knees, opens her thighs wide. She turns on and places the nightstand lamp at an angle on the bed to illuminate her vulva. She props a hand mirror against the bedcovers to reflect her sex nest. With the syringe spike at ready, she locates a vivid blue vein, stabs in the needle and shoots in the dope. She extracts the spike, moans rapturously as she relaxes with hooded eyes in heroin's poisonous womb bliss.

She enjoys her favorite fantasy: She sees Big Louise, her mother, attacked by a nude mob of giggling johns. One of the mob loops his belt around Louise's throat to cut off her piteous screaming. Louise's naked whalelike blubber arches, quivers, and leaps when the mob wrenches her legs agape and gang-rapes her with gigantic organs swathed in barbed-wire-studded condoms. Delphine sees herself mercifully smother Louise with a giant pillow.

Fantasy steeped, Delphine finally picks up the phone receiver on the fifth jangle to Young Joe's basso profundo voice. "Baby Lady, you all right?" he asks.

"Fine and thinking of you, heartbreaker," she coos.

"You gonna pick me up at three?" he says.

"That's right, handsome sugar, at the usual place at three sharp. So don't be late a second or I'll beat your sweet butt, you hear?"

He laughs. "I don't want you doing that, Miss Sugar Ray, so I won't be late. Bye."

An hour later she has showered, made up, and dressed in clingy rust silk with tan ankle-strapped baby doll shoes and matching bag. She dials Whispering Slim at home, makes her third deal in the past two weeks to pick up two bills' worth of "H" within the hour.

She leaves the building, goes to a black battered '41 Ford parked down the block. She guns it away. She purchased it to carry out her plan to rip off Slim's dope cache she believes is in an upper Avalon Boulevard one-bedroom house she's tailed him to on several late evening occasions from the Blue Pit Bar. Then, she had tailed him back to the bar, to fill dope orders, she is certain.

She drives to park a block from Slim's lavish six-bedroom residence on Hoover. She tails Slim to the Avalon house. Ten minutes later, she parks a block away from the blistered frame house. She watches Slim drive his puce Caddie into the drive-way of the house and key into it. Within five minutes, he comes out and drives away.

She decides to rip off Slim's dope and Joe Junior's bank nest egg on the same day in the near future and split to the Big Apple. She U-turns, goes home to exchange cars. She drives to the Blue Pit Bar, enters to slide in across from Slim in a front window booth. The bar is deserted except for a barmaid and the three-way dwarf-ish whore with the epic behind seated with her Popeye look-alike trick at the bar.

Delphine slaps the side of Slim's thigh with the back of a hand palming two C-notes. He takes it off beneath the table, takes a flash look at it before he sticks it into a trouser pocket. He drains his glass of Coke, starts to move out.

She presses a palm against his canary yellow suit sleeve. "How about my merchandise, Slim?"

He whispers, "Easy, girl, I was gonna tell ya, your package is taped under that stool at the far end of the bar," as he leaves the booth.

She sits for a moment, watches him go across the sidewalk to his Caddie and pull away. She goes to sit on the stash stool, orders a planter's punch. She gets the stash, stuffs it into her bosom. She pays the barmaid and leaves the bar preceded by Epic Bottom and her trick.

Ten minutes later she pulls to a stop to pick up Joe Junior, fresh and neat in a pearl gray slax suit. He is surrounded by a mob of idolizing teenagers on a corner across the street from Slater's used car lot. Zenobia's La Salle is absent! Delphine slides across the seat to the passenger side, push-buttons the top down as Joe gets beneath the wheel. They kiss.

As Joe pulls the Continental away, she exclaims, "Candy Daddy, I've found it!"

He says, "What?"

"The location for Delphine's Beauty Box. Go to Vernon Avenue just off Central and I'll show you the frame of my dream."

He drives to park in front of the "for rent" storefront. They get out and peer through plate glass into spacious rectangular, freshly painted purple emptiness.

"Isn't it beautiful!?" she exclaims.

"Yeah, I guess. But ain't it kinda big?" he says as they turn away for the car.

"Probably not big enough." Delphine waves an arm toward the nearby intersection of Central and Vernon Avenues, the ghetto's busiest hub.

It is teeming, even on Sunday, with mostly women window-shopping, alighting from or waiting for east-west or north-south streetcars.

They get into the car. As he drives away she says, "I visualize at least ten booths with really expert beauticians."

He shakes his head dubiously. "That's gonna cost a lotta bucks to set up, ain't it? . . . More'n the four or five bills I maybe could help you with."

She says, "You angel! I won't need your help. I haven't told you the most wonderful part. One of my father's lifelong friends, an L.A. doctor, has promised to back the whole venture with cash and the necessary credit backup with his cosignature. I'm so happy!" She scoots close to him with her cheek against his shoulder. "Let's have a picnic, sweetheart," she says.

"That's mellow! . . . You got goodies packed there in the trunk?"

She says, "No, but we can get everything we need at that delicatessen on Broadway."

When he parks in the crowded lot beside the popular store, he takes out his wallet.

She opens the car door, says, "Baby, this is my treat. My lawyer in the Windy sent me some money against that big money my father left me. He expects to recover most of it from the IRS before the year is out." She exits.

He watches her go across the lot into the store. When she returns with the picnic bag, she folds four twenties and shoves them into his shirt pocket.

He says, "What's this?" as he removes them and stares at them.

She takes them from his palm and slips them back into his shirt pocket. "That's the four weeks' rent you loaned me to save me from eviction. Don't break your promise to let me pay you back. Remember?"

He kisses her, says "Girl, you something else" as he pulls the Lincoln away into traffic.

She says, "Stop at a liquor store."

A half mile later he pulls past a police car besieged by shouting black teeners, into the parking lot of a liquor store at Central and Florence Avenues.

He says, "The juice is my treat. What do you want?"

"I'm in the mood for sloe gin," she says, "but with that hassle on the street shouldn't you get it somewhere else?"

He gets out. "I know those kids. I'm gonna see what's going on. Stay put."

She shakes her head as she watches him walk toward the melee. As he reaches the mob of club and bicycle chain–armed teenagers, a cop hurtles his cruiser away, knocking several of the cursing teeners to the pavement.

"Nigguhs! What the fuck is going on!?" Joe roars.

In utter silence the twenty odd boys turn and stare at Joe. The leader, a six-four brawny giant of sixteen, steps forward with a hostile face. "Kong, we tired of that muthafuckah rousting us all the time," the kid growls.

Joe shoves him hard. "Benny, don't call me Kong no more. Nigguh, you don't know me that well."

Benny's fortress of muscles tightens as he glares at Joe. Joe says, "Jump-frog! I dare you." Then he eye-sweeps the gang, says, "That cop is gonna call in for a firing squad. What you suckers waiting for? A trip to the morgue?"

Benny snarls, "Fuck 'em! We ain't getting in the wind. Ain't that right, guys!?"

The gang cheers halfheartedly.

Joe rams his face into Benny's, shouts, "You chumps don't wanta listen to Benny. This sucker don't know his ass from a stiff in a coffin. Now break up and hit that alley." He dips his head toward it, behind the parking lot. "G'wan, split before the Gestapo shows."

Benny says, "Gang, we ain't fleeing," as he casts apprehensive eyes down the avenue.

Joe seizes him, roughly mock-frisks him.

"What you doing, man!?" Benny asks as he backs up, brandishes a bicycle chain.

"Since you staying to face shotguns, nigguh, I was frisking you for the machine gun you oughta have," Joe intones.

Benny's cohorts snicker. Benny swings the chain at Joe's head. Joe ducks it and decks Benny with an uppercut, snatches the chain and lashes Benny's buttocks.

He helps Benny to his feet. "Now, all you nigguhs hit the alley!" Joe commands as he whirls Benny and boots him in the rear end.

The gang fidgets and stares at Joe. There is a faint yowling of sirens.

Joe says, "Please, nigguhs, get in the wind 'cause I don't wanta bawl like a crumb crusher at your funeral."

They and Benny bolt into the alley and disappear. Joe goes to the Lincoln, pulls it into the street. A block away he pulls to the curb as a half dozen police cars, blasting sirens, roar past on their way to the liquor store.

Joe gets sloe gin at a quiet liquor store several blocks away. They go to a nearly deserted park on the fringe of the ghetto. They spread their kosher corn beef sandwiches, potato salad, and rice pudding on an oaken table beneath shade trees in a cool cul de sac. They top off the food with the fifth of sloe gin. Delphine gets a bedspread from the car trunk. They go into an odorous maw of bushes ringing the clearing and make frenetic love. Then, spent, briefly nap pressed together.

She kisses him awake. He lights her cigarette. They lie on their backs gazing through a lattice of lilac branches at lamb's wool clouds appliquéd against a tapestry of afternoon sky.

She says softly, "I feel so wonderful when I'm with you . . . I want to be with you forever."

He gobbles the dizzying bait, closes his eyes, palpitates at the vision of their wedding. He remembers Zenobia's warning. His eyes pop open. He gazes at the marvel of Delphine's delicately fashioned profile, thinks he'll get the ring, maybe even marry before he somehow gets Zenobia's acceptance of a "pretty" daughter-in-law after the fact.

"What are you thinking about, Daddy?" she says.

"About what a fine fox I got and thinking how wonderful I feel too when I'm with you," he says in a tremulous whisper.

She crawls atop him, feather-kisses every inch of his face as she massages her crotch against his quickening organ. She says,

"You're the first and only man I've wanted to do this to," as she licks and bites her way down to cannibalize him until he bellows in climax.

They rise and dip themselves into a creek, dry off each other with paper napkins. Delphine drives the Lincoln from the park. She cruises the outer fringes of the ghetto.

At a stoplight on upper Central Avenue Joe hears a frantic voice holler his name. He and Delphine look toward a tenement stoop, see a boy teener and girl struggling to lift a drunken old man, in Sunday suit, into the vestibule of the building.

"Delphine, that boy is Lester, usta be our paperboy. Turn the corner and pull into the driveway." Joe gets out and walks past a group of young adult winos lounging on a dilapidated couch in the bottle-strewn yard.

"Me and Sis sure glad you showed, Joe. Them nigguhs is laying to rob Grandpa," Lester says as Joe stoops and picks up the cursing old man.

Joe follows the teeners to a second-floor apartment bedroom, dumps the old man into a bed. His grandkids lock him in, serve Joe a glass of lemonade before he goes back to the Lincoln incongruously parked in the shambled tenement yard.

As Joe gets into the car Delphine says, "Whew! Let's put these streets down and go to a movie. Okay, sugar?"

Joe grins, nods as he drives into brisk traffic.

Six

That same day, several minutes before midnight, terrier Susie and Baptiste appraise his bizarre reflection in a full-length wall mirror in his bedroom. He has costumed himself as an out-of-fashion Sunday-go-to-meeting silk-gloved elderly woman with gray-riddled long wig, black-bustled dress, overtrousers, and ostrich feather–plumed floppy chapeau, all acquired from a Salvation Army thrift shop.

He breaks the hat brim down to obscure his horn-rim-spectacled face, three shades darkened with makeup. The backs of tennis shoes flash beneath the nearly floor-length dress hemline as he bends in close to the mirror to widen and thicken his dainty lips with dark red lipstick.

He steps back, arches his spine a bit in the posture of the very old. He goes to the dresser, picks up a double-barreled derringer. He stares at it in his palm for a long moment. He replaces it on the dressertop. It could dirty a clean, blind grab-and-run heist, he tells himself. But then he realizes his risk against two of them at the drugstore. He thinks that certainly there will be a pistol carried by old man Havelik or his son to protect eight to ten grand in loot. He picks up the gun and stuffs it into his bosom, protrusive with falsies.

He scissors a football bladder in half, dumps three large cans of cayenne pepper into a half bladder. He inserts it between the sections of a foot-long rectangular rhinestone evening bag. He snaps it shut. He points it toward a cologne bottle, squeezes the bag in his palm. Like a bellows, it blows a jet of pepper that endusts the bottle.

He turns, walks toward the door. Susie pirouettes on her hind feet, yelps excitement at the prospect of a walk. She follows him to the back door.

He pauses, picks up Susie, nose-nuzzles her chest, smooches her muzzle, says, "Li'l baby, you can't go with Papa. Take care of the house. I'll be back right away."

He stoops to release her on the floor, steps into the backyard's pitch blackness. He locks the back door and goes into the alley and begins to walk down it with a berserk heartbeat. At the mouth of the alley he halts, peeps at the still brightly lit drugstore plate glass across the street on the corner.

He jerks up the dress to his trousered hips. He darts across the deserted street, moves like a phantom from shadow to shadow cover until he stops, panting and peering from behind the trunk of a giant oak tree twenty yards from the stoop of the drugstore. Excitement and fear twirl a rope of vomit in his gullet when he sees the store lights extinguish.

He glances up at the darkened windows of Erica's apartment above the drugstore. He steps onto the sidewalk with quivering legs, freezes as he sees the door open. He stands paralyzed, loses his nerve for an instant. He sets his jaw, forces himself into the decrepit posture of his role, goes toward them as they step out, turn back briefly for the lockup ritual.

The old man faces him, looks at him curiously without alarm as his son locks the door.

"Lawd a mighty! I come to get Sal Fayne for my toothache and y'all done closed," Baptiste says in a high-pitched voice reeking agony as he presses the back of his hand holding the pepper-loaded purse against his jaw. He extends a dollar bill in his other hand.

The son clutches the target sack as he turns from the locked door to face Baptiste, looks at his father.

The old man shrugs, says, "Unlock the door, Harry. I'll get it for the lady in a jiffy."

Harry turns and unlocks the door. Baptiste sees the glint of a pistol butt rammed into Harry's belt. The old man steps inside. As Harry turns back to say something, Baptiste leans in close and shoots a cloud of pepper into his face. The paper sack falls to the concrete as Harry hollers and plasters his palms against his eyes. Baptiste scoops up the bag. Harry blindly grabs for Baptiste. Baptiste falls, evading him. Harry draws his nickel-plated pistol, fires a wild shot several feet above prone Baptiste as his father dashes to the sidewalk, screams, "Help! Police! Help!"

Baptiste aims the derringer at Harry's head. But his finger freezes on the trigger. Baptiste rises and runs. He falls again, tripped by the long dress. Baptiste scrambles to his feet. He jerks the dress up to his waist as the elder Havelik dashes back into the store. Baptiste sprints away down the sidewalk to the middle of the block. He streaks across the street, pauses into the mouth of the alley that runs behind his house.

He peeps at the corner, sees old Havelik dabbing tissues at Harry's blinded eyes. He glances up at Erica's apartment windows as light flashes on behind the shades. He turns and races down the alley. He goes across his backyard and into his kitchen. He locks the door and collapses on the linoleum.

Susie yelps, tinkles, and leaps in wild excitement around him. He rips open the paper sack and dumps its contents. Traumatic shock and disappointment jiggle his head as he stares at his loot. Strips of newspaper are cocooned inside a dozen odd dollar bills.

He rolls and moans as he weeps. Finally he sits up, drained, his back propped against the refrigerator. He rips the bills into confetti as he stares tear-drenched eyes into space. He listens to the insistent ringing of the phone on the wall across the room. He dredges himself to his feet to answer it.

It must be Erica, he tells himself as he picks up, says "Hello" in a voice gravelly with fake drowsiness.

"Da Dee!" she says in a voice staggering at the crest of hysteria, "there's been shooting! A woman held up Harry and Lou!"

He manages to say calmly, "Don't go down there. Call the police."

She says, "It's all over. She got away." Then she chuckles. "But the joke's on her. Harry always carries the store receipts next to his skin in a money belt around his waist. She got a decoy paper bag for her trouble. Da Dee, I'm coming over as soon as the police leave."

Baptiste says, "I'm going back to sleep, Erica. See you tomorrow."

He hangs up, staggers up the stairs to get something from the medicine chest to relieve the pain in his head that sledges like a dozen toothaches.

At dawn in the guest house behind the Beverly Hills mansion of the Sternbergs, Pretty Melvin, sleepless for most of the night, gets out of bed. He compulsively glances at sleeping Reba as he paces the carpet, tries to think of the kindest way to tell her that their wedding is off.

He sits down on the bedside, lights a reefer. He languidly draws himself high. Tranced narcissistic, he gazes with pleasure at his soft girlish face reflected in the bed's mirrored headboard. He lights another stick. Reefer dangling from his mouth, he shifts his eyes to scrutinize the manicured tips of his long fingers.

He remembers his father's early evening ultimatum: Defer the marriage for premed school or marry and be self-supporting. He is unaware his father meant the ultimatum purely as a test of the quality of his emotional status, of his depth of feeling for Reba and the responsibilities of husband and father.

He grimaces, shivers at the prospect of a gig changing tires at the Greyhound garage his father promised to arrange. He finger-strokes a satiny palm, visualizes it encrusted with calluses, winces. Tears of self-pity sparkle his lacy-lashed amethyst eyes. He shapes a sad rosy-lipped smile as he gazes at Reba's supine naked splendor.

At seven a.m. he makes erotic canine sounds as he grinds his face against her pubic thicket. She awakens, reflexively slams her thighs together to trap his head for an instant. He giggles ecstatically as he scoots up to wiggle his tongue tip in her navel. She cries out, flees to the bathroom.

After breakfast in bed they go to the pool. They swim and frolic until nine a.m. Wetly glistening in the warm sun, they lie embraced on a poolside canvas chaise under the eyes of the elder Sternbergs lying in bed above the pool.

Reba looks into his eyes, says, "What are you thinking, sugar?" as she finger-combs through his water-lanked hair.

His eyes flee to the vault of dazzling blue sky. "Sweetmeat, you wouldn't be happy, respect me, couldn't love me if say I became a funky tire changer for six bits a week to support us and whatsit's name."

She laughs. "The heck you say! I'd love you and be happy and respect you if you were just a bootblack on the busiest corner downtown . . . Why, I'd be your assistant, darling. I'd carry our shine box stenciled 'Melvin and Reba Sternberg.' I'd gig and inhale the foot funk when you got pooped. I'd lug whatsit's name strapped on my back papoose style. So forget the tire wrestling. Popping a public rag is more groovy. And becoming a doctor ain't bad, I want to hip you."

He frowns. "Stop clowning. I'm serious, Re," he says as he wins the struggle to look into her eyes.

"Okay, you called me Re. You never do unless you're angry or worried. So, no, I'm hip you're serious. C'mon, what's got you frazzled, sweetheart?"

She laughs nervously. "Baby maker, you haven't also put one of my zillion rivals in the family way while we were on the outs, have you?"

"Stop it!" he exclaims as he disengages to sit on the side of the chaise with a solemn face.

"Hey, baby, then tell Mommy why you've suddenly become a gloom buff?" she says as she sits up beside him, shakily flicks lighter flame to two cigarettes, lays one between his lips.

"Re, I really love you and need you," he half whispers as he furiously puffs his cigarette with a tortured face.

She says, "Damn, baby, after a thousand years tell me something I don't know. But please darling, don't call me Re anymore in my delicate condition."

She exhales, snuffs out her cigarette in a seashell ashtray. She embraces his waist, is alarmed to feel an almost imperceptible trembling of his torso. He burrows his head into her bosom, heaves an anguished sigh as she finger-strokes his temple. She says, "I can't stand a helluva lot more of this. What's wrong?"

"It's the end of the world and I don't know what to do."

"You mind breaking that down?"

"We can't get married!"

She jerks away to evict his head, locks his head between her palms as she stares into his eyes. "Fathead, we have to get married. Whatsit's name. Remember!?"

He averts his eyes. "We can't!"

"Why?"

He spills it out. "Dad's knocked out the money props, last night. He told me marriage now and premed, no go. He'll give us only a small house we'd have to run on the lousy salary from the tire gig. We can't live like that. We just couldn't make it without Dad's support."

She says, "Cry for yourself, sonny boy. I don't need your father's welfare to enjoy life, to make it with you. I've got a sewing skill, and I'm not lazy. We can make it if you've got the guts to try. Well!?"

He rises to his feet, paces the flagstone edge of the pool under her slitted eyes for a long moment. And also under the anxious eyes of the elder Sternbergs peering through their bedroom curtains at the tableau.

He pauses before her, manages to say stoutly, "I've got the guts not to shove you and the baby through the poverty wringer . . . Dad plans to give you a big check, even take you in, give you and our baby the finest care. I love you! Please under—"

She leaps to her feet, lips curled in contempt. "Your ass, jellyfish! You can't con me. You can't love anyone except selfish lazy number one. YOU! I'd blow my brains out before I'd take a red penny from your father. Tell him that! I'll take care of MY baby and myself!"

She slips off his ring, hurls it against his forehead, stomps away toward the guest house. He follows her inside. He sits on the side of the bed, watches her get her clothes from the closet. She goes into the bathroom, slams the door shut. Shortly, she emerges dressed in the diaphanous pink dress she wore at Joe Allen's main event fiasco. She moves in stockinged feet past Melvin, seated on the bed. She bends to pick up her shoes on the carpet at the head of the bed.

He leans, smooches her buttocks, says, "There, I've kissed your ass to say I love you. Let's talk and work out something."

She snaps erect, steps into her pumps. She whip-turns, eyes radiant with hostility. "Hah! Big deal! You've sucked and kissed asses in motels all over town. We've said it all. We're through!"

She turns, goes quickly for the door. He lunges after her, seizes her around the waist at the dresser beside the door.

"I can't let you quit. I'm your forever man!" he declares loudly as he roughly whirls her, tries to force his tongue into her mouth.

She bites his bottom lip, hard. He bangs his palm against the side of her head. She snatches up a brass stiletto letter opener from the dressertop.

He backs up a step, hoarsely whispers, "Creole witch, you're gonna fuck your man goodbye," as he oozes toward her.

He retreats to the middle of the room as she jabs the blade at his crotch.

"Man!? Pussy freak!" she hisses with chest aheave. She pauses to catch her breath. With acidic sarcasm she lies, "By the way, great lover, since I took you back for the baby's sake, your midget weenie hasn't moved me once. And every time you've given me head, I've nearly puked with boredom."

Wounded, he grits his teeth, glares at her. "You lying cunt!"

"Sissy bastard, it's true!" she says.

He rocks with knotted fists. "I'm going to beat your ass and rape you for lying," he snarls as he lunges.

She fires the letter opener. The point grazes a scarlet rill at his temple, cracks the headboard mirror behind him. Shaken, he stumbles back onto the bed.

She backs toward the door, screeches, "You ever try to touch me or get in my face, I'll kill you!"

She leaves the house, bangs the door shut behind her. Forty minutes later she leaves a cab at the mouth of the alley running past the Rambeau backyard. She walks up the alley, goes through the gate. She crosses the yard to the back door. She starts to turn the doorknob, hesitates. She decides she must be utterly alone in her crisis.

She retraces to a corner of the yard. For the first time in years, she stoops to enter the door of the weather-mauled candy-striped playhouse of her early girlhood. Tears threaten as she eye-sweeps the dusty toys, the quartet of dolls in silk dresses, now time sleazed, seated at a miniature table with dull waxen smiles before a tiny scaled daisy-appliquéd tea service. Misery embattled, she falls to her knees on the mildewed beige carpet beside the table. She smiles oddly as she takes flight through the regressive gates of nostalgia's comforting time warp.

In a child's quaver she says to the diminutive ghostly ladies at tea, "Pretties, I'm so glad to see you again. I've been away on a trip. Can you please forgive me for staying away so long?" She leans, crawls about the table, kisses each of their cool tarnished foreheads in turn, murmurs, "I will always adore you."

A beam of late morning sun fires through a sooted window-pane, illuminates the face of a tiny doll swathed in calico lying in a crib with long-lashed eyes shuttered. Reba crawls to cribside. She takes a cracked thermometer from a toy doctor's bag beside the crib.

She inserts it into the doll's mouth for a moment before she withdraws it, mock-studies it, exclaims cheerily, "Whoopee! Peggy Precious, your fever's gone!"

She crawls to a half dozen naked dolls topsy-turvy on an eye-level shelf, staring blank eyes into space. She tenderly arranges them neatly seated side by side. She takes a square of black silk from a rainbow-dyed straw Easter basket. She drapes it across them to cover their nude torsos.

From the basket, a music box, in the image of Mickey Mouse, issues, for a moment, the tinny lyrics of "On the Good Ship Lollipop."

She gazes at a huge doll dressed in yellowed white satin seated in a rocking chair across the room. She crawls to the rocking chair, stares into the filmy china blue eyes of the doll. She fingers the satin dress hem. She remembers Philippa spanking her bottom raw in angry outrage when she discovered her expensive dress cut up to costume Tawny, the huge doll's name.

Reba stiffens, recoils as she stares at speckles of brown dried blood on the bodice of the doll's dress. The blood of her father, she remembers. One early a.m. it was Philippa that had shed his blood. Philippa had stabbed a nail file into his wrist, splattering her bed and doll when they brawled in the hall and into her bedroom, about her mother coming home drunk with her clothes disarrayed.

She spots a pair of her mother's old high heels that she remembers tottering in when she played grown up. She tries to slip her foot into one of the shoes. She is amazed to discover her triple-A foot too snug now for Philippa's triple-E size.

She rolls a rusted tricycle squeakily across the floor. She remembers the scary blood from a forehead cut when she fell on the sidewalk riding it with her feet on the handlebars, showboating for a gallery of chums. Old sorrow twinges her as she excavates, from the toy box, the rhinestone collar of her beloved Mitzi, the Yorkie, her first puppy, long ago murdered by a Doberman.

Tears flood her eyes as she fondles a pair of sneakers from the box. She was seven, she remembers, when she wore them. She had fled in terror into the midnight from a terrible profane fight between her parents. A sweet-faced elderly man in a big black car befriended her, promised to take her home and stop her parents from killing each other.

Instead, the man drove her to frightening darkness behind a factory. She remembers his suffocating hand over her mouth to stop her screaming. He had ripped off her clothes when the blinding headlamps of a police cruiser interrupted him. She trembles to remember how she sobbed and clung to one of the cops all the way home to Baptiste and Philippa, who played out Academy Award performances as happy, loving husband and wife for the cops.

She picks up a tiny dapper man-about-town doll, in frayed tuxedo, from the toy box. She turns it, frowns as she stares at its too delicate face profile. Almost identical to Melvin's, she thinks. She wrings off the doll's head, collapses in a storm of weeping.

In Reba's bedroom, green satin–pajamaed Baptiste and Erica are packing Reba's clothing and personal effects.

Erica says, "Da Dee, I still feel uncomfortable about not letting Reba pack her own things. After all, she's a woman. And then too there's the question as to whether or not your assumption is valid that she will accept moving into my place, even temporarily."

Baptiste says, "This is an emergency. Look, you know the finance company will come at any moment today to repossess the furniture. The marshal is due to evict us today, no later than tomorrow." He hitches his shoulders disconsolately. "She has to accept your apartment. Like me, she has no place else to go until her marriage."

Erica frowns. "But Da Dee, just like a man, you're overlooking the dynamics of female territoriality. She'll probably have a natural reluctance to move from the spacious privacy of her own home into a cramped two-bedroom apartment where I'm lady of the house. Surely you can't expect her to choke up at the chance to place herself in the position to daily witness her father sleeping with his mistress. She's possessive of you, you know." She sighs. "But we'll see, Da Dee, we'll see."

They go to Baptiste's bedroom to pack his things. Reba leaves the playhouse somewhat composed. Baptiste spots her through his bedroom window. He hurries from the room to go downstairs to cushion the shock of her packed belongings. He races down the stairs. The fifth of whiskey he's guzzled since the heist stumbles him. Flat on his back, he stupidly stares up at Reba. She helps him pull himself to his feet. He shapes a crooked grin of embarrassment, dips his head toward the stairs.

He murmurs, "There's a step with a split in the carpet . . . I uh . . ." Realizing the bad news he must break, he checks himself before he says, "I have to fix it." He follows her toward her bedroom door, says, "Mouse, what's wrong? Your eyes look like you've been crying."

She says over her shoulder, "I cut Melvin loose. And don't call me Mouse."

"Don't tell me the marriage is off," he gasps.

"You heard me!" she says harshly as she steps inside her bedroom.

She halts, reels at the threshold with a shocked face. She stares at the mini-mountain of her luggage and possessions in cardboard boxes stacked on the stripped bed and strewn about the room. She whirls to face Baptiste in the hallway.

"Baptiste, what the hell does this mean!?"

"Now, now, dear, I'll explain. Don't get upset," he says gently as he pats her shoulder.

She jerks away, legs akimbo, green eyes afire. "We've lost the house! Haven't we?"

He averts his eyes, mumbles, "That's the heartbreak gritty of it, my dear. But nothing can stop stepper pals like us, baby." He reaches to embrace her.

She jerks back with a hostile face. "Stepper, you told me two weeks ago that you had won the money to save the house and furniture from those four men who came here to play cards. Is that right!?"

He collapses on the bedside, bent forward, palms pressed against his face. "I lied, baby . . . guess my touch played hooky . . . They beat me, busted me out." He peers pathetic eyes at her through the bars of his fingers.

"Stepper pal, why did you lie, fool me that everything was all right?" she pursues with a hateful face and merciless scorn in her voice.

He laments in a coarse whisper, "I had a sweet backup deal if there ever was one, set up for last night. Baby dear, it's best I don't tell you details. But last night I literally bet my life that deal would fall a royal flush. Hon, I lied to spare you worry." He shudders, wrings his hands. "That deal soured last night and broke my heart. Anybody except a Rambeau Creole would have cashed himself in. You've got to forgive me for lying. I did on the promise of that deal because I love you more than I ever did Philippa or even myself."

He extends his arms toward her, eyes piteous. She heaves a resigned sigh, shakes her head as she eye-sweeps the chaotic room. She drops down on the bed beside him, embraces his shoulders.

"Papa, I forgive you. We're not flat broke. I've got four hundred dollars saved from my sewing. We have to vacate immediately?"

He says, "Yes, it's best we do . . . Hope is dead to save our house." He pauses to say with visceral passion, "If I didn't have you, I'd stand them off with my hunting rifle." Then he sighs, says softly, "I'm ashamed of the way I begged them on the phone today for one more extension."

She whispers, "Papa, I just can't believe this is happening . . . after all the big money I've heard you brag about winning through the years."

He smiles bitterly. "I take the full sucker blame for letting Philippa ruin us. Year in and year out, like an idiot, I let her blow thousands at the racetrack, on clothes from Beverly Hills shops that she didn't need. And when she left after that . . . uh, shooting upstairs last year, she took my strongbox containing an emergency five grand . . . Then to cap off bad breaks, I had that, uh . . . accident to my throat that knocked me out of the big buck sweepstakes. But I promise, dear lamb, to come back stronger. Soon!"

She says, "Well, guess we'll have to check into a hotel until we find a small, clean furnished house to rent . . . Say! We can rent the Allens' back house. It's clean, furnished, and the rent is only sixty a month."

He frowns at her suggestion. He is about to tell her about his plan to move them into Erica's flat when the doorbell chimes. Insistently!

"Damn! That must be one of the bad news bastards already." Baptiste groans as he gets to his feet and leaves the bedroom, followed by Reba.

They go to the door. Baptiste puts an eye to the peephole, is surprised to see Saul Sternberg, wearing a pajama top beneath his blue serge suit jacket. He opens the door, forgetting it's on chain. He reaches to unfasten it.

Reba sees Saul. She shoves Baptiste aside, glares at Saul through the chained aperture. "What the hell do you want? God!"

Saul ashens, says, "Reba, I must talk to you! Please!"

"No! I'm through talking to rotten Sternbergs." She smashes an elbow into Baptiste's chest when he tries to pull her away.

"Reba, let me in. I want to discuss making an equitable arrangement for you and the baby," Saul pleads as he extends his hand through the door to touch her.

She recoils. "Get lost!" as she slams the door on his hand.

Saul's muffled outcry of pain winces Baptiste behind her. Baptiste seizes her shoulders, spins her away from the door. She grapples savagely with him as he tries to go out the door. He breaks free to the porch, sees Saul angrily gun his Mercedes away. Baptiste steps back into the living room, glares at Reba turning from the open front window with smug triumph on her face.

"You dumb hellion! You just blew our chance to save the house!" Baptiste explodes.

"Goddamn the house, Baptiste! To hell with that muckety-muck's welfare."

Baptiste plops down on the couch. "I hope you get some sense when you cool off. The Sternbergs owe you a cash settlement. All you have to do is file a paternity suit to get the payoff."

"Forget it, Baptiste! I'm through with them. Understand!?"

Baptiste groans under his breath. "How could I be the father of such a star natal sucker?"

She turns back to the windows when she hears a familiar truck sound. She sees Senior Joe key off the plumbing truck across the street and go into the Allen house.

"I'm going to rent the Allens' back house," she says as she moves toward the front door.

Baptiste leaps to his feet, intercepts her at the door. "Baby, that won't be necessary. We're moving into Erica's place for a while. Isn't she wonderful to take us in?"

She sets her jaw. "Then I'm renting the Allen house for myself if you decide to shack up with Erica." She pushes him aside and leaves the house as he clutches at her. Susie yaps at her heels.

He goes to the porch, rears his bantam frame erect, shouts to her back. "Baptiste Rambeau will never humiliate himself with those peasant Allen niggers as his landlord!"

Within the hour Reba, with the help of both Joes, transfers kitchen utensils, curtains, drapes, and the haunting contents of the playhouse to the Allen back house. She sits on a sofa relaxing with Young Joe at an Allen living room window watching Baptiste and Erica move the last of his things in the Packard, which Erica had saved by cashing in an insurance policy.

An hour later, Reba sadly watches the finance company movers load the house furniture into a mammoth van and drive away. Within minutes she sees the marshal padlock the house. She breaks into wild weeping. Young Joe takes her into his arms and gently rocks her. He gazes at her fawn face, feels a thrilly quickening. But his absolute belief that she will go back to Melvin, as she has countless times, chills any urge to dream her his. He thinks of Delphine to further insulate himself against Reba.

Shortly she says, "Big Bro, I'm cool now. Think I'll go and start setting up my new pad."

He releases her. She kisses his cheek and leaves the room.

That early evening, Zenobia finishes scouring dinner utensils in a Beverly Hills kitchen. Fatigued and eager to leave, she goes to peep into the dining room. She sees her employer, a shrewish matron, still chewing filet. Zenobia slits her eyes in loathing for the woman who weeks before had cruelly berated her, before dinner guests, for sloshing sauce from a serving dish onto the tablecloth.

Zenobia is about to turn back to the kitchen when she sees the slave driver clutch her throat, make choking sounds as she whitens. Zenobia stares impassively into her tormentor's terrified eyes, ignores her frantic hand beckoning. The woman tumbles to the carpet.

Conscience at bay, Zenobia leans against the door frame, is electrified by a perverse surge of power for a long poisonous moment watching the woman writhe feebly. Zenobia actually turns away, takes a step toward the kitchen before she turns back. She hurries to the blued woman. She lifts the scrawny form, falls into a chair with the woman stomachdown in her lap, her head hanging over the edge of her thigh. Zenobia pounds her fist against the stricken woman's back as she dredges a middle finger deep into the woman's throat.

The woman coughs as Zenobia digs out a small hunk of filet. The woman gulps for air, turns on Zenobia's lap. She sits up, presses her head against Zenobia's bosom as she locks her arms about her neck.

The woman sobs gratitude. "Oh! You saved my life! You're so wonderful, Zenobia. Thank you, darling! Thank you!"

Zenobia helps her to bed. A half hour later she leaves, rewarded with a fifty-dollar bill. She pulls her La Salle away for its ghetto parking space on Slater's used car lot.

She exclaims aloud. "Thank you, Sweet Jesus, for chasing Lucifer before I let that mean white woman die. Thank you, Jesus!"

She thinks of Elder Joe, the Midnight Creeper, and vows not to lose him the next time she tails him.

Seven

Ten days after Reba's eviction and her unprecedented series of phone calls, Philippa is on a midnight flight from New Orleans to pay a surprise visit to Reba in her new home. She has seen Reba once since leaving Baptiste. And then clandestinely in a downtown hotel to avoid Baptiste's certain rage.

She finishes her sixth coffee heavily laced with scotch. Affluent enough to afford first class, she has always preferred to travel coach with the hoi polloi. She feels she relates more comfortably to them than with fat boring business types. Then too, she's discovered to her perverse joy on several memorable occasions that the probability for raw erotic adventure is greater among coach have-nots. The haves in first class are prone to fresher, young stewardesses.

Seated at the nearly deserted rear of the plane, she stares down at the pallid neon of a medium-sized city. She thinks it resembles Shreveport, Louisiana, as she remembers it from the top floors of office buildings that she helped her janitorial French-Cajun parents service from the age of ten, until she was fourteen when her parents were killed in a car crash. Then Rajah, a polyglot ethnic and notorious movie star–attractive badger-game hustler, stole her and turned her out in Baton Rouge on his specialty.

Her reverie is interrupted by the reflection in her window glass of the cutest young soldier she thinks she's ever laid eyes on, staring hotly at her from an aisle seat just across the way. In the cathedral-soft light of the airliner, she appears half her forty years.

Cop, dogcatcher, even Western Union, and especially soldier uniforms, worn of course by comely studs, have always revved her ravenous loins.

She shifts and points her bottom toward the young lecher. Her short tight dress hikes up to her porcelain-hued girlishly voluptuous thighs. Her nude slavemaster behind sheens, defines, through the gauzy white silk like perfectly matched oversized honeydew melons.

She lowers her Sophia Loren look-alike face to a pillow. Her witchy green eyes gleam as she gazes surreptitiously at the young wolf that she suddenly decides to make her prey. She is suspicious, piqued that he apparently plots to tryst with Lady Five Fingers when she sees him remove his cap and place it on his lap. She is certain when he thrusts a hand beneath the cap. His bedroom eyes devour her, glow phosphorescently in his teasing-tan face.

Excitement mauls her as she sits up, gets a cigarette from her purse, obviously rummages through it for a light. From a corner of an eye she sees him fumble to secure his fly before he scrambles across the aisle to lean his lighter flame to her cigarette tip.

"Thank you. That's so sweet of you, Soldier Man," she croons in her heady contralto.

"Your voice is as pretty as you are," he says.

She coyly averts her eyes, remembers that an infatuated Bourbon Street musician lover once described her voice as starlit prelude to opus sixty-nine.

"We're lonely. Mind if I sit down and keep you company?" the dreamboat says in a rich vibrato baritone which gives her the sensation that it rocks the seat cushion beneath her bottom.

"Why no, of course not," she says as she moves her purse from the aisle seat. "I'm terribly patriotic," she continues inanely, wishes she could reclaim the remark as he sits down beside her.

He says, "Thanks. I'm Reginald Lewis, mustered out of the occupation army in Europe. I'm on my way home to L.A. from a Baton Rouge visit with an injured battlefield buddy."

She lies, "I'm Cleo Johnson, happy divorcée from New Orleans on my way to an overnight stay in L.A."

His fierce tawny eyes and sandy coarse-mopped leonine head aura him jungle cat, palpitate her to a sizzling frenzy. She enjoys a tipsy interior giggle, thinks, This is great! . . . The farm boy has his ewe to abuse and this gorgeous lion has me.

They empty the fifth of scotch from her purse and chat minutiae for the better part of an hour. She schemes where, as quickly as possible, she can get her raging brush fire extinguished. To prime him, she opens her thighs to his explorer finger.

She glances at the lone coach stewardess agiggle as she leans in, distracted at the side of a towheaded young soldier seated near the front. Philippa glances at her prey's rigid monster aquiver against the khaki. She asks herself, Should I simply mount dreamboat's lap and impale myself on his jumbo stake? Too risky and restrictive, she decides. She smiles slyly as she abruptly locks her thigh gates, feels the seismic tremble of frustration in his finger ejected.

She rises. As she leg-bangs past him to the aisle, she veils her eyes seductively, whispers, "Lover, I'm going to the little girls' room. I feel so deliciously patriotic."

He leaps up to follow. He enters behind her when she lets herself into the chamber. Panting, and thrilling her giddy with masterworks of tenderly obscene erotic profanity, he mightily humps her dog fashion. She bends, with palms on the john seat. She raises her head to stare into a mirror at his humping reflection, then into his cruel eyes, slumberous and mesmeric behind half-drawn lash curtains.

She exclaims, "Oh yeah! Ride me tough and talk that nasty sweet shit to me, Reg . . . Rex!"

Her ponytailed, wiry red mane swishes madly as she spastically jerks her head and makes high-pitched equine whinnying sounds of rut until their mutual carnal explosion.

Before the plane touches down in Los Angeles, they encore the performance. Satiated, at least for the moment, and scotch maimed, Philippa checks into a downtown hotel for the night.

* * *

*N*ext morning, at the magenta blush of early August sunrise, lethargic Delphine spikes a medicinal speedball of H and C. She rises effervescently from bed. She leisurely packs her belongings for the split to the Big Apple, several days before she planned.

Her double-ripoff timetable had been changed the midnight before. She plucked scuttlebutt off the street grapevine that Whispering Slim had taken a midnight flight south to the funeral of a pal pimp.

She remembers how she seized the chance to crowbar through the back door of Slim's dope stash house. Searching for the dope, she tore the inside of the house asunder. She even crowbarred up a dozen suspiciously loose floorboards. Nothing! Exhausted, she sat on the john stool to tinkle. She had risen, flushed the john when an odd sound of metal scraping against metal caught her attention. She flushed the toilet again as she leaned an ear toward it. She removed its water tank cover, lifted and opened a large coffee can afloat in the water. She had split with the plastic-wrapped kilo of smack from the coffee can.

One down and one to go, she tells herself now, thinking of Young Joe Allen's banked nest egg.

After packing, she showers, grins wickedly as she soaps her sex nest. She thinks of how she has shut out Young Joe from it for over a week to puff his testicles obese with desire, to distract him in her presence later, to trance him during her swindle game in play.

At ten a.m. her arsenal of curves is abristle inside a short, tight, nearly transparent orange silk dress. She pays a pair of loser loiterers on the apartment building stoop to carry her luggage to the Lincoln's trunk. She drives away. Before the Lincoln's engine warms up fully, she pulls through an alley into a Vernon Avenue parking lot behind a building housing a complex of doctor and lawyer offices. She locks the Lincoln and takes a cab back home to her phone.

She dials Young Joe at home, laments, "Oh Joe! I've got bad news. That sweet old doctor, lifelong friend of my father's, just paid me a pre–office visit. He tried to crawl into bed with me on the basis that my 'you know what' would be the fee and the interest for the thirty-five-hundred-dollar loan."

Joe says, "What happened?"

She says, "I threw him out! . . . And the loan. But what else could I do? As you know, today I'm supposed to complete the business arrangements necessary for 'Delphine's Beauty Box' to become something except a dream. I'm so blue."

There is a pit of silence for a long moment before Joe says, "Cheer up. I been thinking ever since you told me about him, that I oughta loan you the money. Without interest!"

She exclaims, "You're wonderful! I'll pay you back every cent."

"You ain't got to pay it back in no big hurry. Pay me back when your Chi Town lawyer unties the geeters your father left you from the I.R.S. I know you'll have it in hand soon."

"I will. Cross my heart!" She sighs. "Damn, Joe! I just remembered more bad news." She hears Joe catch his breath. She continues, "I promised you my car would finally be out of the shop today for our first date in so long. It isn't, and I've missed you so much, heartbreaker."

"We gonna take care of your business and then take care of bed business. Today! We can ride cabs. Okay?"

She says, "I hate cabs! I'd rather borrow a girlfriend's car." Then she laughs. "That is, Daddy Ice Cream Cone, if you don't mind riding in a stone jalopy. Huh?"

"Mind? No, baby, that's mellow."

She says, "Since you want to go to the bank, shouldn't I pick you up earlier than planned? I can't be late for my appointment with my lawyer."

Joe says, "Noon is still cool. I'll walk to the bank when I hang up. It ain't but a coupla blocks from home. See ya, Fox."

She exclaims, "Heartbreaker, I can't wait!"

They hang up. She goes to the battered Ford, gets in, starts to drive away. She keys off the motor, writes a note to Joe. She seals it, with the Ford's pink slip and bill of sale, into an envelope before she drops it into her purse.

She sees him waiting for her, crisp and clean in a blue jean suit, on the usual corner of sun-glutted Avalon Boulevard. As she pulls into the curb to pick him up, she wishes he were an older, tougher, less pathetically vulnerable mark. He hops in, kisses her. His blue-black brutish face is softened and radiant with infatuation as she drives away with her strategically hiked-up dress magnetizing his puppy eyes for a long moment with the satiny exposure of lush thighs.

He looks at his wristwatch, says, "It's just twelve thirty. You got a half hour. I could stand a sandwich. I forgot to eat breakfast."

She drives to park in front of a fast-food restaurant on Vernon Avenue across the street from the building where ostensibly her lawyer has an office. A beer bar sits across the alley from the restaurant.

He says, "Wanta sandwich or a beer?" as he gets out of the jalopy and heads to the sidewalk bustling with pedestrians.

"Maybe a cold Budweiser, baby," she says as she notices the bulge of his father's thirty-eight pistol rammed into his belt beneath his jean jacket.

She watches him lope his giant frame into the cafe. Within minutes, he returns to the car. She sips beer as he wolfs down a pair of hamburgers, washed down with a bottle of beer. He wipes his mouth with a paper napkin. He reaches into his trouser pocket, extracts a fat doubled brown envelope, removes a sheaf of currency.

She casually watches him count out thirty-five hundred dollars in small denominations on the car seat. He replaces the bills in the envelope, shoves it into her purse on the seat between them.

"Thank you, darling! You're a stone-sweet gentleman to come to my rescue," she bubbles as she scrambles across the seat to pepper his face with kisses. "I won't disappoint your faith in me, heartbreaker. I'll repay every cent the day I get that chunk of my father's inheritance from Chicago."

He says, "That's mellow, 'cause my . . . uh . . ." Since he plans to propose to her momentarily, he checks himself before he childishly says, ". . . mama will kill me and drop dead if she finds out that money ain't in the bank." Instead he says, "Well, I remember you said that day we had a picnic that you wanted to be with me forever. So, hold out your hand, Mrs. Joe Allen, which I hope you'll be, soon."

He takes a black satin ring box from his jacket, opens it. A credit, C-note down, twenty a month, white gold-mounted carat diamond blazes quality, blue-white fire. She stares at his happy ugly face through the black windows of her sunglasses. She shifts her eyes to appraise the ring, guesstimates it accurately as an eight to nine hundred dollar item. She is about to extend her hand when the look of pure adoration on his pitifully unattractive pug face stirs her slumbering conscience.

She says, for her surprised ears, "Daddy, yes! You're wonderful! I thought you'd never ask. But please save the ring delight until you know, later when we're at my place with candlelight, champagne, and all. Okay?"

He says, "You sure know what to say, beautiful," as she shoves the ring box into his pocket.

She looks at her wristwatch, leans to kiss his cheek. Half out of the car door she pauses. "I'm so glad my lawyer is qualified to handle everything for me—the paperwork, the buying of all the shop's equipment. Isn't that a break!?"

Joe says, "That's mellow!" as she steps into the street, slams the car door shut.

She gives him the sealed note and jalopy papers from her purse.

"Keep this for me, baby, until I get back. They're terribly important personal papers," she says as she drops the envelope on the seat.

He picks it up. She's half tempted to extend her hand and say, "I can't wait!" and rip off the ring as she watches the envelope go into the ring pocket. Instead she sighs and turns away.

He watches her jaywalk across the street and enter the office building. Almost immediately, his thirst unquenched by one bottle of beer, he gets out of the car and goes down the sidewalk into the beer bar flush with the alley mouth. He takes a stool and sips a beer as he stares into the back bar mirror at the street and alley beyond, leading to the rear entrance of the lot behind the building where Delphine's Continental is parked.

In the meantime, Delphine has hurried through a rear door of the building to her car. She moves it to the alley mouth to make a left turn down it away from Vernon Avenue where the jalopy is parked. She sees a large truck move up the escape end of the alley to block her as she moves the Lincoln several yards into it.

Inside the bar, Joe's eyes balloon in flabbergast as he stares at the reflected rear of the white Continental in the mirror. He is first stricken by mega-surprise, then immobilized for a long moment by the sudden shock of sucker insight.

A graven image of Kong, he watches the Lincoln's backup lights flash on as Delphine backs her car up the alley toward him, then out of sight into the office building parking lot. He leaps off his stool and onto the sidewalk when the truck pulls through the alley toward him on its way to Vernon Avenue.

When the truck pulls free of the alley, he sees the grille of the Continental ooze into view. He trumpets the maniac riff of the fleeced as he halfbacks through a steel line of hurtling doom machines. The torrid sun skitters mini-pebbles of light off his sweat-wet dome, aimed like a blue-black projectile toward the full profile of the Continental. His muscles rope and spasm against the thigh denim as he gallops toward Delphine, fright-paralyzed staring at him.

She finally manages to stomp the engine stallions into a careening left turn at the instant that Joe reaches her. He leaps onto the rear bumper, haunches across the trunk, claws at the top canvas as she torpedoes the jouncing Lincoln down the potholed alley. He draws the pistol, aims it through the rear window at the back of her head.

A star trick, he ironically bellows argot like a killer mack man. "You dirty motherfucking 'ho! Unass my geeters out the window or I'll blow you away!"

He glares into her horrified eyes reflected in the rearview mirror above her as he feels his trigger finger roll the pistol cylinders. But his finger freezes, limply disengages from the trigger. The front wheel of the car, accelerated to seventy miles an hour, suddenly dips violently into a deep pothole, hurling him off to the alley floor. He rolls and tumbles through a pool of old crankcase oil to break his fall.

Oil tarred and feathered with debris and alley grit, he struggles up to sit and watch the Lincoln turn into the street out of sight at the end of the alley. In a fugue of despair and rage he stumbles back to the Ford past a horde of mute gawkers. He sits behind the wheel for a long moment vacantly staring through the windshield. A vision of Reba, his real love, cushions his trauma as he idly pulls Delphine's sealed envelope from his pocket.

He rips it open, reads: "Sorry, stone sweet young gentleman, it had to be you, 'cause you are, no bullshit, the nicest guy I ever met. It's maybe a sad bitch of a present, but I want you to have the Ford from this street poisoned junkie whore who was growing fond of you, and so blue this week, 'cause you got in my way. Believe me, I didn't have to bed you to beat you. Guess you were like the big brother I have always yenned for or something . . . Heartbreaker, please try not to hate and hurt too much and long. Hey, lucky guy, you're worth ten of me!"

He shreds the note into the ashtray, shoves the Ford's papers into his pocket before he guns away to search the ghetto catacombs for the Lincoln until late afternoon.

That same warm afternoon at five, silk-gloved, blue straw–hatted Philippa, cool and impeccable in navy linen and white and blue spectator pumps with matching bag, leaves a cab at the Allen house. Carrying a shopping bag, and an overnight case strapped across her shoulder, she goes to the fence gate. Zenobia, home early from work, stops trimming hedges to let her into the front yard.

"Oh, Zenobia! What a pleasure to see you again," Philippa exclaims.

"Chile, it sure is a treat to see you again looking fine as any magazine model," Zenobia says warmly as they embrace. "Your sweet daughter's home." Zenobia stoops to pick up her trimming shears.

Philippa goes down the walk at the side of the house to the front door of the back house.

Almost immediately, Young Joe chugs the Ford to a stop in front of the house, gets out. Zenobia flings her shears away again, stands staring at disheveled Joe as he enters the yard. She blocks his path to the house, hands on her hips.

"You look scand'lous! You been alley-fightin' again, Li'l Joe?" she asks. "And whose wreck you did in?"

He manages a grin to throw her off. "Naw, Mama, I ain't had no fight. I been working to get that machine started that I stole for thirty dollars. I'm gonna fix it up and paint it up 'til I make it stone-cherry wheels." He pecks her cheek and limps up the walkway and through the front door of the house.

In the living room of the back house, Philippa and Reba embrace and cling together for a long moment. Arm in arm they go to the kitchen. Philippa dumps the contents of the shopping bag on the kitchen table, an assortment of every conceivable delicacy known to gratify the eccentric palate of the pregnant. They put the groceries into the refrigerator and kitchen cabinets.

They go to sit on the living room sofa. Philippa sweeps disparaging eyes about the dismal room, furnished with a grimy potpourri of outdated, mismatched furniture and fake Oriental carpet, pocked with stain and wear spots.

Reba says, "Mama, I haven't had the time and money to fix up the place the way I plan. Next time you visit it's going to be real cozy and bright with color."

Philippa snorts, "Oh, dearie! You can't have serious plans to stay in this dungeon of a house."

Reba says petulantly, "Don't knock my home, Phil. It's all I've got. I'm stuck here for a while."

"Oh, no you're not. I've got a solution. I've come to rescue you. I'll tell you details shortly," Philippa says with a smug face.

She lights a cigarette, offers one to Reba who declines. "No thanks—no good for the baby, I heard on the radio."

Philippa says, "The Devil just pooted, as my mother used to say."

Reba says, "What?!"

Philippa laughs. "It means he's cross because I remembered all those things to bring you and I forgot demon scotch for me . . . Dearie, tell me you've got an aging bottle of mood lifter stashed among the stalagmites in this drag cave."

Reba shakes her head. "I don't drink anymore. The baby. But I'll run up to the corner drugstore to treat you with a bottle." She rises to her feet.

Philippa pulls her between her knees, embraces her waist, plumped inside her flowered print maternity dress.

"Let Mama get her own poison," Philippa says as she looks lovingly into Reba's face, enhanced by the ultra-glow of the pregnant.

Reba bends to kiss Philippa's lips as she gently strokes her abdomen, says, "I want to go; the exercise is good for us."

Philippa releases her waist. "All right. Don't let Baptiste kidnap you." They laugh. Philippa continues, "I have to make several collect calls to New Orleans. Oh yes, bring me Johnnie Walker Red."

Reba nods, goes to pick up a change purse from a tabletop near the door as she leaves the house. Neighbors, in yards and on porches on both sides of the tree-shaded street, greet her or wave as she walks to the corner.

Baptiste steps from the store with a sacked fifth of whiskey as she reaches it. He pauses, fuzzy jaws black with a week's growth of beard, his thinned form dressed in wrinkled trousers, bedraggled bathrobe, and scuffed house slippers.

Rheumy eyed, he grasps her arm, stares ambivalently into her face before he hugs her. "How you doing, Mouse?"

She moves away. "Just lovely, Papa, and don't call me Mouse."

He pats her shoulder, chuckles as he moves toward the street door leading to the stairs of Erica's flat. Reba pauses at the drugstore door, twinged by pity for Baptiste's sorry appearance.

He turns, says, "Give your mother my worst wishes when you get back home."

He disappears behind the door. Reba enters the store in wonderment at the neighborhood's chain-lightning grapevine. She forces herself to be pleasant with Erica, who sells her the scotch. She leaves the store, wonders as she crosses the street if the bluish bruise on Erica's cheekbone was Baptiste inflicted.

She turns her head back to look toward Erica's front windows. She realizes it wasn't grapevine magic that tipped Baptiste to her mother's visit. She sees Baptiste, with binoculars pressed to his eyes aimed down at her, hastily drop the spyglass from sight and grin grotesquely.

Bath refreshed, Young Joe, beetle browed and stripped to the waist in fresh denim trousers, is frenetically mowing the lawn when Reba enters the front yard. Aboil in disenchantment with females, Joe is only half playing when, grimacing ferociously, he chops the mower savagely at her heels as she squeals and scurries away to safety.

Philippa is seated on the living room couch when Reba enters. An audience of cleansed playhouse dolls stare at them through the windows of an antique cabinet. Reba sets the bottle on the coffee table before Philippa, who immediately pours herself a hefty drink into one of several glasses on the tabletop.

"I saw Papa . . . He knows you're here," Reba says as she sits down on the couch.

"What did that clown say about that?"

Reba hesitates, bites her bottom lip as Philippa studies her face. "Not much . . . Just said 'Give your mother my best wishes.'"

Philippa clucks her tongue. "Pshaw! You're a clumsy liar, dearie. Baptiste still hates me! And will until he's banquet for maggots. You know that."

Reba touches Philippa's wrist, says softly, "Now, Mama, I'm almost sure Papa's still in love with you . . . How is Mister Coceau, your new husband? I saw a big picture spread on him a few months ago in one of the local black newspapers as a premier businessman and grand something or other of the New Orleans chapter of the Masons, I think."

Philippa smiles bitterly. "That was then, before supersonic senility swooped. He's now retired as chairman of the board of vegetation. Hey, wait, he's also a biggie in the unroyal order of pee-stinking flannel drawers and dribbled jaws. He's a charm! But then, I never needed him anyway except for his money. Believe me, dearie, I'm not hurting biologically. I've got a hopperful of men."

Reba smiles stingily, studies Philippa's face. The garish wash of table lamp casts cruel angles of light and shadow that mock the face-lift to reveal eye socket wrinkles and the harsh, long-nosed gauntness of her aging face.

Reba frowns. "But Mama, I can't understand the sense of all those men!"

Philippa upends her third double shot glass of scotch. "Sweets, I need lots of men to have lots of cruel fun with. Most men are shyster Romeo bastards like Coceau, who sniffed me first to make sure before he made a serious commitment that I was at least under thirty fresh.

"Coceau married me anticipating regular plunges into a hot sassy volcano. Instead, he got an ice pit where the swirl of scented smoke and raging flame were illusions, a spell cast by an avenging old witch whose gorgeous smile and girlish face were courtesies of a five-grand set of upper and lower choppers and a New York face-lift. The womanizing sonuvabitch has become a rabid fan of the Holy Ghost. It's scrumptious fun having the old reprobate freezing his balls, nailed to a cross of ice. But enough of him—let's talk about you and this trap you're in."

Reba says peevishly, "Trap? Perhaps, Mama, but just briefly for this stepper."

Philippa pours a shot, stares into the amber liquid as she whirlpools it inside the glass. "I hope briefly, Stepper, but don't forget the first strike was called when you stepped up to bat."

Reba exclaims, "What!"

Philippa tosses the shot down her throat. "Dearie, the baby and no husband. The second strike will be when and if you let the calendar mildew your tail feathers before you hook Mister Rich, and security."

Reba shakes her head. "Lots of money would be great, Mama. But I—"

Philippa cues in. "I'm glad you said that. I'll fly you back to New Orleans for a secret abortion before we go on the prowl to nail a rich trophy to the wall. As a matter of fact, I've got a very rich and very old prospect in mind. But you're my younger sister, not my daughter, when I launch you."

Reba struggles against anger. "That's not for me, Mama. I'm having my baby! I'd settle for modest comfort with a man I felt something for. Maybe I am too square, but I want to live respected as a lady."

Philippa, aggravated by rejection of her rescue plan and Reba's plebeian aspirations, gets to her feet, prances to and fro before the couch. Her still-sleek leggy frame twangs frustration. The chic navy linen dress clings seductively to taut curves that long ago magnetized badger-game victims in chrome and leather jungles in a score of cities.

Philippa pauses before Reba to snort, "Lady!? The Queen of England is the only woman in my memory who can afford to be a lady to the bone. Now there's a lady! . . . Wears stays in her street dresses to prevent any racy flash of her upper, lousy legs."

Philippa leans close to Reba's upturned face. "Dearie, the reality is, it takes a tough street fighter bitch to avoid the third strike when too soon that calendar beast claws you and whispers in passing, 'Doll, you ain't seen nothing yet!'"

Reba says, "I'm not old yet. I refuse to panic."

Philippa snorts, "Dearie, you can procrastinate, and not go back with me. But before your calendar string runs out, you better be impure enough and scared enough to juggle your values and turn half beast yourself to escape that well-known black pit."

Reba gets to her feet, strokes her temples. "Mama, I'm gonna take a nap, got a helluva headache."

Philippa places her palms on Reba's shoulders. "All right, nap on my solution to your bind. And please don't forget, survival happens to be the name of the game you're playing, fresh young pet. It's a blood sport! Don't wind up trapped in this dungeon with a slew of kids and a pauper zero for a husband."

Reba kisses Philippa's cheek, starts to turn away for the bedroom, pauses. "Mama, what's the reward playing life your way?"

Philippa smiles. "Gracious living, dearie." She leans to pour a glass of scotch. "And induction into the old bitch hall of fame." She smiles bitterly, and as Reba shakes her head and walks away she says, "Darling, how about some of my gumbo filet for our dinner?"

"I'd love that, Mama," Reba says over her shoulder as she disappears into the bedroom.

At that same moment, in the bedroom of Erica's flat, boozed Baptiste has the problem of dressing for a grocery shopping trip with Erica. She fidgets in the doorway, red poplin rain-or-shine coat over her white store uniform. She watches him crash to the carpet as he attempts to insert the second wobbly leg into his trousers.

She glances impatiently at her wristwatch. "Da Dee, I'm really going to have to leave now. I have only an hour to get back to work. We're short of girls downstairs."

As he hoists himself to sit on the side of the bed to successfully enter the trousers, she says, "It's no use—you can't drive the Packard loaded like you are. Harry can drive me to the market in his Chevy as he has for two years."

Baptiste bullishly shakes his head. "He's not this time! I am! I'm not drunk," he exclaims with bleary-eyed bellicosity as he gets to his feet, slips into a paisley print shirt, inside out.

She delicately stamps a sandaled foot as Scandinavian pique frosts her warm blue eyes. "Ahha!" she jeers. "You can't put your shirt on right. You're too drunk to drive, kiddo!" As he studies the inverted shirt buttons slack jawed she says, "I've got to go without you."

She turns to leave the room. He lunges to seize her wrist. He jerks her back through the door frame, waggles a furious index finger in her face, knifes her dance palace hostess background. "Look, dime-a-dance broad, you can't waltz me around the suckerberry bush. That horny Harry bastard is not taking my woman to the market. If I don't, then call a cab."

She snatches her wrist free. "We can't afford a cab and besides, there isn't time to wait for one. By the way, I'll remind and warn you not to ever again strike me or call me names. Understand, my shabby little gigolo, or is it pimp? I refuse to support you and take abuse in any form."

He says, "Mule, I heard you but I'm gonna chastise you, White Lady, when you get back, if Harry takes you to the market. And say, square, damper that gigolo-pimp lie you telling yourself, because you and your chump change wouldn't make a canker on a star whore's pussy. It takes a big buck to support Baptiste Rambeau the way he's used to. Understand that, star natal square ass?"

She studies him for a long moment, trembles with aggravation before she turns and goes toward the front door. He staggers after her, slams a palm against the door as she reaches it. A sudden twinge of pain at his rear end lurches him, bends him. He sorts out stress, Erica induced, as the cause. He diagnoses rectal cancer for himself.

She watches alarmed before she sees him recover and speak. "Remember, I'm gonna tear your white ass up if Harry takes you," he warns with bloodshot emerald eyes on fire.

"You better not ever strike me again. Don't force me to call those redneck cops back again. They'll nightstick you and throw you out. Remember, they begged me to let them last week when you punched my face."

Fear flits across his face for an instant. "You lynching, cop-hearted snitch bitch!" he shouts. Then he bluffs, "I've got loving Reba and a home waiting down the block. Bitch, I can leave now!"

She says, "I won't call them! I don't want you to leave me."

"I will if you crack cop again."

Cowed temporarily, even as rage pings her, she says softly, "Da Dee, I can't stand to live like this much longer. Let's break this insanity!"

She closes her eyes, rocks dreamily a bit like a little kid hitching a maiden whirl on a carousel. She says, "I'd give anything to make us happy again, make us as we were again together."

He steps aside with a cunning face, says in a sugary whisper, "It's easy, honey kitten, since you know the combination to that new safe downstairs. Why, I could breeze into it, then hammer and chisel it a bit to cover your part. I could score the night before the armored truck picks up the money. Trust me, love me enough to give me that combination. Angel face, you know Baptiste will stay in your corner until the grim reaper yanks me. Erica, I swear that with a fresh bankroll to make my comeback with the cards, I can put myself, and us, back together as we were. Well!?"

She pauses at the door. To placate him she says, "That proposition could be attractive if conditions reversed between us. I promise to think about it, Da Dee. A lot! That is, if you can sweeten up a bit, not drink so much, not strike or threaten me anymore. Please!"

He says, "I'll give you sugar diabetes when you lay that combination on me." He palm-bangs her rear end. "Go on, let that cocksucker take you to the market for the last time."

She goes out the door. Baptiste slams it behind her and scrambles to his binoculars on the seat of an overstuffed chair rammed against a front window.

Next morning, Reba walks to the sidewalk with Philippa. Young Joe, prepared to earn Philippa's windfall fifty bucks, stands beside his newly polished Ford ready to get Philippa's luggage, then take her to the airport. Philippa and Reba embrace waists.

Philippa pleads, for the dozenth time since breakfast, "Please, baby girl, come with me. Don't rot here!"

Reba says firmly, "I'm going to have my baby and stay here, Mama. Maybe I'll visit you after the baby is walking. I love you."

They kiss. Philippa stuffs a thousand-dollar bill down Reba's bosom, says, "For the hospital and a nickel's worth of stuff for my grandbaby." Philippa flees to the car before Reba can protest.

Young Joe gets behind the wheel. He U-turns it to take Normandie Avenue to downtown. Philippa's eyes threaten tears as she waves goodbye to Reba. Then tears burst loose when she glances at the memory-steeped Rambeau house.

Young Joe halts the Ford at a stationary STOP sign at the end of the block facing the drugstore. Joe pulls away under Baptiste's lovesick eyes locked in the spyglass zeroed in through the windshield on Philippa.

A ghetto half a mile away, Reginald Lewis, Philippa's airliner humper, cat-foots silently about a three-room apartment. He completes packing his total possessions. He stares at his snoring, pudgy, and uncomely but faithful nurse's aide sweetheart that he was shacked up with when shipped overseas by the army. A boss cook, but a broke-as-Lazarus lousy lay, he thinks as he remembers his toothbrush in the bathroom.

He pauses in the john to tinkle. He gazes at his jungle cat face in a cabinet mirror as he relieves himself. Rapture bombards him as he kudos himself for catching, at last, a rich, sexy, and beautiful woman. Philippa's vow to take him back with her to New Orleans to live an opulent life blares inside his head with the percussive thunder of a John Philip Sousa march.

He hears the cabbie hit his horn staccato as he goes to the dressertop to write a "Dear Mable" note. Suddenly, Mable's pet cat leaps onto the bed and chews at the curlers in her hair to awaken her.

They stare at each other before Mable says peevishly, "Oh shoot, Reggie. What the dickens you doing out of bed before you keep your promise to give me some homecoming loving? You ain't forgot you fell in bed and died last night soon's you said hello. C'mon, undress, sweetie, and make me holler like you usta."

The cabbie's horn prods again as he looks at his wristwatch, says gravely, "Naw, Big Mama, I'm sorry, but I'm late. I can't stay. This stud is fleeing in the wind to chomp the tall sweet clover. Bye, baby, bye."

She whimpers piteously, leaps from the bed when he picks up his duffel bag and steamer trunk. He moves past her, cosmic eyed.

"I'm gonna put a curse on you!" she shrills. "You a dirty nigger to split on me cold-blooded like this, Reginald!" She pursues, claws at him to the front door, Aunt Jemima face maniacal.

He swings the duffel bag hard against her chest. She falls backward to the carpet. He steps into the sunshine, bangs the door shut. He whistles himself to the cab, loads his gear and himself into the rear seat. As it pulls away, from the only friend and home he has anywhere, he stares at Mable weeping her heart out, standing nude, in the open doorway.

Reginald arrives first at Philippa's hotel. Young Joe's jalopy has been slowed by a traffic jam. Reginald drops his bags at a window couch. He goes to the desk to be informed that his dream inamorata is absent from her C-note-a-day suite. He goes to sit on the couch. Head aswivel, he alternately hawk-eyes the bustling street and rear lobby entrances for Philippa's arrival.

Joe pulls into the hotel's rear parking lot. Philippa gets out. Reginald spots her, fresh as dew-washed daisies in yellow silk, as she comes through a rear door toward him. He catapults from the couch. But his gazelle-smooth streak across the lobby stonewalls against the gouted foot of a portly gent who calls him "crazy nigger" in strident Swedish.

He lies in a sweatbox of embarrassment under the stares of passersby and the neoned eyes of his voluptuous bonanza. His sky fallen in, he closes his eyes and chickens out fetal for a mini-instant before he sensuously acrobats to his feet, guided by the velvety crutch of her hand.

Cold-blooded amusement skates her icy eyes as she volleys him with giggle bullets. But he forces himself impervious. Philippa injects his lips with one of her cobra kisses that breaks him down sloppy like a sawbuck shotgun. His "Howdy Doody" mouth slobbers to threaten her "Ingenue of Camelot" makeup scam.

"I missed you too, gorgeous," she whispers as she ducks her fragile mask away and steers him back to the window sofa.

They sit and gaze at each other a spell before she says, "I've got bad news."

His voice shakes. "Bad news? . . . Uh, about us?"

She lifts his hand, smooches the back of it, "Don't look so distressed, Soldier Man. It's just that we can't fly to New Orleans together today."

"What!? Why?" he exclaims.

"My mother called me from New Orleans last night to alert me that my crazy ex-husband will be staked out all day at the airport to beg me back." She straightens a stocking seam on a Grable-quality gam as she continues. "Lover, it seems to me you'll simply have to take a later flight, perhaps in several days to give me time to clear the damn fool out of our way. Don't you agree?"

He frowns, drops her head. "Yeah, sure, but I've got a problem."

She finger-lifts his chin. "Your problems are my problems, honey lamb. What's worrying you?"

He heaves a heavy sigh. "I'm, uh . . . almost flat broke, with just a few bucks for food . . . lost my mustered-out money gambling on the troop ship coming stateside. I don't even have a place to stay."

She laughs gaily. "Cheer up, poopsie. You don't have a problem." She rises. "You can stay in my suite until I wire you money for plane fare in a day or so."

He follows her, with his bags, to pick up her key, then to an elevator. She watches him freak out when they enter the ultra-posh suite.

"What a terrific pad!" he loudmouths.

She goes to the bathroom to get her makeup to pack into her small suitcase. She suddenly strips nude, falls supine to the airy carpet. Her mega-notched, fat-lipped, whiskered glutton winks at him. He shucks out of his clothes, sports a quality erection which she promptly rips off with bitchy yaps of joy. Then she mounts his face, humps it savagely, smears it, with bared teeth.

Leaving the suite, she embraces him and fantasizes her slashing teeth hemorrhaging his lips and tongue. He yelps in pain, recoils free.

As she steps into the corridor with her bag she reassures him. "I adore you! I'll be in pure misery until I meet your flight in New Orleans."

He hippy-dips, "Everything boss cool with the landprop?"

She says, "Will be, for the time we'll need after I stop at the desk."

She turns away. Quim maimed and drained, he teeters on rubbery legs, gazing at her witching him again with the ball-bearing wiggle of her honeydews through sheer yellow silk. She disappears into an elevator. She goes to a pay phone near the lobby's rear exits.

She calls the desk, says, "This is Mrs. Tomlinson, registered in suite six-ten. Please don't disturb Mister Tomlinson with messages or phone calls before he checks out at two p.m. today."

She is suddenly assaulted by an imp of madness. She pauses, reflected at the door glass. She twists her face into a cretin sneering monster, then an idiot slut, with scotch-purpled tongue lolled out like a gangrened penis. After a tensioned tussle, she rousts the gibbering imp and moves into the parking lot. She instantly becomes an animated portrait of laid-back élan, perhaps inspired by the card-carrying sanity buffs moiling about her.

Cruel to say the least, but Reg is easily one of your most creative hangings since you strung up adorably hung Miguel, she tells herself. You couldn't let a mere busboy illegal alien hook your heart so you fingered him to the immigration cops. You beautiful, perfect, genius person you. She goes across the lot to Young Joe moving the jalopy through dazzling sunlight toward her.

She gets in. As he pulls away for the airport she says, "A priceless day like today makes life worth living, doesn't it, darling?"

He says, "I maybe can say yes today. But no way yesterday. I'm getting hip to take the bitter with the sweet."

She leans her head back on the seat cushions, closes her eyes, muses, "Good thinking, Joe . . . We have to use our memories of the candy and orchid days of our lives as cushions for the catastrophes."

"Ca . . . what?" he says.

"People-caused disasters, Joe, as for instance the bride or groom is no show for that road show of elderly shoes and rice," she says bleakly as she thinks of Reba's split-off-from-Melvin dilemma.

"Yeah, I dig you now," he says softly as he remembers Delphine's ripoff with a hot poker stab of psychic pain.

He flogs the crippled jalopy into autopsy-hazardous traffic with typical Young Joe Allen derring-do and, with soul-based, brute machismo.

Eight

Under the deepening cover of September twilight, a month to the day since hapless Reginald's hotel lynching, Zenobia sits parked in her La Salle. Her falcon-bright eyes are welded to the Hoffmeister plumbing firm building a half block away. She waits to tail her eel-elusive Midnight Creeper. Driving skills honed and Holy Ghost vibrated, she flirts with the conviction that she will bag the Midnight Creeper this tail out.

A church member's trio of preteen daughters pause and stoop beside the La Salle's sidewalk side open window to startle her with a stoutly chorused "Hi, Miss Zenobia!" before they boogie away.

She stares at the departing trio and the rather tackily dressed stepsister Maude. Zenobia's ruined doll face is thoughtful and softened in the fallout of lavender light. She watches ebonic Maude, in cheap black dress, become nearly invisible at the corner between the high-yellow natural sisters, butterfly vivid in starched dresses. Zenobia remembers the church gossip about the sinful and cruel way the widowed mother of the daughter trio favors her blood offspring over Maude, the family chore slave.

Zenobia's mind takes flight to painfully grope the past. She remembers when she, at Maude's age, was the despicable, anxiety-wracked, wet-the-bed, family lackey. She remembers the sweaty summer nights she lay on her washboard-rough rag pallet. She'd lie there bruised on the pine floor in the one-room cabin. She'd dream herself into her sisters' feather-mattressed brass bed, gleaming like gold in the rush of moonlight through the open door.

She remembers shedding a billion tears, lying there wishing she wasn't so heart-grindingly blue-black so her stepmother would touch her, hug her, love her as she did her silky-haired mulatto daughters. She had wished them all dead and stinking a thousand times. Even her lovable but jelly-spined tar black father when he cajoled, pitifully begged her half-white stepmother, Ora, for sex behind the leaky privacy of a gunnysack curtain.

Rejected and hopeless, she often death-wished that the Big Dipper would scoop her up through the star-shot gates of Paradise. She remembers that when trouble and hurt burdened her unbearably, she would sneak from the sharecropper cabin to a clump of forest to rendezvous with a hallucinated only friend. Childishly, she had secretly named him Mister Firefly Face for the warm light that always suffused his unearthly kind face when he came to hold her, rock her, kiss her to tranquil slumber beside a musical brook.

Her stepmother, next morning, always razor-strapped her bottom raw for that before her daily, fatiguing chores. Her father's feeble protests were always blown away by the blast of her step-mother's ex–moonshine joint B-girl spew of profanity.

She remembers the midnight the carping voice was stilled forever, and those of the others in the cabin. She was awakened brookside by the banshee screams of her tyrant stepsisters. She raced to the flame-shrouded cabin, watched their terror-hideous, hated yellow faces through a curtain of door flame. Cotton-slave neighbors arrived too late at the cindered scene. She had guessed correctly that it was her father's usually carelessly tamped-out presleep pipe that had started the fire.

She remembers the cratered face of her father's cousin bellying against her, clutching her horny eyed and scary in the glow of flame. "Baby girl, I ain't gonna let them mean peckerwoods stick you in no prison orphanage," he whispered, rattling her skinny frame with terror. "I'm gonna be ya pappy 'cause I hear Cousin Frank begging me to be, jus' as clear."

She hurts to remember her shrieks of blackout pain when he drunkenly butchered her maidenhead with shaft-long slams of his wrist-thick meat slab. She felt he had split her into two bloody halves. She remembers that she tried to drink herself dead when, years later, he deserted her, pregnant with Young Joe, for a new infant concubine.

Now, she sees Elder Joe come out of the plumbing building. She watches him get into the truck, drive away, decked out dapper in blue suit with matching homburg rakishly cocked on his square head. She eases the La Salle away in pursuit.

She follows him to a Hollywood bar adjacent to a fancy motel. She watches him park the truck a hundred-odd yards from the La Salle on the street near the front of the bar. She drives to the other side of the street to spy into the psychedelic murk of the place. She sees the Creeper sip several drinks on a stool at the bar near the open door as he darts anxious glances toward the sidewalk.

She stiffens, white-hot jealous, as she sees Joe grin, lean back, and stare at the stately Marguerite Spingarn getting out of her fuchsia Caddie. She is *Vogue* gorgeous in a powder blue, blue fox–trimmed suit and matching baby doll shoes. Emotion sweat drenches Zenobia as she watches them kiss and cling in the manner of the long-term lovers they are.

She remembers how Joe's creamy tan handsomeness and bawdy jocker/baby boy personality had shucked her out of her potato sack drawers. She remembers it was sweet right away in that cricket-serenaded bush bedroom. He had pushed her love button as he rode her on palms and toe tips with only a blue sash of moonlight to cushion their pelvic smashes.

Now, she sits paralyzed with hurt as she watches Joe leave her ritzy rival at the bar to go to stand behind a pair of customers at the next-door motel office window and wait to rent a room. She thinks of the scythe in the La Salle's trunk that she earlier picked up razor honed from the sharpener to chop down a patch of backyard weeds. For an insane instant, before her Sweet Jesus routs Lucifer, she visualizes Marguerite's decapitated head on the barroom floor to shock Joe when he returns.

She sits and cries like a scalded baby for a long time after she sees them go into room 210. In a red haze of revenge lust she stumbles to a nearby sidewalk pay phone cubicle. She dials the operator, blubbers she wants the police to arrest a murder fugitive. But when the operator connects her to the voice of a desk sergeant, she hangs up. She stares across the street at the neon ripple of the motel's telephone number on its shocking pink facade. She dials. The motel switchboard operator connects the call.

Inside, the lovers disengage from their favorite sex-snack position. They stare stupidly at each other for a long bit before Marguerite picks up and says, "Hello."

Joe sees her ashen, puts his ear to the back of the receiver, hears Zenobia's flat voice say, "Put Joe Allen on this phone, ya filthy Lucifer's pet!"

"That isn't possible, lady. There's no Joe Allen here," Marguerite manages to say coolly before she hangs up. "Oh God!" she exclaims as the lovers scramble to peer through a slit in the room's drapes at an empty public phone booth near the entrance to the parking lot.

They are speed-dressing when the phone jangles them rigid. They stare at the phone for three blasts before Joe again glues his ear to the back of the receiver when Marguerite tremulously picks up to Zenobia's voice. "Ya lyin' strumpet! Tell my convic' husban' he better fly outta there 'cause I'm gonna drop a nickel to the poleece so's they can ship his 'scaped butt back to the Georgia chain gang for killin' that white man."

Marguerite drops the receiver to the nightstand with a clatter as she collapses with a color-drained face onto the side of the bed. She rocks as her fingers work like vipers massaging her temple pits. He drops himself down beside her. She recoils when he tries to loop an arm around her shoulders.

Her bleak maroon eyes stare into his eyes that flee to an intense interest in the taffy carpet when she whispers, "Tell me it isn't so, Joe," with the pathos perhaps of the legendary moppet baseball fan who long ago begged that Black Sox player to deny his thrown-game guilt.

Joe's silence confesses, whips her to her feet to finish dressing with her milk chocolate cat-body barraging "We're through!" vibes.

Half dressed, he rouses from trance, wild eyed. He leaps through space, arm-shackles her at the cracked door where she fearfully eye-sweeps the lot darkness, infested by portly, black, razor-ready shadows haunched in the jungle of guest cars. He roots his face into her pounding clavicle, Paris perfumed.

Like the crotch-deep cry of a lynch mob amputee, he squalls, "I can't let you quit me, Marite!"

She struggles, says harshly, "You fool! Let me go before the police break in here to arrest you and destroy my reputation."

He shucks his careful grammar to babble. "Sure, I kilt that redneck. I'll kill him a thousand more times if he could make it back after what he did. I crawfished tellin' you 'bout it 'cause I was scared you was gonna spook and quit me. Lissen, lemme 'splain how I ain't in no true sense a real killer. You woulda kilt him yourself in my place! Lemme 'splain!"

"I'll call you at the plumbing office . . . sometime . . ." Marguerite wiggles free and streaks across the lot to the sidewalk with her fingertips hiking up her dress hip high and her shoes tucked beneath her armpits. She halts to double-eye-sweep the street before she puts on her shoes and goes to hurtle her car away.

Zenobia sees Joe race from the motel to gun the truck away in pursuit of Marguerite. Zenobia sputters inside the La Salle frustrated by sudden bumper-to-bumper traffic that prevents her U-turn pursuit. She stares up at the reflection of Joe's truck until it evaporates in the La Salle's steamy rearview mirror.

Twenty minutes after Marguerite's arrival at home, she sees Joe bring the plumbing truck to a grinding stop in front of her house, leap out, and dash up the walkway to ring her doorbell and frantically drum his knuckles against her front door.

"Have you gone mad?" she shouts through the double-locked door. "Your wife will give the police your truck plate number for an A.P.B. They will arrest you here, arrest me on charges of harboring a fugitive. Please, Joe, go away!"

He shouts back, "I won't! I've got to talk to you. Now!"

In the racket of doorbell and his door pounding, she mulls calling the police to report his presence to protect herself from arrest. She goes to the phone, lifts the receiver. What if Zenobia hasn't informed the police, she asks herself as she replaces the receiver.

She goes to the door, opens it on chain, says, "I'll give you a few minutes after you move that truck out of my block."

He turns and goes to drive the truck away. Minutes later she lets him into the crystal-chandeliered entrance hall. He follows her into the spacious living room, furnished with expensive contemporary mahogany pieces, an elegantly color-schemed cream carpet, and rich sable velvet drapes. They seat themselves on a chocolate satin couch before a silver coffee service on a tan leather–topped coffee table.

She says, "Cup of coffee, Joe?" as she lifts her interrupted cup of black brew to sip.

"No thanks," he says as he scoots close to her.

She turns her face away from his emotion-fouled breath. "Say it quickly, Joe. I'm in a terrible strain with you here." She studies his sweat-glossy face impassively from a narrowed corner of her eye.

"I lied about my roots to impress you, Marite," he confesses. "My preacher, sharecropper pappy was never a wealthy general store owner down South. He was just a pauper on the forever tab of the general store in town. It was owned by the white man who owned the cotton land we twelve Allens worked for fatback and beans." He bitterly chuckles as he pauses. "We were so poor the mice and roaches nixed our cabin . . . On my pappy's last day we picked up some beans and molasses and a couple of gunnysacks of dung fertilizer at the general store one July afternoon when I was ten."

He pauses to light a cigarette with a tan leather–covered table lighter. "Pappy was a half-inch shy of seven feet tall, and skinny as a string of cotton with a core of steel wire. He was country dap strutting in swallowtail coat and brand-new overalls. He caught the eyes of all the white folks in town when our buckboard, pulled by old Hettie the mare, went through on our way back home.

"Almost all of the God-fearing white folks respected him and the thick brass-bound Bible he kept tucked under his arm, shining like a slab of gold. He was a Christian showboater to the bone, and the town's Kluxers hated him for it. Oh! He was half God himself with bass drums in his throat and violins in his bosom. He preached his sermons from his pulpit beneath magnolia trees every Sunday morning." He pauses to wipe tears from his eyes. "I loved and worshipped Pappy. He was my god!" he exclaims as he continues with his eyes locked on Marguerite's inscrutable face.

"Our buckboard was skedaddling down a narrow dusty road a short piece from home when a rut in the road flung off a bag of fertilizer. It busted when it rolled down a little hill. It hit smack dab into goodies spread out on a tablecloth on the grass beneath shade trees by several of the town's nigger-hating toughs with their wives and kids. Pappy stopped the wagon and we hotfooted down the hill to the picnic spot to apologize and save what fertilizer was left in the busted bag . . ."

Marguerite says, "Excuse me for a moment," as she rises to go to the bathroom.

Joe pours himself a water glass half full of bourbon from a silver decanter on the coffee table. At first sip, the phone rigs on a stand at his elbow beside the sofa. On the throne, Marguerite reaches to pick up the receiver off the wall phone beside her. Joe stares at the silenced phone for a long moment before he eases it off the hook to his ear.

"My dear, I'm in my chamber taking a cigar break. I hope I didn't interrupt something important with my call." Joe is certain the voice is that of Judge Evans.

"No, darling, talking to you is much more important than getting that final fitting by Mrs. Phelps, my dressmaker, for the blue sequined cocktail dress I've raved to you about."

He says "Come in" to a faint knock sound. Then to Marguerite, in a stage whisper, "Honey, a defense counsel just came in. I'll call you after court."

Joe mops a sudden rash of sweat bubbles off his forehead.

Marguerite returns to sit, blue taffeta housecoated, at the far end of the sofa, twanging impatience as she exhales a gust of cigarette smoke, says, "I don't want to be unkind. But please finish so I can take the bath you interrupted. Now, you and your pap . . . uh, father had unfortunately crashed a redneck picnic . . ."

He emotes it, replete with face ballet, dialect, and poignant hand play as he goes on. "They all, even their kids, looked fit to kill us when Pappy snatched off his derby hat and said, with his soft drawl and rough English, 'Gent'men, ladies, I 'pologize for that sack of dung that's done spoiled yo outin'.' Pappy dug a couple of dollar bills from his frock coat. He held it out to the nearest mean-faced white man, Jeff Jenkins. He was rumored to be the head dragon of the local Klan.

"'It sho ain't 'nough to pay for all them vittles that bag ruint,' Pappy said as we looked down at the piles of smoked pork chops, ham, and potato salad sprinkled with dung dust. 'Please take it, suh, in the spirit of restushin. Ah gwine pay you soon's I can, the 'mount you tell me.' Pappy pointed the Bible toward our farm windmill on a slight rise a short piece away. 'Stop by after harvessin' an' ah sho gonna pay ya ever penny whut y'all tell me now ah owes.'

"'Whup hell outta 'em!' one of the women said. Pretty soon the rest of them, even the little kids, started shouting, 'Whup the nigguhs! Whup the nigguhs!' while Pappy just stood smiling offering Jenkins the two dollars on his palm.

"I thought the big vein on Pappy's neck would explode when Jenkins spat a gob of tobacco spit into Pappy's hand and broke his silence. 'Nigguh, we gotta git a piece of you long black ass! . . .' Then, Jenkins looked long at Pappy's famous Bible before he said, 'Lessen ya puts up colatrul to covah thurty bucks' worth o' vittles ya done ruint. Nigguh, gimme yo Bible 'til harvessin' time!'

"Pappy said, 'No suh! Cain't and ain't gonna do that!' as he stooped to wipe the spit off his palm on the grass. I screamed, 'Look out, Pappy!' too late for him to duck Jenkins' boot kick to his jaw that coldcocked him flat on his back with his crooked mouth leaking blood. I got down beside him and wiped the blood off with my bandanna. Last I remember was Jenkins popping Pappy's head with a stone from a pile the brats had been playing with from a gravel pit at the edge of the clearing.

"Then, before I blacked out from a stone to my forehead, I saw and heard all of them laughing and stoning us. Pappy was dead when I came to myself around dusk. I was all alone and Pappy's Bible was still gripped in his cold hand. At the five-minute inquest that week, Mama made me describe a gang of strange hoboes instead of the Jenkins mob for fear of revenge.

"Well, every day and night, until I was seventeen, I thought about killing Jenkins. One night I was coon-hunting with my dog, old Count, when I got my chance to square accounts with Jenkins. He and his dog had treed a coon. I recognized him in the beam of his flashlight that was aimed up at Mister Coon. Wasn't no use to try to sneak up on him with his dog by his side, excited and barking. So I just sashayed right up to his back and said, 'Howdy, Mister Jenkins, suh. It looks like you done had good coon luck.' He laughed and without turning his head, not knowing it was me, said, 'Sho have, boy. Whoopee!'

"I put a 30-06 bullet through his dog's head first before I leaped back a piece. Jenkins spun around to face me with his flashlight on my face. He screamed at sight of my face—the image of Pappy's—and tried to swing 'round his shotgun to blast before I shot out his blue eyes lit up like hell's fire.

"Idus, my oldest brother, sneaked me food where I hid in a cave for a week before a powerful white man Mama cleaned house for brought me safely in for trial. I was just turning twenty-one when I escaped a life sentence from the chain gang."

Weakened by desperation, he lowers himself to the carpet on his knees before her. He buries his face in her lap. His arms jail her legs as he pleads piteously, "Say you understand, Marite. Say you're still mine!"

His heart cycle jumps with joy to feel her hands tenderly stroke his neck and shoulders. He raises his hopeful eyes to see love in her face. Instead, he sees only decadent, raw pity that pierces his pride, forces him to struggle to his feet to crutch his invalided manhood straight and tall.

"Guess we're through with each other, Miss Marite, 'cause I sure don't want you since you don't want me." He turns away for the front door.

He pauses to pick up and cock his thrift shop blue homburg at an insouciant angle on his square head.

She murmurs softly to his back, "You've got the last ounce of my sympathy. I'll keep your secret. Forgive me, but I'm so sorry, Joe. I can't risk sacrificing my reputation, my son's life and law practice for us." Her voice breaks. "Good luck always."

He thinks of the phone call from the wealthy socialite Judge. He checks himself before he turns back to lash her. A vision of the truck staked out by cops chills him inside his Robert Hall suit of blue as he moves on marshmallow-soft, sable carpet through the richly appointed room. He steps into the night bleaked by the mournful sighs of the weeping willow trees flogged by Santa Anas.

At that same instant, bathrobed Baptiste and the pile of his belongings are starkly illuminated on the stoop of Erica's flat by the spotlight of a police cruiser. Young Joe Allen, on his way home from a trick tryst with a Delphine look-alike Central Avenue whore, parks his Ford and joins Reba among the knot of neighborhood gawkers at the scene.

Erica weeps at the doorway as she gingerly fingers a fat, livid bottom lip before she turns and disappears up the stairway followed by a cop.

The other uniformed cruiser cop trembles as he leans his red, hostile face close to Baptiste. "Boy, you ain't got long to get you and your stuff out of my sight. You heah!?"

Reba sleeve-tugs Baptiste a few paces aside. "That cop is itching to beat you up or kill you. Oh, why did you hit that white woman?"

Baptiste growls, "I slugged her for kicking me and cursing me . . . after I caught Harry playing stink finger with her in my Packard behind the store."

Reba says firmly, "Well, I don't care what you say now, we're moving your stuff in Joe's Ford, to the back house." She turns to Joe beside her. "Can we, Joe?"

He shrugs. "That's okeydokey with me."

Baptiste drunkenly stares at the heap of his possessions on the sidewalk. Then he gazes lustfully for a moment at the Havelik safe, glossy black-lacquered virgin squatted at the rear of the store.

He grins ruefully, his eyes sparkled by tears. A Jolson fan, he apes his idol with outflung arms. "Heah I is, baby mammy. Take me home! I'm yours!" he whispers into Reba's ear as he embraces her.

Reba laughs as she shoves free. Reba and Young Joe load Baptiste's stuff into the Ford and take it and him to the back house.

Inside the Allen house, Elder Joe sits chain-smoking in his bedroom after correctly deducing that Zenobia, after shooting her wad of anger on the telephone with Marguerite, has not finked on him to the cops. But he wonders about the whereabouts of Zenobia as he goes to the kitchen.

At that moment, following a fruitless comb of the ghetto for sight of the plumbing truck, Zenobia sees it parked at the house and pulls the La Salle up behind it. She goes wearily into the house, goes straight to the kitchen at the sound of Joe's movement. He shuts the refrigerator door, turns toward her with a glass of orange juice as she enters the kitchen.

They glare at each other before Zenobia moves a waggling index finger in close to his face. "Don't evil-eye me, Mister Slick Stuff. I gave you fair warning. You gonna make a fool outta me enty mo' with her? What's that fancy butt's name?"

His quivering hand slops orange juice from his glass to the linoleum as he stares at a pipe wrench on the table behind her. He vibrates with lust for the consummate orgasm. Murder.

He smiles hideously as he whispers hoarsely, "It's all over with . . . uh, Grace Webb." He shrugs. "You win. But I got to remind you, Madame Dick Tracy, that misery that goes around comes around. Will for sure for what you did."

She snickers, "Mister Creeper, I'm glad you in misery. You gonna be in chain gang misery if you jivin' me 'bout breakin' up with you woman Grace. Yo muckety-muck sweetie was gonna quit yo low-life convic' butt soon down the line anyways. So nigguh, don't threaten me no more in no kinda way. If I weren't stove up and ailin' critical, I'd bung yo head bigger'n a Georgia watermelon 'bout you and thet tramp."

He glares fury at her as he attempts to move past her. She shoves him hard against the refrigerator. His face is demonic as he splinters the glass of orange juice against the linoleum.

She says, "I hope you mad 'nough to hit me, bad nigguh, so's I can sic Li'l Joe on you. He's snatch off yo arms and legs, nigguh, an' throw 'em in the garbage can for the pickup man if he jus' even knew 'bout me ketchin' you cheatin'. If you don't straighten up fast and fly right like the song says, I'm gonna tell Li'l Joe 'bout you and Grace Webb bussin' his mama's ailin' heart."

She shifts her eyes to stare through the kitchen window at Young Joe leaving Reba's back house.

Elder Joe turns to see him, hurries past Zenobia to leave the kitchen as she says, "I'd tell him now on you if I could stand the sight of blood."

Young Joe enters the kitchen, hugs Zenobia as she starts to stoop to pick up the broken glass. He says, "Mama, let that slide. C'mon, sit down and let me lay the latest Baptiste happenings on you." He leads Zenobia to a chair at the kitchen table.

At the front of the Allen house, the Reba-smitten Reverend Felix Junior, preteen preaching whiz, pulls to the curb in his chauffeured black Cadillac limousine. His cute face is radiant with anticipation as he gets out to pay Reba a social visit under the pretext of offering her his newly created position of assistant church secretary.

Nine

In the spring of the following year of 1948, Zenobia, the great thoroughbred workhorse, lies retired and sleepless in the quiet of midnight. Medicine bottles on a nightstand glitter in a spot of early May moonlight like the flash of silicone gems on a headstone.

Elder Joe, in his bedroom down the hall, flicks on a nightstand lamp to torture himself with a recent edition of the black *Los Angeles Sentinel* newspaper. Tears well as he scans, for the dozenth time, one of its society pages devoted entirely to pictures and copy of the Acapulco marriage of Judge Evans and Marguerite Spingarn, adorable in peach peau de soie and lace.

Joe silently screams, "Oh Marite!" as he stares into the depths of the mesmeric eyes of her paper image. He groans, feels a hybrid twinge of loss, rage, and guilt for Zenobia's Christmas Day stroke while serving her white woman's dinner party.

He painfully remembers his creative nastiness until her stroke, calculated to punish her and zoom her blood pressure. This, of course, in the long absences of Young Joe, full time on his stepfather's plumbing job and part time as a night watchman. He rises to check on Zenobia, dead from the waist down, who is unaware of her inoperable cancer of the pancreas. On cane, he goes to her cracked door, hears her softly praying.

She sees his shadow. Bitterness deforms her mouth, closes her eyes to feign sleep as he comes to sit on the side of the bed. He whispers, "Zen, I know you ain't 'sleep . . . you all right? Can I do anything, get you anything?"

She turns to focus malevolent eyes on him as she rasps, "Lemme alone, ya dirty cruel nigguh! Ya gonna pay! G'wan and git 'cause I got Li'l Joe and Reba to do alla nursin' I needs."

She gouges fingernails into the back of his hand when he pats her dead thigh, screeches, "Git! Ya crippul motel snake! I'm gonna tell Li'l Joe 'bout the cause of his mama's stroke iffen ya don' stay outta my face."

He rises, struggles back to his bed on arthritis-quaked legs.

Across the hall, Young Joe gazes at Reba's nude body beside him. He thinks she is almost back to normal curvaceousness after the birth of Pretty Melvin's stillborn baby in early March past. He feels himself palpitate wildly after his maiden ride between her banana yellow thighs. His ride ticket was validated a week to the day ago since he slipped the pain-stained Delphine diamond on Reba's finger. He had kept the ring as a lodestone to attract visions of Delphine and to keep the memory of her grifter yapping at bucking climax masturbating through his mind.

A mellow fit two ways, Joe had thought, and anyway, ain't no doubt Reba has always been my wet-dream queen. Now he closes his eyes, moans to himself, "I done had enough hurt to make the angels wanta bawl, as Mama's always saying. Sure hope Reba don't lay no grief on me. You choose wise and fast 'cause ain't no other fox fine as Reba nowhere, no time, gonna hook up with you, my man, 'cause you the ugliest nigguh in L.A. Baby Kong, you maybe the world champ of ugly." He smiles stingily at his bitter humor.

His eyes are puppy soft as he watches Reba slip into her quilted housecoat at the side of the bed. They kiss before she silently opens the door, carefully closes it behind her. She peeks at Zenobia through her cracked door as she moves on tiptoes to the stairway.

Clean-shaven Baptiste awaits her, piqued, on the living room couch, a sight to gallop Philippa's cruel maverick heart, attired as he is in the neat silver-buttoned cop blue uniform of the rent-a-night watchman firm that has employed him for two months and Young Joe for several weeks. He stands and wears the supporting belt of the holstered pistol low on his slim hips, perhaps in the fashion of an aging star in the fast-draw blood sport of the Old West.

His silver-braided coplike cap glints brightly as he dips his head toward the Allen house. "Jeez, they are breaking you down. You look awful bad, Mouse. I can't get why you drain yourself nursing her for free."

Reba studies his face as she lights a cigarette. "It's easy, Papa. She's my friend. I like her a lot—no, love her a lot. And Papa, don't call me Mouse!"

He takes her hand, stares at Young Joe's engagement ring for a moment before he looks deeply into her eyes. "I can't get it why you accepted that ring. He's not one point your type. You couldn't ever love that klutz as a husband."

She frees her hand. "I can try, Papa. It's my life. In lingo you can get, I'm Joe's royal flush catch. He has worshipped me and loved me since I was ten. But best of all, he's a stone man. I'm through with the self-centered sissified Melvins of the world. Get it!?"

Baptiste slowly nods his head, kisses her forehead before he leaves the house for his lumberyard shift.

A month later, in the hush of predawn, Young Joe, awakened by Zenobia's loud delirium, hastens to her bedside. Sorrow trembles him as he stands staring down at her writhing, sweat-drenched figure, wasted skeletal inside her flannel nightgown.

She laughs as she jerks her head in excitement. Young Joe watches the long braids of her hair whip about her head. Her braids in motion remind him of the snowy bunting whipping on the facade of the Allens' Down Home Cafe dream that came true on that windy day of its grand opening when he was just a gangling kid.

His face hardens as he hears her babble, "Lookit you sweet patootie's chopped-off haid layin' there, Mister Midnight Creeper . . . Ya cryin' over Grace! . . . shucks! . . . Fool, you need to cry, 'cause ya ain't never cried over me . . ." She breaks into tears, blubbers, "But ya gonna pay, Joe Allen, 'cause ah'm tellin' Li'l Joe how ya and yo sneak sweetie near dropped his mama dead layin' up in that motel."

A moment of lucidity focuses her eyes on his face. "Promise Mama ya gonna stop the ring fightin' an' marry my play daughter an' git kids."

He exclaims, "I promise with all my heart, Mama! But I need you!"

Suddenly she bolts erect against her pillows, arms reaching, eyes bulging, hypnotized by divine visitation. She claps her hands, shouts, "Hallelujah! Prechus Lamb! Ya done come to take me home!" as she gazes at her Sweet Jesus, golden tressed and sky blue eyed, framed in white flame by a nimbus bright as an exploding star. She sees him smile beatifically as he beckons from the doorway.

Joe drops onto the bed, embraces her waist to restrain her feeble lunge from the bed. He buries his face in her bosom, sobs, "Mama, you ain't seeing him for real. Please don't die and leave me for no jive Holy Ghost, Mama! Even if He's real, He's gonna Jim Crow you up there like He did down here. He's gonna have you slaving up there for the white folks!"

She struggles with eyes on fire. "Hush up you blasphemin' mouf, Lucifer, an' let me loose!" She stiffens, then falls back limply on the pillows, whispers, "Ah'm so tired . . . Lemme go!" She closes her eyes and heaves a mighty sigh before she dies.

Joe takes her into his arms, rocks her as he pleads, "I love you, Mama! Please have mercy on poor me and come back. Oh Mama, come back to your child!" He weeps piteously as he cradles her shrunken body. "Mama! Mama! Mama!"

He releases her corpse, whirls on the bedside when he hears an explosion of bleating weeping. He tenses, slit eyed as he glares at Elder Joe as he shakily rides his cane to bedside, his contorted face flooded with tears.

He blubbers, "Oh, son! Zen's Sweet Jesus has snatched her from us!" He puts a hand on Joe's shoulder.

He slams his fist down on the back of Elder Joe's hand with such force that he howls with pain through his weeping as he staggers backward into a chair.

Young Joe springs from the bed to lean into his face. "Nigguh, don't you never touch me again!" he shouts as he seizes Elder Joe's crooked arthritic hands and crushes them in his gargantuan hands. He tightens the vise until the screaming old man's defecation backs him away.

"Son, you crazy!? Why you abusing me like this?" he croaks as he struggles up to his feet on cane.

He cringes away from Joe's maniacal face and snarling indictment, "You and a broad named Grace kilt my mama, motherfuckah!"

"Me? Killed Zen!?" the accused whines.

"Yeah, for a piece of pussy, you busted her heart and planted that cancer in her. You need killing!"

Elder Joe scuttles for the door, his guilty face pleading "no contest" to the crime.

Young Joe seizes his shoulders, spins him, says in a vicious stage whisper, "Stay outta my face forever 'cause I'm gonna kill your old crippled ass if you don't. Understand, murderer!?"

Elder Joe frantically dips his gray head as he eases away to the safety of the hallway. Joe slams the door shut behind him. He turns and bellows grief until he can only whisper, "Mama! Mama!" as he stares into Zenobia's blank eyes.

It was several days later that the standing room only funeral was held, with preaching prodigy the Reverend Felix the Second presiding. The esteem and love of the congregation felt for Zenobia is poignantly exhibited by the number of mourners that burst into tears as they file past her black lace shrouded remains in her coffin beneath the pulpit.

But it is Elder Joe, a bitter pawn of guilt, who charges the somber air with gasping melodrama when he screams, seizes and crushes the remains to his chest.

He rivets his hostile eyes on a twice-life-sized bronze image of Christ looming from an alcove above the choir stand and bellows, "You let 'em stone my pappy dead and now you've gone and let my dear old girl die! Send me to them! Kill me now if you got the power, Holy Monster!"

The blasphemy leaves a sea of shocked faces in its wake and mutterings of outrage. He is barely restrained by mortician aides and ushers, who lead him whimpering back to his front pew seat. But then at gravesite he tops his maudlin church sideshow by a lunge to the lip of the yawning grave as the casket lowers.

He is again restrained as he bleats, "Bury me with my Zen Saint! I don't want to live without her!"

All the way home from the cemetery, in the family limousine, Young Joe compulsively darts evil eyes at Elder Joe, seated trance-like on the back cushions between Reba and his stepson.

That night Elder Joe awakes from eggshell sleep popping panic sweat. He recoils from the sight of Young Joe rising from the side of the bed staring at him as mute tears glisten on his oddly serene face.

He gets out of bed when Young Joe murmurs, "Good night, Creeper," and saunters from the room. He laboriously hip-pushes the dresser across the door.

He stares at a picture of himself and Young Joe, at twelve, fishing from a riverbank. He picks up and gazes at a picture showing him riding Young Joe, at four, on his knee. He weeps as he removes his pistol from a dresser drawer. He lets himself down into a chair facing the door with a grim face.

Within a week he flees the horror prospects of his death or his murder of the stepson he has always loved with blood-bonded passion. He finds refuge in a spare bedroom of Panther Cox's apartment above his Cox's Freeway Fresh Fish Market. It sits in near abutment to one of the main traffic arteries at the end of a ghetto business street. Elder Joe clerks part time for grocery and pocket money.

A month after Zenobia's funeral, the church is again S.R.O. for the wedding of Joe and Reba. Reba is dressed in a curve-clinging bridal gown of rose satin which does not yet reveal that she is "in the family way." Happy Joe is a resplendent giant attired in a tailored indigo tuxedo.

Baptiste begrudgingly gives the bride away. He leaves the church immediately after the "I do's" for his Packard.

The couple move through kisses and congratulations and a rice blizzard to Zenobia's La Salle, gleaming richly in the fiery June sun. They drive away to a week's honeymoon in San Francisco, blessed effusively by a hundred-word telegram of good wishes and love from Philippa, bedded, but finally recovering from a bout with a recurring and mysterious malady.

Near the end of 1948, a week before Christmas, Panther Cox sits at the Allen kitchen table. He sips Sunday morning coffee with bathrobed Young Joe, who feeds his month-premature but healthy, two-week-old carbon replica, Joe Allen the Third, purring contentment on his lap.

Housecoated Reba washes breakfast dishes at the kitchen sink as she glances at coveralled Baptiste busy beneath the hood of his Packard in the alley behind the Allen house. Supervisor Susie yaps on a fender.

Cox's Original Man's face is serious as he breaks a long silence. "Li'l Joe, you're grown and I'm not here to pressure you no kinda way into a decision about your dad. But, like I told you, he's gonna wind up in the state joint for crazies soon. He's bad off. He doesn't gig in the store anymore. He just lies in bed with a spooky look on his face mumbling to the ceiling. I been locking him in when I leave the pad to keep him from playing traffic roulette in his pajamas like he did last week.

"He's bad off, Li'l Joe . . . Maybe if you could find it in your heart to forgive him. I know he cares about you and your family because when his head is clicking on all cylinders he quizzes me about you and Reba and his grandkid. You know, pay him a visit to let him know you care about him, at least a little. Will ya please, Li'l Joe? Now?"

Joe's face softens as he glances at Reba motionlessly staring at him. "Poor Pops! Mama loves him in her grave . . . She'd want me to go . . . think I will since it's Christmastime and 'cause Pops was once my main man before he . . ."

Reba shouts "Hooray!" as she leaves the sink to splatter Joe's face with kisses.

"Be cool, Reeb. You win again. But I can't go until you get back from church." Bitterness clouds his face for an instant. "'Cause I got to baby-sit to keep your precious kid, Felix, from having conniptions and calling here to check up on my wife like he did last Sunday when you didn't show at church. So I can't try to make up with Pops until you get back from church. Right!?"

Reba laughs. "Wrong, Daddy Joe! Take the baby with you to visit his grandpop. Right?"

"Right, 'cause ain't no way you gonna stay away from that little bullshit shyster and his choir two Sundays in a row," Joe says petulantly as he transfers the dozing baby to Panther's lap and rises to dress for the street in a fresh salvo of Reba's reward-control kisses.

Within the hour Cox and Young Joe, with the baby, ascend the creaky stairway to the apartment. They hear a weird keening sound as Panther keys into the living room, whispers, "Sounds like he's hunting coons and killing that redneck down in Georgia again. He thinks he can set up coon studs with that sound of a bitch coon ripe to lay out her poontang." Panther heaves a sigh. "Hurts my heart when he's flipped out on the dark side."

The coon call suddenly stops.

Panther whispers, "Joe's spell of crazy is probably over. But only for a little while."

As they move toward the bedroom door, Young Joe falters, stares at a tan plaid shirt draped across the back of a sofa. He feels a surge of renewed hatred for Elder Joe as he remembers that Zenobia gave Elder Joe the shirt for Christmas almost a year ago. Her last one. Young Joe tells himself that he won't try to reconcile with his stepfather, that he'll turn and go back home. But the pathetic portrait of Elder Joe roots him at the threshold when Panther unlocks the bedroom door, swings it open, steps into the shade-drawn murk of the room.

They stare at pajamaed Elder Joe, who stares eyes luminous with terror at Young Joe. He cringes in a corner. He darts a hand between the mattresses for his pistol, confiscated by Panther. Then he snatches up his shotgun-barrel-thick, heavy-headed cane.

"Lemme alone, Li'l Joe! I'll kill you! I ain't gonna let you hurt me. You better heed, Li'l Joe, and lemme alone. I'd kill God before I'd let him harm me. Lemme alone, Li'l Joe!" Elder Joe whips his mock rifle to his shoulder, squints down its shaft, aimed at Young Joe's heart.

"Oh shit, pally! Get yourself together. Your boy has brought your grandson for you to meet. Li'l Joe ain't gonna harm you," Panther says as he moves to take the cane, helps Elder Joe to sit on the side of the bed.

Elder Joe warily watches as Young Joe approaches the bed with the baby. Young Joe smiles as he extends his hand for a long aching moment before Elder Joe limply handshakes. Young Joe sits down on the bedside, places the baby on Elder Joe's lap. He lifts a flap of blanket, gazes at the tiny face. The baby stirs, gurgles as he opens his enormous dark eyes that stare into Elder Joe's eyes glittery with tears as he hugs the baby to his chest.

Panther eases from the room.

"You wonderful little sonuvagun!" he exclaims. "Your grandpa is sure glad to meet you. But shame on you for making me cry." He looks at Joe Junior. "And thank you, son, for coming and bringing him."

"Pops, we gotta dump the past . . . so . . . uh . . . well . . . Oh shoot! I want you to be my main man again. Okeydokey with you?" He warmly puts an arm around the old man's slumped shoulders, shaking with emotion.

Elder Joe's eyes study every plane of the earnest, brutish face before he whispers, "Okeydokey, son, if you really done forgave me. If you sincere and want old Pops around you again."

Young Joe leans in eyeball to eyeball, whispers raggedly, "I'm on the dead level, Pops . . . want you to come for Christmas dinner with your family, even move back under the roof that you and Mama slaved to get and keep. You coming, Pops?"

He leans his head against Young Joe's shoulder, blubbers, "You won't have to pick me up, son, and Panther don't have to bring me. I'm gonna throw away my stick and do the fox-trot all the way to that Christmas dinner."

Young Joe stands, hand-helps the old man to his feet with the baby. The old man breaks into weeping when Joe lifts the baby into his arms, leans and kisses Elder Joe's cheek.

As they step into the living room Panther says, "Say, Li'l Joe, Melvin's cousin is cracking for a rematch."

Young Joe barks, "Mama retired me from the ring. But tell that pussy any alley in town he picks will do to bust his ass wide open 'stead of his jaw. And Panther, maybe you better bring Pops with you Christmas Day so's the cops won't bust him fox-trotting."

They laugh.

Elder Joe tiptoes, whispers into Young Joe's ear, "Son, if something happens to me, just let 'em burn me and scatter my ashes in my tulip bed in the backyard at home."

"Come offa that crap, Pops. You got boo-koo years to go before you cash in," Young Joe whispers.

"Promise, son?" the old man persists.

"Yeah, I promise, Pops," Young Joe says as he locks an arm across the old man's shoulders.

Panther, with tears in his eyes, follows, embraces them both at the front door before Young Joe leaves for the La Salle parked behind Panther's long chippie-enticer convertible.

Early Christmas Eve night Panther Cox scrutinizes his dapper six-two reflection in his bedroom door mirror. He smiles satisfaction, bares a cache of gold-nugget teeth gleaming in his cave-dweller, coal dust black face. His vanilla suit is lumped across the shoulders by daily conditioned muscles that long ago powered the punches that swept him into contention for the heavyweight boxing crown of thorned orchids for his brain clot coronation bid in the roped pit with the Manassa Maniac, who kayoed his dreams of fistic glory.

He cocks a tan-banded porkpie lid on his glittery boulder head, mossed straight and black by a fresh process and dye job. He blazes his fingers with a half dozen fake diamond rings from his jewelry box. He steps into the living room, pauses to study

Elder Joe seated on the sofa tapping his foot to radio music as he plays solitaire on the coffee table.

Joe raises his eyes to give Panther a level look. "Stop eyeballing me, old buddy, and make your run. My head is cool and mellow, as Li'l Joe would say."

Panther smiles. "Ain't got no doubts about that, pally. I'll be back in a coupla hours. Want anything from the streets?" he asks as he moves to the front door.

With a cool grin and tragic eyes Elder Joe says unlightly, "Yeah, lug Marguerite Spingarn back with you if you bump into her."

They manage to laugh bleakly as Panther leaves the apartment. He remembers, on his way to the street, how he met Elder Joe ten years before. He was a penniless and hungry hobo off a freight train from Alabama. Joe had fed him in the Down Home Cafe because of his resemblance to Jack Johnson, his idol, when he wandered in. He remembers the mountainous stacks of dishes he volunteered, the next day, to wash in the furnace heat of the cafe's kitchen for meals, a modest salary, and shelter in the Allen back house before he won the small fortune at craps to set up his fresh fish market a year later.

He steps into the incendiary sunlight torching red skyrockets off his new Buick. It reminds him of the red-painted shoeshine box he hustled the streets of Birmingham with when he was an escapee from the last of many foster homes at fourteen.

Twenty minutes later, fishing the streets for sexpot strikes, he brakes the Buick sharply at a streetcar stop to reel in a flirtatious mulatto barracuda, hooked by the lure of his prepossessing red trawler and the big buck sparkle bait of his paste gems.

Later at the apartment Joe awakens from a nap as night's black broom sweeps away the last lavender debris of twilight. He takes a glass of milk to the coffee table to resume his game of solitaire. He pops anxiety sweat as his eyes seem to zoom in on and away from the cards he turns in the manner of a berserk movie camera.

He closes his eyes, groans as he sees the queen of spades transpose into the angry visage of Zenobia, whose paper lips move to threaten, "Ah'm gonna send ya to git yo leg julry back on the chain gang, Mister Midnight Creeper."

He flings the deck of cards to the carpet. He goes to the window, jerks it open to the whine of freeway traffic at the bottom of the tree and brush covered incline below. He stares at headlights flitting through the brush curtain like coon hunters' flashlights as he inhales deeply of the rush of crisp air. He whimpers, wrings his hands in panic to see the scene zoom in and out, then shift into the Georgia locale of his revenge slaying long ago. He recoils, struggles against incorporation into the phantasmagoria of his madness, but it absorbs him, drops its black murderous hood over the portals of his mind.

The excitement of murder lust is magical therapy that bolts his arthritic legs to the front door, cane unaided, without a scintilla of pain. He lurches through the door before he remembers he'll need his shotgun for his mission. He hurries back to the sofa to snatch up his cane. He goes to climb over a fence in the backyard. He flops, panting, into the mini-jungle. He crouches as he stares through the forest with his shotgun cradled at ready.

A motorcycle cop zips into traffic from a car parked on the shoulder of the road below. Joe scrambles down the incline toward the ticketed motorist, walking back to enter his car. The motorist freezes in surprise at the sight of the bathrobed apparition materialized on the shoulder of the road ten yards away. Joe stops, stares into the captive blue eyes of the motorist, terror glowing in the headlight glare of his car.

Joe puts the cane to his shoulder, squints down its oaken barrel as he aims it at the head of his target. His trigger finger scratches the cane fruitlessly to blast out the blue eyes as the motorist leaps behind the wheel of his car. Joe reaches it, splinters the windshield with a violent roundhouse swing of the cane before the motorist bombs his car away into brake-grinding traffic. Joe pursues the fleeing car into the wind-tunnel traffic that whips his bathrobe to his naked waist, baring his mocha tan, twisted limbs, and organ erected by his aphrodisiacal frenzy of murder.

By ironic coincidence, it is a black La Salle that smashes him airborne. His scream pierces the traffic roar when he crashes to the pavement to be disemboweled beneath the multiple wheels of a tractor-trailer truck. A nest of his entrails writhe and glisten hideously on the pavement like Medusa serpents. He sprawls motionless in the freeway cacophony of rear-end collisions and screeching panic braking of cars.

Through a gout of claret, he burbles, "Marite!" Then death shutters the bedroom eyes that shucked young Zenobia out of her potato sack drawers down in Georgia long ago.

Ten

*Y*oung Joe was severely guilt shaken by his belief that in revenge for Zenobia's death he had nudged his stepfather into the grave. He had narrowly escaped a nervous breakdown. But time, five years of it, has diminished the angst of his neurotic guilt. That is, except when he finds himself within eyeshot of Elder Joe's backyard tulip bed, sprinkled with his ashes, and pauses to flay himself.

It is a fat-mooned midnight in the year 1953 when Joe is awakened by the racket of a neighbor's squabble with his wife. A moment later he hears five-year-old Joe Junior flush the toilet, then patter past in the hallway on his way back to his bed in Elder Joe's old bedroom. Joe lies free of the imp of his guilt in the paradise of his mind created by the vision of his Creole Goddess, Reba, beside him in Zenobia's master bedroom. He gazes at her and the derby-hatted knight of his man-prince rears a blue-black awesome shadow across the moonlit valley of her sleek gold-dusted thighs, still sheening the illusion of girlish attraction.

He poises a callused palm above her nipple on the lam through the lace bars of her nightgown. He glances into a double crib at bedside, gazes at miniatures of Reba, twin girls, two months old. He tussles with the paranoid notion that his ugliness is so potent that at least some tiny bit of it should show on the twins if he is really their blood daddy. He twiddles his thumbs as he remembers that their mutual colic has drastically cut into Reba's sleep for several nights. And too, he remembers, Reba still complains of too much soreness for intercourse since the twin's birth. He left-jabs his monster for creating the frustrating emergency.

Behind the sham of closed eyelids, Reba quakes and mentally crosses fingers that she won't be summoned to perform the most onerous of her marital duties. She flinches when his Brillo Pad palm scrapes across her nipple. One of his sandpaper caresses before he mounts me to batter-ram me, she tells herself bitterly.

She listens to Joe's coarse pooch panting and remembers Gibran's heady lyrics of love that Felix, her teenage wizard of woo, would be breathing at this juncture. And she remembers, with heart pit excitement, how then Felix's vicuña-soft hands and tongue would caress her and thrill her to her jade-painted toenails. She snarls when one of Joe's meat hooks gouges a hunk of her buttock.

But she is grateful that Joe the baby-sitter, with his aversion to a Felix-related event, has threatened to boycott the picnic for a beer bash and catfish fry at Panther Cox's. Since Joe is the only sitter she will trust, her two-month cherry will languish at home, unplucked by Felix in the picnic jungles. They had giggled like demented felons at the doomsday risk, with the vision of sleuth Joe handcuffed by Junior and twins while they pull off their caper in the woods.

She turns toward him on her side, seething, green orbs lash curtained. When Joe's mouth descends to slobber-kiss her face, she holds her breath in the gust of decomposed supper liver and onions on his breath. She remembers the baby-sweet breath of Felix.

He moves her to her back. "Baby, I can't wait no longer," he groans as he drops himself between her thighs. She tenses, remembers her promise to Felix to preserve her posttwins cherry for their daredevil thing tomorrow in the woods. For a year she has used tactics to limit Joe's bumpkin raids on her treasure box. The better to lavish it on her now nearly six-foot humping doll, Felix. And generous he is to a fault with money she launders and banks through the cover of her steady sewing revenue.

She had stubbornly decided not to let the bubbling fountainhead of her sexuality wither and evaporate through lack of frequent replenishment. So, what the hell! Why not cuckold Stone Age Joe, she tells herself, since Joe, from the beginning, closed his mind to improvement of his sexual performance. He refused to read Doctor Van de Velde's popular book on marital love play and the genital kiss. She had bought it and diplomatically suggested *they* read it.

"I ain't gonna stick my head in no pussy like your nasty freak usta be nigger Pretty Melvin did," she remembers Joe had exploded after scanning the table of contents and then a hasty, beetle-browed skim of the "kiss" section.

Then, she had let inept Felix seduce her in the parsonage after the death of the Elder Felix the year before. She remembers how she had opened herself to young Felix out of just plain desperation for someone she thought attractive to give her an orgasm. Felix had been an ultra-avid trainee, and in her opinion has surpassed the once regarded peerless Pretty Melvin Sternberg as a lover.

Since Joe is clearly responsible for her adultery, God will reflex-forgive her for gratifying his God-given superpowerful sex drive, Felix and she have assured herself, to anesthetize her guilt pain. But agnostic Felix feels neither guilt nor terror of divine retribution for his adultery with Reba.

As Joe haunches to pile-drive his first bludgeon stroke into her, she grimaces and violently jars the crib with the bump of a spread-eagled leg. The twins, Belle and Sadie, squall her off the bangee hook. She leaps up, gathers them into her arms. She dips her head toward the domestic bedlam riding the hot humid air through the open bedroom windows.

"Sorry, Joe, we have to rain-check it. I'll try to put them back to sleep on the other side of the house in your old room," she says as she leans to kiss his pursed lips.

She starts to turn away. She pauses, is panged by pity for Joe, so much nitty-gritty man, so faithful, but so flawed by his lackluster lovemaking. She turns away and leaves the room, and Joe to commit benign adultery with Lady Five Fingers as he has since the birth of the twins.

As she goes down the hall with the twins clasped close to her bosom, the Madonna of her woman-princess pains with the realization that she has, in five short years, drifted far left of her moral center. And she is fearful of the probability, she tells herself with a shiver, that Philippa has genetically doomed her to follow in her wanton bitch pattern.

She goes to lie on the moon-dappled bed in Joe's old bedroom. Within the hour, she rocks Belle and Sadie to sleep in her arms. She closes her eyes, tries hard to drift into sleep. But she fails to turn off the spigot of apprehensive second thoughts about her promise to Felix to make love in the woods next day. She shudders as she visualizes their discovery by Joe or even by a church member. She carefully releases the twins from her arms, eases from the bed.

She goes down the hallway to peek at snoring Joe before she cat-foots down the stairway to the living room telephone. She sits down on Zenobia's cherished horsehair sofa, feels it prickle her bottom through her nightgown silk. She picks up the phone receiver. She hesitates dialing Felix in the parsonage to call off the risky rendezvous as she stares through a front window at the former Rambeau residence across the street.

Once the beautifully landscaped showplace of the block, it is now a run-down weed-glutted halfway house for female ex–drug addicts and paroled convicts. She sees a curfew-fracturing light-skinned Philippa look-alike resident leave a cab, remove her high heels before she goes down the concrete walk to key through the now scabrous front door into the house. She is jolted by painful déjà vu as she remembers herself on the other side of the door. She sees herself on countless awful mornings as a child awakened when tipsy Philippa the sex glutton was assaulted by enraged Baptiste as she tried to sneak through that front door.

As she finishes dialing Felix, she sees Baptiste and the now elderly terrier Susie walk with June, his comely married white sweetheart, to his Packard. It is parked in the newly constructed concrete driveway near the newly built garage housing the Allen

La Salle. The Delphine Ford jalopy gift-sits in the backyard—Joe's rusting derelict bitter keepsake.

Baptiste backs the Packard out to the street and drives away to take the woman to her Inglewood home as he has done on weekends for several months.

"Hello. God bless you, friend," Felix answers in his habitual way but in a surprisingly alert voice for two a.m., Reba thinks with a twinge of savage jealousy as she catches the faint sound of a throaty female voice in the background. She strains to hear an even more dulcet sound of violins.

"May He bless you and save your butt if I've interrupted chippie business," she says edgily as she loses sound of the voice.

Alone in the parsonage on his bed, Felix smiles mischievously after he silences his radio, stage-whispers, "Shut up, Joyce, it's you know who." Then he says to Reba with a chuckle in his voice, "Babykins, be cool. I was just listening to sweet radio music and thinking about you and tomorrow."

Reba says, "I think I'll sneak over to check you out."

He turns his radio volume up very softly, then down and up again. "Sssh!" he hisses, then laughs, titillated by her jealousy of the apparent presence of a rival whose sexy voice happens to be that of a popular DJ who is delivering a lengthy and sultry commercial for a line of cosmetics whose use is guaranteed to grovel the object of one's affection.

Reba says, "You bastard, aren't you cute?" as she suspects his hoax and turns on a table radio beside her.

She quickly spins the dial until she hears the violin-accompanied DJ voice.

"Darling, I don't think we should take that chance in the woods tomorrow," she says.

"What!? You chickened out, huh?" he snorts. "I told you there's nothing to worry about."

"It's too risky. We've got too much to lose if he catches us. He'd kill you! And almost as bad would be if a church member or some child spotted us. I think we'd better forget it and meet later, in the evening in the parsonage."

Felix's voice shakes with exasperation. "Trust me, baby. There is absolutely no chance we can be seen or caught together if you will just follow our plan. All right?"

She sighs. "I'm not sure . . . We'll see tomorrow. Good night. Talk to you."

They hang up. Reba takes a portable TV upstairs. She watches half of an old 1935 movie, *Riffraff* starring Tracy and Harlow, on the tiny screen before she drifts into sleep beside the twins.

Next early afternoon Joe sits near the center of the gala Love Picnic on a bench ideally located for Reba-Felix watching. He sits in the moil of fifteen hundred men, women, and children enjoying the rental Ferris wheel, loop-the-loop, and the flared-nostril pygmy steeds on a merry-go-round. Its calliope lilts "Stairway to the Stars" into the sun-splashed clamorous air.

Portly church matrons, in sauce-and-soot tarnished white linen dresses, baste and turn slabs of barbecued ribs, salivating mass mouths with charcoaled gusts of smoked ambrosia. Other church men and women operate the penny pitch and spin the wheel of fortune booth with plaster Kewpie dolls as prizes. Other church member women and their husbands sit on the grass and on benches. They apprehensively hawk-eye sons and nubile daughters running and squealing in contact and chase games with east of Avalon Boulevard teenage ghettoites accompanied by their parents. They are guests invited by Felix to promote love and understanding between many snobbish middle-class members of his congregation and their poverty-trapped black brethren.

Joe, on his bench, Joe Junior beside him, and the twins in a double stroller before him are harassed by church people of all ages who pause to kiss, fondle, or tweak the cheeks of the bawling twins. Before he flees, Joe glances at Reba, in black linen shorts, umpiring a softball game between church teenage girls and a team of ghetto rough and tough Central Avenue area girls. He rises from the bench, locates Felix, the martial arts buff, demonstrating elementary moves of the craft to a group of church youths in a far corner of the grassy grounds near a thick forest.

Joe, with Junior in tow, wheels the stroller to the La Salle, parked on a roadway on a slight rise overlooking the picnic revelry. He swings open the curbside doors of the car for ventilation from the ninetyish temperature before he and Junior seat themselves on the front seat. Joe hums a lullaby and gives the twins bottles to put them to sleep on the back seat.

Joe's mouth drops open in flabbergast when he eye-sweeps to relocate Felix, who has vanished. He sees Felix's group of youths meander back toward the central hub of the picnic. And Reba, Joe discovers, has vanished as umpire of the softball game, replaced by a substitute. Galvanized by suspicion, Joe leaps from the car with Junior in hand and goes fifty yards before he realizes he can't leave the twins unattended. And he decides he won't wake them and drag them back into the crowd.

He returns to his post in the car. He sits and strains his eyes to cull the crowd several hundred yards away for sight of Reba and Felix.

Minutes later, Sister Sarah, the twins' ancient godmother, parks her flivver down the road from the La Salle. The white-haired old woman leaves her car and comes to the La Salle. "How are my babies?" she says as she peers at them.

"Oh fine, Mother Sarah. They and Junior need you for a while. I need to stretch my legs some. Will you look out for them?"

The old woman says, "Sure will, son," as Joe moves out to let her take his front seat post. He kisses the old woman's forehead before he turns and goes quickly toward the crowd.

Reba moves deeply into the forest toward the roar of a waterfall as per Felix's instruction. She reaches it, stares at the white-capped cascade of water.

She suspects typical Felix pranking when she hears his muffled voice echo, "Oh please! Somebody help me!"

She moves to stare in puzzlement into the churning pool of water at the bottom of the falls, the seeming locus of his voice. Suddenly he steps into view from behind the falls on a ledge of rock. He laughs as he beckons her to him. She ascends a mossy incline to his side. They cling and kiss before he leads her into the cool murk of a cave behind the falls. He pulls her down on a pallet of moss and old brown leaves with a rolled-in hollow that pings her with jealousy.

She says, "How cozy this is . . . you dirty dog!"

He laughs shakily. "Not guilty. My old man was the dirty dog that I trailed here with that sexy old Sister Matthews last summer just before he died."

Reba is stunned speechless for a moment. "Oh, horsefeathers! I just can't believe that about your father. Why, he carried himself like a saint."

Felix shakes his head. "I peeped on them petting in the parsonage a dozen times after my father made her church business manager. And, as you know, her husband is a senior deacon of the church who was also my father's best friend."

Reba says, "C'mon now, you don't have to tar-brush your dad in his grave to cover up for yourself. What you did before we started our thing doesn't matter to me. So, don't jive me, sugar pie."

He heaves a heavy sigh. "No, it's true about Sister Matthews. Believe me, he was evil for as long as I can remember." Reba's caressing fingers invade his fly and for the first time fail to inflate his flaccid organ.

"Darling, I believe you about this cave and your father," she says tenderly.

He says, "Maybe our meeting here wasn't such a groovy idea after all . . . This cave has me hung up on memories of that tyrant bastard. I'm thinking of how he let my mother die. Ah! She was the saint!"

She holds his head against her bosom. "Oh baby sweets! You never told me bad things. I thought you were very happy growing up. Since you're hurting, it doesn't matter that we don't make love here. Let's go . . . ," she whispers into his silky ringlets of curls.

"We can't now!" he exclaims as they stare through the curtain of waterfall at a pair of teenage lovers who enter the clearing and almost immediately bed down in tall grass. They fuck violently and keen the air with their erotic outcries as startled birds flash like feathered neon through the jade panorama of forest.

Felix nests his face on Reba's bosom as he bitterly muses, "Now I'm sure I love and trust you enough to tell you the truth about my rotten old man as my mother told me so many times. He was a Harlem faith healer–atheist, a con man hypnotist. He swindled the superstitious poor and sick with John the Conqueror roots, love potions, and magic oils he sold from a store that he claimed could cure all diseases, including cancer, enslave sweethearts, and ward off evil spells of enemies."

Reba's face is shocked. "He was a warlock!?"

Felix says, "Baby, now you get it. He also got his following and fame removing spiders, snakes, and scorpions from beneath the skins of curse victims that crawled only in their minds."

"And your mother," Reba says softly, "was she one of your father's customers when he met her?"

"No. She was only a fifteen-year-old schoolgirl when she caught my father's eye. She was the only child of Black Solomon, my father's chief enemy and rival for the Harlem witchcraft trade. Black Solomon was an egomaniac. He challenged my father to a public riddle bee in a large Harlem auditorium that was filled with their followers.

"My mother said that after three hours they were tied, neither stumped by each other's mind-stretching riddles. Then, my mother told me, my father pointed at her seated in the front row and asked Black Solomon, 'Your lovely daughter is fifteen years old. You had your sixtieth birthday celebration last week. You've bragged publicly that she was born when you were forty-seven years old. On her first birthday you were forty-eight times older than she was. Tell me, Black Solomon, why is it that now you are only four times her age? And why is it that forty years from now should she reach fifty-five and you a hundred, you will not even be twice her age?' Mother said her father's black face turned gray as he pondered the question for a half hour in the silence before he left the hall, crushed and preoccupied with the riddle."

Reba whistles. "Whew! I've got a headache just hearing that riddle."

"Mother said her father swore to fast until he solved it," Felix continues. "Finally his mind snapped and he wound up in a Bellevue padded cell and my old man wound up with all of his clients and my mother as his love slave."

Reba says, "I'd bet the solution to that riddle is mathematical. Did you ever lay it on any of those eggheads at UCLA before you graduated last year?"

He chuckles. "Sure, several theorized actuarial mumbo jumbo and compound interest years as the solution. But maybe the real solution could be as mysterious as the slow-aging time warp of an outer space traveler."

Reba says, "Could be. But what do I know . . . How did your father wind up in L.A., the founder of the Universal Holiness Church?"

"He came out here when I was five after he finished a two-year sentence in Attica for practicing medicine without a license. A powerful Harlem politician discovered after the death of his sister that she had been my father's patient. She died from a brain tumor he had treated as simple migraine with powdered bat hearts and black healing candles. My mother's appendix burst and she died our second year in L.A. He had treated her for a week for indigestion with herb tea.

"Oh, how he abused us! He beat me with a razor strap and forced me to memorize the Bible. I'm not even convinced God exists. I'm just an actor reciting lines in the pulpit. He forced me to preach at five . . . The novelty drew a mob of members to his church when it was just a storefront on San Pedro. I hated him! I despise him in his grave. If there's a hell, he's—"

They jerk rigid, stare at Joe entering the clearing. They watch him walk to within yards of the waterfall, stop, swivel his shaved bullethead to locate the teenagers' outcries of copulation in the tall grass.

Joe goes to the thrashing bed of grass, peers down at the couple, mumbles "'Scuse me" before he turns and goes deeper into the woods.

The teenagers rise and hurriedly leave the clearing. Felix leaves the cave, followed a moment later by Reba. She jogs to the perimeter of the picnic area. She is about to leave the woods when she encounters several preteeners chasing and snaring butterflies. She gets an idea to allay Joe's suspicions.

"Kids, I saw lots of the prettiest butterflies I've ever seen deeper in the woods. Come on, I'll show you!" she exclaims as she leads them back into the woods.

She leads them to Joe frantically searching thick underbrush. He whirls at the sound of their voices with a stupefied expression on his face. Reba saucers her eyes to feign amazement to see him.

She moves to his side, whispers harshly, "Joe Allen, what the hell are you doing out here? Where are our children?"

He shifts his clodhopper feet as he exhales tension relief to discover her apparently innocent. He averts his sheepish eyes to mumble, "Aw, Reeb, I was just taking a light hike . . . The kids are with Mother Sarah . . . They're all right."

Reba hisses, "She's old and ailing. Joe Allen, will you please get your big black ass back to the kids? Now!"

He nods his head. As Reba turns and moves away with the preteeners she says loudly, "All right, kids, let's go get those pretty butterflies among those sunflowers over there."

From the corner of an eye she sees Joe hurry back toward the picnic grounds, vows to herself never again to be persuaded to take such a foolish risk with Felix.

*R*eba kept her vow to herself not to hype up her affair with Felix with brink-of-doom thrills through high-risk shenanigans. The lovers have become so cautiously sub-rosa that Joe's suspicion of them is in almost total remission.

Joe feels contentment, a euphoric rush of happiness as he holds Reba in his arms on the front seat of the La Salle at a drive-in theater. They watch the gas chamber end of the new hit 1958 crime movie *I Want to Live!* starring Susan Hayward in the real life role of Barbara Graham.

Ten-year-old Joe Junior, fast asleep on the rear seat, holds his five-year-old sleeping twin sisters, Belle and Sadie, in his arms. The couple show only a slight stomp of time. Joe's shaved bullet-head has a two-day sprout of prematurely gray stubble. But his flat brutish face is unlined. And his steely muscles still writhe sinuously beneath his panther black skin. And, except for slightly thickened thighs and middle, Reba is still head-swiveling pretty.

Joe kisses her earlobe, whispers, "Ain't we happy, Reeb?"

She says softly, "Yes, Joe honey, very happy . . . My sewing customers are growing and at two hundred bucks a week you're the highest-paid field employee old Hoffmeister has. And best of all, you're home nights and not on that night watchman gig."

He says, "Ain't that the truth? Sure is mellow that old wolf ain't lollygagging 'round our door and we got healthy kids." He squeezes Reba so hard she gasps. "Oh, Reeb, I love ya! Happy is sweet!" he exclaims so loudly that the kids jar instantly awake.

Reba climbs over the seat to take the twins in her arms. Junior climbs over into the front seat to Reba's place beside Joe. They watch the executioner's cyanide pellets drop into the bucket of acid. Fatal vapors swirl about Hayward, strapped into the death chair.

Joe replaces the car speaker on its stand, keys the La Salle engine to life, drives hurriedly toward an exit to avoid the end-of-movie glut of cars.

But Pretty Melvin Sternberg, lonely physician, in the family Beverly Hills mansion is neither happy nor still pretty as he shoots a shot of Dilaudid, a morphine derivative, into a main arm vein. He withdraws the empty syringe, places it on a new nightstand as he reclines his obese bulk against the bed pillows. His face is jowly, blotched, and seamed. His once enormous sparkling gray eyes now seem piggish in his once handsome face that had sex-vibed legions of chippies. That magnet face has vanished, is uglied by fat and debauchery.

He scowls furiously as he looks about the bedroom he had to completely refurnish a month ago as he had been forced to do to nearly every other room in the mansion. He glances at his wristwatch—only seven p.m. He decides it's too early to leave for another of his ritualistic Saturday night searches of the black ghetto vice jungles for Roxie Jackson, a beautiful teenage whore he'd become slavishly infatuated with and retired, he thought, when he moved her into the mansion to share his bed.

In recent years, he remembers, he has given fat fees to a wide assortment of street girls for hire from Hollywood to Watts. But only pain freak Roxie proved to be the perfect superstar foil for his bondage and S and M games, requisite to gratify his cruel and rapacious sexual appetite. So he feels excruciating Roxie withdrawal misery as he stares at her huge nude image commissioned in oil on the bedroom wall.

He is unaware that it was the now king of black L.A. pimps, Whispering Slim, her secret boss, that had used a crew of Central Avenue losers and a pair of rental moving vans to strip the mansion of heirloom furniture, tapestries, paintings, Oriental carpets, and gold tableware left Melvin by the elder Sternbergs, who had died six months apart several years before.

Roxie had been cleverly programmed to dupe Melvin's lone house servant, Tessie, an elderly black jack of all household labor, away from the house. Tessie had accompanied Roxie on a supposedly heavy shopping trip in midday to allow the cleanout thieves' dream access to the Sternberg treasure. Roxie had ditched the old woman in the Beverly Hills shopping center after the burglary was completed.

Melvin had persuaded Tessie to keep Roxie's presence in the mansion and her part in the robbery a secret from the police and insurance snoops. He had reasoned that his white, affluent patients would desert him en masse were the sordid details of his involvement with Roxie revealed by her apprehension by police.

Dilaudid freaked out, he flirts with the mad idea that when he finds her he'll kidnap her and hold her prisoner in the wine cellar under key and steel bar for his pleasure and her extended punishment.

At eight p.m., he gets out of bed to dress himself in a casual black slax suit for the ghetto search. He forgets his wallet on the dressertop. He rams a snubnose thirty-eight under his belt before he goes to the guest house, site of his breakup with Reba years before. He tiptoes in and lifts the key to sleeping Tessie's nondescript black 1950 Dodge off the dressertop as he has for a month of weekends.

At the moment that Melvin drives Tessie's Dodge away from the mansion through the balmy August night, vice king Whispering Slim brushes his mop of processed hair before a Sternberg dresser mirror. He strokes his glossed head, tells himself, "Player, your mop is so slick and perfect a fly would bust his ass lighting on it."

He glances at stable pet Roxie Jackson lying on the heisted Sternberg emperor bed. His white stucco six-bedroom Hoover Street headquarters is luxuriously furnished with the other stolen loot. The house was built as a residence for a major oil company's executive years before when the now black neighborhood was exclusively upper-middle-class white.

The other five girls of Slim's southeast L.A. stable pause in the master bedroom doorway, street-jungle sexy in outrageously short, tight, and noisy dresses. Their fierce dark faces in the scarlet wash of hallway light auras them war-painted Mau Mau maidens, murder stained. "Happy birthday, Daddy Slim," they chorus.

The other six, the white half of Slim's stable, live, hump, and shoplift in the shops and hotels of the Hollywood and downtown fast tracks.

"Hey, Daddy Slim, we creamin' to hit them streets. We gonna starve them other nigger pimps' 'hos shitless tonight," his straw boss Rubenesque warrior bitch enthuses with shapely black net stockinged gams aggressively akimbo.

"G'wan, Sharlene, take them 'hos and git in the motherfucking Hog," Slim commands as he admires his mauve and shocking pink decked out image in a mirror. He sees his squad of john flippers disappear behind him down the hallway on their way to his new puce and ivory Caddie.

He gazes at Roxie. His diamond-glutted hands pretend to adjust his custom silk tie. It depicts the hand-painted copulation between a kneeling alabaster sexpot and a gargantuan black German shepherd. He watches Roxie, with lime chiffon gown hiked to her porcelain-hued belly, perform her dazzle-daddy, leg-pumping, bicycling, quim-flashing exercise. A mane of tousled platinum hair frames her Kim Novak look-alike face, infant innocent in the soft blue ambience of nightstand lamp. Gossamer gowned and violet eyed, she is haunting, as ethereal in the blue mist as an escapee nymph from Botticelli's *Allegory of Spring*. Roxie Jackson, teenage queen of black ghetto hookers, the polymorphous perverse favorite bitch of an interracial swarm of street tricks.

My pussy money tree, Slim thinks as he turns from the dresser mirror to prance to bedside, to say goodbye until dawn.

"Daddy, please lemme hit the streets, like tonight, before I flip out. Please! Huh?" she huskily pleads with a cheek pressed against his fly in protest to her thirty-day house quarantine since the Sternberg wipeout caper.

She gazes up into his face. He lags his response to bang the pain junkie with suspense jollies as he stares into her face. He remembers how he had stalked her for four years, since she was fourteen. He trapped her the year before when she turned eighteen. He remembers how he first moved into the Jacksons' lives by buying a river of cheap grape for her mulatto wino father before he passed the year before. He had hipped her alcoholic white mother how to get welfare checks under multiple names and addresses. The fur-choked, Caddie-blessed mother waxed horny gratitude. He'd then whammed his costly meat freebie into the buxom mother periodically, he recalls, to cover his four-year obsession to make Roxie his whore. He shapes a cunning little smile as he remembers how he fingered the mother to welfare investigators to get her a jail sentence so he could turn out Roxie on the fast track.

"Talk that get-down shit to your daddy, sweet freak bitch star," he whispers as he slashes a fingernail across her nipple.

He leans as she shivers to grind her bottom lip between his teeth. He sees a vision of her à la Melvin Sternberg inside ripoff of the biggest dope dealer in Harlem. The ancient ex-pimp dealer, monikered Joy Boy, already has been scouted with Roxie's final briefing and planned Apple flight to cut into the mark only a week away.

"Girl, ain't no way I'm gonna put you down in them streets to get your head busted or chopped off by one of that sucker croaker's scalpels. Be cool and concentrate on that three, maybe four, kilos of Joy Boy skag we gonna score for in the Apple. Lissen to me, bitch, and be patient."

She pouts her rosebud mouth. "Sharlene told me my star trick was on the scene last night with his dick in his hand looking for me. You know, Daddy—Chuck, the peckerwood, that ex–marine hero that always spends a C-note. Sharlene is gonna give him my phone number if he shows tonight. Can I turn him, Daddy? Please!

I'm so fucking bored! I feel like crapping on the carpets to get some action."

He studies her upturned face before he whispers from his ruined voice box, "Yeah, you can turn him at the Circle. Bitch, the king don't allow no tricks turned in his castle. Maybe later, when the Pit closes, I'll call you and you can cab to my birthday party. That is, Miss Frisky, if you make that trick bring you back home fast, with no detour into no cabarets."

"I promise, Daddy," she says as she kneels on the bed, unzips his fly with her snowy teeth. She mouths in to tow out his cable-veined womb sweeper. Her epic chest humps with excitement as she reaches to a nightstand to hand him a snaky whip and handcuffs. He locks her hands together behind her and whistles the whip across her back.

She moans ecstatically, "Ooooh! Wheeee!"

He violently whip-welts her buttocks and back while she fellates them to mutual climax. She collapses supine, gaspy, her kiddie face wet with sweat. He unlocks her hands, goes to the adjoining bathroom for a moment, steps out. He gives himself a final checkout in the dresser mirror, blows her a kiss as he leaves the bedroom.

Shortly before one a.m., in suburban white Lynwood, Chuck Haggar, Medal of Honor winner in World War Two, civic leader, and father of preteen boys, lies wide awake beside his sleeping wife. He is feverish, erected by raging Roxie itch. He stares at his beloved but inhibited wife, feels a twinge of resentment for her no-suck, missionary-position, sexual concrete that forces him to find Roxie, the sexual circus.

He speed-dresses in slacks and sports shirt, leaves the bedroom to move quietly down the hall past the bedroom of his sleeping sons. As he leaves the house, he remembers that while lying alone in his suite during a six-week lecture tour, it had been erotic thoughts of Roxie, not of Tricia, his wife, that had driven him into the night to find a succession of whores that had only half satisfied his carnal hunger. Chuck tells himself he has to somehow break the expensive and risky Roxie spell as he drives the new family Pontiac toward the black ghetto.

Melvin Sternberg sits in Tessie's parked Dodge a half block from the Blue Pit Bar. He watches the parade of street people and the interracial johns on foot and cruising in cars to spot Roxie. He skin-pops a load of Dilaudid into a forearm, swoons for a moment under the jolt.

He shifts his scrutiny to the Blue Pit. "Oh, how I hate the scurvy low-life bastards!" Melvin exclaims aloud as he stares, with a mean face, at a knot of whores and peacocking pimps high-jiving on the sidewalk in front of the bar.

Twenty minutes later Chuck parks his car near the front of the bar behind Slim's new Caddie. He hits his horn. Sharlene breaks away from the knot of scufflers on the sidewalk. She comes to lean into the Pontiac from the sidewalk side with a toothy grin on her painted face.

"Hi, Sharlene. You got good news?" he says with excitement shaking his voice.

"For real, Chuck sweetie!" she exclaims as she digs into her bosom and lays a matchbook cover with Roxie's phone number on the seat. "Roxie's phone number, baby. She's gonna pee on herself with you call 'cause, no jive, she's missed you like a motherfucker while you was outta town."

He picks up, studies the matchbook.

"Ain't you gonna tip me?" she asks as she pouts her heavy-lipped, sensual mouth.

He peels off a ten spot from the wad. She grins, takes it, and stares at the battered car of a regular trick, an elderly black man, just pulling into the curb behind Chuck's Pontiac. She dips her head toward the Circle Motel on the corner, a few yards from the Blue Pit. She snake-hips down the sidewalk toward the motel, followed by the gimpy old man togged out in a baggy ice cream suit.

A half hour later, stable straw boss Sharlene emerges from a motel trick room at the moment of Roxie's arrival, by cab in the motel parking lot.

"Oh you lucky bitch! I ain't had nothing but ten-buck nigguh dates humping my pussy sore to win a home and you got Chuck waiting in number five to pop off like Br'er Rabbit for a C-note," Sharlene says as Roxie steps out and the cab pulls away.

Chuck looks at them from the window of room 5, his craggy face lit up with anticipation.

At the sight of Roxie, Melvin hurtles the Dodge into traffic. He narrowly escapes multiple collisions as he crosscuts against fast traffic to career into the motel lot as Roxie walks toward number 5. Melvin squeals the Dodge to a stop near Roxie. She whirls, stares at his rage-deformed face struggling to smile sweetly through the windshield. He swings open the car door, starts to get out.

She screams, "Sharlene! Get Slim!"

Chuck opens the room door. "Roxie, is that your boyfriend!?" he hollers.

"Shit no! I don't even know that nut!" she shrills as she darts into the alley behind the motel.

Chuck charges from the doorway. He dashes toward the Dodge, shouts, "Hey there! You! What the hell is going on!?"

Melvin misses him by inches as he guns the Dodge across the lot and down the alley in roaring pursuit of Roxie. She is caught in the spew of headlights as she cuts into the lot behind the Blue Pit. She stumbles in her high heels, falls as she nears the half-open back door. Melvin stops the Dodge, lunges from it as she gets to her feet. He bear-hugs her waist as she flees toward the blue murk of the noisy bar.

She screams, "Slim!" as Melvin picks her up and carries her struggling and screaming back into the lot.

Slim and several of his pimp friends race into the lot and grab Melvin as he tries to force Roxie into the Dodge. They tear Roxie from Melvin's arms. Slim's full nelson holds Melvin as the others curse, punch and kick him from head to ankles.

Chuck cruises his Pontiac down the alley, stops to watch the brutal tableau, vivid in the glow of full moon. Sharlene, on scene, embraces Roxie. Roxie's red organza dress is torn in several places.

Sharlene hustles Roxie into Chuck's car, which he bombs away down the alley.

Slim releases Melvin, winks at his fellow assailants ringed about the victim. He draws a pistol from his waistband. He removes the bullets, dumps them into a suit coat pocket. Melvin, fallen face down, is half stunned and paralyzed with pain. And then he trembles in fear when Slim stoops beside him, presses the snout of the pistol against the back of his head.

"Roll over, lard ass!" Slim commands in a vicious whisper.

Melvin rolls to face Slim on his back. His blood-streaked face ashens when Slim jabs the pistol snout between his eyes.

"Please, mister, don't kill me!" Melvin gasps as he sees Slim's trigger finger roll the pistol chambers.

"Nigguh, you put the gorilla on my pregnant stepdaughter. I got to kill you!" Slim whispers with his face twisted in mock rage.

"Brother, don't ice the fat man. He ain't nothing but a poor ugly raper or mugger out to grease his dick on a freebie or score some grits and greens for his big gut. Maybe he's gonna 'poligize and ask forgiveness," a fake commiserant pleads.

"I'm sorry! Forgive me!" Melvin begs with wide eyes locked on the barrel of the gun between his eyes.

"That don't move me. I got to kill you, nigguh!" Slim intones as he again rolls the pistol cylinders. "'Sides, he tore my stepdaughter's three-hundred-dollar dress. I got to kill this gorilla!"

One of the mob kneels beside Slim, his whippet face a con mask of anxious compassion. He cracks, "You ain't gonna have to waste Fat Man 'bout your stepdaughter's vine." Whippet leans into Melvin's fearful face. "Fool, up the three bills to the man for the vine you ruint and git in the wind."

Through puffed lips Melvin mumbles, "Left my wallet at home . . . got a ring . . . Take it!"

Melvin slips off the gypsy-mounted diamond ring. Slim takes it, examines it for a moment. To cover the fact that he knows Melvin's identity, he first glances disdainfully at Tessie's battered Dodge, then he rolls the pistol chambers.

"Driving that junk, ain't no way this rock is real. Nigguh, who are you and what kinda work you do?" he whispers harshly.

"I'm . . . uh . . . Franklin . . . uh, Franklin Armstrong . . . I'm . . . uh . . . a tire changer at the Greyhound garage," Melvin stammers.

"How you buy this ring on a sucker salary?" Slim asks as he and Whippet stand.

"It was my late father's ring. It's real!"

Whippet says, "Give Fat Man a break, brother, and take a chance on the hoop for restushun for the vine."

Slim bends down close to Melvin, waggles the pistol in his face. "Nigguh, I'm gonna let you live 'til I see you again anywhere on this side of town. You hip!?"

Melvin nods his head furiously, starts to rise on his elbows. Slim kicks Melvin against the side of his head, stuns him. Slim leads the others to the Dodge. They search it and overlook Melvin's pistol stashed beneath the dashboard. Slim unfastens his fly as he leads the mob back to a tight circle around Melvin, just coming to.

"Let's baptize this gorilla!" Slim stage-whispers. The others undo their flies, aim their organs down on Melvin. They grunt like swine at swill to pressure-tap their bladders for a long moment before they drench him from face to feet. Melvin rolls in a fetal ball under the awful rain. They hee-haw as they turn away for the Pit back door belching jukebox blues.

Melvin weeps wildly, watches his attackers disappear through the steel back door that somebody closes and bars with a heavy clank of metal. Melvin hears a bell toll two a.m. as he struggles to his feet. He hobbles to the Dodge, gets in. He uses wads of Tessie's paper tissues to wipe his burning eyes and to blot his dripping hair. He sees a bamboo blind drop across a steel-barred back window, sees several pinholes of blue interior light in a corner of the blind.

Maybe I can put one through the head of that skinny bastard, he thinks as he starts the car, backs it close to the window. He leaves the engine running, gets his pistol, and gets out. He leans against the car; the stench of urine triggers vomit until his guts dry-lock. He stumbles to the window, peers through a blind pin-hole into the noisy blue murk. He sees a towering black bouncer usher through the front door a half dozen outsider black and white men in conservative suits. The bouncer locks the door, drops steel blinds across it and the front windows.

Melvin watches Slim blow out the fifty candles on a huge frosted cake on the bartop. He draws a bead on the back of Slim's head. His trigger finger pulls carefully. He sobs in frustration when Slim abruptly goes to join Sharlene and her stablemates in a distant front booth. The jam of street people cheer and raise their glasses to toast the guest of honor.

Melvin's face is horrible with hatred as he scans the cluster of dope-snorting whores and pimps for Roxie's presence. Rage maddened, he decides to use his semi-automatic hunting rifle to blast justice Slim's way. And with luck, to his other assailants, he thinks, as he turns away.

He gets into the Dodge and punches it away, decides not to go to Beverly Hills to get his rifle. Instead, he goes to park in the earlier stakeout spot up the street. He shoots a heavy load of Dilaudid to quiet his shrieking nerve ends. He rests his stinking head against the seat back, stares malevolently at the darkened facade of the Blue Pit. Go home, clean up and stay there, forget those maggots over there, reason dares to whisper in the boiling bedlam of madness. But his lynched manhood overrules, rants for revenge, murder. Mass.

He starts the Dodge, U-turns on the nearly deserted street. Two miles away he finds an open station. He parks the Dodge a half block away, walks to the station. He pawns his wristwatch to the attendant for gas and a red five-gallon can. He grins oddly as he watches the unsuspecting attendant fill the can with gasoline. His face is a Halloween fright mask as he drives back to park on a side street facing the bar fifty odd yards away.

He violently sings snatches of an old-time hit ghetto ditty, "I'll Be Glad When You're Dead, You Rascal You," as he wicks the firebomb with six-inch-long wadded strips of tissues jammed into its uncapped top.

He grunts and sweats his way to the glass front door of the Pit with his lethal burden. He stands stock still for a moment in the blast of raucous whore gaiety and profane ribaldry from the other side of the door reflecting his hellish, piss-steeped image of death. He casually strikes a match, lights the wadded fuse to the drum. He lifts it above his head. He hears the gurgle of the bomb. He grits his bared teeth and crashes it through the glass door. The steel blinds stop its flight short on the shock-silenced other side of the door.

Melvin scrambles away across the sidewalk, halts, stares at Roxie kissing Chuck goodbye before she leaves his car, which is pulled in behind Slim's Caddie parked yards away. Roxie freezes, stares saucer eyed at Melvin for a long moment before she whirls and leaps into the Pontiac through the open front seat passenger window. The firebomb explodes, blows out the front window plate glass behind Melvin as he draws his pistol and scuttles down the sidewalk toward the Pontiac. Chuck desperately maneuvers the machine from the tight spot, starts to U-turn down the street when Melvin reaches the car.

Melvin thrusts the pistol through the open window into Roxie's face and screams, "Stop, Peckerwood! I'll blow this double-crossing bitch's brains out!"

Chuck lurches the car into the U-turn, knocking Melvin off balance for an instant. Melvin recovers rapidly, fires five shots into the Pontiac. Two of them plow into the back of Chuck's head. His dead foot slams down on the accelerator. Another bullet pierces Roxie's throat. The Pontiac rears across the sidewalk on the other side of the street and crashes, like a howitzer shell, into a closed greasy spoon.

Melvin stares at the Pontiac, winces as it explodes in flames. He glances back at the bar front, bursting flame and smoke. Screeching pandemonium in the bar trembles the air as Melvin hurries to the Dodge. He speeds away for his Beverly Hills mansion at the instant that the elderly white owner of the Blue Pit arrives to check the evening's receipts. He sits in his Caddie De Ville double-parked in front of the bar. He wrings his hands as he stares at Slim and his stable cindered by Melvin's firebomb that rolled to within several feet of their booth and exploded. They, the only dead casualties, are fused together in a blackened mass engulfed by flames. The bar owner sticks his head out of the car window and vomits.

A last trampled trio of mack men survivors crawl retching from the stench of burned flesh and billows of black smoke through the back door, unlocked at the blast by the bar porter to set out garbage. Squealing sirens chorus as the street's residents pour out to witness the holocaust.

Twelve

A ghetto mile away, sleepless Reba burns with jealous suspicion of Felix. He is two days overdue back from a two-week conclave of ministers in Chicago. A young new church member, ravishing Ruta Jones, went with Felix as secretary Reba's substitute. Oh, you ugly, jealous bastard, Reba exclaims to herself, remembering how Joe foamed at the mouth when she hinted that she should be taking the trip with Felix. She glares at snoring Joe beside her, too pooped to awaken soon from his bumpkin after-the-movie sex calisthenics, she decides as she eases from the bed to the living room phone to call Chicago.

Upstairs, several minutes later, Junior is frightened awake by nightmare visions of Hayward's realistic portrayal of death in the gas chamber. He awakens Joe as he groggily climbs across him into Reba's vacant spot in the bed. Joe takes him into his arms, rocks him to sleep. Joe eases himself free to go to the bathroom, stops in the hallway at the strident sound of Reba's voice chastising someone that Joe is certain must be Felix. He goes to the head of the stairs, sees Reba slam down the receiver and look at him with a flabbergasted face.

He scowls, a pajamaed image of Kong. He growls, "Reeb, daybreak is on the turn. What the F you doing down here with the phone?"

"Massa, I'se done made a call. And I'se grown, 'member, Massa?" she bluffs with a hollow laugh. "I'se couldn't sleep, Massa, worrying 'bout Sarah Godmother. She's still hanging on, praise de good Lawd," Reba continues as she rises from Zenobia's horse-hair couch.

"Girl, don't lay no more pickaninny rap on me," he says as he descends the stairway with catlike quickness to intercept her as she moves toward the kitchen. "Reeb, you feel like you a slave with me?" he harshly whispers as he seizes her shoulders and spins her to face him.

"Shit no, Massa! . . . 'cept when you turn gorilla on me, like now. Look, Massa, I'se gwine stick a knee in your balls if you don't unass your paws from my body. Massa suh," she says as he lets her wrench herself free.

"Slick Topsy, I'm gonna call Godmother and give her some more love since you just had to wake up the dear old soul. In the a.m.!"

Her mouth flaps open for a pounding instant as she pauses, watches him plop on the couch, dial the phone. As she retreats into the kitchen she hears him ask someone about Sarah, then exclaim with a sob, "What! Man, did you say Mother Sarah passed away at the dinner table early last night?"

A moment later Joe moves to stand statue still in the kitchen door. He glares at weeping Reba, seated at the kitchen table.

"Reeb, you heard. Too bad about Mother Sarah," Joe says softly as he goes to seat himself across from Reba at the table. He takes her doll hands in his, whispers shakily, "Why'd you lie, Reeb? Girl, I love ya! You can tell me the truth about anything and I'll be cool and mellow."

She says, "You're sure, Joe?" as she dabs a napkin at her tear-glistened eyes.

"Sure as Ike is humping Mamie in D.C.," he says as he flashes his jumbo perfect teeth in a cunning little smile. "Try me, Reeb!"

She withdraws her hands from his. The consummate liar against the wall, she forces herself to make unblinking eye contact as she sensuously finger-strokes the backs of his hands. "Baby, my call was to Reverend Felix, collect. I was so worried about him with nincompoop Ruta in Chicago. I felt guilty because I let you pressure me from making the trip. Ruta is just a girl and he's really just a boy, very insecure. I'm his right arm, maybe even his mama figure. And I swear, Joe, that's where it's at between us. I lied about the call 'cause you know why, jealous baby. Believe me, Sugar Joe?"

He lies, "Uh-huh," as he takes her hands, presses them against his cheek. "Reeb, I got a deal for you that's gonna solve everything the mellow way. Okay?"

She nods.

"Awright, since you ain't sweet on the nigger, cut him and his church loose. If you—"

To interrupt him she jerks her hands free, clasps them rigidly on the tabletop.

"Lemme finish the deal, Reeb! If you cut him loose, I'm gonna promise, on sweet Mama's grave, to join a new church with you and the kids. Now try to be cool, Reeb, 'cause I'm gonna shock you silly. Reeb, I ain't guaranteeing, but I'll even try like a sonuvabitch to get converted if the Holy Ghost is for real and ain't just preacher con. We got a deal, Reeb?"

She snickers, "You a church member, a convert?"

"If your rotten daddy could get religion, anybody can," he says with a smirk.

She says, "Sounds great! But no deal, Joe, unless you join my church. I won't leave my church, my friends. I can't cut loose the kids from their Sunday school friends and teachers."

She rises, goes to the sink to draw a glass of water, sips, stares out the open window overlooking the backyard and guest house. She sees bathrobed Baptiste and age-enfeebled Susie. The terrier squats near Elder Joe's cherished bed of tulips, sensuous golden dancers in the blue footlights of summer moon.

To change the subject Reba says, "The tulips are so lovely . . ."

Joe comes to embrace her waist from behind. "Reeb, we ain't got no deal 'cause you sweet on the nigger and been a long time. Ain't that right?"

She stiffens. "I'm sweet on everybody, Joe . . . even on you. And believe me, that's tough to be when you don't trust me . . . Maybe we ought to call it quits . . ."

He roughly spins her to face him, digs his fingernails into her shoulders. "He's got you mojoed like Melvin! But ain't no quitting, Reeb, 'til the graveyard cuts us loose. Please don't make me waste that shit-colored sissy!"

She fouls him, low. "Now, now, be cool and mellow, Massa. You're six feet nine with ten inches of . . . uh . . ." She lets him twist, gape jawed, for a moment in the wind of suspense before she fouls him lower. ". . . of uncircumcised battering ram, to put it kindly. Massa suh." She continues, "Hey, you 'fessing up you so scared of a sissy stealing your woman you ready to go to the joint?"

He violently flings her away. The back of her head bangs against a dish towel rack on the wall. She snatches a steel potato masher from a wall rack, hurls it. It thuds against his chest. She backs away from his maniacal face as he moves forward with black bludgeon fists clenched and quivering at his sides.

"I'm gonna chastise your chippie ass for that crack!" he roars as he pursues her to the center of the kitchen.

Baptiste peers through the open kitchen window, darts away.

"C'mon, punch me out, gorilla, and blow me and the kids out of your life forever. Do me that favor! Please!" she screams as she halts flight.

Her connoisseur curves twang defiance through the orchid gauze of her nightgown. His number thirteens brake. He stares at her slack jawed in the thunderous silence. She moves in, assaults him with a barrage of tiny fists.

He seizes her wrists. "Reeb, you got the best hand. You win, girl, like usual," he croaks as he releases her.

She tiptoes her face into his. "I'm gonna cut you loose if you ever again accuse me of Felix or even just threaten to harm me. Understand, gorilla!?"

He nods, thinks, Awright, high-powered Mama Slick, I ain't saying nothing, ain't doing nothing to you and your sweetie 'til I catch you dead-bang wrong. He turns away with garage door shoulders slumped in shamed defeat to face Junior, cringed in the doorway with a startled face. He scoops him up into his arms. Violent knocking on the back door whirls him.

He and Reba stare at each other, hear Baptiste shout, "Open the door!"

Joe carries Junior to the door, unlocks it, glares at Baptiste wielding a shotgun.

"You all right, daughter dear?" Baptiste asks as he looks around Joe at Reba.

"Everything is cool, Baptiste," she says with an annoyed face. Baptiste's ubiquitous Bible peeps from his robe pocket.

Joe lets Junior down to the linoleum. "No it ain't, Gray Ass. I'm hot!" Joe explodes as he grabs the shotgun, smashes it into two useless pieces against the door frame. "Dingbat, what you doing at my door with your shotgun?" Joe says as he seizes the lapels of Baptiste's robe, yanks him close. "Nigger, your Bible is drove you crazy."

"I . . . uh . . . heard Daughter scream . . . uh, thought a prowler had broken in," Baptiste gasps.

Joe shoves him away, says, "I oughta beat your ass for lying. You know ain't no nigger in the ghetto with the balls to break into Joe Allen's pad."

He slams the door in Baptiste's frightened face and bolts it.

"Massa, I'm gonna quit your black funky ass if you don't straighten up. Soon!" Reba warns as Joe takes Junior's hand, leads him from the kitchen to the doorway of his bedroom.

Joe squats, looks into the half-scale mint image of his own face for a long moment as he embraces Junior's waist. Joe sees raw ambivalence flicker in Junior's narrowed eyes, detects tension in his strong lanky body. Remorse twinges Joe as he realizes that Junior must have witnessed most of his fracas with Reba. Joe glances at a light punching bag suspended from the ceiling in a corner of the room.

"C'mon, Junie," Joe says as he straightens from his squatting position and goes to hit the bag with rhythmic violence.

Junior comes to his side, watches with a solemn face.

"G'wan, take your turn, Junie, so's I can check out your timing," Joe says as he steps back from the bouncing bag and picks off a pair of lightweight training gloves hanging from the top of the dresser mirror.

Junior hesitantly slips out of his pajama coat, extends his hands for Joe to lace on the gloves. Joe sits on the arm of a red leather chair and watches Junior bang the bag briefly with half-hearted fists. Junior steps back from the bag, extends his fists toward Joe to be ungloved.

"How was I, Papa?" Junior inquires in a bored voice, with a lackadaisical slump in his body.

"Rotten, Junie!" Joe needles. "Maybe you'll do better with me as your target. G'wan, try to K.O. me with a good combination."

Joe raises his palms defensively, smiles as he sees Junior's body twang enthusiasm, sees his eyes glow with odd excitement. "You really mean it, Papa, and you won't get salty if I nail you good?" Junior chortles, and grins as he dances and feints joyfully before Joe, perched on the arm of the red leather chair.

"Sure ain't gonna, tiger. I ain't shucking you. Lay your best shot on me," Joe tells him as he tucks his chin behind the cover of an elevated shoulder ridge.

Junior steps in to unleash a ferocious two-fisted attack to Joe's bobbing head with amazing force and speed for a fledgling gladiator. For several minutes the leather splats viciously against Joe's palms as he picks off the bombs, slips others with deft evasions of his head. Then Joe deliberately lets Junior score hard hooks and crosses to his head and face before he lets himself topple off the chair arm into its seat with his nose dripping claret, his bottom lip ballooning from a whistling right cross.

Joe flops lifelessly in the chair, legs sprawled out awkwardly, feigning a K.O. as he peeps through apparently closed eyes at Junior still dancing excitedly before him. Then Joe sees concern replace the savage joy on Junior's face as he leans in, desperately teeths loose a glove lace, yanks off the glove beneath his armpit. He removes the other glove with his free hand, dashes into the bathroom across the hall. Joe hears the flood of tap water. He sees Junior sprint back to his side with a dripping towel. Joe closes his eyes tightly, feels Junior press the cold towel against his forehead.

"Papa! Papa!" Junior exclaims in alarm when Joe doesn't respond.

Then Joe feebly stirs with a groan, spastically blinks open his eyes, stares up blankly into Junior's distressed face.

"Damn, Sugar Ray Junie! That was one helluva sweet combination you took me out with," Joe mumbles as he pulls himself to his feet, gingerly strokes and moves his jaw hinge.

Junior embraces Joe's waist to steady him on his faked rubberized legs. "Papa, you awright and sure you ain't salty?" he says softly as he slips into his pajama coat.

"Naw, baby, I told you to lay it on me," Joe gasps. "Say, man, I got to go to bed. Would you do Papa a light favor?" Joe whispers.

"Yeah, Papa," Junior says as he tiptoes to put his arms around Joe's neck.

"Mellow, Junie. Then go to bed and get some solid doss. Okay? Now, gimme some good-night sugar." Joe half squats with pursed lips.

Junior nods, kisses Joe's lips, then gnaws his own bottom lip. "Papa, you wouldn't for real beat up Mama, would you?" Junior asks with desolate maroon eyes locked on Joe's.

"Naw, man. I was just shucking and jiving to keep Mama from beating my butt."

They laugh, kiss again, disengage. Joe palm-smacks Junior's pajama seat.

As he turns away for his bed Junior turns back as Joe straightens up. "Papa, would you do me a light favor?" he asks with piteous eyes.

"Sure, baby man, anything."

"Well please, Papa, don't shuck and jive like you gonna beat up Mama no more. It scares me! . . . Promise?"

"I promise, Junie. You ain't never gonna hear me do that number again with Mama. Son, I love Mama too much to harm her, even if she beats the pee outta me. I mean it!" Joe solemnly finger-crosses his heart.

Junior's face is thoughtful for a moment before he chortles, "Gee, Papa, I'd feel so good if I could punch out mean Grandpa Baptiste. Can I?"

Joe grins. "No, Junie! Your mama would have a stroke. 'Sides, he's gonna be cool 'cause I told him, last week, I was gonna set his old butt on fire with his own razor strap next time he hit you with it."

They laugh. "I love you, Junie," Joe says as they slap palms.

Junior says, "Me you too, Papa," before he turns and leaps into bed.

Joe says, "Good night son," as he closes the bedroom door.

He goes down the hall into his bedroom holding the cold towel against his leaky nose. He gets into bed. He lies listening to radio music. He hears Reba go into the twin's room down the hall for the rest of the night, as usual after a spat. Shortly, the music soothes him into ragged sleep.

At daybreak he awakens to go to the toilet. He starts to slide from bed when the voice of a newsbreak announcer demands his attention. He listens to a report of the grisly Blue Pit story.

Thirteen

In Beverly Hills, Melvin emerges from the whirlpooling of water in his black marble bathtub after soaking his bruised body and napping there since his arrival from his spree of murder. He towels off, goes to lie nude on his emperor-sized bed with a chaotic mind, but in merciful amnesia for all of his actions after he left the gas station with the can of gasoline. He flips on a table radio, bolts upright in bed, listens with rising panic to a detailed news broadcast of the Central Avenue horror. He bites his fingernails to the quicks as he connects himself in total.

"Oh my God! My watch! With my initials on it!" he screeches aloud as he rolls his pain-wracked blubber out of bed.

He shakes uncontrollably as he slips into a gold-brocaded robe and house slippers. He snatches his wallet and Tessie's Dodge key off the dressertop as he hastens from the room. He stumbles, nearly crashes down the stairway on his way to the car. His shaking hand fumbles to insert the ignition key for a full minute before he finally manages to speed away for the black ghetto gas station.

"Gas chamber, Patek Phillippe! Gas chamber, Patek Phillippe!" the engine's roaring whisper seems to taunt inside Melvin's head.

A half mile away from the ghetto, it occurs to Melvin to prevent identification of the Dodge's license plates. He pulls the car into a curb. He gets out and bends the plates unreadable. He drives the long way toward the station to avoid the immediate area of his crimes.

Two grizzled Mutt and Jeff veterans of the LAPD Homicide Division, staked out in the office of Melvin's gas station destination, sit on steel chairs and sip Cokes. Unfortunately for Melvin, they have given his watch, a moment before, to the lieutenant leader of the Blue Pit investigation. He had immediately phoned in to downtown Homicide Division the serial number of the expensive clue to trace ownership.

The officers watch the beanpole black attendant pump gas into a pickup truck. The detectives had arrived an hour before while combing a three-mile-square area for witnesses and also for the seller of the gasoline that had been quickly established as the substance used by the arsonist-murderer to torch the Blue Pit death trap. The cops' unmarked blue Ford sits concealed from easy street view inside the adjacent lube-repair shop.

"Think our nut will show to take his biscuit out of hock?" Jeff asks his partner, Mutt, as he balls up his Coke paper cup and arches it into a wastebasket.

"He's compelled to show. And when he does, walking or riding, our boy out there will drop the rag and we'll get him. But he won't show, as you know, if he's a thief who doesn't have to worry that a checkout of the watch will finger him," Mutt replies as he misses the wastebasket with his crumpled Coke cup.

Jeff shrugs. "And he could have panicked and split the state." His forehead wrinkles in thought as he rises from his chair, paces the office concrete. "Yeah, odds are he stole it. I don't see a two-grand watch bought by a guy who wears cruddy clothes and stinks of piss. We could be wasting—"

Jeff's excitement cuts him off as he sees the attendant cut his eyes back toward the office when Melvin pulls the Dodge in behind the serviced pickup truck. Both detectives move to stand with guns drawn, peep through a corner of the office door glass for the attendant to drop his wipe rag as the positive identification signal. The attendant is also under instruction, in the event the suspect arrives by car, to immediately raise the hood and rip loose the distributor cap.

The truck owner pays, drives away onto Central Avenue. The panic-stricken attendant freezes, stares bug-eyed through the windshield at Melvin's grim face. The several dollar bills from the truck owner flutter from the attendant's palsied hand. The signal wipe rag dangles forgotten from his hip pocket.

Melvin reads his responses as intended. He lifts his pistol off the seat beside him, points it at the attendant through the windshield, waggles him to the car.

Their field of vision blocked except for a view of the Dodge's rear end and the beanpole's upper torso, the detectives hesitate, think the attendant hasn't made a certain ID of their suspect.

The trembling attendant goes to the open driver's side window, leans in his head. "Yas suh, fill 'er up?" he blurts out in a squealy voice as Melvin jabs the pistol snout into the hollow at the base of his throat.

"I want my watch you took in pawn," Melvin says in a deadly whisper.

"Oh shucks! I thought you was the guy. Yas suh, gimme a minute to get it from the office soon's I check under your hood."

Melvin watches as the attendant lifts his head and cuts his electric eyes over the car top toward the office. Melvin says, "Forget the hood, man! Get my watch!"

"Yah suh! Yah suh!" the attendant exclaims, and dips his head so frantically that Melvin stiffens, locks his eyes on the attendant's image in the rearview mirror, sees him nervously look back over his shoulder as he trots toward the office.

The attendant belatedly jerks the signal rag from his rear pocket and flings it away. His red shirttail fans out from his rear end like a fiery mini-missile liftoff blast as he accelerates past the office to disappear down a side street.

Melvin sees the rag action and then the detectives bursting from the office with guns pointed toward him. He stomps the Dodge onto Central Avenue in a rain of bullets. He careens the Dodge south. Mutt and Jeff hasten across the station lot to get their car to follow.

A mile down Central Avenue near Florence Avenue, Melvin hears the old Dodge's engine miss, sputter, and then stall under the punishing stress. He leaps from the rolling machine, stumbles and crashes to the pavement with pistol in hand. He lies gasping for a moment. He struggles to his feet, scuttles into an alley as a police cruiser arrives and skids to a stop. Melvin crouches behind an apartment house trash bin, fires two rounds at Mutt and Jeff as he crouches and zigzags into the alley with drawn service pistol.

Jeff drops to the alley floor, rolls to cover beneath an abandoned car in a vacant lot twenty yards away from Melvin's trash bin cover across the alley. He fires three rapid shots at Melvin when he breaks from cover, and hears him howl with pain as he clutches his gun arm, sees Melvin's pistol fall to the alley floor.

Melvin disappears around the corner of the apartment building. Jeff sprints after him with a chilling smile on his face.

Fourteen

A nightmarish mix of hoodlum passion and puckish fate in 1963 colored the Felix-Allen triangle. Red. Joe, the gluttonous humper, forced to scrounge for the Felix-staled crumbs of Reba's sex cake, is puffed with constant rage, starved on a frequent fare of sexual hardtack. Masturbation. Ironically, Joe lances the boil of his aching jealousy and long frustration in the evening of an historic November day of gore. Exactly on that day, the New Frontier dreamer disciples were betrayed when Oswald Iscariot cross-haired their Christ of Camelot.

But in the early afternoon of the day, Joe and Panther Cox are portraits of unalloyed joy as they watch undefeated fifteen-year-old Junior outbox a Latin opponent in the light-heavyweight competition of the Southwest Golden Gloves finals. Junior seems a cinch to become division champion. Joe remembers, with a pang of sadness, his last pro fight and Elder Joe's anguish when his dreams of fistic glory went down the drain in this very ring long ago when he lost his temper and knocked out Melvin's cousin between rounds.

But now their joy is short-lived, replaced by despair. Junior's crafty, older opponent sees him telegraph a left hook with an almost imperceptible hitch of his left shoulder. He decks Junior with a crunching counter right cross to his chin at the bell. Panther and Joe leap through the ropes into the ring to assist groggy Junior to his stool. His handlers frantically sharpen his dulled mind, derubberize his legs with smelling salts and brutal massage.

"Junie, stop hunching your shoulders before the left hook. You hear!?" Joe shouts above the cheering din of Mexican partisans.

Shapely fox Dorothy Lewis, Junior's girlfriend, screams from ringside, "Please throw the towel in, Mister Allen!"

Junior shakes his shaved bullethead, leaps off his stool to his feet before the bell. He violently pounds his gloves together as he glares mayhem across the ring at his smirking opponent seated coolly on his stool.

Junior snarls, "Lissen to the chili bellies cheer that lucky fart. But this round I'm gonna make 'em bawl when I K.O. his ass."

Joe says harshly, "Chili bellies!? Nigger! You sound like the damn KKK. Get your head together. Fool!"

Junior lunges toward his opponent at the sound of the last-round bell. Joe and Panther groan.

Panther shouts to Junior's back, "Be cool, baby boy! Don't blow the fight—you done won!"

Headhunter Junior throws a reckless right-hand lead that his opponent slips, then counters with a left hook that quakes Junior's legs. As Junior backpedals, he darts fearful eyes past his opponent across the ring into Joe's eyes.

"Panther! Looks like Junie's ticker is turned chicken shit first time he's really tested," Joe whispers with hoarse anguish.

His opponent traps Junior in a corner, slams his midsection and face with a sizzling combination. Junior slips to his back on the canvas, stares apprehensively across the ring at his grim-faced opponent dancing impatiently in a neutral corner. The elderly referee tolls the count. At the seven count, Junior halfheartedly dredges himself to his knees, feebly clutches at the ropes before he collapses on his back at the T.K.O. count of ten.

Joe and Panther rush into the ring to help him to his stool. They silently ply him with smelling salts and cold wet sponges. They escort him through absolute Latin pandemonium into the dressing room to shower and dress in heavy silence.

Junior goes to open the dressing room door, pauses. "I'm sorry I let you both down . . . got a bad break, I guess . . . Dottie's got her daddy's car. See ya later, Papa," he says with downcast eyes as he steps out into the corridor.

"See ya later, Junie," Joe says softly as Junior closes the door behind him.

They step out into the corridor behind Junior and Dottie, watch the couple walk out the front exit. Joe and Panther leave the building for Panther's new chippie-catching red Buick hardtop parked in a lot across the street. As Panther tools the machine toward the ghetto, he cuts concerned glances at Joe slumped on the front seat with his eyes half closed in obvious deep depression.

"Joe, we both got a right to have the blues after what happened to Junior. But cheer up. There's a bright side. Every young fighter is—"

Joe cuts him off, completes an Elder Joe old saw, ". . . lucky, Panther, if he gets his ass kicked good up front to chastise him for thinking he's three times better than he is so he can be taught to be five times better than he is . . . or to hip him he ain't got the ticker to make the big time."

They laugh hollowly. Joe's disconsolate face still vibes the blues.

Panther says, "Say, buddy, let's stop off at that new joint on Vernon for a taste of blues chaser before I take you home."

Joe glumly shakes his naked head. "Naw, Panther, a ocean of booze couldn't chase my blues."

Panther says softly, "Reba?"

Joe mumbles, "Yeah, and Felix."

Panther exhales noisily. "He's with Reba down South?"

"Naw, Panther, not that. In a way it's worse 'cause like they say, 'The hand of fate has wrote' and hipped me, with no doubt 'bout that snake banging my woman.' That shit-colored sissy is got her hoodooed!"

"Joe, I don't know and don't want to know who snitched to make you sure. Lemme throw this out. I lost the only broad I ever truly loved when I believed the lies about her a stinking snitch laid on me to steal her. You gotta be careful, Joe. You can't be sure unless your eyes see it," Panther says as he pulls into the Allen driveway behind Joe's La Salle.

Reba's new pink Thunderbird gleams beneath a carport at the rear of the front yard. Joe smiles bitterly. "Panther, I been ninety percent sure 'bout 'em for years . . . would've busted into the parsonage and caught 'em humping dead bang a hundred times 'cept for that goddamn ten percent I'd be wrong and cinch lose Reeb. Until a short while ago, my sucker ticker wouldn't let my head think 'bout living without Reeb. But she and her nigger done hurt me so much and so long I guess they done numbed me and made me strong 'nough now to play the hand of power Reeb dealt herself."

Panther's face creases in puzzlement. "Power hand, Joe?"

Joe starts to answer, but ten-year-old twins Belle and Sadie spill through the front door in starched white cotton dresses and red shortie coats, to Joe's side of the Buick, and chorus, "Hi, Daddy and Uncle Panther!"

"Daddy, will ya be sweet and give us some money for Popsicles?" Belle, the more aggressive twin, asks as they lean in and kiss Joe's cheek.

Joe pats the pockets of his blue slax and black leather jacket. "Ain't got no change on me, honey bunny. Wait a minute 'til I finish talking to Panther."

They dash around the other side of the car when they see Panther quickly excavate a half dollar from a trouser pocket of his robin's egg blue plaid suit.

Panther grins, says, "Now don't you gorgeous li'l foxes blow all this bread in one place," as he drops the coin into Belle's extended palm.

They lean in and hastily smooch his cheek. They scamper away for the now black-owned corner drugstore, sold several years before by newly wedded former store manager Erica and Harry Havelik after the death of the elder Havelik.

Panther lights a cigar. "Joe, you was gonna run down the power hand you got."

Joe lights a cigarette, leans back thoughtfully against the seat. He exhales a gust of smoke, muses in a tensioned voice, "Miss

Slick Reeb called me from New Orleans . . . 'round nine this
morning and told me she was flyin' in sometime tomorrow . . .
said she was gonna get a cab home and wasn't no sense in me
picking her up at the airport 'cause tomorrow is my busiest day
on the plumbing gig. Philippa's old housekeeper called me just
before you picked up me and Junie . . . said Reeb had packed and
left town to visit a cousin in Baton Rouge for a few hours . . . before
she flies back to L.A."

Joe pauses to snub out his cigarette in the ashtray. "Tonight!
Get it, Panther!?"

Panther says, "Yeah, looks like she's planning to spend the
night in L.A. on the Q.T. Maybe you're right about her and the
preacher."

Joe exclaims, "Ain't no maybe! They ain't fucked for three
weeks 'cause she's been down there burying Philippa and taking
care of some business to cinch that coupla hundred grand soon's
the probate court dishes it out. They so hot to screw tonight, I'll
bet both of 'em is so slippery between the legs, they can't walk
for trotting. But their thang is over 'cause I'm gonna bust in on
'em and get the power to keep the kids if I don't keep her. I'm
gonna fix Bitch Face. Real good! She'll stay with me and the kids
'cause he ain't gonna be worth doodly squat to her after I catch
'em."

Panther frowns alarm. "Joe, the kids! They gonna hurt some
bad with the notoriety and the shame. They might wind up hat-
ing you."

Joe says in a quiet monotone, "Panther, I been thinking 'bout
that . . ." He heaves a mighty sigh. "I been worried 'bout that for
a zillion years, seems like. Guess I ain't made no kinds move to
shuck my pain 'cause o' that. You ain't been me, Panther, playing
possum boo-koo times she's come in way late . . . don't take no
bath 'cause she's done had one after he finished jugging in her.
She hits the bed and dies just like some bitch dog that's done let
a mob of mutts ram her. I done sniffed her sleeping, Panther, and
done smelled that sonuvabitch stinking in her pores right past
her bathing.

"I done trapped her and killed her a hundred times in night-mares, Panther, like so real I gotta scoot outta the bedroom when I wake up. I'm so happy I bawl 'cause I ain't really harmed her and don't wanta wake her up and upset her. Panther, I ain't 'shamed to say I love Reeb's dirty drawers! That's why I'm gonna bring all this shit to a head before I think I done woke up from wasting her in my sleep some night and get hipped I ain't been asleep. That's the long big pain I gotta spare the kids and me. You dig? I owe that preacher the worst!"

Panther gravely shakes his head. "Joe, I agree with you, he deserves the worst. But I'd grieve to see you up in the state joint doing it all 'cause of temper. And don't forget the punk is a black belt. He might press you in a humbug and you might acciden-tally ice him to keep him from icing you."

Joe explodes. "I'll tear his wings out at the sockets if he flaps any of that karate jive in my face!"

"Joe, I know you and you'll ice that punk in a hassle. Please, don't blow every—"

Joe cuts him off. "Hush up, Panther! I'm a sucker, but I ain't a star natal sucker. I ain't gonna do nothing 'cept make him look like that humpback in the tower . . . uh, you know, Queezy Moto. Shit! Reeb's gonna think I'm pretty. And she's gonna see lotsa me 'stead of being his flunky 'ho secretary every other minute of the day and night. I'd bet a C-note 'ginst a lead nickel alla her pre-cious so-called friends vote to throw her ass outta that church after I do my thang."

Joe opens the door, steps out. "So long, Panther. I'll call you after I . . ."

Panther says, "All right, buddy. But I hope you change your mind and do what I been begging you to do for a long time be-fore you blow your cool and do something bad to Reba."

Joe's face hardens as he shakes his head. "Naw, Panther, I ain't never gonna cut Reeb loose, and hope she never cuts me loose. She's my forever woman. I ain't never gonna harm her. Other-wise, long time ago I'da tore off her head and dribbled it to the police station, as much hurt and shit as she's done put on me. And 'sides, my poor mama loves Reeb in her grave."

As Joe turns away Panther says, "That snake housekeeper broad that snitched on Reba worries me. Maybe she's in cahoots some way to cross you and Reba so she and somebody will have a shot at all that bread."

Joe turns back, chuckles. "Panther, the old lady ain't no snitch. She called to tell me Reeb had forgot her big ring of keys so Reeb wouldn't be upset 'bout 'em when she got home. She said she was airmailing them to L.A. tomorrow morning."

Panther exclaims, "Ain't that a bitch of a cold break for Reba?"

Joe grins stingily. "Ain't it!? But sweet for me. Pops was dead right—what goes 'round comes 'round."

He turns, walks away several paces before he turns back to the car. He looks into Panther's eyes as he says solemnly, "Panther, ain't no use for me to jive myself that you ain't been like my papa since Pops passed away . . . ain't that right?"

Panther nearly whispers, "Yeah, Li'l Joe, that's right. And got feelin's for you like you my son."

Joe shifts his feet uneasily, sheepishly averts his eyes for an instant before he stammers, "Well, I . . . uh . . . I been doing lotsa heavy thinkin' lately 'bout my bed work with Reeb . . . She laid a sex book on me a long time ago . . . wrote by a doctor. I ain't never read it good 'til lately . . . He's gotta be a freakish mother hisself 'cause he swears a stud ain't nothin' but a amateur in bed if he . . . uh . . . don't suck his lady's poony! You older than spit and maybe done had more pussy than them Hollywood humpers, Gable and Flynn, put together, quiet as it's kept."

They laugh.

"Well, uh . . . I got a real kinda personal question to ask you that maybe I ain't 'sposed to ask. But if you get salty, I'll under—"

Panther cuts him off. "Li'l Joe, that doc's book is on the pussy money. Up front, I gotta confess, I been thrilling the girls goofy with my jib for sixty years, since I was fifteen in fact. So ask me anything, son."

Joe gnaws his bottom lip before he blurts out, "You puke your guts out the first time, Panther?"

Panther grins. "That first time I was like a hog at the slop trough, that broad's pussy was so clean and sweet. Delicious! 'Course, later I run into a few pukey butts that I throwed outta my bed. You been nixing something great, son, 'cause scarfing a sweet one is good for your health, maybe got a lotta vitamins even."

They burst belly laughs.

"A wise scarfer once said, 'Show me a chump that ain't scarfing his woman's snatch and I'll show you a chump I can steal his woman from.' So Li'l Joe, let ya conscience be ya—"

The noisy arrival of the twins, at Joe's side, cuts off Panther.

"I wanta thank you, Panther! You sure done helped me make up my mind 'bout somethin' important," Joe chortles as he slaps palms with Panther.

He scoops the Popsicle-wielding twins into his arms, turns away.

"Bye, Uncle Panther!" the twins exclaim and wave over Joe's shoulders as he carries them across the yard.

Panther waves, watches until they disappear through the open front door. He backs the Buick into the street to go to his apartment above his Freeway Fresh Fish Market.

At twilight, Joe, swathed in warm black woolen slacks and a Zenobia-knitted sweater, sits chain-smoking on a battered milk crate. He is concealed in the midst of thick bushes in the alley behind Felix's church grounds. He stares intently at the front door of the parsonage, a three-story mansion unconnected to the white stone church. A spirited confection of choir practice voices drips into the grape-hued haze through half-opened stained glass windows. Felix's new gold El Dorado coruscates outside the parsonage door, parked beside his formal limousine firing black rockets of light from its highly simonized hull.

Joe's car is parked two blocks away down the alley. Certain the lovers would bed in the parsonage as usual, he'd decided not to tail Felix if he made the airport trip to pick up Reba for fear that one of them might discover his tail driving a now rarely seen collector's item La Salle.

Shortly, the choir members spill into the parking lot, chatting as they go to their cars. They drive away, leaving only the church's elderly caretaker's scabrous blue Pontiac on the lot. Joe upends a pint of vodka. His throat locks when a gang of teenagers pound past his bush blinds pursued, seconds later, by a hurtling police car that strafes the bushes with alley grit.

A moment later, Joe tenses as a cab pulls into the church lot, pulls to a stop near the parsonage door. He relaxes, amused to see bottle-curvaceous Ruta, Reba's hated much younger rival, alight tipsily from the cab. Blue fox encased, she wiggles and staggers her curves up stone steps to the parsonage door as the cabbie drives past Joe down the alley. Joe watches her impatiently jab the doorbell for a long moment before robed Felix opens it with an expression of utter consternation on his face, frothed with shaving cream.

They stand glaring at each other before Felix grabs her hand and yanks her inside, bangs the door shut. "You're breaking the rules, Ruta. A, you're drunk, and B, I told you I wasn't receiving your calls or your company until tomorrow. You can't stay!" he exclaims harshly as he hurries away across the lavish pink and beige motifed sunken living room for the first-floor bathroom.

Mean faced, she pauses in the entrance hall, eye-sweeps the half dozen bouquets of pink orchids reposing elegantly in crystal vases about the living room. She stomps to the bathroom doorway, evil-eyes his face reflected in the cabinet mirror as he straps his straight razor. She shapes a crooked little smile of defiance as she lets her fox coat slip to the carpet.

"I'm staying!" she slurs as she kicks off her rhinestoned blue velvet pumps, whirls her nude curves away down the hallway leading to the kitchen.

Joe's curiosity lures him from cover. As he creeps around outside the house, he is attracted by a flash of light in the kitchen. He goes to peer through a partially opened window. He sees Ruta open the refrigerator door, stand glaring into it.

"Aha! I knew it!" Joe hears her exclaim as she snatches out a silver tray of caviar canapés, dumps it on the floor.

Several minutes later, Felix razors off the last patch of stubble, hears the pop of a champagne cork. He races for the kitchen clutching the razor strap. He stands at the kitchen door quivering with a mixture of outrage and irritating excitement as he glares at her rear end. She squats at the open refrigerator door above the open neck of a jeroboam of mums intended to celebrate Reba's return. He watches, rooted in the doorway, as she dribbles droplets of tinkle into the bottle and onto the floor.

"You filthy tramp! I'm going to punish you!" he rages as he charges her with the razor strap twirling and whistling above his head.

Outside at the lace-curtained window, Joe is spellbound as he eavesdrops and ogles the raw tableau. He aches for a camera to document it all for Reba's eyes.

Ruta spins away from the strap, loses her balance, falls on her back as Felix reaches her. He welts her thighs with a violent slash of the strap. She rolls, evades a rain of strap licks that pop against the floor.

"Why!?" he pants as he pauses to catch his breath when she escapes to a refuge under a bolted-down breakfast nook table.

"I hate your old square-ass main bitch!" she shouts from beneath the table.

He stoops to drag her out by the heels. She kicks savagely at his face to force him away. He stands for a moment in glowering frustration before he goes to the sink. She peeps at him with a sly face as he turns on the hot water tap until steam billows from the sink.

As he fills a large pot, she says icily, "Miss Swinger, you'll be sorry if you're filling that pot for me."

He stiffens, glances at his wristwatch, grits his teeth. He falters as he turns toward her brandishing the pot. He stoops at eye level with her. "You've got ten seconds to crawl out and get out!" he warns as he monitors his watch with a draconic face.

"Douse me and I'll snitch you out of your pulpit," she warns.

He sloshes water from the kettle as he jerks rigid on his knees, glares at her, sneers, "Hah! Your credibility is zero minus . . . You've forgotten, Miss Nympho Klepto, that your folks dumped you out here on your late grandmother after that last of a dozen busts in Harlem. I'd swear my only interest in you has been paternal to rehabilitate you in my church since you were sixteen. You couldn't sell any scam on me. You've got two seconds!"

She throws her head back, laughs. "My suicide letter will explain how you corrupted me to try death. That will give me a hundred-plus credibility. Get it, Miss Preacher Bitch! . . . Then after I scribble the letter, I'll drop a few reds and dial an operator. I'll mumble what I've done and my address before I let the phone crash in her ears. What the hell, I wouldn't mind my stomach pumped to get you smeared. Then wanta bet everybody wouldn't believe the truth about our threesomes with Hollywood lesbians and jocks. Do you want it known that you like dick? You double-sexed bastard! Huh?"

He ashens; his fingers curl into karate claws as he glares mayhem.

"Be cool, tiger. I'm coming out," she says.

He leans aside to let her crawl out and stand with legs akimbo. Her body twangs soot black triumph above him frozen on his knees.

"You know I'm mad about you, cutie . . . It's your old square-ass bitch that makes me evil. You don't need her. Cut her loose!" she whispers sweetly as she grinds her crotch against his cheek.

He recoils. "I won't!" he exclaims as he pulls himself to his feet.

She shrugs. "All right, I'll give you another out. I won't put us in the papers if you will treat us equally from now on. Well!?"

Stricken speechless, he nods, quivers with rage as he stares into her frosty eyes.

"I'm not riding any more cabs. This week I want a new 1963 arctic white Thunderbird, with all the extras she's got on her car," she intones fiercely.

He studies her obdurate face for several beats before he says, "You got it. Get out!"

She shakes her head. "Not before you do me . . . Let her have the garbage after me for a change."

She leaps atop the breakfast nook table, jackknifes her thighs against her chest. He darts an alarmed glance at his wristwatch. He sighs resignation as he pulls up a chair, drops into it. He stares petulantly at her sex nest before she roughly seizes his ears. He moans as she yanks his head into her fat-lipped valley floor.

Nauseated, Joe hurries back to the cover of his bushes. A half hour later, he sees the couple get into the El Dorado and leave with Ruta behind the wheel.

Forty minutes after dropping Ruta at her apartment Felix leaves his car in an airline parking complex to wait near the disembarkation point of Reba's flight. Several minutes later Reba, chic and voluptuous in a ginger Saks dress, shows with skycap and bags. They yelp rut as they fly into each other's arms. Six feet of wiry power, Felix carries her heavy luggage almost effortlessly to the El Dorado.

"Darling, how did everything wind up down there?" he asks as they enter the car.

"Splendidly, except for the sadness . . . I buried Mama with her husband in his crypt."

They pet and kiss torridly until an airline security officer braces them courteously, but firmly. "Pardon me, folks, but will you please consider the facilities of a hotel down the road. Now!"

They grin coming out of steamy trance. Felix guns the El Dorado away for the parsonage. He slows at a hotel driveway turnoff down the road. But he decides to pass up its sterile accommodations for the orchid-strewn warmth of the parsonage.

"Oh baby! I'll never again stay away from you," Reba croons as her hand caresses his organ swelling against his trouser gold silk.

Felix stops at a liquor store for champagne. Moments later they arrive at the church grounds.

An instant after Felix parks in front of the parsonage, the elderly church janitor, his duties performed, walks to his Pontiac heap. He gets in, grinds the starter. He gets out and raises the hood to tinker underneath.

Joe watches the pair start to get out, then freeze for an instant before they relax on the car seat. Joe watches their silhouettes merge, red hot and starved for each other. He sobs and snots like an infant. He screams silently; his teeth ache and chatter. He leaps from cover, streaks his two hundred and fifty pounds of assassin rage toward them with teeth bared. He is phosphorescent, a doom poster animated in the "black light" of ultraviolet stars. He brakes, peers into the car's posh murk. He growls in his throat as he stares at Reba.

She pecks, like a gluttonous bird, at the preacher's long worm, risen through his open fly. His eyes are shuttered in bliss. His diamond-glittered right hand convulsively squeezes Reba's writhing buttocks. His silky locks jounce on his head, moving in sync with Reba's bobbing head.

Joe opens and rips off the Lincoln's door. He hurls it away like a Frisbee. They jerk rigid on the seat with chalky faces at the terrible wrenching sound of the severed door. Their eyes are gargantuan, electric with shock, staring up at him. He sees the preacher's hand snake a nickel-plated pistol from beneath the seat. Joe grabs Felix's gun hand and hears the wrist splinter as he slams it down on the steering wheel. Joe catches the flying gun, flings it away over an ox shoulder to the concrete.

The stench of the preacher's B.M. churns Joe's stomach. His gout of vomit fouls the preacher's gold silk suit. Felix chops a left-hand karate blow at Joe's throat that cracks against Joe's dipped chin. Woozy, Joe slugs his temple. The preacher's teeth gouge a hunk of flesh from his hand. Joe punches a geyser of scarlet from the dainty nose.

Joe screams, "You freakish devil! I'll kill you for God!"

Reba hollers, "Police! Please, somebody help us!"

Joe jabs her mouth bloody. Reba leaps to the sidewalk clutching the bottle of champagne. Joe's face is hideous with joyful killer vengeance as he seizes the preacher's bloody head and jerks him from the car. The preacher's head makes a smashed-melon sound striking the concrete. The gray, lover boy eyes glaze and close. Joe straddles him, grunts as his hands rip the corners of the cute mouth deeply into the cheeks. He jackhammers his knee into the preacher's scrotum. Reba's screams are deafening in Joe's ears as he tries to twist off the preacher's girlish head.

Lights in nearby houses flash on. People gape from their windows at the carnage.

Joe feels Reba straddle his back, bucks violently as she claws rills of fire on his neck and naked skull. He falls away, stunned for an instant, as Reba clubs his head with the giant bottle. He feels his blood ooze hot and wet down his face. In a red mist, he hears the bottle glass shower to the street. He turns to see Reba's wildcat face as she poises the dagger neck of the bottle to strike at his throat. He hurls his fist and sees her jaw pop askew like a gate wobbly on its hinges.

She drops lifelessly on her back, thighs gaped open. For a mini-instant, he stares into her crimson-lined sex snare that for years she has stingily rationed out, starved him mad for. She loves to suck off the preacher but gives me cold kisses on my cheek, he tells himself.

Refueled rage galvanizes him out of all control. He whirls back to murder Felix. He hears a chorus of horrified cries from shadowy spectators. He seizes the preacher's throat, chokes him as he bangs his head against the concrete. Felix's head seems afloat in a pool of claret.

The racket of sirens, the screech of police car brakes shudder the night air. Then, even cop fists, their batons, their hoarse commands cannot loose his death grip. Only the dark curtain of oblivion releases him from his psycho frenzy of rage.

Fifteen

For his mindless twenty-odd minutes of vengeance, Joe got eight days in the jail ward of County Hospital and three years' probation. For three months, under its terms, he has lived out of the Allen home with Panther in his apartment above his fish market and has had no contact with Reba.

Joe lies in bed, reads by coffin gray morning light, for the dozenth time, a letter from Reba's lawyer which notified him, the day before, of her action to divorce him. He lights a cigarette. He torches a corner of the letter with the lighter flame, drops the flaming paper into an ashtray. His cop-scarred face is satanic in the glow of fire as he stares into it, has murderous thoughts of Felix until the letter shrivels into ashes.

He violently slaps his thigh in frustration that the private investigator's report of Felix is lagging. His only chance to sour Felix's continuing affair with Reba. Joe makes a mental note to demand action from the sleuth or a refund of the fifteen-hundred-dollar fee borrowed from his boss.

He rises to go to the bathroom, hears Panther snoring as he steps inside to bathe and shave. Afterward he gulps grits and eggs. Then, with lunch pail in hand, he goes into the chilly February morning wearing his plumbing coveralls over a Zenobia-knitted sweater. He pauses on the sidewalk to engorge his lungs with crisp air. A sudden foul drift of exhaust fumes from the cars humming by on the nearby freeway stings his nostrils, knifes him with the memory of Elder Joe's fatal fracas with phantoms on it long ago.

He goes to secure the wind-mauled tarpaulin covering the recently overhauled and painted La Salle. He gets into the plumbing truck parked on the street in front of it, spends a sweaty twenty minutes getting the ailing truck to start, drives jerkily away. He is thankful that as a bonused twenty-four-hour troubleshooter, he'd received no phone calls dispatching him to work using the crippled truck.

A half hour later he chugs the truck into the plumbing firm's lot, bustling with a dozen trucks and drivers preparing for the workday. He greets and slaps palms of most of his interracial coworkers as he moves across the parking lot into the one-story sprawling redbrick building housing offices and truck maintenance space. Joe steps through the open door of old man Hoffmeister's office and nearly collides with him and his son leaving the room. After warm greetings, Joe explains his truck problem.

The lanky towheaded son, crisply neat in fresh blue coveralls, says, "Joe, I'll check with the mechanic to see if number nine is ready for service," as he strides away down the corridor.

A silver-crested leprechaun with laughing blue eyes, the elder Hoffmeister, impeccable in a blue serge suit, pauses. "You look drawn, son . . . no new personal problems, I hope?" he says as he and Joe stroll down the corridor.

"Naw, Otto, ain't no recent grief, and I ain't stewing but a little these days, even with the news yesterday that Reeb's gonna divorce me," he lies.

The old man clucks sympathy, pats Joe's shoulder as they step into the parking lot. "You're still young enough to make yourself happy with someone new. Like your papa was before arthritis laid him low. You're the best I've got . . . Come and talk to me if you feel yourself about to get into more trouble. Will you do that, son?"

As they shake hands Joe says, "Yeah, sure will and I wanta thank you, Otto. I 'preciate you but I'm gonna be all right."

He goes to the replacement truck, gets an assignment sheet from the younger Hoffmeister before he drives away. At noon Joe excitedly leaves the Vernon Avenue office of the private investigator with the report on Felix he's agonized a month for.

A week later, during Joe's lunch break, the sun bolts through an acrid wall of smog to illuminate an early-bird young hooker working Western Avenue. Joe sits and gnaws at a meatloaf sandwich as he gazes through his plumbing truck windshield at the hot-gaited vision switching miniskirted hips down the sidewalk toward him.

Joe's stress-sunken eyes sparkle as he cocks his naked head and scans the neat curves and svelte planes of the bantam sex kitten wiggling closer, smiling at him. What a fine young fox, he thinks, she's got Reba's green eyes, the whole li'l cute Bambi smear. His scrotum tingles when she stops and sticks her head inside the truck. He gazes into the slumberous eyes of the infant mudkicker.

"Hi, big 'un. I'm Jill, and you?"

"Joe," he mutters.

"How about a light lift?" she asks in a smoky-sweet voice.

He nods. She gets in beside him with a pulse-leaping flash of satiny thighs and braless to the navel cleavage. His testicles ache with long-term pressure as he keys the truck to life. He drops his mutilated sandwich into his lunch pail on the seat between them.

"Where can I take you, Jill?" he hears himself ask raggedly.

She lifts his lunch pail to the floorboard. She scoots her curves against him and finger-strokes his earlobe, pinches his rod on the rise.

She says, "To that motel around the corner from McDonald's. That is, if you want to sin with me for ten . . ." Then she whispers a standard hook. "Just did sixty days. I wanta come, Joe!"

He pulls the truck away to the corner, turns into the motel lot. As Jill slides across the seat to get out she says, "All right, Daddy darling, give me ten and four for the room."

Something in the "Daddy" salutation, the way her young voice quavers for an instant, chills and turns him off, reminds him of Belle and Sadie. He bites his lip, stares stupidly at her child's palm extended. He digs into his wallet, passes a ten-dollar bill into her palm.

As he starts the engine he says, "Baby girl, I'm sorry I took up your time. I've changed my mind. I gotta cut you loose."

She gets out of the car, confused, and watches as he drives from the lot. He glances at his wristwatch through a blur of tears forced by a sudden jolt of Reba loss. He drives furiously to his twins' grade school. He parks across the street from the school. He switches on the radio to Lou Rawls' "Natural Man" lyrics. His elephantine foot unconsciously sledges the floorboard in time to the tune. He lights a cigarette that dangles, after a puff, from his fat lips. He blots his eyes with his shirtsleeve. He uncaps a pint of vodka, sucks half down his gullet.

He hears the bedlam of kids flooding the schoolyard across the street for recess. He sticks his head out through the truck window. He stares through the fence into the moil of kids searching for a glimpse of Belle and Sadie.

He spots them. Their gleaming auburn tresses lash their shoulders as they skip into the schoolyard behind the last of the other kids. He thinks he sees them dart glances toward the familiar truck. They're laying the cold shoulder on me, he thinks. Reeb's poisoned them against me.

He honks furiously to force their attention. His heart sprints as they mope poker faced to the fence. They stand, shifting feet, staring at him. He waves, throws extravagant, frantic kisses. They are statues for a long heartbreaking moment. They exchange looks before they wave hesitantly, halfheartedly blow back kisses. Then abruptly they scamper away to play. He is sure they despise him. I've lost them! he thinks.

His eyes harden. His hands quiver madly as he glances at his work sheet. He drives away, feeling like his own grandpa, to unclog a toilet on Vermont Avenue near Sunset. He finishes the job at noon. He thinks of Junior. His need to see him overrides his shame and fear of rejection.

He drives toward an open-air lunch stand near Manual Arts High School. The school building looms like a redbrick repository of his youthful memories. He remembers his long-ago heartaches, the misery of comely and affluent Melvin's conquest of Reba. He scowls as a mulatto jock cruises by in a gaudy Chevy crammed with girls. He is reminded of how he suffered to see Melvin and Reba cruising by in his low-riding purple chippie catcher.

He parks down the street from Junior's taco stand hangout. He is surprised to see the stand deserted. Farther down the street he sees an excited mob of students at the mouth of an alley cheering wildly. He leaves the truck and goes down the sidewalk to the alley. He peers above the head of the mob into the alley.

Junior is nose to nose with a sneering dandy who taunts, "Dottie is our broad. Chump!"

Junior shoves him and starts to exchange blows with the powerfully muscled young adult. The grunts of the combatants resonate the alley.

Joe watches quietly, with rising irritation, as Junior's counter-punching opponent beats Junior to the punch again and again with sucker overhand rights to the head. He winces as Junior falls to the alley floor glassy eyed.

Dottie, a dazzler with a child's face and a woman's full-blown curves, wails and throws her arms around Junior. Junior shakes his head like a poleaxed steer as he tries feebly to regain his feet. His opponent kicks at him.

Joe bulls through the silent crowd into the arena. He seizes the kicker and hurls him against the side of a building. The kicker bounces off the wall and falls to the alley floor, gasping for air. Joe stoops to help Junior to his feet. Junior glares at his unfaithful fox. She paws, throws herself at Junior. Junior slaps her away.

As Joe leads Junior away toward the sidewalk she pleads, "Please, Jo Jo, don't be salty. I ain't never gave that funny-time nigger no action. Honest, I ain't lying!"

Junior brushes past, turns to blow a gob of bloody spit at her feet. He says, "We're through, scumbag!"

She screams, "Fuck you, ugly ass!" Then she whirls, with a pouting mouth, back into the alley to comfort and coo over Junior's comely rival.

Joe says, "Son, I'm glad you woke up to Dottie. You'll forget her."

Junior glances back. Stops. Joe's fist grinds into Junior's back as he forces him down the student-clogged sidewalk into the truck. Joe roughly uses mouthwash and tissues to cleanse Junior's wounded face. Junior lights a cigarette.

They sit silently for a long moment before Junior mutters, "Papa, I coulda beat the pee outta that turkey if I wasn't just up from the flu."

Joe smells the cheap wine on his breath. He says harshly, "Don't jive me, Junie. You got the crap knocked out of you 'cause you been messing 'round with low-life chippies, cigarettes, and wine, and you still twitching that left shoulder before you throw the left hook. I've told you and told you about that. Why shit, when I was your age I'da run that sucker back up his mammy's belly with my first combination.

"Know why? . . . 'cause when I was in my teens I had my nose wide open to win. I stayed away from cigarettes and hooch. I trained and listened to my papa's boxing teaching. I stayed hungry for Pops' advice. It's why I didn't take a drink or smoke a coffin nail or lay a broad until I was nineteen. Believe me, baby, I could've made heavyweight champion of the world if I had been hip enough to stay on the boxing track. But Pops got arthritis and I got double-trapped. First doing his plumbing gig, and then by my nose wide open for your mama. Get yourself together, son. Make me proud. Gimme a boost so I can have hope for you, so some of my misery looking back will make some kinda sense."

Sadness veils Joe's face as he sighs and pauses, then continues. "Funny thing, I can't forget how I bawled at Pops' funeral until my guts ached . . . been to lots of funerals of folks dead before their time. Know something? I can always put the finger on the killer. It's the bastard that bawls the most!"

Junior's bottom lip trembles as he looks into Joe's eyes and whispers, "Papa, I'll make you proud. I will! I ain't copping out, but I ain't been myself since you left home . . . needed your advice lotsa times . . . called your boss, left messages a whole lotta times since you . . . uh . . . had that hassle with Ma and the preacher."

In a long silence the brute-faced twins stare into each other's eyes. Joe says softly, "I'm sorry, son. I thought you hated me, would be better off without me after what happened . . ."

Junior says, "Wanta tell me your side, Papa, about what happened that night?"

Joe remembers how in court he had, against his lawyer's advice, kept the secret of Reba's fellatio of Felix.

Joe almost whispers, "What did Reeb say happened?"

Junior's Adam's apple yo-yos in his throat. "That she was sitting in Reverend Felix's car with a bad headache from working on the church books . . . Mama says he was just massaging her head and shoulders to ease her pain. Then you come up on 'em . . . blew your top thinking they was doing a horny number. Ma told the truth, didn't she, Papa?"

He pats Junior's arm. "Yeah, son, she told the truth. Guess my eyes told me a lie. How is Reeb's jaw? . . . That was an accident. She got in the way."

"Ma's jaw is healed up swell."

"Junie, I'm sad and sorry as hell 'cause the whole thing happened . . . Does the preacher come 'round, call the house much? . . . Reeb get out much?"

Junior shakes his head. "Naw, Ma stays in, don't even go to church no more and the preacher don't call no more, don't come to the house or nothing."

Joe eye-locks him. "You sure, Junie?"

"Yeah, I'm sure, 'cause I'm home all the time helping Ma clean and stuff, 'cept when I'm in school." Junior glances down on the seat. "Guess I lost my bag of lunch hassling in the alley with that nigger."

Joe puts his lunch pail on Junior's lap. He watches him wolf down the contents. Joe dips his head toward the students streaming back to their afternoon classes. Junior jumps from the truck to the pavement. He says, "Papa, you make better lunches than Ma."

Joe shapes a bitter smile. "I'm a lot better in a lotta ways than Reeb. See you tomorrow, right here."

Junior reaches in to slap palms before he slams the door. Joe watches him sprint down the street and into the school building. He lights a cigarette. He mulls the cruel injustice of how he lost his goddess, Reba.

He pounds his thigh in frustration, tells himself that Reba has no solid love or affection for Felix, that Reba is simply a dazzled victim of the preacher's evil magnetism. And Felix? I'd bet he's getting ready to cut Reeb loose 'cause she's maybe old stuff now in his book, he comforts himself. "Hey! Cheer up!" he exclaims aloud. "Reeb's a lead-pipe cinch to quit him when she eyeballs the cheating scam on him."

The thought of Felix out and himself back in with Reba swoons him for an instant as he fishes his exposé ace-in-the-hole from his coveralls. He opens the dog-eared manila envelope containing the private detective's pictures and reports.

He studies a picture of the preacher at a table in a Hollywood nightclub. The teenage daughter of an elder church deacon gazes into the preacher's eyes with slavish passion in a bar booth. Another: Ebonic Ruta, Reba's bitter rival, is pictured clinging starry eyed to Felix as they leave a Hollywood bistro. Another: The preacher sits sloe eyed with a young black giant and a young white Apollo beneath the huge umbrella of a sidewalk cafe.

He heartens with hope that Reba will wake up, get the strength to cut Felix loose forever as she had her heartthrob, Melvin. He shoves the envelope back into his pocket. But hope drains away as he remembers Reba's years of total infatuation with Felix, the way she defended him the carnaged night he trapped them.

The crackling voice of old man Hoffmeister comes over the truck's shortwave. His heart jumps rhythm. An emergency call to a burst pipe two blocks from the Allen home. He torpedoes the truck away. He waves at acquaintances as he drives for a mile through the sun-swept streets of southwest Los Angeles, with its neat houses and manicured lawns.

He reaches Reba's block. He glances down it as he drives toward his job address two blocks farther south. He sees Reba's new Thunderbird parked in the driveway of the pink stucco house. A moment later, the corner of his eye snares a gold machine in the alley behind the house. His palms drip sweat on the steering wheel as he jerks the truck to a stop. He reverses the truck with a howl of gears. He brakes the truck with a violent slam of foot. He sits in a palsy of rage as he slit-eyes the preacher's El Dorado parked down the alley behind the Allen house.

He shakes uncontrollably as he soft-shoes the truck down the alley to the rear bumper of the El Dorado. It is the preacher's! A neighbor's garage prevents view of the truck from the Allen house. He gets out to the alley floor, stares up at the upstairs master bedroom. The drapes are half drawn! Faint strains of a Bobby Blue Bland ballad waft out on the sunlit air.

The sub-rosa voices of vodka and his cuckolded man-prince rant a savage pitch: That bitch face is freaking off with my wife. In my bed! Fuck probation! Deal the snake justice! Stomp him in half, up the crotch like a wishbone. But the thunderous voice of reason checks his blind fury, persuades him to cunning.

Then, nonchalantly, he gets a Luger from beneath the seat as he remembers that the preacher is a karate black belt who carries a pistol. As he goes casually to the gate, he checks the Luger, rams it into a coveralls pocket. He pats the private detective's evidence in his pocket, thinks perhaps he won't have to kill Felix to break up the romance. But no, he decides, the only certain way is to waste him in a way that will leave him free to resume his life with Reba.

His face is expressionless, his pulse calm now with deadly purpose. He hesitates at the gate, tells himself, This time I'll leave him naked and dead in my bed.

He removes his shoes and eases himself through the gate across the backyard toward the house. He is thankful that Zenobia is not alive to be disgraced to have birthed a killer. Sorrow and guilt reel him as he glances at the tulip bed repository of Elder Joe's ashes. He glances into a back house window. He sees Baptiste, Bible on his chest, mouth agape, sprawled drunkenly asleep on a battered sofa. He curls his lip as he stares at the trampish old man for a moment before he moves on.

He pauses at a trash bin, lifts and fondles a rusted tin trophy he won in his teens as an amateur heavyweight boxing champion. A pair of blue jays chatter recognition as he moves beneath their house in a weeping willow tree. A sentimental lump clogs his throat as he pauses to retrieve a battered doll from the dust. He gazes at it for a long moment. He remembers Sadie's ecstatic squeal two Christmases ago when she unwrapped it. He tenderly places the doll on the teeter-totter. He glances at the tiny slab of black marble above the grave of Susie, deceased for several years.

He retrieves from the dust his and Junior's favorite fishing poles. He leans the poles against the side of the house beneath a kitchen window. He turns, stares bleakly for a moment at the weather-blistered carcass of Delphine's Ford gift. Then he checks to find all the kitchen windows locked. He goes to the side of the house and removes louver panes of glass from a window. He climbs into the living room.

He pauses stock-still in the familiar atmosphere. The house odors, the atom-deep pain and sense of intangible treasures threatened by Felix jackhammer his temples, make him vibrate with the compulsion to execute his tormentor.

He moves past the gaudy clutter of Reba-selected modern furniture and Zenobia's carved horsehair couch. The heady aroma of Reba's Creole gumbo filet wafts from the kitchen as he moves with the stealth of his Masai warrior bloodline across the living room blue pile carpet toward the hallway that leads to the staircase.

He halts, startled by the feral-faced stranger reflected in the mirror over the fireplace. Curiously, alternately now, he watches himself, feels himself the avenging subject of a documentary movie camera. He soundlessly opens a closet door at the foot of the stairs. Reba's dress-up gowns and furs coruscate like perfumed swatches of rainbow.

He stands and gazes up the spiral staircase. He struggles to turn back, to awaken from the nightmare. The sorcerous sun beams cathedral-soft light through a stained glass staircase window on his tortured face, softens it, gives it the beatific aspect of

an ugly saint. He cocks his pug-ugly head. His maroon eyes os-
cillate in the manner of a killer watchdog as he hears the dulcet
lyrics of Reba's voice.

He stiffens, thinks he hears a noise in the kitchen, strains his
ears to confirm. Decides he hadn't. The erotic drumroll of the
preacher's mellifluous baritone catapults him up the staircase
carpet on the balls of his stockinged feet. Bombs of rage concuss
his brain as he swelters in his straitjacket of hate, bleeds flaming
sweat.

Baptiste, having awakened with hunger pangs and come to
the front house kitchen, moves from the kitchen to the foot of
the stairs. He blinks, not sure in his alcoholic haze that he had
really seen a flash of monstrous stockinged feet on the stairway.
He tiptoes up the stairs.

Joe glides down the hallway. He stops and presses his ear
against the door of the master bedroom. He hears the sound of
the shower rain beneath their carnival of joyful grope. He draws
the Luger as he inches the door open.

Baptiste reaches the second-floor landing and peeps down the
hallway. Instantly sobered, he sags against the wall aghast as he
sees Joe enter and shut the bedroom door behind him. Baptiste
turns and creeps down the stairs. He flees the house to his back
house telephone. He excitedly makes a "man with a gun!" call to
the police.

Joe stands inside the bedroom door for a long moment watching their nude yellow bodies soaping and groping each other
through the frosted glass of the shower door. He must defang the
preacher, he thinks. He moves to search the preacher's clothes,
hanging on a chair beside the turned-back canopied bed, lush
and sexy with fresh pink silk sheets. He snuffles his nose against
the silk. She's perfumed and talced the bed! He carefully searches
the floor, the bed area, and between the mattresses for a gun.

He rips the telephone cord loose at the baseboard box before
he conceals himself behind velvet wine-colored drapes across a
walk-in closet. He peers at them through a slit as they emerge from
the shower. While they are toweling each other off, he sees them

sucking and licking each other. He raises the Luger and draws a bead between the preacher's sultry eyes. But no, he might hit Reba, the mystical snake's innocent victim, he tells himself. Besides, he must stick to his plan. He lowers the gun.

He thinks, with painful envy, of his own misshapen and uncircumcised organ as he sees Reba heft and kiss the preacher's sleek circumcised dick head. The preacher scoops Reba up into his arms, tongues her ear as he carries her to the bed. She squeals when he hurls her onto it. Felix dives onto the bed, licks his way from her toe tips to her chest. Joe draws a bead on the back of the preacher's breast-suckling head. His maverick finger caresses the trigger. Prematurely.

Joe watches the preacher work his fingers gently and deeply into Reba. He extracts his glossy fingers, sucks them ravenously. Reba giggles, sucks his tongue with such force that he whimpers. She goes down to deep-throat him for a long moment before she falls back on the bed supine. He tongue-flicks a trail across Reba's belly down toward her heaving crotch.

She pushes his head off trail and moans, "I want you inside me . . . all of you. Now!"

He haunches over her with a rigid weapon. Reba moans impatience as she holds her knees against her bosom, thighs atremble to receive him. Joe strains his ears to hear the preacher cooing into Reba's ear. He thinks it sounds like the sissy drivel of that poet, Gibran, that Reba goes ape for.

Joe stares at the preacher stroking into Reba. He dances a silent hot cha-cha of rage on the closet floor. For an instant, like Elder Joe before him, he lusts for the Epicurean orgasm. Murder. Through the lens of hurt and madness, he sees them in red soft focus, in slow-motion grunt and groan action.

Reba shouts, "Fuck me! Fuck me, pretty daddy!"

He remembers the preacher's chop on the chin that nearly decked him outside the parsonage. He tells himself to wait for Reba to bleed the snake of his lightning karate venom. Then he'll be easy to stomp into a bloody mush, he thinks. I'll cinch kill him slowed down. I'll let him bung me up enough to prove at the coroner's quiz that I beat a naked black belt in my wife's bedroom. This time Reeb will help the bear, me, he thinks, after I lay the private eye documents on her. He smiles at the perfection of his plan.

Joe struggles against the impulse to blow them both away when they bellow ecstasy as they climax. Together. They lie locked together, panting. In a lance of sun their golden bodies are sparkled by crystal gems of sweat. Reba's auburn glory gleams like a cache of Aztec copper.

Joe starts to step out of the closet, doesn't. He stares mesmerized as Reba's wizard of woo performs his postcoitus wrap-up.

Felix's lips feather-stroke Reba's lacy eyelashes. He croons baby talk, "Da Da's star eyes?"

"Yes, darling! Oh yes!" Reba exclaims.

His teeth gently nip her tip-tilted nose. "Da Da's magnificent doll nose?"

"Yes!" she gasps.

He sucks her cupid-bow lips. "Da Da's confection mouth?"

"Oooeee! Yeah!"

He swoops to suck and teeth-rake her nipples, rose tipped. He tongue-flogs her mound of Venus. "You're so fucking marvelous, such a gorgeous cunt you have!"

"It's yours, Daddy Good Dick!" she whispers rapturously.

He moans, "I love you!" Then prophetically, "I'd die for you! Oooh!" he exclaims, "You sweet bitch Madonna." Then he tongues the backs of her satiny knees.

Joe winces in the closet to see Reba's face deform with passion. She whines as Felix cannibalizes her feet with lips and teeth.

She moans, "Felix, you gotta fuck your baby again."

The preacher moves to haunch over Reba with his reinflated weapon ready to encore. Poor Reba, how could she stand off that freakish devil, Joe thinks.

Joe springs from the closet with a hoarse cry. "No you don't! You bitch-faced sonuvabitch, unass my wife!"

They stare at him in total shock as he moves to the bed and points the Luger at them. The preacher rolls away toward the rim of the bed as if to take to his feet.

Joe savagely whispers, "Go on, cocksucker, move another inch so I can blow you away."

The preacher collapses on his back, eyes wild, chest heaving. Reba scoots up to a sitting position on the bed. Her lips work soundlessly as her voice fails. A distant chorus of police sirens keens feebly in the silence.

Joe seats himself on the chair four feet from the preacher. He extracts the manila envelope and throws it into Reba's lap. She stares at it with a puzzled frown.

The preacher says softly, "Look, Brother Allen, these things happen. It isn't really the sordid thing it appears to be. We love each other. We plan to be married after Reba's divorce from you is—"

Joe leans with a ferocious scowl and levels the Luger at the preacher's head. The preacher gulps.

Joe growls, "Shut up, you conning faggot! You ain't got no more chance or time to marry nobody. I'm gonna kill you! Reeb, dig that scam about this snake."

Reba picks up the envelope and pulls out the contents.

The preacher glances at it apprehensively and mumbles, "Joe Allen, you can't kill me and not go to the gas chamber. The D.A. and the Mayor are personal friends of mine. And I still happen to be Bishop of the Southwest Conference of Ministers. Put that gun down and I'll prove how much man I am."

Reba's face drains color as she studies the photographs. Joe sees the preacher's muscles tense. He leans and slugs the barrel of the pistol against his kneecap, says, "Relax, sissy. You'll get a shot to prove how bad you are."

Reba glares venomously at the preacher as she shoves the pictures under his eyes. Joe frowns mild concern at the now strong wail of sirens.

Reba's outrage quivers her as the preacher takes the pictures. Just a flicker of guilt touches his face before he tosses them aside. He says blandly, "Oh, Reba darling, can't you see he has obviously framed me with a double?"

The preacher tries to lay a placating hand on her thigh. She claws furrows of blood on his hand. The preacher stares at the wound with mouth agape.

She shrieks as she punches and claws at his head, his chest, his crotch. "It's you, Felix! You low-life cheating bastard! I'll kill you myself!"

Joe leans back with a wide grin as he watches the preacher cringe and cover up from her attack. He pleads, "Bunny love, please! Please give me a chance to explain."

A couple of the pictures fall to the carpet in the fray. For an instant, Joe's eyes leave the preacher as he bends to retrieve them. In that instant, the preacher snatches an automatic from the tie-back ruffles of the bed's canopy.

Joe hears Reba scream. He glances up into the yawning hole of the gun pointed at the center of his forehead. He hears the deafening boom, sees the orange blossoms of fire as he flips his head down and away a mini-second in time. He feels the pain of a thousand toothaches as the volley of white-hot bullets rips through his cheek and gums.

He leaps towards the bed, grabs the preacher's gun hand, falls between the preacher's spread-eagled legs, smothers the preacher's flailing body like a ponderous lover copulating. His jaw agony, the odor of their love juices gag him, rev up his rage to maniacal peak. He shoves the snout of the Luger up the preacher's rectum. He squeezes the trigger. Felix trembles and surrenders life with a soft sigh.

Joe struggles off the bed to his feet, clutching the Luger. He stares, awed at the steady splash of scarlet on his blood-soaked coveralls. He cocks his head, listens to an alarming rising racket on the stairway. Curious, he stumbles toward the door. He opens it, sees a mob of cops double-timing toward him. He shapes a grotesque crimsoned grin, holds out the gun like a naughty child surrendering contraband.

He burbles through a blood-glutted mouth, "Officers, I'm Big Joe Allen . . . caught my wife and Felix the preacher screwing . . . He shot me! . . . had to kill him!"

The police halt. "Drop that gun!" the leader cop shouts.

Joe stares into the cop's face. Long-term hatred glues the gun to Joe's hand as he waggles it in the face of the leader cop as he struggles to drop it. The cop fires several rapid pistol rounds into Joe's lower torso. Joe reels, feels, as oblivion looms, that killer bees have stung him, poisoned him woozy and weak. Joe crashes to his knees, crawls back into the bedroom screaming, "Reeb! Reeb! Tell these crazy rollers what happened! Tell 'em, Reeb!"

The black chasm sprouts jaws and devours him.

Sixteen

Convict Joe Allen half awakens. He bolts upright at the climax of a frequent nightmare. He trembles on his sweat-drenched upper bunk in a cell on a lifers' tier in state prison. His teeth bare in a black leopard snarl as he recoils from a guard's firebomb flashlight exploding through the bars into his eyes.

"Reeb! Tell these crazy rollers what happened!" he shrieks.

The elderly hack's white harlequin face, framed by his metallic braided uniform cap, glows eerily in the macabre light of his flashlight. Still not fully awake, Joe has the delusion that a psychotic cop is brandishing a flamethrower.

"Hey there, Big Joe! Wake up!" the hack commands. "You're giving the cell house the weemies with that hollering in your sleep."

The hack lowers the flashlight. Joe rubs his eyes with the heels of his palms. He shivers as he mumbles, "I'm awake now, Mister Balansky . . . had a bitch of a nightmare."

The hack says, "Sounded like the same kind you been having for years."

Joe sighs. "Yeah, the lousy preacher kind."

The hack stoops to peer at Joe's snoring cellmate on the bottom bunk. He clucks and shakes his head. "All that racket you made but Old Percy snoozes on like he's in the Fairmont's Presidential Suite."

The hack moves away down the tier on his rounds of the darkened cell house. Joe lights a cigarette. The firefly tip is tremulous in the shadow-haunted gloom of the cell. He feels the roil of diarrhea. He swings off the bunk to the stone floor with astonishing grace. The crushed bridge of his flared nose and broad face are measled with cop-inflicted scars.

He has a cobweb of fine wrinkles around his eyes and on his forehead. He also has a white stubble on his now jowly face. But he has kept his fortress of muscles taut. His two-fifty weight is at free-world level. This through rigorous exercise and training as the prison's heavyweight boxing champ. He is also straw boss to the civilian supervisor of the prison's sports program.

He pulls down his scratchy cotton shorts and seats himself on the icy throne of the john. His shaved bullethead shines dully in the anemic light. He watches a humpbacked rat on the tier pause, rear on hind legs, fix bright malevolent eyes on him. Then the rubber-soled thud of the hack's feet on the tier above and his monstrous shadow on the cell house wall spook the rodent convict away.

A sleeping triple murderer of poker flimflammers revisits his orgy of blood with ear-rending screeches of rage. Epidemic farting, monologues of profanity, roaring of flushing toilets, and bellowed expectorating resonate the cell house as the kitchen cons arise early to set up breakfast.

Joe watches infant gray fingers of dawn ease through the ancient grime of cell house windows. He stares hypnotically at the sleeping face of his beloved cellmate, his kindred soul of betrayal, misery, and murder. The spade-nosed, cruel-lipped face, even in leathery repose, has a savage cast. The face is a living logo of its long years of caged pain, the madness of its scorched blackness, while the old man was a lost slave child beneath the blowtorch sun in cotton wildernesses. The thick woolly hair fires-light in a laser of dawn like a platinum halo sanctifying a visage of Lucifer.

The cellmate's hands flutter on his chest like panicked bats. His eyes suddenly open and stare into Joe's. They are enormous, shockingly soft ginger-cookie eyes buried in his awful face.

He shapes a ragged grin. "Gimme a puff of that pizen, son."

Joe passes the cigarette to him.

Percy wiggles his nose. "Ain't ya nevuh gonna flush that hole!?"

Joe pushes the button.

Percy struggles up to sit on the side of the bunk. "I'm gonna dreen pee down my leg if ya don't hurry, Joe."

Joe says, "In a minute, Pops. I got the galloping shits."

Percy scowls. "Ya musta been spankin' the preachuh again 'bout Reba's pussy."

Joe nods. "Yeah, sneaked in on me 'round four this morning. For ten years, that bastard is been fucking with me. I gotta find a way to cut him loose!"

Joe cleans himself, punches the button and draws frigid water into the washbasin and sponges off. He gets a pack of cigarettes off his bunk and tosses it on Percy's as he sits on the side of it.

Percy goes to empty his bladder into the john. As he does, he says, "Joe, for seven years in this cell I been ya stand-up friend. I ain't nevuh jived ya, even if it hurt ya and made ya salty . . ."

Joe laughs. "Sure, that's what held me together. Kept me from going back to the nuthouse or icing a screw. Pops, I've told you a zillion times how much I 'preciated it, after I cooled off."

Percy punches the john button. "Well, I got a bone to pick with ya, son, 'fore breakfast."

Joe shrugs. Then as is their habitual custom after washing up, they dress early and quickly in joint gray and make their bunks. They sit on Percy's bottom bunk in the gloom and smoke while waiting for the imminent explosion of wake-up lights. Percy's face is wry and sad as he gazes into the contaminated light of a new zombie day filtering into the steel cage.

Joe takes a note from his shirt pocket, delivered the afternoon before by a hospital runner. By the glow of dim cell house lights he reads its shaky, too neat, almost feminine handwriting for the dozenth time: "Joe, please make sick call in the morning. I have to rap with you. I'll lay a lid of Mexican smoke on you just to show. It's a life or death matter. If you can get past how you feel about me, you can score for two grand in cash. Doc Mel."

Joe rises from the bunk, paces the cell, frowning in deep thought under Percy's glare of disgust.

Percy says, "Let's pick that bone. Tell Old Percy why ya gittin' a hard-on for that faggot's two grand."

"I'm broke as Lazarus, with no B.R. for the free world when I hit it. I gotta think 'bout two grand!" Joe says stoutly as he shreds the note and flushes it down the toilet.

"Aw shit! Ya done flipped and got a yen for a pine box parole 'stead of walkin' through the front gate," Percy taunts as he rises to confront Joe as he turns from the john. "Betcha the Arin Nashun is done put a contract out on that snitchin' nigguh. They gonna hit ya bad ass too if ya butt in . . . 'member they got the joint brass and mosta the hacks backin' 'em 'ginst nigguhs and spics. Do I gotta run down how them Arin peckuhwoods is got even some of the screws leery of gittin' hit on and 'sides, that—"

Joe knocks Percy's hand off his arm. "Lay off, old man, 'cause the reasons you cracked for me not going to rap with Melvin is the reasons I gotta go. You think the paddy that delivered Melvin's kite ain't tipped off them Aryan cocksuckers? I ain't scared of a motherfucker in here, or a slew of 'em if they assholes is pointed to the ground . . . Now, lemme rent your shank for a taste of that grass, reefer freak!"

Percy shrugs. "Ya got it, bad ass," he snorts as he starts to slip out a six-inch shiv fashioned from a file and honed to razor sharpness from the hollow of a makeshift leather scabbard sewn onto the underside of the heavy leather belt behind his spine.

"I ain't got no cool blade stash. Gimme your belt and take mine," Joe says as he pulls his off to exchange for Percy's armed belt.

Suddenly the strident clang of the wake-up bell, accompanied by a blast of lights, shocks the cell house to full bedlam life. Shortly, the bars above the cells slide away and the cons step out onto the tiers and file from the cell house for breakfast in one of the mess halls.

Nude Doc Melvin, wolf mother queen of the joint, relaxes in his cozy hospital quarters. He smokes the day's first reefer, reclines on a candy-striped satin sofa after a breakfast of strawberries and waffles. He exhales a chestload of acrid smoke, kisses the parted lips of his naked roommate-orderly, Lucy, a Lilliputian flame-mopped near double for the slender and zany comedienne. Except that his curves are more "wow," his violet eyes more sultry, haunting his rose petal face from lacy-lashed shadows.

Melvin gnaws Lucy's nipple as he gives him a draw on the pot stick. Lucy whines, loops a girlish arm about the long yellow neck of his lover. Lucy grinds his top-trophy buns against Melvin's hirsute lap as their extended tongues duel furiously for a long bit.

"I'm gonna miss the piss out of you, Daddy Doc," lisps the former Hollywood "chicken" and convicted burglar.

"Not for long, Honey Meat. Trust Daddy's long bread and boss connections. You'll be hitting the bricks right after your parole hearing sixty days away." Melvin pauses to suck on the pot stick, which sparkles his hazel eyes in his gaunt face. "Then baby, it's me and you in our Beverly Hills castle living happily ever after."

Lucy chews his bottom lip, runs fingers through Melvin's silky mop of white hair in the heavy silence.

Fear flickers Lucy's face. "Sounds fabulous. But sixty days is gonna be a bitch-kitty long time with my old ma—uh, ex–old man and his Nazis out to ice me."

"Lucy, I won't let them! The baddest con in the joint is coming to see me this morning to arrange for your protection," Melvin croons into Lucy's delicate ear.

"Kong!?" Lucy exclaims.

Melvin nods. "But never let him hear you call him that," he warns.

Lucy pouts his fragile mouth. "I'm still scared! Right now there could be one of them with the swampers or who knows, planning to hit us. I—"

Melvin bear-hugs him. "You'll be transferred only two days after tomorrow, Monday, to the gym right under Joe's wing after we make our deal this morning. How about that, baby?"

Lucy says, "That's great!" as he scoots off Melvin's lap to his knees between Melvin's legs, sleeked and firmed by years of ruthless diet and conditioning on the basketball court.

Their swap-out sucking of each other is interrupted five minutes later by the chuck wagon with its rubber tires rumbling off the elevator from the first-floor hospital kitchen.

They cling together, deep-kiss before they disengage to speed-dress in white shoes and snowy starched-linen uniforms. Melvin stands behind Lucy, squeezing his bottom as he brush-flogs his red shoulder-length mane before a mirror in his bunk cubicle in a corner of Melvin's large one-room kitchenette/cell.

Melvin strolls away to pour a glass of papaya juice from a six-foot gold refrigerator stocked with health foods. Then he flops down in a leather easy chair to get the early morning news on TV. Lucy comes to glance occasionally at the screen as he quickly makes the bed, tongue-brushes Melvin's mouth before he sways from the love nest to hurry down the corridor to dispense morning medication to the thirty-odd inmates on the ward.

Melvin is startled by the jangle of the phone on a table at his elbow. He picks up to the sonorous voice of the prison switchboard operator, who connects him with the hungover slur of his boss and benefactor, elderly Doctor Miliken, the prison's chief medical official. "Good morning, Mel. But since I'm deprived of it by you know what I won't be in until noon."

Melvin laughs. "Good morning. I can dig it, Doc. Relax, I've got the snake pit covered."

"Thank you, friend!" the doctor exclaims feebly before they hang up.

Melvin rises from the chair, goes to stare out a lace-curtained, steel-barred window at serpentine lines of gray-clad cons crawling across the yard toward their work buildings. Other sparse lines of sick call cons, accompanied by blue-clad guards, file out of cell houses toward the hospital.

He stiffens as he hears the uneven rubber-soled gait of Sweeney, the racist and treacherous night guard, slap the parquet floor in the corridor outside his room on his way to the elevator. Melvin watches him scuttle to the yard below dragging his right leg, his right hip maimed by an iron pipe wielded by a Black Muslim before he and other members of a goon squad had beaten the con to death several years before.

He waves at elfish Krute, the elderly closet fag warden, dapper in taupe moleskin suit, as he cuts roguish blue eyes up at Melvin before he strides into the administration building with supermasculine gusto.

Melvin smiles as he remembers how he won his prison power base through bribes and nude freakouts with the warden behind his locked office door when he was the warden's runner at the start of his bit. Up until his emergency transfer to the hospital several years before, to assist alcohol-hobbled Miliken with a rising glut of inmate patients, he remembers as he stares at Joe Allen entering the hospital behind a long line of cons.

Melvin sticks a glassine bag of grass and a sheaf of C-notes into his socks. He goes to the examination room across the corridor lined with sick call cons on benches. He examines throats, rectums, legs, arms, teeth. He passes out cough syrup, pills, salves, and psycho placebos until he reaches Joe, purposely last in line. He listens to a stethoscope pressed against Joe's naked chest under the gimlet eyes of a hack on a bench across the hall.

"How's Reba and the family, Big Joe?" Melvin says pleasantly, only to regret the inquiry an instant later when Joe's heartbeat bombs in his ear.

"Lissen, Melvin, don't never let Reba come outta your jib. Get to your business point, nigguh!" Joe intones in a raspy whisper.

"All right, Joe, be cool and get in the buff for a complete examination to cover our rap," Melvin says softly with an amused smile and mischievous eyes.

Joe strips off nude with a wary scowl, goes to lie prone on the steel table. Melvin loops a blood pressure sleeve about his left arm.

"I have a secret to share with you, Joe. I'm going out of here Monday coming on a special parole," Melvin says as he studies the gauge reading. "My attorneys arranged it at a private session of the Adult Authority Board. I received the news by telephone yesterday."

"Melvin, you gotta be dreaming unless you done copped a miracle past the head D.A. in L.A. that's been nixing your parole every time you went to bat, along with the kind folks of that white man you wasted," Joe says doubtfully.

Melvin grins. "No dream, Joe; no miracle either. Chuck Haggar's only survivors, his wife and sons, were killed several months ago in a car crash on Pacific Coast Highway. My D.A. nemesis retired a year ago to France. Long bread and lawyers with political muscle finished turning the release trick for me, Joe."

Joe says, "You a lucky nigguh, Melvin . . . Now, 'bout that bread you cracked in your kite?"

"The two grand is your fee for guarding Lucy against head Nazi Stregner and his gang for sixty days. And especially against rape!" Melvin says as he probes Joe's scrotum with jabs of his manicured fingertips.

Then he jabs Joe's slab of meat. He seizes and squeezes his bullish testes. Joe cringes, drums fists against his chest. A round-ball buff, Melvin shapes a bitchy smile. He titters at the thrilly imagery of Reba's pink-rimmed hoop under the slam dunks of the hammer-headed stuffer.

Joe punches his hand away, growls, "I'm gonna beat all the bitch outta you, nigguh, if you touch my swipe again . . . Now lissen, we ain't got no deal if I gotta get transferred up here in all these germs to look out for that fairy."

Melvin says, "I'll arrange to have Lucy transferred to the gym and to your cell house tier Monday, no later than Tuesday. Deal!?"

Joe gets to his feet. As he starts to dress he says, "It's a deal for three grand, Melvin."

"Three grand!" Melvin exclaims.

"Yeah, that's what I cracked. I go to the Board myself in sixty days. I could make them streets by Christmas. I ain't gonna take the risk of icing a Nazi guarding that punk for less'n three grand. Deal!?" Joe says as he buttons his shirt.

Melvin extends his hand. "It's a deal."

They step out of eyeshot of the hall hack momentarily for Joe to conceal his payoff grass and cash in his socks.

As they walk toward the door Joe says, "Melvin, we ain't never been nothin' 'cept cat and dog with one another from way back . . ." Joe pauses at the doorway, looks into Melvin's eyes as he rumbles in a near whisper. ". . . but like I was 'bout to say, you wasted them people and then come up a winner and still alive after fifteen years in the white folks' cold-blooded joint . . . Well, I uh . . . wanta say, since you a brother and just a nigguh like me even with them big bucks, I gotta congratulate you, Melvin, and wish you stone-good luck out in them streets."

Melvin's green agate orbs mist as they shake hands.

"Joe, that was nice to hear . . . from you. Thank you . . ." He pauses, sets up to needle with a perverse twinkle of his eyes. "Joe, in appreciation I want to do something for you out there."

Joe shakes his head. "Naw, Melvin, thanks. I'm hittin' the bricks myself 'fore long."

"Oh, come on, Joe, there has to be something . . . Perhaps, with your permission, I could take roses and cheer, and of course any message of yours, to Reba," Melvin says just before he recoils from Joe's mock-furious face.

Joe steps back, hurls a lights-out right hook that he pulls just short of Melvin's jaw. He grins. "Melvin, I know you glad that hook was hip you was just jivin' 'bout Reeb."

"Oh yeah!" Melvin exclaims as he saucers his eyes the way his favorite comedian does when using the line.

They step out into the liver-spotted face of the day hack, alerted off his corridor bench by Joe's right-hook byplay.

"C'mon, Big Joe, and get your sick call pass stamped," the hack says over his starved shoulders as he turns away for his desk near the elevator with his shiny blue serge uniform flapping on his emaciated frame.

As Joe splits off from Melvin to follow, a corner of his eye snares the harsh face of a white con peering into the corridor through a glass window on the ward door. The bulldog face nearly deposits recognition in Joe's memory bank before it ducks from view. Joe follows Melvin past a barrage of mops swung by convict swampers to the ward door across the corridor. As Melvin opens it, Joe sees the dwarfish young peeper leap into his bed at the middle of the ward, grab up a magazine, and pretend to be utterly engrossed in its pages.

"Say, Melvin, who is that half-pint con with the magazine?" Joe asks to halt Melvin.

"He's fish, fresh out of quarantine . . . a transfer from Atascadero. He came in from the print shop yesterday or the day before with intestinal flu. Why?" Melvin says as he stares at the con.

"He vibes me bogus. I almost made his ugly mug a minute ago spying through the glass," Joe says as he rummages his memory.

Melvin laughs. "Him a hit man! Shit, I can handle that skinny punk if he gets down wrong. Besides, he's been searched, even his rectum. But Lucy and I will watch him closely."

"Even while you sleepin', Melvin?" Joe says as he turns to go down the corridor to the day hack's desk.

Melvin follows for several paces, stage-whispers from the side of his mouth, "No need to, Joe. The ward is locked at night and only I have the key. Doc Miliken's rule. Even Sweeney, the screw, has to wake me up in an emergency."

Joe nods, eyes straight ahead locked on the watching hack, as he goes to get his pass time stamped for passage back to his boxing coach duties in the gym.

That early evening, after lockup and the count, Joe and Percy throw a grass party. Each alternately posts himself at the cell bars, with a sliver of mirror, to monitor the tier. This to alert the smoker to guard rounds while he repeatedly flushes the john to suck away the smoke as he exhales it into the open top of a newspaper cone covering the john hole.

Spent, after a gut-tickling roundelay of free-world vignettes and dirty jokes, they luxuriate on their bunks in the rose-glowed transport of the high-grade pot when the cell house lights extinguish at ten. Joe, on his top bunk, feels a rhythmic vibration from Percy's bunk.

"How you feelin', Pops?" Joe whispers.

"Like a lucky lollipop gittin' sucked off by a Chinese doll in Red Joyce's 'ho house 'til ya snatched me back offa them streets . . . Now please, nigguh, dummy up!"

Joe chuckles, closes his eyes to an instant vision of Reba's magnified sex snare as faithful Lady Five Fingers strokes into action.

Just before dawn, Sweeney, the hospital night hack and racist ally of the prison's Nazi mob, smiles as an amber light flashes from ward bed nineteen on a board beside his desk. He gets to his feet, dragging his crippled right leg. He goes to carefully open Melvin's kitchenette door. Sweeney eases across the room. He goes around a hand-painted silk screen, stares at the sleeping couple embraced on the bed.

Melvin's face is serene. He is unaware that mere hours before several thousand of Chuck Haggar's outraged VFW buddies, tipped off to Melvin's imminent release, had forced an emergency meeting of the parole board to rescind Melvin's parole, "for future consideration" against the livid opposition of Melvin's brace of big buck fixers.

Too bad about that fucking nigger-loving kid, Sweeney thinks, as he stares at Lucy's face on Melvin's chest. But further remorse is routed an instant later as he reminds himself that he has been prepaid five bills and the goodwill of the feared Nazi cons to play his role in the hit scenario.

After an eye-sweep of countertops he takes the ward key from the pocket of Melvin's trousers on the foot of the bed. His giant frame quivers with excitement as he scuttles from the kitchenette to the ward door. He recoils, startled by the fiery blue eyes of the grinning assassin staring ghoulishly at him through the darkened door glass. Sweeney averts his eyes as he keys open the spring lock, turns quickly away from the apparition to replace the key in Melvin's trouser pocket. Then he goes to the john at the end of the corridor.

The hit con stuffs a wad of toilet tissue against the lock to jam it. He slips off his gown before he steps out into the corridor. A razor-sharp dagger, prestashed by a Nazi electrician in the ward two days before, gleams wickedly in his rubber-gloved fist as he darts down the corridor to Melvin's door.

He steps inside, shuts the door. He pads his bare feet to bedside. He locks eyes, for an instant, with young Saul and Mai Ling Sternberg smiling warmly at him from a wedding picture on a bedside nightstand. Predawn light filters through the peach window curtains. It softens the planes of Melvin's hard con face, magically lifts it to the dazzling comeliness that lubricated slews of black ghetto foxes long ago.

The hitter leans in close to the bed. He shakes in a psycho frenzy of excitement and hatred as he stabs the dagger to the hilt into Lucy's ear. Lucy shivers. He hammers the blade handle horizontally with the heel of his hand as Lucy convulses, gouts brain blood, dies on Melvin's chest.

Melvin stirs as the killer jerks the dagger from Lucy's butchered brain. Melvin's big hazel eyes flash open. He throws up a defensive palm too late to parry the violent plunge of the dagger into an eye socket. Melvin dies with a mighty sigh that spews the killer with blood.

He slashes his victims' throats from earlobe to earlobe, mincemeats Melvin's crotch before he dashes away past the ward door to the swampers' mop and broom closet door. He enters it, wipes the blade on a hanging mop head. He throws the blade and bloody rubber gloves behind bottles of cleaning agents on a shelf. He hastily scrubs his blood-splattered body and hair at a sink with cleaning rags and strong detergent before he steps out into the corridor. He gives Sweeney, emerging from the john, the A-OK sign with a looped index finger before he enters the ward and removes the wad of paper that lets the door lock behind him.

He slips into his gown. As he goes to his bed, he vainly eye-sweeps the beds for a wakeful con in the bleak light of breaking dawn. He climbs into his bunk, lights a cigarette. Assassin rapture trembles him as he relives, gloats over the awful artistry of the murders. He grins, certain that he will not be among the suspect thirty-odd swampers, typists, and other hospital workers dormed in the building after the corpses are discovered by Sweeney just before he goes off shift.

Leaving the john, Sweeney pauses at the kitchenette door on his way to his desk for a slug of nerve-therapy whiskey. But morbid curiosity forces him to enter the door, go gingerly to peer around the silk screen at the horror scene. He retches with a bellow as he flees the grisly chamber for whiskey tranquilizer.

Within the hour, the prison's wake-up whistle shrills. An instant later, lights blast on in Joe's cell house. He sleepily rises from his bunk to sit on the icy porcelain throne.

At that instant, in a four-man cell on the all-white fourth-floor D tier above, Kurt Stregner, Aryan commander, sits in shorts on the side of his bunk. He stares into a square of mirror as he squeezes a blackhead on his ruddy, classic Nordic countenance. Painted bust portraits of his idols, Nazi bigwigs from Hitler to archfiend Himmler, scowl from the walls. His trio of general staff stare from their bunks at the cell door as a guard's key rasps in cell locks on their tier.

Stregner leaps off his bunk to the cell door as a grizzled guard unlocks the cell, pauses, hisses, "The both of 'em!" before he moves away.

"Shit yeah! Got them bastards!" Stregner and his cellmates shout as they stomp the cell floor.

Their revelry triggers a guttural chant of the word from other cells on the tier housing sect members.

On C tier below, a middle-aged black guard who is a Manual Arts High School acquaintance of Joe and Melvin's unlocks Joe's cell. He pauses, dips his head up toward the din from the tier above. "Listen to the cocksuckers celebrating," he whispers hoarsely.

Joe's belly aches with the answer even as he exclaims, "What!?"

The sad-eyed guard says softly, "Melvin and Lucy got cut to pieces this morning."

Joe goes to the bars. "Who!?" he exclaims with wild bright eyes. "Who, Jimmy!?"

The guard shrugs. "Coulda been anyone of close to thirty hospital cons. Nobody finks in here and lives . . . so it's just another prison case to mildew in the unsolved files. Poor Melvin," the hack says before he turns away to unlock the next cell.

"I'm gonna deal justice to that Stregner bastard for Brother Melvin!" Joe venomously whispers as he leans close to Percy seated on the side of the bunk.

"Nigguh, git outta my face talkin' that suckuh shit and ya ain't got but two months 'fore ya parole shot. Ya scored three gran', Sweet Gravy! Lucky fool, ya cain't owe no dead fag nothin'!" Percy whispers savagely as he rises to brush past Joe to take his turn on the throne.

Joe lets himself down on the side of Percy's bunk. He lights two cigarettes, leans and passes one to Percy. The old man inhales as he glares at him.

Joe rises to pace the floor. "Pops, I ain't stupid. Maybe you right. I don't owe Melvin nothin', since he chumped off his life for some fairy hole and also 'cause he ain't in no shape, croaked, to care 'bout or 'preciate me layin' revenge on Stregner. Ain't no doubt, that's stone logical. But Pops, I ain't gonna let that Aryan cocksucker slide after crossin' a nigguh I knowed into the grave and then cheer out loud, knowin' Big Joe Allen, a nigguh, is listenin'. 'Sides, me and Melvin wasn't no enemies when they hit him. No, Pops, I gotta make that fuckin' Stregner and his hit midget shit some bloody turds."

Percy exclaims, "Hit midjut!?"

Joe pauses before Percy, grimly smiles. "Yeah, I dug him eyeballing from the ward. I made his ugly mug like a vision late last night. I saw his pic and read in the *L.A. Times* over a year ago 'bout him almost wastin' one of them L.A. Jewish militants with a sniper rifle."

Percy exclaims, "I 'member his pichur leavin' court, a Arin lookin' jus like a bulldawg."

"That's the dude," Joe says as he goes to sponge off. "He musta picked the lock on the ward door and outfoxed whiskey-head Sweeney, or maybe Sweeney—"

Percy interrupts. "Yeah, Sweeney coulda laid the shiv on the jokuh and looked the othuh way."

They laugh feebly, then wash up and dress in silence.

Minutes later as they wait at the door to step out onto the tier for breakfast, Percy says, "Please, son, don't fuck with them peckuhwoods and blow ya parole shot."

Joe says firmly, "Sorry, Pops, I ain't gonna let 'em slide. I gotta at least cripple one of 'em. But I think I got a way to trick 'em into gettin' down tough on me so's I can harm 'em in self-defense. I'm gonna be pat for 'em the first Sunday it rains and we have cell house rec."

They step out into the moving line of cons on the tier. Joe's line stalls at the cell house door while the last of D tier's cons file slowly through. Giant Kurt Stregner pauses at the door, sneers as he eye-locks Joe.

Joe leans toward him and sets up the trap challenge with a savage whisper. "Motherfucker, for Melvin, I'm gonna run you back up your white 'ho mammy's ass the next time we got rec in the cell house."

Stregner's lupine lips whiten at the corners before he hideously grins. "Hooray! We got a date, maybe sooner, Shine Liver Lips!" he stage-whispers as he moves away through the cell house door.

Two Sundays later, incessant heavy rainfall forces boisterous cell house rec after lunch. The cell doors are open to permit the cons to stroll the tiers and main floor to visit friends and play board games together. Others play sexual games between infrequent rounds of several hacks. The hacks tear themselves away briefly from a television set on the cell house keeper's desk, tuned in to a pro football game they've bet on between themselves.

Fully dressed, Joe lies on his top bunk faking a nap. His face is turned toward the steel wall, his feet point toward the open cell door. His right hand grips three feet of lead pipe as he waits to spring the trap. Percy, shiv armed, lies propped up on his bunk. His face and torso are hidden from tier view by the newspaper he pretends to read as he watches passing traffic on the tier through a slit in the paper.

"Son, I think one of them Arin bastids jus' sashayed by and copped a gander at us," Percy whispers.

Joe chuckles. "They gotta be peeing their pants 'bout now to chastize me."

In his cell above, lifer Kurt Stregner and his trio of Nazi cellmates sit on their bunks chain-smoking as they stare grimly through the open cell door at passing cons on the tier. Kurt fondles a one-shot zip gun in his lap.

The young Nazi scout that Percy made enters the cell twitching excitement, blue eyes radiant. "Kurt, he looks asleep!" the muscular blond exclaims.

"Otto, I'd bet that jigaboo is playing the possum game. That's good!"

Otto's face is puzzled. "Good?"

"Yeah, good. At least for a second or two he'll be a still target for a surprise head shot. He won't have a prayer to make physical contact . . . What about the old darky?" Kurt concludes as he stands.

"He's got his nappy head stuck in the funny papers," Otto replies as he stands.

Frank Klepper, the hospital hit con, enters the cell.

"Klepper, let's go bag the jungle bunny," Kurt says as he rolls the zip gun inside a magazine and steps out on the tier followed by half-pint Klepper and the others.

They go to the rear of their tier, take a back stairway down to Joe's tier. Stregner and Klepper make con small talk as they stroll toward Joe's cell followed by the quartet of backup cons. They pause to peep over the railing near Joe's cell at the hacks clustered about the TV set on the desk.

Stregner turns to scan the tier. He sees it deserted except for his four henchmen casually walking toward him in pairs. They spy into raucous cells they pass from corners of their eyes to protect their rear against attack by any Joe sympathizers who might alert from poker and blackjack to join a fray.

"Klepper, he's tough! He may even be tough enough to attack with just a twenty-two long in his knot. So you gotta charge the cell when I fire to give him a heart shot with your shiv. Then we'll ice Old Percy whether he butts in or not. He's the only con in the cell house nuts enough, and with a reason strong enough, to finger us," Stregner instructs from the side of his mouth as he pushes a potato silencer over the plumbing pipe muzzle of the zip gun.

The pair soft-shoe to the side of the target cell. Stregner inches his head to peer through the bars at Joe still faking a nap on his side. Percy sees nothing through the slit in the funny paper, Stregner's head blocked out by the underside of Joe's bunk. Stregner moves to rest the gun's barrel between bars as he draws a bead on Joe's head.

Percy suddenly spots the gray trouser legs, leans from his bunk to get a full view of Stregner squinting down the gun barrel. Percy shouts, "Joe! He's got a piece!"

Joe pops his eyes open to stare for a mini-instant into the gun barrel before he jerks his head backward toward the rear of the cell. At that instant, Stregner fires a muffled shot that deeply creases Joe between the eyes, half blinds him with a gush of his blood.

Klepper races into bunkside to deliver the shiv coup de grace as Joe scoots his back up against the rear cell wall. He rocks as he paws the blood from his eyes with his left hand. The pipe in his right hand clubs at Klepper, weaving and dodging as he stabs Joe hard in the upper chest.

Percy leans in from his bunk to plunge his shiv upward to the hilt, into Klepper's heart, as Stregner charges into the cell, blue eyes demonic as he slashes at Joe's throat. Klepper, dying on the floor, spurts blood as Percy leans from his bunk, tries vainly to wrench his shiv free of Klepper's chest.

Joe bangs the pipe against the side of Stregner's head. Stregner flees the cell, his head bursting blood. Joe lunges off the bunk in pursuit, slips in blood at the cell door, falls, sprawls on his belly on the tier. He seizes Stregner's ankles, crashing him to the floor of the tier. Joe struggles to his feet, lifts dazed Stregner and hurls him over the railing to the concrete two stories down.

The sharp smash sound of his skull commands the attention of the football fan screws, who dash from the television set up the front stairway for Joe's tier. The cell house keeper rushes to Stregner.

The quartet of backup Nazis swoop on Joe with shivs. They stab him repeatedly in the back and upper torso before he bloodies them and drives them down the tier with a violent pipe assault. Joe collapses into the arms of Percy and several cons as the guards pound onto the tier.

After blood transfusions and a month of patch-up in the prison hospital, and then thirty days in solitary, neither Joe nor Percy were indicted by a grand jury, which ruled the killings defensive. But Joe's parole consideration was deferred for a year. At the end of that year, he makes parole. But now Percy is secretly distraught and envious at the prospect of the imminent release for Christmas of his long-term comrade on their last morning together.

Percy says softly, "Now, the white folks is cuttin' ya loose tomorrow, for Christmas . . . Ya owe 'em the rest of ya life back heah if ya fuck up out there."

Percy pauses to light a cigarette. He exhales a poltergeist of smoke that jailbreaks through the cell bars toward a half-open window.

"Say, son, git on the earie 'cause I'm gonna spiel some bitch phalasphy so's ya can git wise to life and 'hos in them streets."

Joe, at the basin, turns to face him with a serious face as he brushes his teeth. He fakes rapt interest to please the old man in the short time they have together. Percy pounds his fist against the bunk beside him. Joe sits down, starts to speak.

Percy spiels, "Don't say nothin', boy, 'til I finish. Ya ain't but forty-five, son, still a baby. Like Old Percy, ya in heah on a damn fool's hummer. A cunt hummer. Son, for ya survivin' ya gotta git it solid in ya noggin all gash is the same, hairy or bald, tight or loose, and don't make no mattuh if it hangs on a two-buck 'ho inna half-buck flophouse or a sweet stinkin' high and mighty so-called lady on Nob Hill. Alla 'em is 'hos in they pizen pumps. Alla 'em gonna stink like a shit house in China if they don't wash they nasty double-crossin' asses. Gash ain't nothin' but 'looshun inna chump's skull. Lissen, say iffen the ugliest dog they is stashes inna dark room and 'nother, the mos' beautifuless dog they is, sticks out her head and 'vites ya to come in jus' 'fore she ducks 'neath the bed, ya gonna go in and shoot jism in that ugly bitch like a elephant, swearin' ya done scored for the bes' cunt they is."

Percy gets a sliver of mirror from a shoe box at the head of his bunk. Joe sits down beside him on the bunk. Percy makes a monster face in the mirror before he holds it for a moment in front of Joe's face.

Joe glances into the mirror. "What's your point, Pops?"

"My pint is you and me is the ugliest nigguhs ever was. Black or white dogs and alla 'em 'tween, that's hooked up with ugly jokuhs, rich or poor, is dreamin' secret 'bout wrappin' pussy 'round some cute jokuh's dick. Alla 'em is schemin' when they open they legs to hog-tie a suckuh and win a slave. The black dogs dream 'bout pretty nigguhs . . . or peckuhwoods, pretty or ugly.

"That mean mistreatuh I kilt was the prettiest black dog that ever peed 'tween fifty buck slippuhs . . . Mebbe I ain't told ya how I 'scaped the white boss's cotton fields down in 'Sippi . . . come north and built my six-truck gardenin' company . . . give her everything she wanted 'fore she asked for it . . . double-sawbuck bubble wine for breakfast, Russky fish eggs at night. I loved that 'ho's spit and shit. I 'dored that dog like she was a princess lady. I ain't tol' ya what happened that night I . . . ?"

Joe's heard it before but he shakes his head to afford the old man a grim pleasure. "I don't think so, Pops, just that you wasted your wife and a man."

"Well, she's in Hell now wigglin' her ass for the Devil, jugglin' her noggin in her hands . . . caught her with the ugliest peckuhwood in Frisco . . . uglier than me! She was sweet-talkin' him and hollerin' hot whilst he was pumpin' his pink dong up her turd cuttah . . . Ah shit! But I made the muthafuckah twins with my axe 'fore I chopped off her muthafuckin' head . . . and I swear on the Pope's faggot ass, that 'ho's head rolled on the rug and stucked out its tongue and winked at me like she had ran a game, played a dirty joke on me . . . guess the bitch did . . .

"I'm near 'bout ninety . . . been locked up forty-some years . . . I ain't jivin', I mebbe woulda let her slide if she'd been cheatin' with a nigguh, 'speshully a ugly nigguh . . . just couldn't take the peckuhwood after what I'd took down South . . . what I seen my poor mama and pappy take down there. Don't forgit, son, that slut I kilt is the cause I'm here! So's lotsa more cons for sluts. So take a damn fool's advice and don't let Mis Reba dump ya in hot grease agin. Alla the pussy they is ain't worth a secon' in this cage."

Joe says, "But Reba was different, on the square, Pops, before she got sucked into the preacher's trick bag. I don't think she's leery of me or hates me no more. You know how she's sent me food packages and birthday cards for the last three years. Why, I just got a classy Christmas card yesterday . . . unsigned, but I'd bet it was Reba's. 'Sides, I heard her ticker is on the bum. Maybe she and me—"

"Dummy up, boy!" Percy fiercely whispers. "Ain't no names never been on mosta that stuff ya got 'cept ya son's and true-blue Panthuh's 'fore he busted his pump strings and croaked coupla years ago ridin' that chippie. Ya jus' a hurt junkie. Ya thinkin' she's been out there ten years with her pussy itchin' for ya? 'Sides, them game-playin' elephant dick nigguhs out there is likely what's done drug her ass. Ya goin' out there and kill 'nother nigguh?"

Joe says, "Pops, I've changed. If I harm another joker out there about Reba I will 'cause he's mistreating her, not on a pussy basis. Guess this long bit has dried up my jism well . . . don't even care if Reba's love machine throwed a rod."

Percy sneers, "I hear ya but that don't signify she's got no sweet feelin' for ya jus 'cause ya hooked on her pure like she's the Mary Virgin. Next ya gonna git 'ligion, huh?"

Joe frowns. "Shoot, the way God treats nigguhs I wouldn't go to Heaven 'less he dies or gets evicted."

Percy goads, "Let's git back to them 'nonumus kites and goodie boxes. Mebbe ya muckety-muck daughters been sendin' ya that stuff on the Q.T. Why ain't Reba been writin' ya every week, comin' to see ya like ya son? Ya ain't got no win with Reba! If she sent the stuff, it ain't nothin' but a cross. Mebbe ya the onliest slave she can still catch."

Joe stubbornly shakes his head. "Pops, don't bad-mouth her no more. You ain't reading her right. She only made one mistake. The preacher! I've forgave her for that . . . Maybe she's forgave me for her pain and disgrace. I think maybe in her older age she's come 'round to be a smidget like she was before the preacher hooked her. Maybe she ain't even playing 'round. She might even be lonely and needing me with the kids grown. So Pops, I mean it, don't run her down no more. Don't make me chastise your old crazy ass. I ain't denying it's a long shot but I think that we could—"

The old man's eyes narrow in icy contempt as he hawks and spits a gob of phlegm at Joe's feet. His face contorts to a fearsome mask of rage and disgust to cut Joe off. He goes to the basin, furiously splashes water on his face. Joe watches with a stunned expression.

Joe murmurs, "What the hell you salty about, Pops? I gotta gamble a shot with her again. It's my life . . . I gotta try to be with her again! Now dummy up about her! . . . Nigguh, pull for me to be happy, if you my friend."

Percy turns, his eyes mad balloons as he weirdly jiggles his head and grunts derisively. He leans into Joe's face and violently taps a gnarled index finger against his pursed lips. "S-s-s-sh! Suckuh!"

Joe shrugs. "You're full of Reb-time shit on this one, Pops."

Joe rises to dress. Then he rolls up his bedclothes and packs his possessions. Percy perches on the throne; his slitted bright eyes watch Joe as he shapes a chilling smile. Finally he gets off the throne and washes off. For a moment Percy shuts his eyes, cackles obscenely as if watching an interior geek bite off heads. Then he winks compulsively, jiggles his head weirdly as he dresses and makes up his bunk.

Joe remembers that Percy spent ten years in the state asylum at Atascadero after his double-murder axe caper. He shudders, remembering his own horror commitment there for the first three years of his bit after he blew Felix away. So he lies atop his bunk intently watching Percy as he furiously sweeps the floor and jiggles his head in that weird way.

The cell house lights bomb on. Joe glances away from Percy for an instant toward the exploding ribbons of lightbulbs on the tier. A shadow swoops the trapdoor in the corner of his eye. The fingers of his right hand, toying with the twine on a shoe box, reflexively tighten on the twine and jerk the box to his chest as a silver light streaks down.

Joe hears a slash sound, feels the box jounce over his heart. He seizes Percy's wrist, poised for a second strike, in midair. Percy grips a razor-sharp stiletto. Joe crushes and twists the old man's wrist until he squeals with pain and falls to his knees. The shiv clatters to the floor. Joe leaps off the bunk. He bends the shiv into a circle. Then he throttles Percy, shakes him so violently his dentures bounce to the concrete.

Joe harshly whispers into Percy's upturned face. "Ding-a-ling muthafuckah, you so lucky! . . . lucky you my play pops. Why!? Why!? You 'sposed to be my friend."

Joe flings him away against the john. Percy lands on his bottom, chest humping. He gasps, "I'm ya true friend! . . . wanted to save ya from the misery ya headin' for out theah . . ."

The wake-up bell clangs. The harsh clicking of the hacks' keys unlocking the cells on the tiers is like the sound of a colossus banging away at a mammoth rusty typewriter.

Joe helps Percy to his feet. He says, "Crazy grayass, get yourself together. You ain't God!"

A hack pauses to study a slip of paper after he unlocks their cell.

Percy whispers, "Ya shoulda did me a favor, son, and kilt me."

The hack says, "Big One, on your way to breakfast, drop your stuff into the dress-out cell, A-5, on the flag. Return to that cell after breakfast."

Joe nods. The hack moves on.

Joe picks up the fallen dentures and rinses them off at the washbasin before he gives them to Percy. Percy squeezes adhesive on them and pops them back into his mouth.

Convicts start to rumble past the cell as the steel-lock bars above the cells slide back. Joe picks up his gear, starts for the door, turns back, stands at Percy's bunk. Percy is a rigid knot on the side, his face turned toward the cell wall.

Joe says gently, "Pops, I hope you don't mind me saying goodbye to you."

The old man turns slowly. He creaks himself to his feet. He blinks away tears as he extends his bony hand.

As Joe squeezes it in a giant paw Percy says hoarsely, "I was a mule's ass, son. I . . . forgive ya for chastisin' me . . . Look out careful for ya'self. I'm pullin' for ya . . . Didn't ya say her . . . Reba's peepuhs was green?"

Joe's face is puzzled as he nods. They embrace for a long moment before they disengage and Percy flops down on his bunk.

As Joe moves toward the door he says, "Pops, you gonna pass up the Sunday morning coffee cake?"

Percy mumbles, "I ain't hongry this mornin'. I'm makin' sick call. Gonna try to skip the tailor shop today. So long, son."

Joe steps from the cell, smiles back at the old man, who flaps a clawlike hand goodbye. Joe disappears into the line of gray-clad cons slogging down the tier.

Percy clambers off his bunk. He digs feverishly into the bottom of a paper carton for a treasure hidden for seven years from Joe. He excavates a half-century-old goldleaf-framed picture of a ravishingly beautiful and curved high-yellow heart stomper in a sequined chemise dress. He sits on the side of his bunk with the picture atremble on his starved knees. His withered loins sparkle and spasm as his soft ginger-cookie eyes gaze rapturously into the green witch eyes of his beheaded inamorata.

Seventeen

Reba Allen sits tensely in her driveway with dashing twentyish Theodis Grant on the front seat of his white Jaguar. His light tan comely face is twisted with frustration as he gazes at her obdurate profile. She is still uncommonly attractive but her once proud shoulders have been slumped a bit by the long-term ravages of alcohol and general unhappiness.

"But baby, give me one logical reason why you can't be my girl anymore. I love you!" he pleads, then lights a cigarette and puffs furiously under her solemn scrutiny.

She heaves a sigh. "You've just given me the one important reason, Theo—I'm not a girl. I've known all along you've been seeing . . . sleeping around town with girls young enough to be my daughters. That's all right—boys should have lots of girls. I don't need you and, my dear, you certainly don't really need me. I've reached a point in my life where I have to be needed!"

She opens the car door with a sad little smile. He clutches at her. She escapes to the pavement and slams the door shut.

He scrambles across the seat, sticks his head through the open window. "Please, Reba! Don't cut me loose. I need you, baby!"

She shakes her head. "I'm sorry but it's over, Theo . . . Please return my door key."

He pats his pockets. "It's at home. Baby, I'll bring it when I pick up my suit. But we can't quit!"

"We already have," she says. "Goodbye." She touches the back of his hand. "Give up, Theo. It's over." Reba turns and goes up the driveway toward her front door.

She goes through the door, inhales the lush pine fragrance pervading the living room. Elderly Baptiste and his granddaughter Sadie string the last of the glittery ropes of tinsel, hang the final shimmery red, blue, and golden balls on an opulent Christmas tree. They stand back to admire their art in the flare of fireplace flame.

Lean Sadie strolls into the adjoining den with the sensuous grace of the fashion model that she is. She sits in a chair near a front window. She lights a cigarette and watches as steady rain drizzles from the overcast Sunday afternoon sky. Reba goes to the bathroom to shampoo her hair.

Baptiste, dissatisfied, shakes a silky forelock of platinum hair from his bifocaled eyes. Old Crow whiskey staggers him a bit as he continues to rearrange the baubles.

Shortly, Reba returns to the den. She sits in a chair beneath a hair dryer. She sips on a Tom Collins as she cranes her neck to see the tree. Beauty salon owner Belle, the more rounded twin, and newly divorced, sits on a sofa near Reba. She lights a cigarette, sips a bit of Reba's drink. She kisses her mother's cheek as she returns the glass to the table.

She says, "Just five minutes more, Mom."

Belle's baby stirs, opens big liquid eyes, in the rocking horse crib beside her. She pushes the crib into motion. The baby girl shutters her eyes and slips back into slumber. Sadie sees Joe Junior pull the battered La Salle to the curb in front of the house between Belle's new El Dorado and her own Porsche. Belle moves the dryer aside to check Reba's hair.

Sadie, as she starts to rise, exclaims, "Junior just drove up, Mama."

Reba says, "I know—the racket of that La Salle is unmistakable . . . Let him in, Papa."

Baptiste continues his tree fiddling and grunts, "He's got the key you gave him." Then under his breath, "Gonna clean us out one day with that key."

The doorbell rings insistently. Baptiste mutters obscenities as he shuffles to the door. He opens the door, nods and scowls as always at Joe Senior's carbon image. Junior scowls in retaliation as he pushes past him to the den.

Baptiste says to his back, "Even a heathen would speak to his grandfather."

Junior growls over his shoulder. "Not if the heathen's evil-ass grandfather greets him with rocks in his jaw."

Junior enters the den with a toothy smile. He bolts for Reba, arms outflung. "Hi, Mama Sweets! Prettiest mama in the world!"

They hug.

Reba laughs. "Jiver, I hope that compliment is a freebie 'cause I'm broke. Lose your key?"

"No, left it at home." He boogies from Reba to his sisters with sloppy kisses as he vises their faces between his gigantic palms. He sprawls on the sofa beside Belle. He ignores Belle's protestations as he scoops baby Constance from her crib onto his knee. Constance awakens and bawls wildly for an instant before she recognizes him. She rolls her green eyes at him and coos when he kisses her. She falls asleep on his bouncing knee.

Reba says, "How are Dottie and the kids?"

"Great!" Junior exclaims unconvincingly.

Belle swivels the dryer head away to reveal Reba's clean, still luxuriant but gray-riddled mass of auburn glory. The vibrant eyes are slightly dulled, sunken a bit in the finely boned face that is under imminent threat of a double chin. Her glowing skin is not quite as taut as before but the slave-master curves that inflate her orchid peignoir are intact.

Belle expertly begins to style the still damp hair with comb and scissors. Baptiste sips whiskey from a water glass as he stares balefully into the den from a living room chair.

Reba says, "Junior, I'm warning you that I'm not going to give you your family's lovely presents to take to them this year. I'm expecting you to bring them to Christmas dinner this weekend coming to receive their presents."

Junior glances at his watch, lifts Constance tenderly back into her crib. His thick Afro grazes the chandelier as he stands.

He says, "I'm leaving at midnight to pick up Papa at the joint in the morning . . . Which one of you rich folks is gonna loan me the price of two rear tires and two tanks of gas?"

Belle says, "Junior, you'll never make it to San Francisco in that thrashing machine. I can do without my car until Tuesday. Go in it so you can be sure you and Papa will make it back to L.A."

Junior says, "Thanks, Sis, but my driver's license is expired. I don't want to put you against the wall with your insurance company in case some chump hits me or something."

Baptiste grunts and stomps disgustedly toward the kitchen. Sadie gets her purse off the carpet, digs into it.

"The best and safest way, Junior, is to wire Papa money for a plane ticket. What if he breaks your jaw and violates parole at the gate when he sees the raunchy condition of his forever La Salle?" she says as she extends a twenty-dollar bill.

Junior laughs shakily as he hops over and grabs it. Then he screws up his face in terminal anguish. "Sadie, I should slap your jaw about cracking that Papa's nuts!"

Reba says sharply, "Watch it! I don't allow even play gorilla under this roof."

Sadie says, "Ree, Junior won't and hasn't hit me since I split his head open with your big steel skillet when I was ten."

Junior laughs. "You didn't K.O. me. I coulda come back and harmed you 'cept I loved your rotten butt . . . and hey! You cracked a plane ticket for Papa. Wouldn't you dig me picking you up in person if you were hitting the bricks after a ten-year bit? Now somebody lay forty more on me so I can split and get together for the trip."

Reba leans and extracts bills from the drawer of her professional sewing table. Junior takes the bills, stuffs them into his black leather jacket pocket. He pecks cheeks all around and moves toward the front door. He pauses at a rack near the den archway loaded with tagged garments. He fingers a man's stylish light blue leisure suit.

"Damn!" he exclaims. "This is bad! With a little alteration it could fit me." He examines the tag. His eyes sparkle with mischief. "Theodis Grant," he reads. "Mama, ain't that the young post office stud that's been on your case to be his woman?"

Reba smiles. "Some young men think they want to make out with a motherly type with a nickel's worth of looks left. He's just a customer, Junior. Drive carefully on the trip."

Junior opens the door, hesitates. "Mama, can I bring Papa to Christmas dinner?"

Reba sighs, glances at Belle and Sadie. They shake their heads. Reba says, "Maybe . . . I'll let you know."

Junior grins and blows a kiss as he steps through the door. Reba fills her glass to the brim from a decanter of Collins on the sewing table. She drains the glass half empty. Belle, snipping at Reba's locks, frowns at her in the wide makeup mirror on the table. Reba glares back as she lights a cigarette.

"Ree," Belle says softly, "after your last heart a . . . uh, illness, we all were told that alcohol and cigarettes were like poison for you. Please, Ree! We don't want to lose you."

Sadie comes to stand at Reba's side. Reba ignores them and puffs at her cigarette. Baptiste drifts back into the living room with a fresh glass of whiskey. He sits down in a chair and opens his tattered Bible.

Sadie presses her cheek against Reba's as their eyes meet and hold fast in the mirror. Sadie says, "Mama Belle's right on. And God knows you know how much we love you. Mama, I . . . ah, would never try to dictate to you. But it seems clear to me that to let Papa come here Christmas, in your condition, is well, absolutely mad . . . after what he did to us all . . . Papa was a maniac up there." She dips her head toward the bedroom chamber of horror, padlocked and boarded up since that afternoon.

Sadie continues, with heat. "Well, let's face the truth . . . I'll say it! Mama, you just can't logically expect anything except more trouble and grief from any contact with Papa. Mama, he spent three years in a hospital for the criminally insane! Then seven years in a cage!"

Belle says, "Sadie is right, Ree. Can't you see it? Papa loved us, loved you in his own sad way. But don't you see? It was a crazy charade, a bomb that exploded because you never loved Papa. You don't owe Papa anything, darling!"

Reba empties her glass, stares through their faces in the mirror at the specter of long years of secret guilt as she says, "Ladies, no offense, but let me live my life. I'm hip drinking and cigarettes are nudging me into my prepaid real estate at Forest Lawn. But who the hell, except punishment freaks, want to live on this rotten mother forever?"

"Please, Mama!" Sadie exclaims as she rakes fingernails across a sudden rash of hives on her wrist.

Reba takes away Sadie's wrist, touches the welts with her lips. "Baby, I didn't mean to upset you."

Reba leans back and embraces their waists. They stand, their auburn tresses fashionably coiffed with bangs and long bobs. Their beautiful faces are solemn. They look successful, trim, and chic in their navy and black Lillie Anne suits watching their shaky savior.

Reba squeezes them close, closes her eyes, tipsy now, as she passionately muses, "No, it's true, I never loved Joe with a 'C'mon, sock it to me, Sweet Daddy' kind of feeling. But I know now, I loved the security of his ugliness, loved him better, stronger for his manhood, for his honesty, his scars, his bad, crazy nigger toughness . . . and tenderness, loved him because he adored me, worshipped me! . . . and I could trust him! You hear me! I could depend on him! But he couldn't depend on me to be faithful. I should have been patient. I should have cared enough to teach and guide him so he could've filled my sexual needs. He deserved that!"

She catches her breath, wrings her hands in despair before she continues. "In or out of the nuthouse or a cage, I'd bet Joe Allen, right now, is more real man than most of the high-jiving jerks out here . . . He wasn't even a maniac that day upstairs . . . didn't touch me when he caught us . . . He was sane, ladies! Why, Felix could have gotten off with just a whipping if he hadn't panicked . . . Looking back, I've convinced myself Joe Allen was never the villain. I'm the one who crapped in our nest. We all owe Joe our love and respect. Your father will be welcome for Christmas dinner!"

They stare at Reba aghast as she casually pats her hair. "It's beautiful, Belle! Thank you, hon," Reba says as she glances at her watch, stands and kisses their cheeks. "I'm going to get some coffee to perk me up for a long grind on the sewing machine. Want a cup?"

They shake their heads as they turn to gather up the baby and their raincoats.

Reba trills, "See ya, dolls," as she leaves for the kitchen.

They chorus, "Bye, Mom."

The sisters go into the living room and peck Baptiste's cheeks. He follows them to the door, watches them tool their machines away in the rain. He shuts the door and goes to the den. He sits on the sofa, swathed in a white silk robe, a combative expression on his lined but still comely face. His gaunt frame is tense as he sips his whiskey.

Reba returns and sets a coffee cup and saucer on the table-top. She ignores Baptiste as she swings up the sewing machine to the surface, flips on its light. She picks up a pinned garment draped across a chair beside the table, examines it.

Baptiste, irritated, characteristically wobbles his dentures to make a clicking sound that always annoys Reba.

Reba takes a sip of coffee, puts the unfinished garment aside with extravagant deliberation, turns and glares at him. "All right, paragon of fathers, give me your licks."

He leans in. "You're a star natal fool if you let that crazy nigger come to this house. And you're killing yourself drinking and it's not fair to get salty with me for caring about you. God don't love ugly."

She laughs in his face. "Saint Whiskey, I've been salty with you since I was a little girl for not really caring for anything except robbing suckers with crooked cards."

Baptiste takes off his glasses. His voice trembles. "I got my throat cut and risked my life trimming suckers to support you and that strumpet in her grave. Where would you be if I hadn't been a stand-up father?"

She laughs. "Chained to a sewing machine somewhere to keep a roof over my head."

"It's your own fault that you don't have any money left from your mother's inheritance. You brought that string of lazy worthless niggers into this house to support and live in sin with you. You're the big shot boozer who set up the house in every sucker trap in town. Then you blew broke on those Vegas trips and on those clothes, diamonds, and luxury cars for that last low-life pissant parasite. You could've bypassed all your grief if you had heeded when I warned you way back when you hooked up with Felix to quit Joe. There's always a misery backlash when you live like a bitch dog. I want to belt the hide off you when I think about how your notoriety fouled up the twins' chances to be well-married high-class ladies in this community."

Reba ashens. "They own the largest beauty salon on Crenshaw Boulevard. That makes them respected and successful business ladies in this community!"

Baptiste snorts. "I know, they're not on welfare, though after your example it's God's miracle they aren't flipping tricks on Central Avenue. But Belle is divorced from a garbage collector, the best she could do for a husband. Sadie, well, I'll bawl sure as hell if I dwell on the bunch of dressed-up bums who courted her. Like that idiot Pullman porter she just broke up with who gets busted out every payday by craps hustlers. Face it, the twins have been blackballed by all the eligible young black professionals they really deserve."

Reba laughs nervously. "My girls aren't complaining! Shut up about them and Joe!"

Baptiste sneers. "You fool! Go on, let him back into your life. He'll kill you sure for those years of misery. I almost feel sorry for him. God and I are warning you. Don't let Joe Allen back into your life and mine. Hear us!?"

Reba's face is a cold mask of defiance. "And hear me! Joe Allen is welcome to come to this house for Christmas dinner." She turns and jerks up the garment. The machine whirs madly as she stitches.

Baptiste stands shakily, intones icily, "I'm paying my way with my pension check and Social Security to help keep this property that you mortgaged to try to get even in Vegas. It's my house too! I'm going to get a box of shells for my shotgun. I'm going to protect myself. If Joe Allen raises his voice or tries to gorilla us, I'll blow him to pieces."

Baptiste moves past Reba on his way to the kitchen to get a whiskey refill. Reba stops her sewing, loses color, presses a palm against her fluttery chest, gulps for air. Her hands shake as she unscrews a vial of pills. She pops one and chases it with coffee.

Eighteen

*J*oe walks through San Quentin's steel release gate dressed in a well-cut but cheap glen plaid suit tailored by Percy. He pats Melvin's C-notes, stashed by Percy beneath the tailor shop flooring for over a year, in the inside coat pocket. He carries an accumulation of personal effects under his arm in pasteboard cartons. He stands hesitantly, blinks spastically like a Gila monster on the concrete landing.

In the sudden explosion of free-world sun, he glances down at the first step. He balks with pounding ecstasy. His hand shades his eyes like a salute to the dazzling expanse of free-world marvel, the shapes of current-model automobiles that he has only seen on TV and in magazines, parked in live color in the visitors' lot.

He does not spot Junior in the La Salle! Desperately he rescans the chromed jungle. Paranoia slams him. Well, I guess Junior has cut me loose, he thinks. Guess his wife Dottie poisoned him against me. She's afraid to have a murderer under her roof.

He eases a foot down on the first step, in a kind of sneaky assault, perhaps in the manner of a novice high diver fearful on the lip of the board. Then his other foot follows, then with successive attacks his feet take him down the concrete stairs and into the parking lot.

His heart drums. Now it's clear why Junior didn't show. A golden Venus alights from a Pontiac at the far end of the lot. Reba has come to take him home. It is! his mind shouts. It is! Her auburn tresses fire skyrockets in the sun. Her mane flogs her shoulders as she jerks her head in that characteristic way as she turns to lock her car.

It is Reba! Tears of happiness drown his eyes as his feet flail the concrete toward her. Her back is still to him as she fiddles a key into a faulty lock. "Reeb! Reeb!" he groans six feet from her, giant hands reaching, when she turns with a startled, strange face and hurries past him.

He mumbles inanely, "'Scuse me, lady," as he collapses, drained, on a car fender.

Then he hears, "Papa!"

Or does he? Warily he glances about. No illusion this time! He rushes toward Junior, who is sprinting toward him from the La Salle. The colossi collide, embrace as passersby stare to see such monsters cry before they get into the car, which Junior scrambles to the highway for L.A.

Joe tussles with the impulse to criticize Junior for the deplorable condition of the La Salle. But Junior's run-over shoes and struggle-hardened face makes him decide to let him slide.

Joe breaks a long silence. "Junior, you sure it's all right with Dottie that I'm staying a while in your house?"

Junior's face screws up terminal anguish. "Papa, she's fixing your favorite dinner—macaroni and cheese, short ribs, yams, and homemade biscuits. And even when she's eight months gone. And evil! Now, you tell me if you ain't welcome."

"How are my grandkids, and Sadie and Belle?"

Joe smiles. "All are well . . . Evil-ass Baptiste is still around with a gutful of whiskey and rocks in his jaw . . . Everybody is invited to Christmas dinner at Mama's . . . You too, Papa, I'm pretty sure."

Joe cracks his knuckles. "You asked her to let me come, didn't you? She told you she wasn't sure?"

Junior fidgets behind the wheel. "Well . . . yeah . . . but Papa, it's gonna be all right."

Joe lights a cigarette, smashes an irritated gust of smoke against the windshield. "I'm sorry you had to do that, Junie . . . wish you hadn't . . . I want you to know, I didn't leave my balls and pride back in that cage . . ."

Junior laughs. "Who you hunching, Papa, who you hunching?"

Joe says, "The meatpackers put you back to work?"

"Not yet . . . still on welfare. I got lots of company."

"Guess I'm lucky to get a parole gig with old Hoffmeister's son," Joe says as he snuffs out his cigarette.

Joe closes his eyes to secretly find his compass in the frightful chaos of the newly freed. His head aches. It's too soon to try, he decides. The hum of the tires lullaby him to fitful sleep. A pothole lurches the La Salle. Joe opens his eyes with the reflex convict impression that his cell has somehow become mobile. He shakes his head in the frantic manner of a pooch emerging from a dip in a creek.

He says, "Junie, maybe now you can answer the question you sidestepped in your letters and visits. Didn't Reeb send me those unsigned food boxes and cards?"

Junior grins sheepishly. "Yeah, Mama sent the cards, made me promise not to tell. She, Belle, and Sadie took turns sending the packages."

Joe cuffs Junior's shoulder. "I won't spill it. Now look, I'm not uptight or planning to mess in Reeb's personal life, but is she on the hook with some guy in a serious way? Junie, I know everybody needs somebody to keep from being lonely."

Junior shakes his head vigorously. "Nobody, Papa, nobody for several years. She seldom leaves the house. Only her sewing customers visit. Belle and Sadie beg her to let them take her to shows and stuff to take a break from her machine . . . Papa, Mama's ticker is bad . . . and she's drinking something awful. It scares me!"

Joe starts to speak when L.A. looms him silent. He waves Junior into a Ralph's parking lot. They fill a shopping cart with meats, staples, and delicacies.

He sits, an alien being, in a trance staring at L.A.'s hyped-up pace and urban phantasmagoria as the La Salle moves through the city. The city, he thinks, that shot my every dream down before it dumped me into a dungeon. And poor Junior's dreams too, he thinks, as Junior parks in front of a rickety, time-blistered hovel of a house off Central Avenue.

A wan, three-girl, two-boy group of staircase faces stare at them through a sooty window as they go up a dingy, buckled walkway to the front door. Dottie, Junior's pregnant ex-sexpot, unkempt in a tattered robe, opens the door with a grotesque smile. The smile, her face, reveal to Joe the brutality of her own sentence in her minimal-security dungeon behind invisible walls in the so-called free world.

Joe and Dottie embrace. They carry the groceries into the kitchen. His five timorous one- to eight-year-old grandchildren stare up at him in fearful awe as Dottie introduces him and they shake his hand solemnly in turn.

Junior shows him through the barren three-bedroom house. Joe drops his possessions on a lumpy bed in the rear of the house, then glances about at the peeling wallpaper, lopsided dresser, and ragged carpet. He follows Junior into the mildewed living room. They sit on a saggy sofa and light cigarettes as they watch a newscaster on a snowy TV screen report that Tom Bradley will be interviewed shortly on the station.

His grandchildren dart in and out of the room, peep at him from door frames as they chew potato chips. He catches glimpses of Dottie's cumbersome bulk as she clatters pots and pans and he is reminded of Reba, pregnant with Junior.

Joe finds dinner surprisingly delicious, given his first and lasting impression of Dottie as a worthless campus chippie in that bloody alley eleven years before.

Next morning, promptly at ten, Joe walks into his parole officer's office. An elderly case-burdened Mister Sheehan recites the usual cautions against felon company, demon drink, drugs, and gambling. A handshake and ten minutes later Joe walks out to the La Salle with the understanding that on January the second he will start employment for Hoffmeister Plumbing.

Joe treats Junior to a spaghetti western he's been dying to see. Junior pulls Joe out to a poolroom midway through it when he realizes the gore and blasts of gunfire are making Joe nervous, perhaps rekindling terrible memories. Junior pool-cues rusty Joe into sweaty exasperation as they guzzle a six-pack of verboten stout malt liquor.

Dottie fires evil eyes at them when they walk in arm in arm bellowing, off-key, Ray Charles' "Going Down Slow." She grins and fries them pork chops when they grandly present to her a pint of Courvoisier.

The week goes swiftly to Christmas Eve for Joe in the role of grandfather, in the warmth and fun of grandkids who discover that he is really gentle Grandpa the lovable clown, not a bogeyman killer.

Joe lies across his bed at noon, smoking a cigarette. As usual, he thinks about Reba. Two days before Junior had called him to the phone. He remembers how his knees quivered at the sound of Reba's voice asking how he was doing, inviting him to come to dinner on Christmas Day. Instantly as he hung up his excitement, his hope soured with the thought that Junior had probably begged her to talk to him, invite him to dinner.

Is that Junior and Dottie squabbling in their bedroom down the hall? He gets to his stockinged feet and creeps along the hall to ear range.

"Goddamnit, Jo Jo! Don't keep bugging me about that motherfucking dinner! You go to your mammy's dinner looking like a fucking bum, but me and my raggedy-ass kids are staying right here in this motherfucking roach heaven."

"Mama's got a slew of presents for all of us, Dot. Please, baby, go!" Junior pleads.

"Fuck your mammy's presents! Now stay out of my face, nigger, with that dinner party shit!" Dottie shouts.

Joe goes back to his room. He shaves. He goes to the living room to find Junior sitting disconsolately staring out at the scabrous terrain of the nearly deserted ghetto street.

Joe slugs an affectionate fist against his slumped shoulders. "Spunk up, soldier! Let's make a run," he commands as he pulls astonished Junior through the front door with him.

Their first stop is the May Company, where, guided by Junior, Joe purchases mini-wardrobes for Dottie and the children.

He remembers gifts for Reba and the twins, even an atrocious necktie for Baptiste. Next stop is Dorman's Men's Shop and indigo raw silk suits for themselves. Then, down the block, Stetson blue suede shoes and boss accessories. They make the last stop a Thrifty Discount Store on Central Avenue. They leave the store with a Christmas tree and decorations and a complete layette for Dottie's unborn baby.

They walk to a knot of people at an alley mouth near the parked La Salle. A wizened old bootblack, dressed in a red ragged doorman's suit, turns from the ring of gawkers, exclaims, "Big Joe!" as he steps to the sidewalk beside his one-chair stand to pump Joe's hand.

Joe grins. "Hey, Cootie!" he says as he and Junior peer into the alley over the heads of the crowd at a white-haired old man in bloodied overalls, struggling in a full nelson applied by a burly black uniformed cop. "What's going on, Cootie?" Joe says as he moves into the alley followed by Cootie and Junior.

"Grandpa Sylvester just stabbed a 'ho older than bedbugs a zillion times," violence-jaded Cootie says almost casually as Joe spots the bloody heap of a gray-haired woman sprawled on the alley floor. An incongruous purple satin ball gown, its tarnished sequins dully agleam, is hiked up to her apricot thighs, pocked with black needle tracks.

"Why'd he waste her, Cootie?" Joe almost whispers.

He shoves through the crowd to within a few feet of the bare-footed corpse, with uncommonly shapely legs for an old woman, sheathed in well-ventilated nylons.

"She jumped outta the alley on him and cut his wallet outta his ass pocket with a razor. She fell and busted her noggin 'ginst a telephone post gittin' in the wind down the alley. Give Sylvester a chance to git her and rassle with her a while for his poke 'fore he started hittin' her with his switchblade after she hit him a coupla deep licks with her razor."

Joe trembles as he stares down into the dead feline gray eyes sunken in the gargoyle face of the bloody corpse. His heart jumps cycle to see apricot light glint from the scraggly mass of dirty gray

hair, to remember how the rosebud mouth cannibalized him with
pro artistry in the hot shadows of her trick trap. He shakes to rec-
ognize the doll feet that spurred his back when he galloped to
climax between her notorious thighs long ago in the youth of his
man-prince.

Delphine! he groans silently to himself as he staggers back to
the sidewalk. He strides quickly away to the La Salle.

Junior says, "Did you know her, Papa?" as they put packages
into the car trunk.

Joe heaves a sigh. "Naw, thought I did for a moment . . . feel
sorry for an old mudkicker like that, iced for stealing."

They get into the car and Junior pulls away for home as a city
meat wagon and a pair of police cars shriek behind them.

Within an hour, the children dance and clap hands around
the lit-up Christmas tree as Dottie tries to hide her tears. At midnight he slips away to his bedroom. He undresses and examines
his fractured bankroll. He shrugs, grins, and falls into bed to
dream about Reba and the dinner party the next afternoon.

The Allens arrive on time Christmas Day, in early afternoon.
Junior parks the freshly polished La Salle; its glossy finish reflects
Baptiste's carefully arranged plaster statuary that depicts the Na-
tivity scene on the lawn. A backdrop of shrubbery rings the pink
stucco house. Baptiste glares at them from a living room window
as they alight and start up the walkway.

Belle spots them from a den window. She goes to the door.
Baptiste moves his loaded shotgun a bit farther into concealment
in the folds of window drapes behind his chair. From his chair,
he is virtually camouflaged behind the Christmas tree but has a
total view of living room, den, and dining room.

The Allen children chatter in their pastel finery. They are butterfly garish in the gray funereal overcast. The Allens move past Sadie's
and Belle's Porsche and Caddie, parked in the driveway, to the open
front door. They enter the house and walk a gauntlet of holiday
kisses, hugs, and words of affection from Reba, Belle, and Sadie.

Joe is aswoon for a pounding moment as white satin–clad
Reba embraces him and broils him giddy with the perfumed pres-

sure of her curves. Joe, Junior, and Dottie seat themselves on the den sofa. Electricity crackles the air as Reba flits in and out of the den, compulsively eye-locks with Joe.

The children go to admire the tree. They spot Baptiste and cry out. He smiles painfully and staggers out to dole out half-hearted pecks and hugs before he retreats back to his lair.

Shortly, they serve themselves and the children from a buffet table in the dining room. It is loaded with steamy mounds of golden browned turkey, salads, candied yams, ruby cranberries, and airy homemade rolls. Ice cream and several frothy desserts cap off the feast.

Joe, Junior, and Dottie drink heavily and sit silently after dinner. Dottie rises and frowns aggravation at the muffled sound of the kids in mischief. She hurries from the den to squelch a forbidden romp through the upstairs part of the house. She returns with them in tow.

Reba leads everybody into the living room to open the mountain of presents banked beneath the tree. Baptiste scuttles away until the squealy furor is over before he returns to his command post to open his presents.

At twilight Belle and Sadie dance the last time to the music of the den phonograph. They say goodbye and leave. Moments later Dottie screws up her face and complains of headache and nausea.

Reba puts an old dance record on the turntable that hit the charts when she was a teenager. She turns and stares into Joe's eyes, which he shyly averts.

Dottie thanks Reba for everything, gathers the children and gifts. The Allens move toward the front door. Reba opens the door and kisses the children, Dottie, and Junior as they move out. Joe lowers his cheek for her to kiss. Baptiste half rises, quivers with rage on his chair.

Reba kisses Joe and tipsily whispers, "Joe, unless you have a hot date, you don't really have to leave now . . . do you?"

Joe looks into her eyes as he whispers hoarsely, "Reeb, you've been drinking . . . Baby, please don't say anything to me you don't mean."

She laughs. "I'm serious . . . I'm inviting you to stay. I'm . . . ah, curious to know if you can still cut a bad rug."

Junior glances back, smiles as he steps back to the doorway. He winks mischievously as he says, "Papa, if you gonna keep Mama company a while longer, I'll take my people home and come back to get you later . . . much later."

Joe nods. Reba shuts the door. Joe takes her into his arms. He dances her into the den to nostalgic strains of music they haven't danced to together since they were teenagers. Baptiste glowers, puffed with righteous indignation in his lair.

The couple laugh, drink, chat, and dance under the baleful scrutiny of muttering Baptiste until midnight. They collapse on the den couch after a dance. Reba rests her head on Joe's chest. He blows into her ear as he runs his fingers through the silky brambles of her disheveled hairdo.

Reba giggles, whispers, "Sweetie, I need a nap. Besides, that evil old watchdog won't go to bed until he sees you leave . . . Dance me one more time to the sewing table."

They do. Reba fumbles as she slips a front door key from the tabletop into Joe's suit pocket. She whispers, "Come back in an hour or so . . . I'll be in the front bedroom."

At the door she says loudly, "Good night, Joe. There's a cab stand on the corner."

She shuts the door. Joe walks to a corner go-go joint. He sips whiskey at the crowded circular bar. He scarcely watches the half-nude hip slingers on the stage for watching the clock. He contains himself until two a.m. to make certain that watchdog Baptiste is down for the night.

Unsteadily Joe makes it down the block toward the house. He notices that only dim night-lights are on in the living room and in Reba's front bedroom. He halts on the sidewalk, stares at Theodis, tipsily fumbling with the fence gate.

"Hey you, nigguh!" Joe hollers as he walks up into Theodis' face.

"You addressing me, mister?" he asks as he recognizes Junior's scarred double.

"Yeah, you. Who you looking for this time of night?" Joe says as his narrowed eyes sweep the dapper figure of the handsome young dandy.

"Jerry Bradshaw!" Theodis blurts out. Reba's door key slips from his sweaty hand to clink against the sidewalk. He stoops to retrieve it. "Car key," he mumbles as he straightens up.

"Shoot! You're drunker than me. His folks live two houses down," Joe says with a grin as he points a wavering index finger toward the house.

Joe moves into the yard, goes down the walkway to open the front door. He steps inside the darkened living room, freezes. He stares at Baptiste emerging from the shadows with his shotgun trained on his chest.

"I saw that harlot give you the key. But you're not lighting here tonight. Now drop that key and let that door hit you in the ass before I blow you in two."

Sobered considerably, Joe grins and drops the key to the carpet. He says, "Sure, Baptiste, you win." He turns, takes a step through the door before he whirls back with a backhand to Baptiste's chest. The shotgun flies through the air with Baptiste. He glares at Baptiste struggling to pull himself from beneath a coffee table.

Joe says, "I should chastise your gray ass for trying to bar me from the house where I was born. Next time you get on my case, I will. Go to bed, nigguh, and stay out of trouble."

Joe picks the shotgun and box of shells off the carpet. He moves into the hallway leading to the staircase. He goes up the stairs to the landing. He stands, for a long moment, gazing at the boarded-up rear bedroom. He turns and looks through Reba's half-opened bedroom door.

Reba is lying on the bed in a diaphanous berry red gown. His Goddess's Bambi face is ethereal in the rose glow of the night-light, smiling at him, arms outstretched to him. He snorts like a frenzied stallion, steps in and closes the door behind him.

Downstairs, Baptiste's nose, banged against a leg of the table, spouts blood as he dials the police.

Veteran 77th Division Sergeant Ray Leski, within a half-mile proximity, is dispatched by his station to investigate the "man with a gun" complaint at Reba's house. He slams down on the cruiser's gas pedal, blue eyes electric in his jowly face.

"I'll remember that address until the grave," he says to his rookie partner on the seat beside him. "Caught a bullet in my chest that ricocheted to within an eighth of an inch of my heart."

His lean young partner says, "A bandit in a hole?"

Leski shakes his gray head. "No, a crazy spade caught his old lady screwing a hotshot preacher. Put his lights out . . . Say, it's been more than ten years . . . wonder if that fucking Adult Authority has put that crazy nigger back on the street? Orsini, call in for some backup just in case they have."

Orsini completes the call as the cruiser races silently down Reba's block. The cruiser eases into the curb in front of the house next door. The pair of police ease to the sidewalk with service pistols in hand. Potbellied Leski shakes.

Excited Baptiste dashes off the front porch down the walk toward them with blood-smeared face, shirtfront, and hands. The nervous cops scramble back to cover behind the swung-open doors of the cruiser. They level their weapons on Baptiste.

Leski shouts, "Halt!"

Baptiste stops and babbles, "I'm the one called you, Officers! Joe Allen beat me up. He's got a shotgun, gonna kill my daughter!"

Leski taps an index finger against his lips for silence as he signals Baptiste to the cruiser with waggles of his pistol. Orsini's boyish face pops sweat.

Reba stiffens in Joe's arms. She raises herself to a sitting position. "Joe, I thought I heard Papa screaming out front."

Leski darts from the cruiser to cover behind the hedges at the front of the house. Joe goes to the front window. He sees Baptiste and the rookie officer crouched behind the cruiser's door. He decides to rebut any treacherous tale Baptiste told.

He sticks his head out of the window in the glow of street lamp and shouts, "Hey, Officer, what's going on? You can't believe that old fool. I'm gonna come—"

Leski fires a round from the shrubbery that grazes Joe's head. Joe sees the muzzle flash, jerks his head back, reflex furious at the splash of his blood on the windowsill. Shocked, he grabs up the shotgun, fires, sees Leski flush from the shrubbery. Orsini fires into the bedroom window. At a side window Joe sees Leski scramble to the back of the house.

Baptiste screams, "Officers, please don't do no more shooting! My daughter's up there!"

Junior drives the La Salle abreast of the house. He sees the action and stops the car in the middle of the street. He leaps out. A chorus of sirens screech in the distance. Junior's eyes are afire as he rushes toward Orsini, who is squeezing off another shot into Reba's bedroom.

A dresser mirror splinters. Reba gasps and falls back limply in bed.

Junior's fist clubs the gun from the rookie's hand. He seizes his throat and shakes him violently as he shouts into his face, "That's my mama's bedroom! You nuts, motherfucker?"

Orsini rams a knee for Junior's groin that grazes his belly. Orsini grabs Junior's privates. Junior howls and hurls him away against the street. He screams as Junior stomps a gush of blood from his face with a gigantic cleated shoe.

"Get in the wind, Junie!" Joe shouts from a window.

Leski stoops and rushes from the rear of the house. He pauses in the darkness at the side of the house, extends his arm, aims at Junior's chest, fires. Joe groans at the sound of the shot. The slug rips through Junior's heart. His huge body crashes to the street, motionless, dead.

Joe, with shotgun, dashes from the room and down the stairs. His eyes double-check the shadows for Leski as he moves through the house to the back door into the backyard.

Joe hears an elderly neighbor scream, "Lawd Amighty! The poleece done kilt Junior Allen!"

Joe peeps around the side of the house. He levels the shotgun on Leski's silhouette. His head. Leski ducks into the shrubbery beneath Reba's bedroom at the instant that the shotgun explodes.

Joe moves down the side of the house toward him. Leski lies on his belly in the shrubbery, listening to Joe's footsteps, as he aims his pistol with two jiggling hands at the corner of the house.

Joe halts six feet from exposure at the sight of police cruisers descending with bansheeing sirens. He dashes to the first floor into the kitchen. He bolts the back door. He sees a squad of SWAT officers slip through the back gate in boots and combat garb. He hurls the refrigerator against the door and races for the stairway. He lunges up it into the bedroom to Reba's side. Her face is composed, waxen. He cries out, feels her silent wrist for a pulse, presses his ear against her mute heart.

He screams from the pit of his gut, "Reeb! Reeb! Baby! Darling! You hear me? Don't leave me! Please come back!"

He weeps as he cradles her in his arms. He goes to peep through the shattered window. Awful sobs wrack him as he watches ambulance attendants load Junior and haul him away. He hears a police loudspeaker command, "Joe Allen, this is the police! This house is surrounded! Come out with your hands on your head! Don't jeopardize your ailing wife!"

Joe places Reba gently on her back. He savagely stacks the dresser and chairs against the door. He goes to the bathroom and rips the ancient bathtub from its moorings and partially barricades the window. He peers around the tub at the street, deserted except for police shadows moving behind the cover of their cruisers. He hears their stealthy feet downstairs. He looks at Reba asleep forever on the bed. The bed, he remembers, where a midwife delivered him from Zenobia.

Maybe I'm dreaming, he thinks. He bangs his head against the tub to flee his nightmare. Maddened, he scrapes his wrist to the bone with the shotgun sight, licks the blood to realize he really isn't dreaming. The shotgun smokes and bucks as he barrages the shadows, blasts out cruisers' windshields in mad frustration and misery.

The phone rings. He cringes from the jangling, further proof that he isn't dreaming. He picks up, waits with painful hope that somehow merciful reality will break through his nightmare.

A familiar woman's saccharine voice issues, "Hello, hello. Reba, are you there?"

His voice drags like a dirge. "Yes and no."

The voice says, "Joe! . . . I didn't know you was . . . Is Reba there?"

Joe mumbles, "Sorry, Hattie, Reba's sleeping," before he rips the phone from the wall.

He hunches behind the bathtub, blasting the shotgun at phantoms, ignoring the stentorian voice of the loudspeaker until sunless daybreak.

He shapes an eerie smile as he thinks about Old Percy caged in state prison. "He was my wise, true friend after all, bless his heart. Too bad he missed my ticker," he tells himself.

He leaps to his feet at a sound in the hallway. He goes to the barricaded door, flops on his belly. He peeps through the clearance at the bottom of the door. He sees cop feet milling. He breaks down and checks the shell box. Empty! He stands and rocks as he squeezes his skull between his palms to stop the doomsday roaring inside his head.

He goes to sit on the side of the bed. His face is radiant. He smiles oddly as he lifts and fondles the shotgun, decides to dream the sweetest dream there is. He rams the shotgun barrels into his throat.

The irrepressible Los Angeles sun explodes through the ramparts of coffin gray clouds like a golden cannonball to illuminate the Bambi face of his misery Goddess. Zenobia's child gazes at her as he slams his giant thumb down on the trigger.